SUPERMAN ADVENTURES

last son of KRYPTON

Written by:
Mark Millar
David Michelinie

Illustrated by:
Aluir Amancio
Ron Boyd
Terry Austin
Mike Manley
Neil Vokes

Colored by:
Marie Severin

Lettered by:
Phil Felix

P9-BZY-255

Superman created by Jerry Siegel and Joe Shuster

Dan DiDio
Senior VP-Executive Editor

Mike McAvennie
Editor-original series

Frank Berrios
Assistant Editor-original series

Bob Harras
Editor-collected edition

Robbin Brosterman
Senior Art Director

Paul Levitz
President & Publisher

Georg Brewer
VP-Design & DC Direct Creative

Richard Bruning
Senior VP-Creative Director

Patrick Caldon
Executive VP-Finance & Operations

Chris Caramalis
VP-Finance

John Cunningham
VP-Marketing

Terri Cunningham
VP-Managing Editor

Stephanie Fierman
Senior VP-Sales & Marketing

Alison Gill
VP-Manufacturing

Rich Johnson
VP-Book Trade Sales

Hank Kanalz
VP-General Manager, WildStorm

Lillian Laserson
Senior VP & General Counsel

Jim Lee
Editorial Director-WildStorm

Paula Lowitt
Senior VP-Business & Legal Affairs

David McKillips
VP-Advertising & Custom Publishing

John Nee
VP-Business Development

Gregory Noveck
Senior VP-Creative Affairs

Cheryl Rubin
Senior VP-Brand Management

Jeff Trojan
VP-Business Development, DC Direct

Bob Wayne
VP-Sales

OCT 2 6 2006

37777002345239

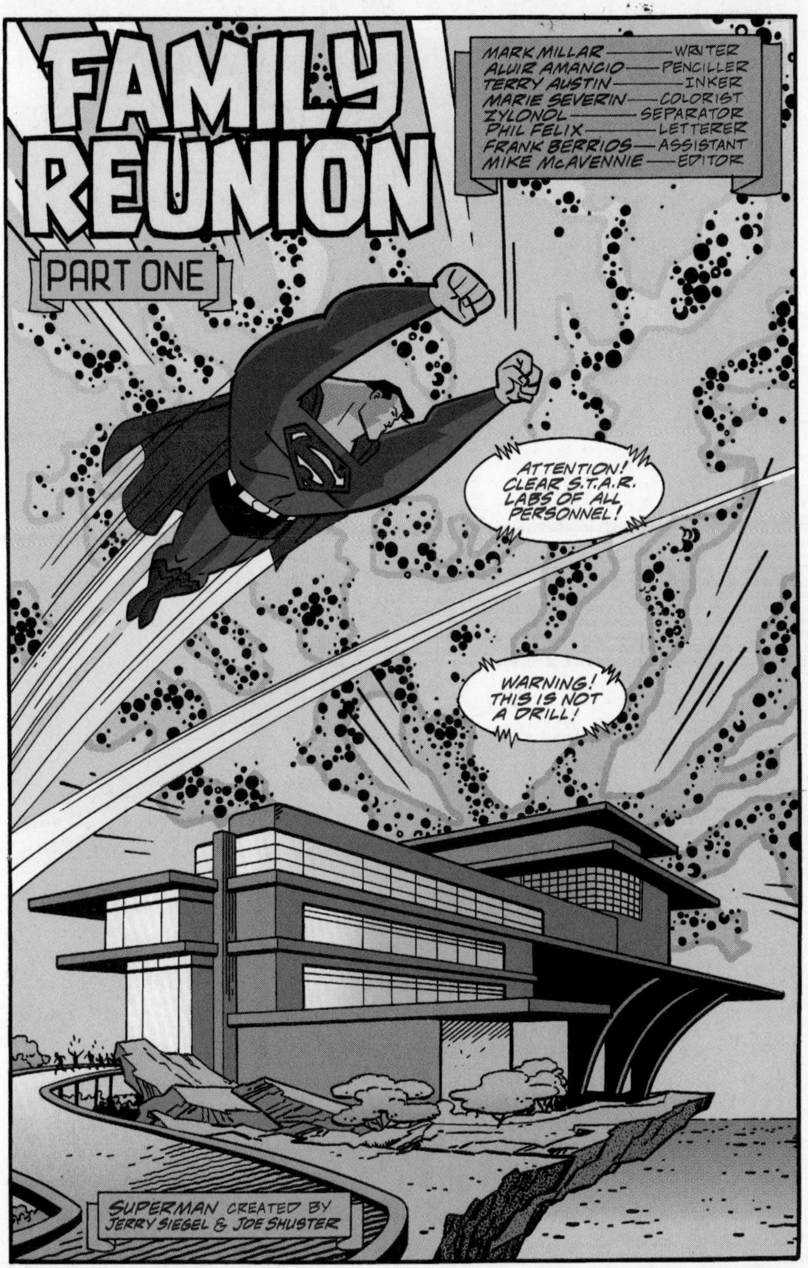
FAMILY REUNION
PART ONE
MARK MILLAR—WRITER
ALUIR AMANCIO—PENCILLER
TERRY AUSTIN—INKER
MARIE SEVERIN—COLORIST
ZYLONOL—SEPARATOR
PHIL FELIX—LETTERER
FRANK BERRIOS—ASSISTANT
MIKE McAVENNIE—EDITOR
ATTENTION! CLEAR S.T.A.R. LABS OF ALL PERSONNEL!
WARNING! THIS IS NOT A DRILL!
SUPERMAN CREATED BY JERRY SIEGEL & JOE SHUSTER

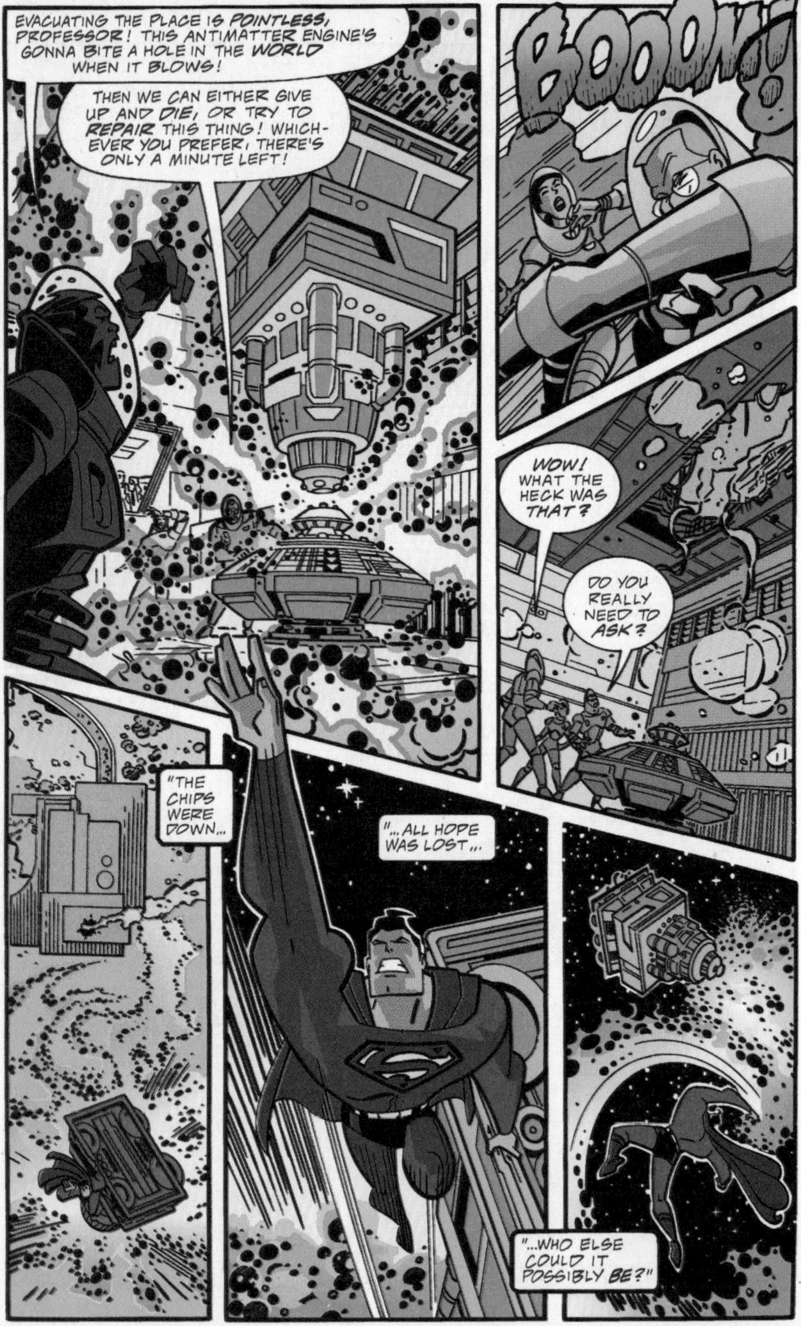

EVACUATING THE PLACE IS POINTLESS, PROFESSOR! THIS ANTIMATTER ENGINE'S GONNA BITE A HOLE IN THE WORLD WHEN IT BLOWS!
THEN WE CAN EITHER GIVE UP AND DIE, OR TRY TO REPAIR THIS THING! WHICHEVER YOU PREFER, THERE'S ONLY A MINUTE LEFT!
BOOOM!!
WOW! WHAT THE HECK WAS THAT?
DO YOU REALLY NEED TO ASK?
"THE CHIPS WERE DOWN...
"...ALL HOPE WAS LOST...
"...WHO ELSE COULD IT POSSIBLY BE?"

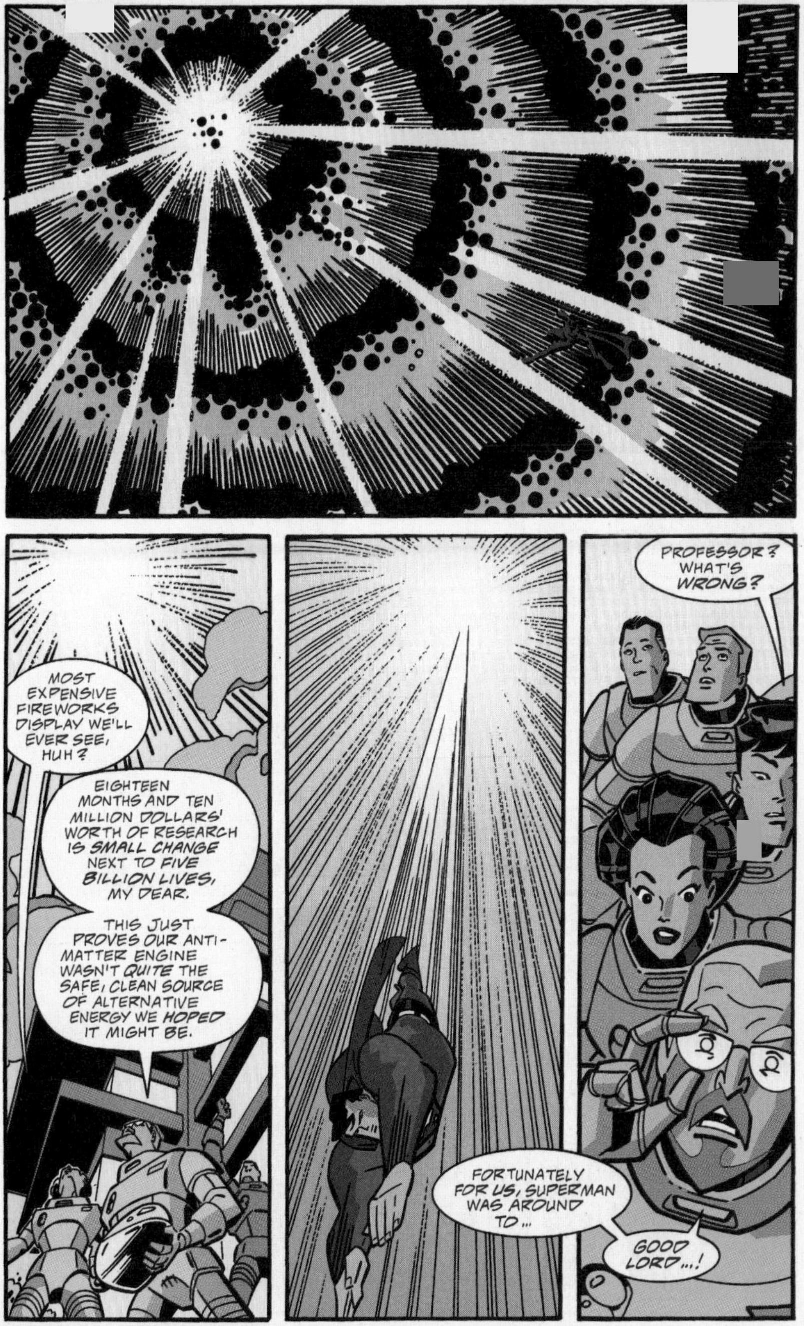

MOST EXPENSIVE FIREWORKS DISPLAY WE'LL EVER SEE, HUH?
EIGHTEEN MONTHS AND TEN MILLION DOLLARS' WORTH OF RESEARCH IS SMALL CHANGE NEXT TO FIVE BILLION LIVES, MY DEAR.
THIS JUST PROVES OUR ANTI-MATTER ENGINE WASN'T QUITE THE SAFE, CLEAN SOURCE OF ALTERNATIVE ENERGY WE HOPED IT MIGHT BE.
FORTUNATELY FOR US, SUPERMAN WAS AROUND TO...
PROFESSOR? WHAT'S WRONG?
GOOD LORD...!

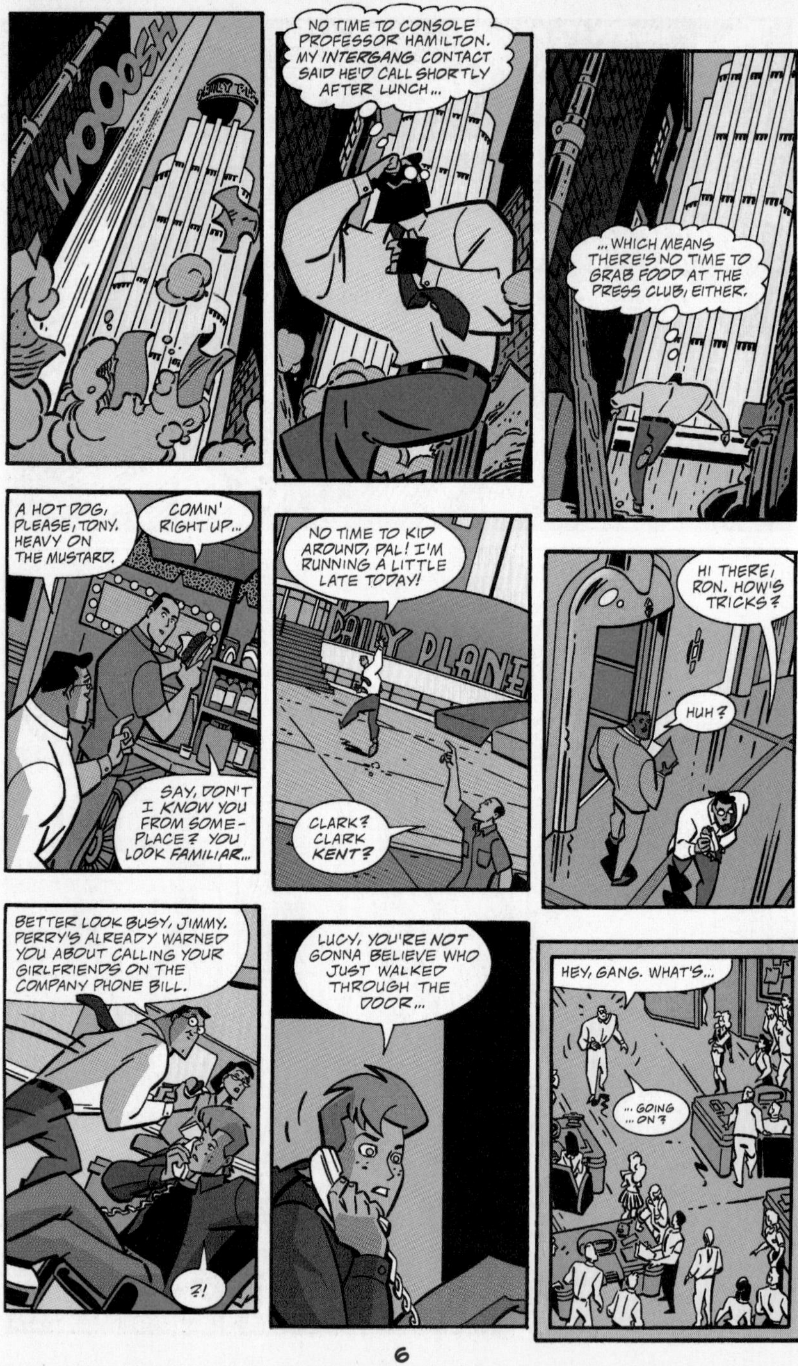
WOOOSH
NO TIME TO CONSOLE PROFESSOR HAMILTON. MY INTERGANG CONTACT SAID HE'D CALL SHORTLY AFTER LUNCH...
...WHICH MEANS THERE'S NO TIME TO GRAB FOOD AT THE PRESS CLUB, EITHER.
A HOT DOG, PLEASE, TONY. HEAVY ON THE MUSTARD.
COMIN' RIGHT UP...
SAY, DON'T I KNOW YOU FROM SOME-PLACE? YOU LOOK FAMILIAR...
NO TIME TO KID AROUND, PAL! I'M RUNNING A LITTLE LATE TODAY!
DAILY PLANE
CLARK? CLARK KENT?
HI THERE, RON. HOW'S TRICKS?
HUH?
BETTER LOOK BUSY, JIMMY. PERRY'S ALREADY WARNED YOU ABOUT CALLING YOUR GIRLFRIENDS ON THE COMPANY PHONE BILL.
?!
LUCY, YOU'RE NOT GONNA BELIEVE WHO JUST WALKED THROUGH THE DOOR...
HEY, GANG. WHAT'S...
...GOING ...ON?

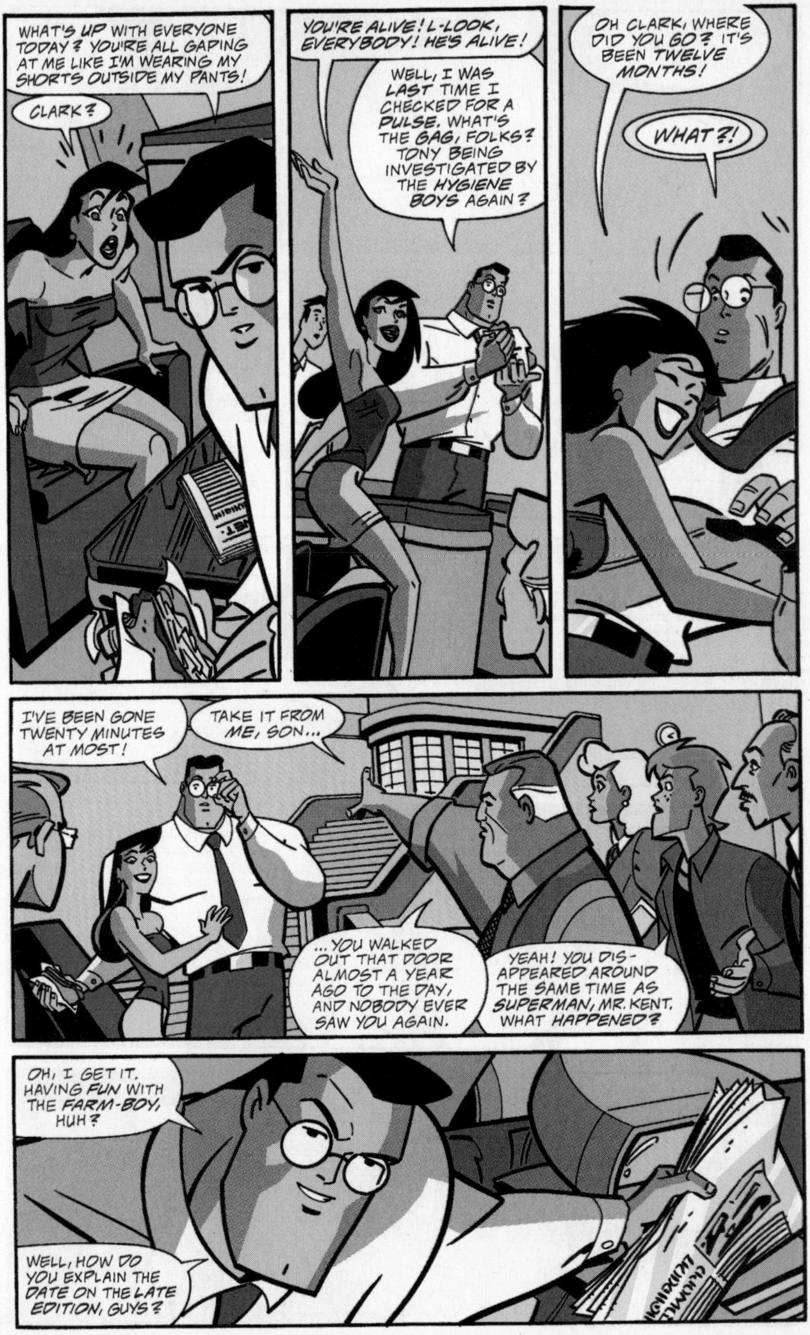
WHAT'S UP WITH EVERYONE TODAY? YOU'RE ALL GAPING AT ME LIKE I'M WEARING MY SHORTS OUTSIDE MY PANTS!
CLARK?
YOU'RE ALIVE! L-LOOK, EVERYBODY! HE'S ALIVE!
WELL, I WAS LAST TIME I CHECKED FOR A PULSE. WHAT'S THE GAG, FOLKS? TONY BEING INVESTIGATED BY THE HYGIENE BOYS AGAIN?
OH CLARK, WHERE DID YOU GO? IT'S BEEN TWELVE MONTHS!
WHAT?!
I'VE BEEN GONE TWENTY MINUTES AT MOST!
TAKE IT FROM ME, SON...
...YOU WALKED OUT THAT DOOR ALMOST A YEAR AGO TO THE DAY, AND NOBODY EVER SAW YOU AGAIN.
YEAH! YOU DIS-APPEARED AROUND THE SAME TIME AS SUPERMAN, MR. KENT. WHAT HAPPENED?
OH, I GET IT. HAVING FUN WITH THE FARM-BOY, HUH?
WELL, HOW DO YOU EXPLAIN THE DATE ON THE LATE EDITION, GUYS?

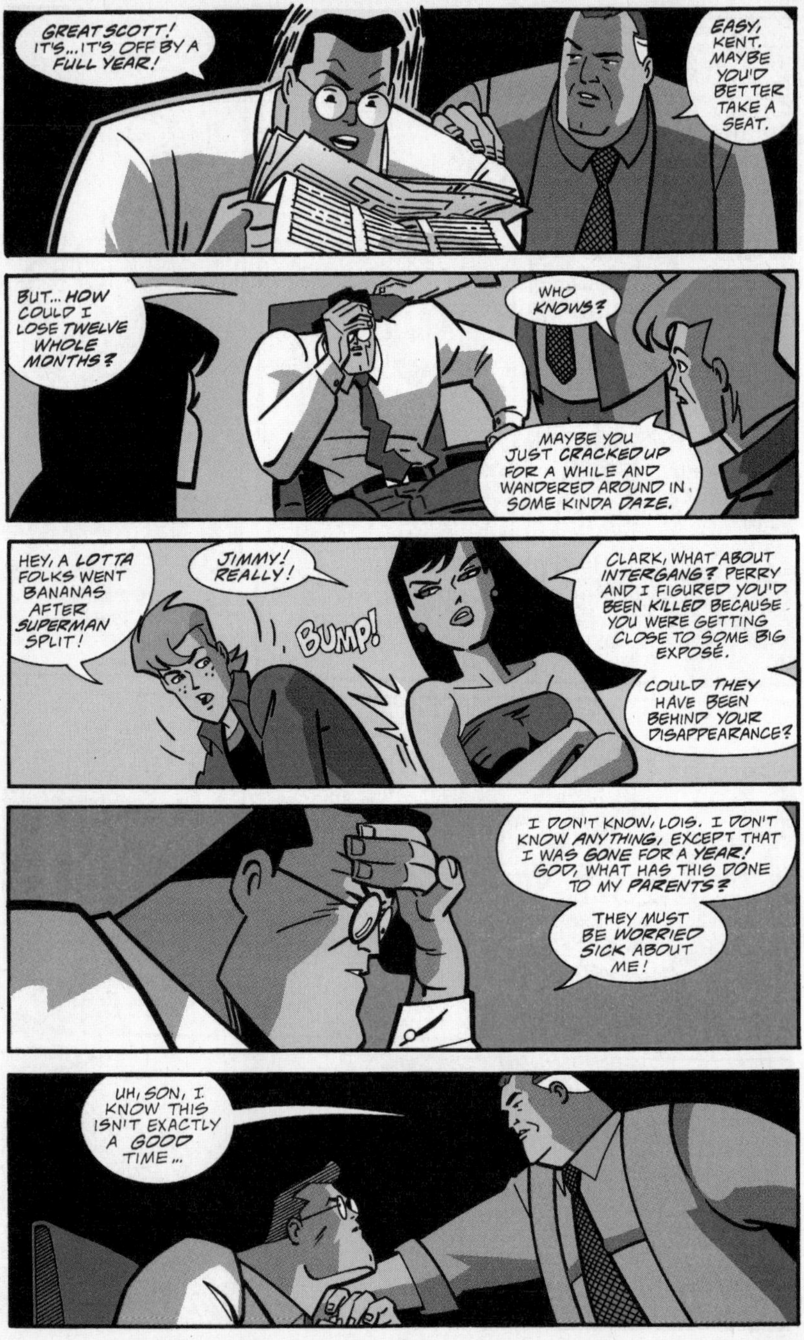
GREAT SCOTT! IT'S...IT'S OFF BY A FULL YEAR!
EASY, KENT. MAYBE YOU'D BETTER TAKE A SEAT.
BUT... HOW COULD I LOSE TWELVE WHOLE MONTHS?
WHO KNOWS?
MAYBE YOU JUST CRACKED UP FOR A WHILE AND WANDERED AROUND IN SOME KINDA DAZE.
HEY, A LOTTA FOLKS WENT BANANAS AFTER SUPERMAN SPLIT!
JIMMY! REALLY!
BUMP!
CLARK, WHAT ABOUT INTERGANG? PERRY AND I FIGURED YOU'D BEEN KILLED BECAUSE YOU WERE GETTING CLOSE TO SOME BIG EXPOSÉ.
COULD THEY HAVE BEEN BEHIND YOUR DISAPPEARANCE?
I DON'T KNOW, LOIS. I DON'T KNOW ANYTHING, EXCEPT THAT I WAS GONE FOR A YEAR! GOD, WHAT HAS THIS DONE TO MY PARENTS?
THEY MUST BE WORRIED SICK ABOUT ME!
UH, SON, I KNOW THIS ISN'T EXACTLY A GOOD TIME...

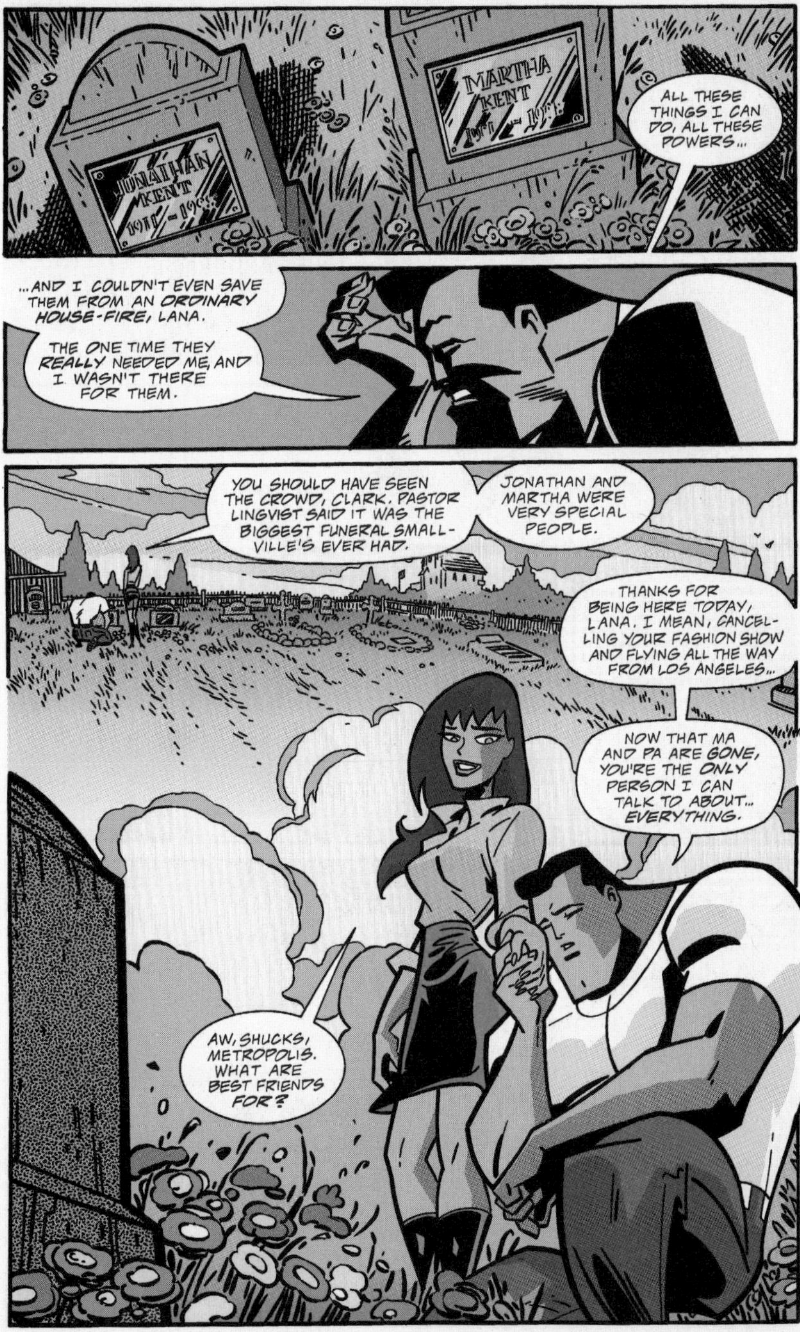
JONATHAN KENT 1911-19
MARTHA KENT 1911-19
ALL THESE THINGS I CAN DO, ALL THESE POWERS...
...AND I COULDN'T EVEN SAVE THEM FROM AN ORDINARY HOUSE-FIRE, LANA.
THE ONE TIME THEY REALLY NEEDED ME, AND I WASN'T THERE FOR THEM.
YOU SHOULD HAVE SEEN THE CROWD, CLARK. PASTOR LINGVIST SAID IT WAS THE BIGGEST FUNERAL SMALLVILLE'S EVER HAD.
JONATHAN AND MARTHA WERE VERY SPECIAL PEOPLE.
THANKS FOR BEING HERE TODAY, LANA. I MEAN, CANCELLING YOUR FASHION SHOW AND FLYING ALL THE WAY FROM LOS ANGELES...
NOW THAT MA AND PA ARE GONE, YOU'RE THE ONLY PERSON I CAN TALK TO ABOUT... EVERYTHING.
AW, SHUCKS, METROPOLIS. WHAT ARE BEST FRIENDS FOR?

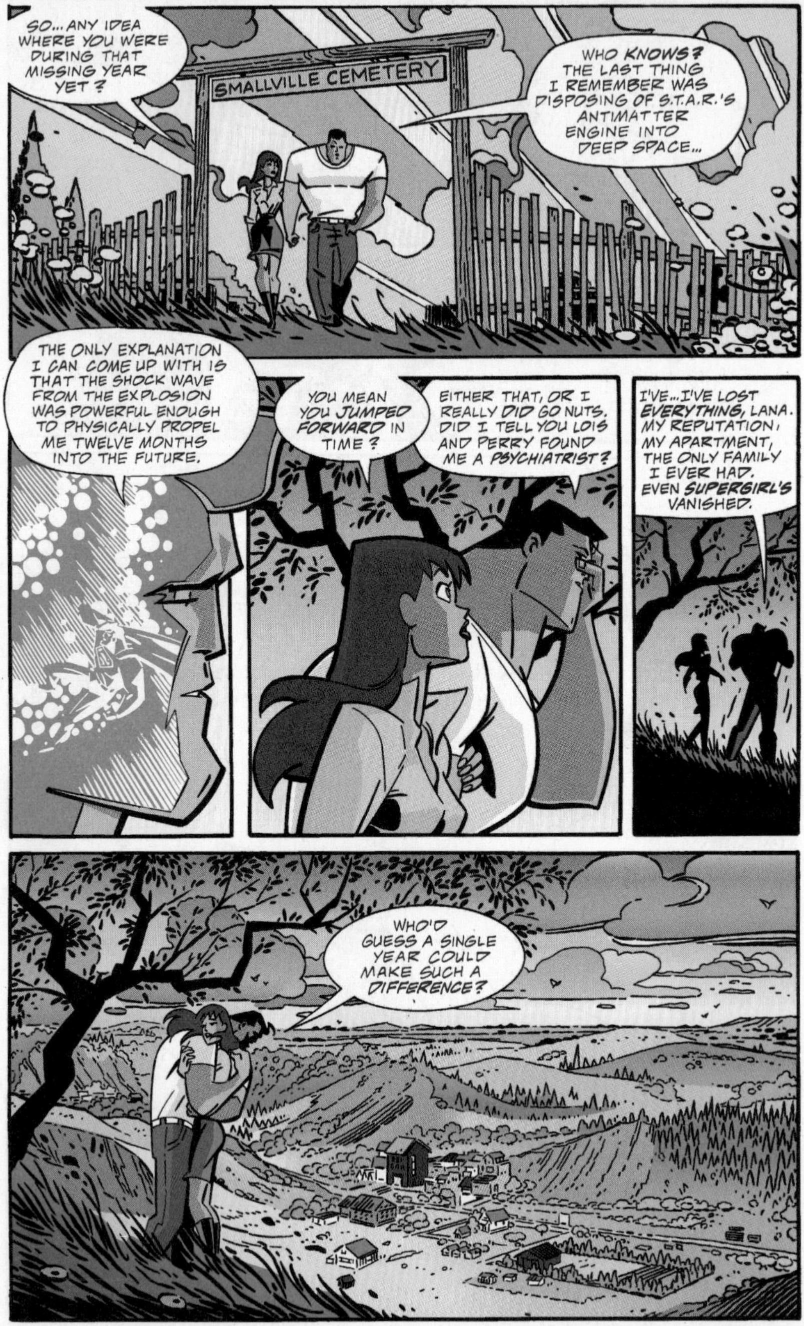
SO... ANY IDEA WHERE YOU WERE DURING THAT MISSING YEAR YET?
SMALLVILLE CEMETERY
WHO KNOWS? THE LAST THING I REMEMBER WAS DISPOSING OF S.T.A.R.'S ANTIMATTER ENGINE INTO DEEP SPACE...
THE ONLY EXPLANATION I CAN COME UP WITH IS THAT THE SHOCK WAVE FROM THE EXPLOSION WAS POWERFUL ENOUGH TO PHYSICALLY PROPEL ME TWELVE MONTHS INTO THE FUTURE.
YOU MEAN YOU JUMPED FORWARD IN TIME?
EITHER THAT, OR I REALLY DID GO NUTS. DID I TELL YOU LOIS AND PERRY FOUND ME A PSYCHIATRIST?
I'VE... I'VE LOST EVERYTHING, LANA. MY REPUTATION, MY APARTMENT, THE ONLY FAMILY I EVER HAD. EVEN SUPERGIRL'S VANISHED.
WHO'D GUESS A SINGLE YEAR COULD MAKE SUCH A DIFFERENCE?

ROCKETED TO EARTH FROM THE EXPLODING PLANET KRYPTON, SUPERMAN ARRIVED HERE MANY YEARS AGO AS THE LONE SURVIVOR OF A DYING WORLD.

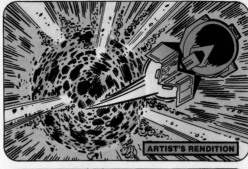

ARTIST'S RENDITION

OUR YELLOW SUN AND LIGHTER GRAVITY BLESSED THE MAN OF STEEL WITH FANTASTIC ABILITIES. FOR A TIME, HE USED THESE GIFTS TO FIGHT A NEVER-ENDING BATTLE FOR TRUTH AND JUSTICE.

BUT THE GOOD TIMES COULDN'T LAST FOREVER. SOONER OR LATER, THE FAIRY TALE HAD TO END, AND ONE DAY, OUT OF THE BLUE, OUR HERO VANISHED, LEAVING THE SKIES EMPTY ONCE AGAIN.

TODAY MARKS THE FIRST ANNIVERSARY OF THE MAN OF TOMORROW'S DISAPPEARANCE. TONIGHT, *METROPOLIS EDITION* ASKS HOW WE'VE FARED IN SUPERMAN'S ABSENCE... ONE YEAR LATER.

ONE YEAR LATER

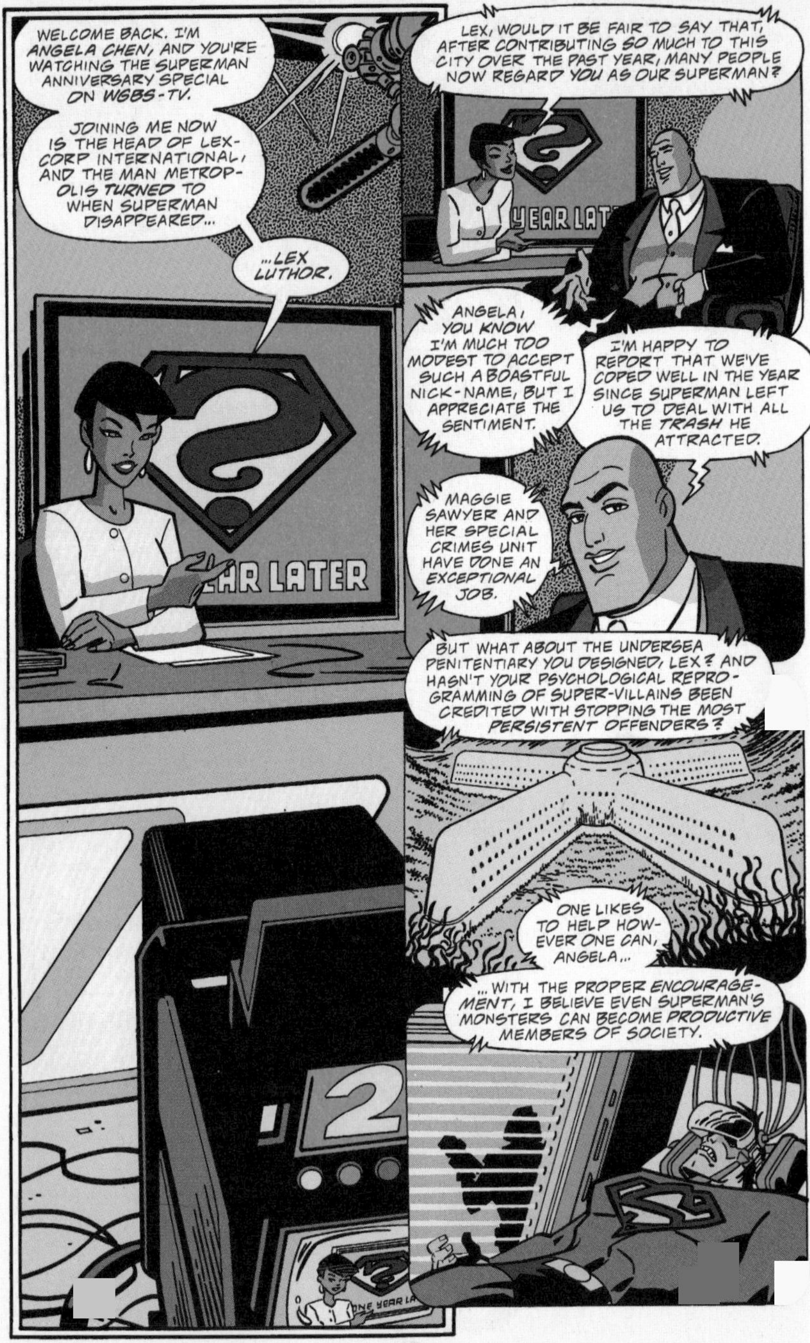

WELCOME BACK. I'M ANGELA CHEN, AND YOU'RE WATCHING THE SUPERMAN ANNIVERSARY SPECIAL ON WGBS-TV.
JOINING ME NOW IS THE HEAD OF LEX-CORP INTERNATIONAL, AND THE MAN METROPOLIS TURNED TO WHEN SUPERMAN DISAPPEARED...
...LEX LUTHOR.
EAR LATER
LEX, WOULD IT BE FAIR TO SAY THAT, AFTER CONTRIBUTING SO MUCH TO THIS CITY OVER THE PAST YEAR, MANY PEOPLE NOW REGARD YOU AS OUR SUPERMAN?
YEAR LAT
ANGELA, YOU KNOW I'M MUCH TOO MODEST TO ACCEPT SUCH A BOASTFUL NICK-NAME, BUT I APPRECIATE THE SENTIMENT.
I'M HAPPY TO REPORT THAT WE'VE COPED WELL IN THE YEAR SINCE SUPERMAN LEFT US TO DEAL WITH ALL THE TRASH HE ATTRACTED.
MAGGIE SAWYER AND HER SPECIAL CRIMES UNIT HAVE DONE AN EXCEPTIONAL JOB.
BUT WHAT ABOUT THE UNDERSEA PENITENTIARY YOU DESIGNED, LEX? AND HASN'T YOUR PSYCHOLOGICAL REPROGRAMMING OF SUPER-VILLAINS BEEN CREDITED WITH STOPPING THE MOST PERSISTENT OFFENDERS?
ONE LIKES TO HELP HOWEVER ONE CAN, ANGELA...
...WITH THE PROPER ENCOURAGEMENT, I BELIEVE EVEN SUPERMAN'S MONSTERS CAN BECOME PRODUCTIVE MEMBERS OF SOCIETY.
2
ONE YEAR LA

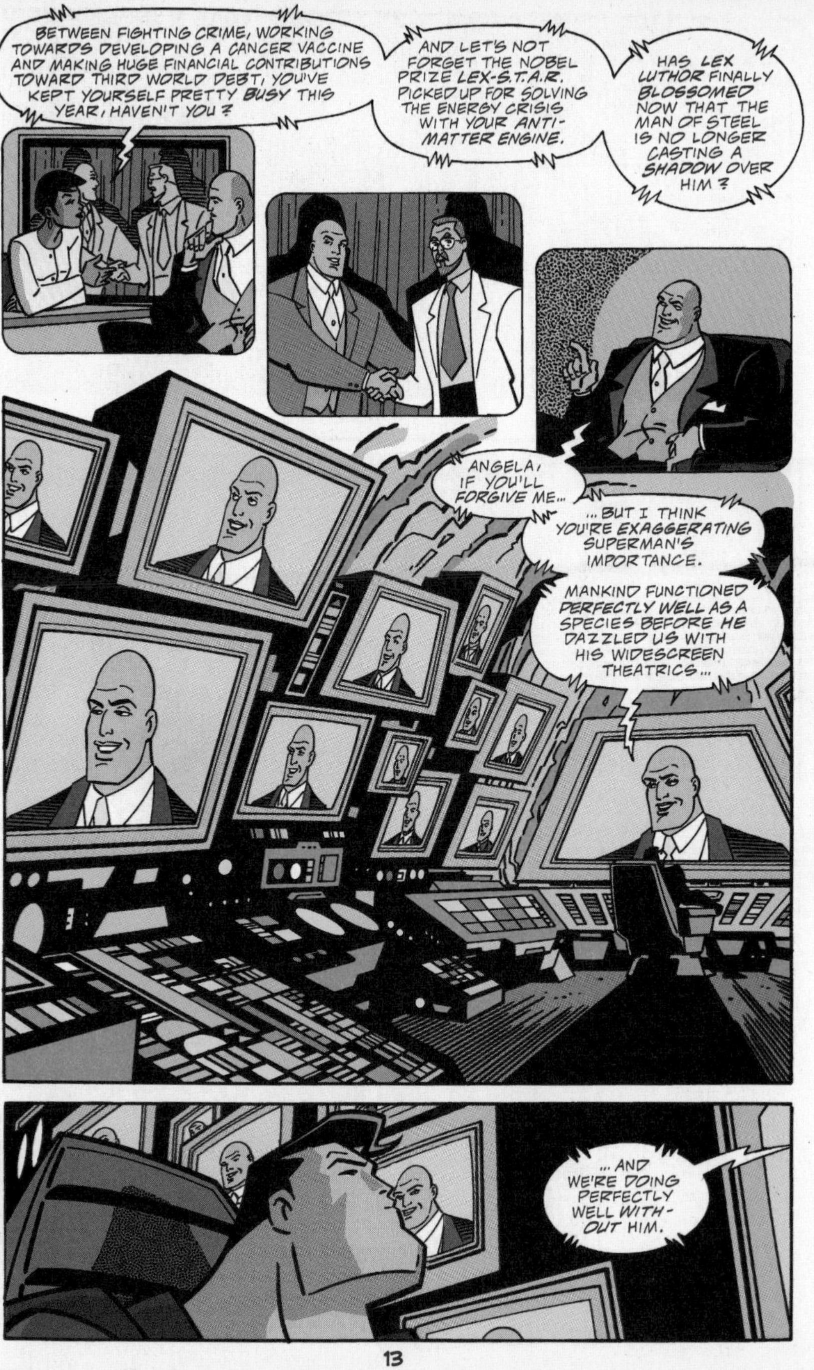
BETWEEN FIGHTING CRIME, WORKING TOWARDS DEVELOPING A CANCER VACCINE AND MAKING HUGE FINANCIAL CONTRIBUTIONS TOWARD THIRD WORLD DEBT, YOU'VE KEPT YOURSELF PRETTY BUSY THIS YEAR, HAVEN'T YOU?
AND LET'S NOT FORGET THE NOBEL PRIZE LEX-S.T.A.R. PICKED UP FOR SOLVING THE ENERGY CRISIS WITH YOUR ANTI-MATTER ENGINE.
HAS LEX LUTHOR FINALLY BLOSSOMED NOW THAT THE MAN OF STEEL IS NO LONGER CASTING A SHADOW OVER HIM?
ANGELA, IF YOU'LL FORGIVE ME...
...BUT I THINK YOU'RE EXAGGERATING SUPERMAN'S IMPORTANCE.
MANKIND FUNCTIONED PERFECTLY WELL AS A SPECIES BEFORE HE DAZZLED US WITH HIS WIDESCREEN THEATRICS...
...AND WE'RE DOING PERFECTLY WELL WITH-OUT HIM.

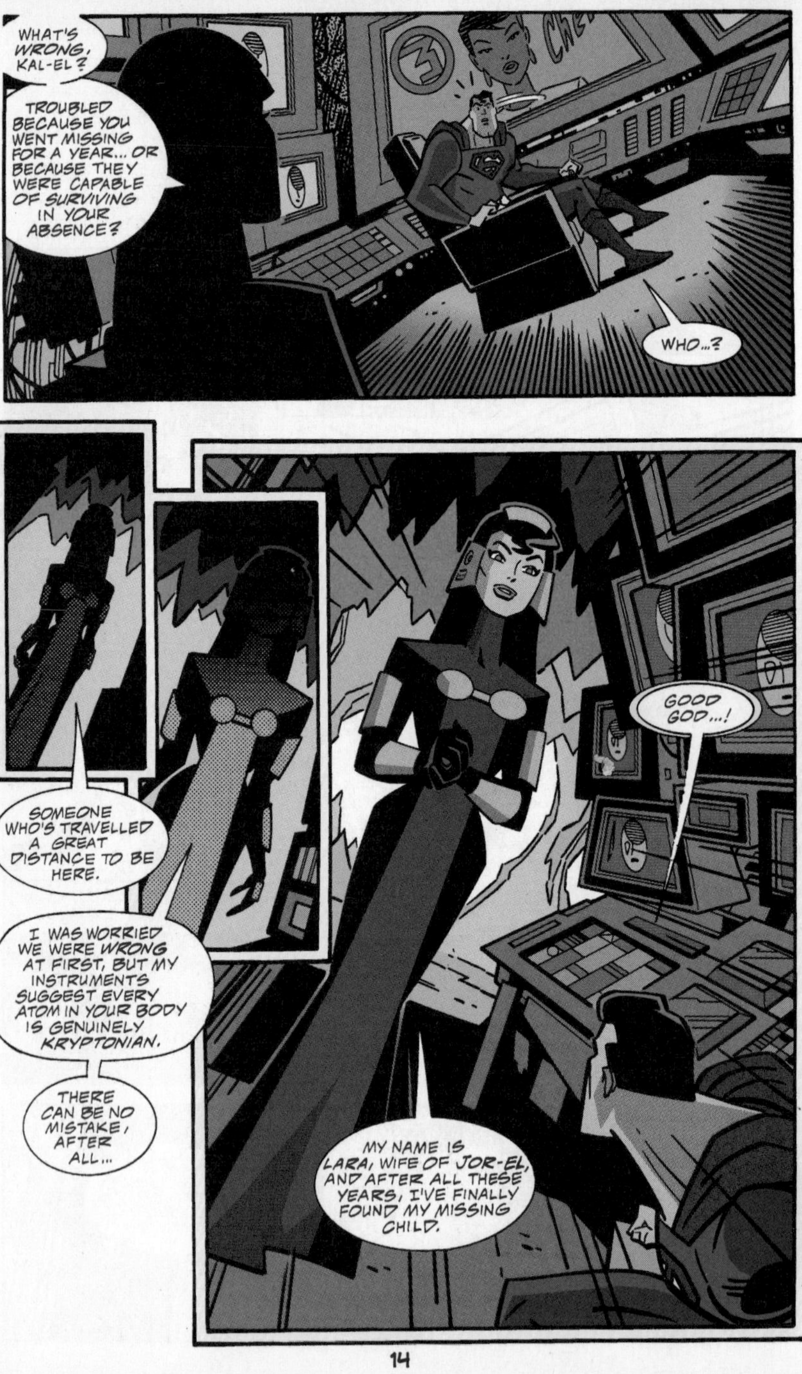
WHAT'S WRONG, KAL-EL?
TROUBLED BECAUSE YOU WENT MISSING FOR A YEAR... OR BECAUSE THEY WERE CAPABLE OF SURVIVING IN YOUR ABSENCE?
WHO...?
SOMEONE WHO'S TRAVELLED A GREAT DISTANCE TO BE HERE.
GOOD GOD...!
I WAS WORRIED WE WERE WRONG AT FIRST, BUT MY INSTRUMENTS SUGGEST EVERY ATOM IN YOUR BODY IS GENUINELY KRYPTONIAN.
THERE CAN BE NO MISTAKE, AFTER ALL...
MY NAME IS LARA, WIFE OF JOR-EL, AND AFTER ALL THESE YEARS, I'VE FINALLY FOUND MY MISSING CHILD.

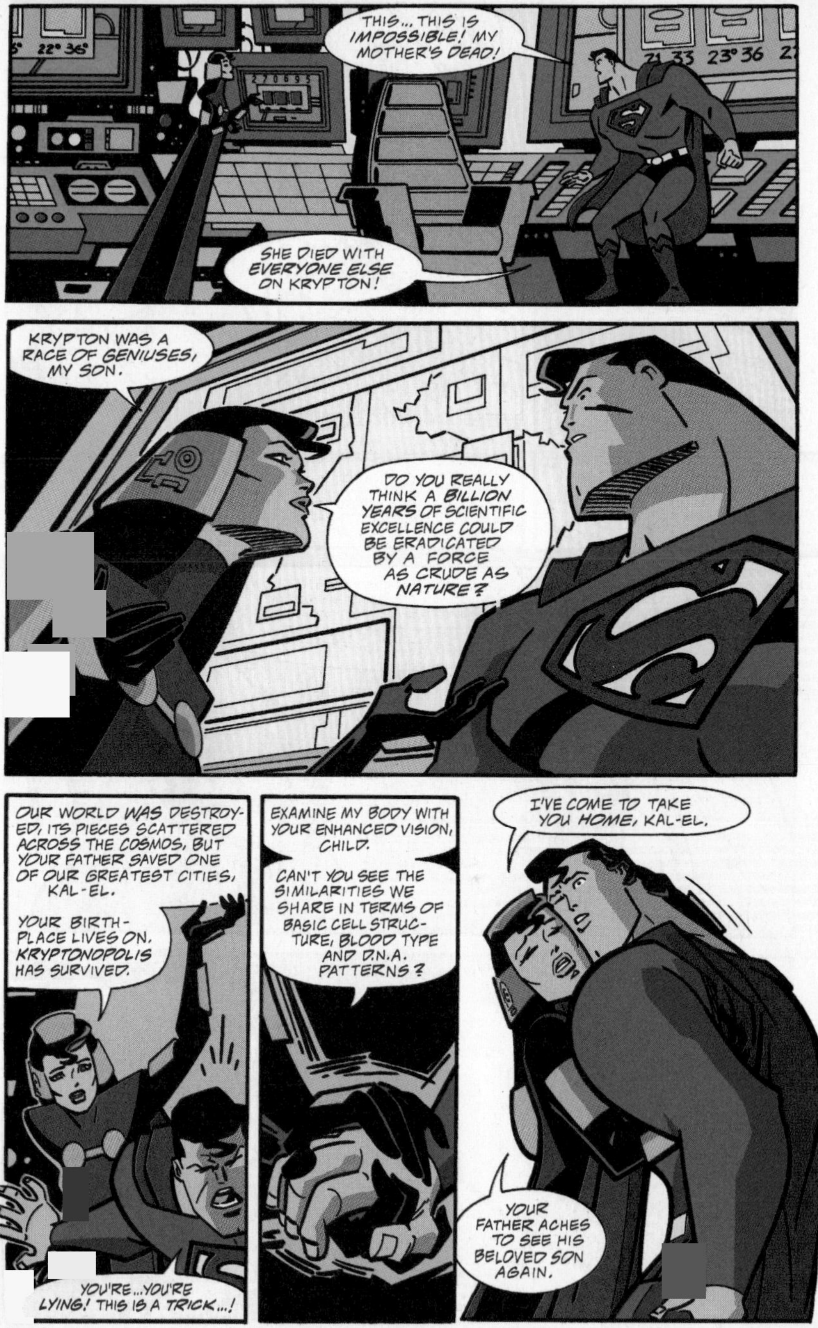
THIS... THIS IS IMPOSSIBLE! MY MOTHER'S DEAD!
SHE DIED WITH EVERYONE ELSE ON KRYPTON!
KRYPTON WAS A RACE OF GENIUSES, MY SON.
DO YOU REALLY THINK A BILLION YEARS OF SCIENTIFIC EXCELLENCE COULD BE ERADICATED BY A FORCE AS CRUDE AS NATURE?
OUR WORLD WAS DESTROYED, ITS PIECES SCATTERED ACROSS THE COSMOS, BUT YOUR FATHER SAVED ONE OF OUR GREATEST CITIES, KAL-EL.
YOUR BIRTHPLACE LIVES ON. KRYPTONOPOLIS HAS SURVIVED.
YOU'RE... YOU'RE LYING! THIS IS A TRICK...!
EXAMINE MY BODY WITH YOUR ENHANCED VISION, CHILD.
CAN'T YOU SEE THE SIMILARITIES WE SHARE IN TERMS OF BASIC CELL STRUCTURE, BLOOD TYPE AND D.N.A. PATTERNS?
I'VE COME TO TAKE YOU HOME, KAL-EL.
YOUR FATHER ACHES TO SEE HIS BELOVED SON AGAIN.

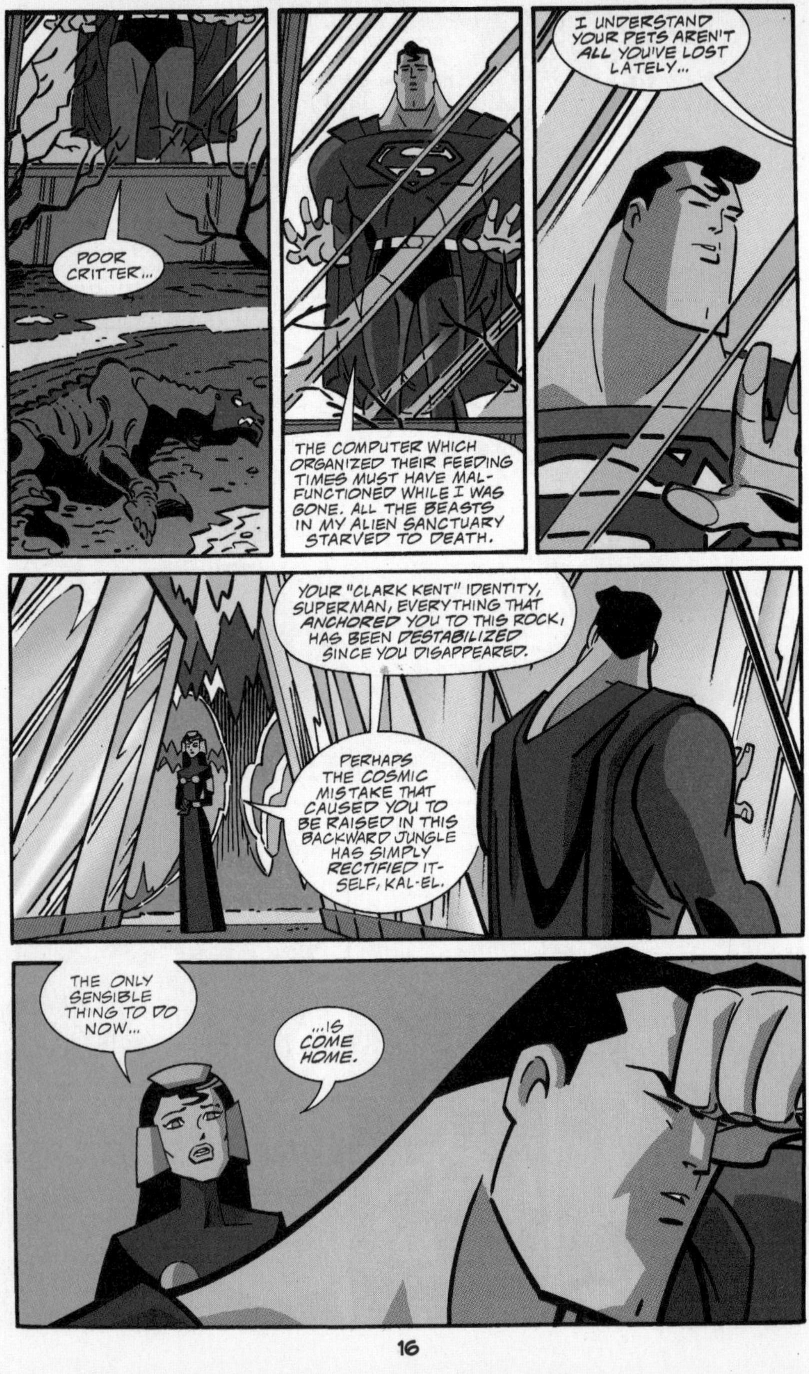
POOR CRITTER...
THE COMPUTER WHICH ORGANIZED THEIR FEEDING TIMES MUST HAVE MAL-FUNCTIONED WHILE I WAS GONE. ALL THE BEASTS IN MY ALIEN SANCTUARY STARVED TO DEATH.
I UNDERSTAND YOUR PETS AREN'T ALL YOU'VE LOST LATELY...
YOUR "CLARK KENT" IDENTITY, SUPERMAN, EVERYTHING THAT ANCHORED YOU TO THIS ROCK, HAS BEEN DESTABILIZED SINCE YOU DISAPPEARED.
PERHAPS THE COSMIC MISTAKE THAT CAUSED YOU TO BE RAISED IN THIS BACKWARD JUNGLE HAS SIMPLY RECTIFIED IT-SELF, KAL-EL.
THE ONLY SENSIBLE THING TO DO NOW...
...IS COME HOME.

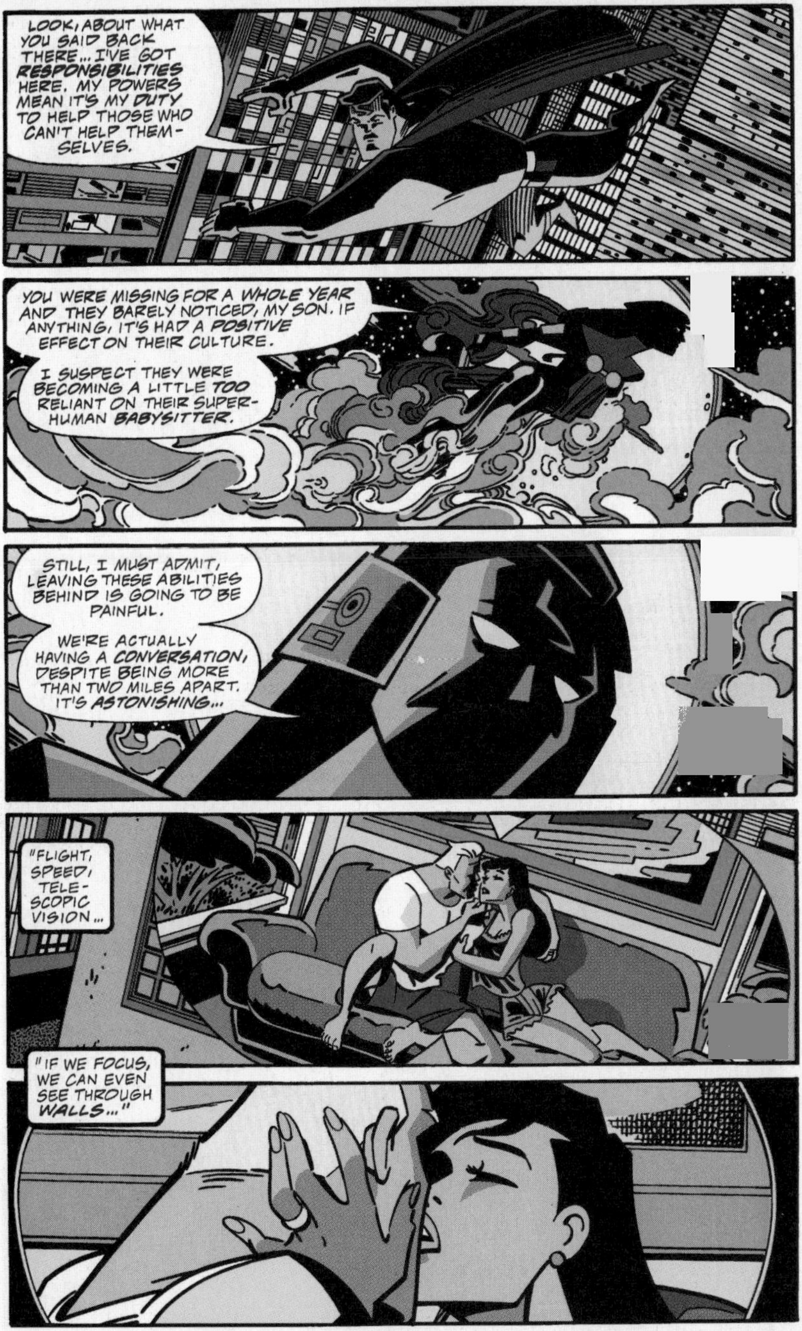
LOOK, ABOUT WHAT YOU SAID BACK THERE... I'VE GOT RESPONSIBILITIES HERE. MY POWERS MEAN IT'S MY DUTY TO HELP THOSE WHO CAN'T HELP THEM-SELVES.
YOU WERE MISSING FOR A WHOLE YEAR AND THEY BARELY NOTICED, MY SON. IF ANYTHING, IT'S HAD A POSITIVE EFFECT ON THEIR CULTURE.
I SUSPECT THEY WERE BECOMING A LITTLE TOO RELIANT ON THEIR SUPER-HUMAN BABYSITTER.
STILL, I MUST ADMIT, LEAVING THESE ABILITIES BEHIND IS GOING TO BE PAINFUL.
WE'RE ACTUALLY HAVING A CONVERSATION, DESPITE BEING MORE THAN TWO MILES APART. IT'S ASTONISHING...
"FLIGHT, SPEED, TELE-SCOPIC VISION...
"IF WE FOCUS, WE CAN EVEN SEE THROUGH WALLS..."

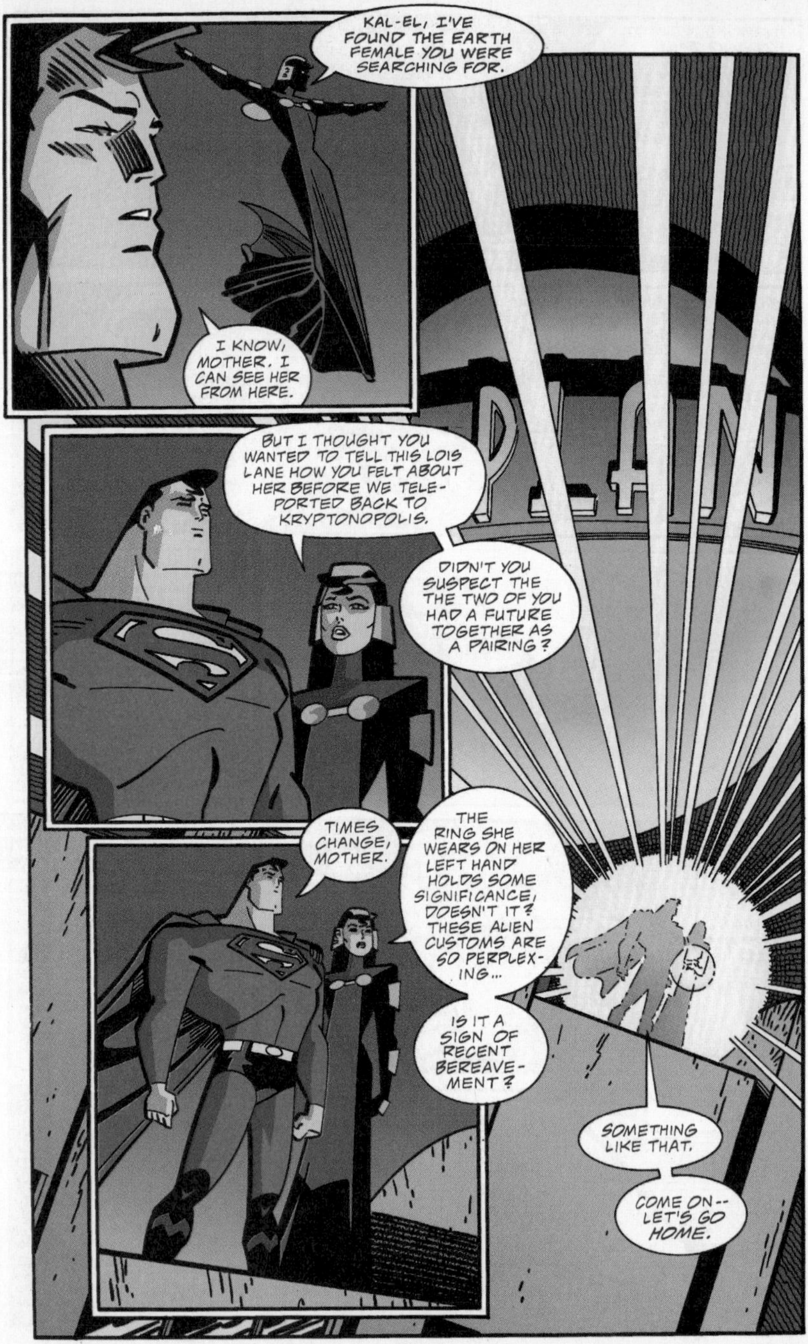
KAL-EL, I'VE FOUND THE EARTH FEMALE YOU WERE SEARCHING FOR.
I KNOW, MOTHER. I CAN SEE HER FROM HERE.
BUT I THOUGHT YOU WANTED TO TELL THIS LOIS LANE HOW YOU FELT ABOUT HER BEFORE WE TELE-PORTED BACK TO KRYPTONOPOLIS.
DIDN'T YOU SUSPECT THE THE TWO OF YOU HAD A FUTURE TOGETHER AS A PAIRING?
TIMES CHANGE, MOTHER.
THE RING SHE WEARS ON HER LEFT HAND HOLDS SOME SIGNIFICANCE, DOESN'T IT? THESE ALIEN CUSTOMS ARE SO PERPLEX-ING...
IS IT A SIGN OF RECENT BEREAVE-MENT?
SOMETHING LIKE THAT.
COME ON-- LET'S GO HOME.

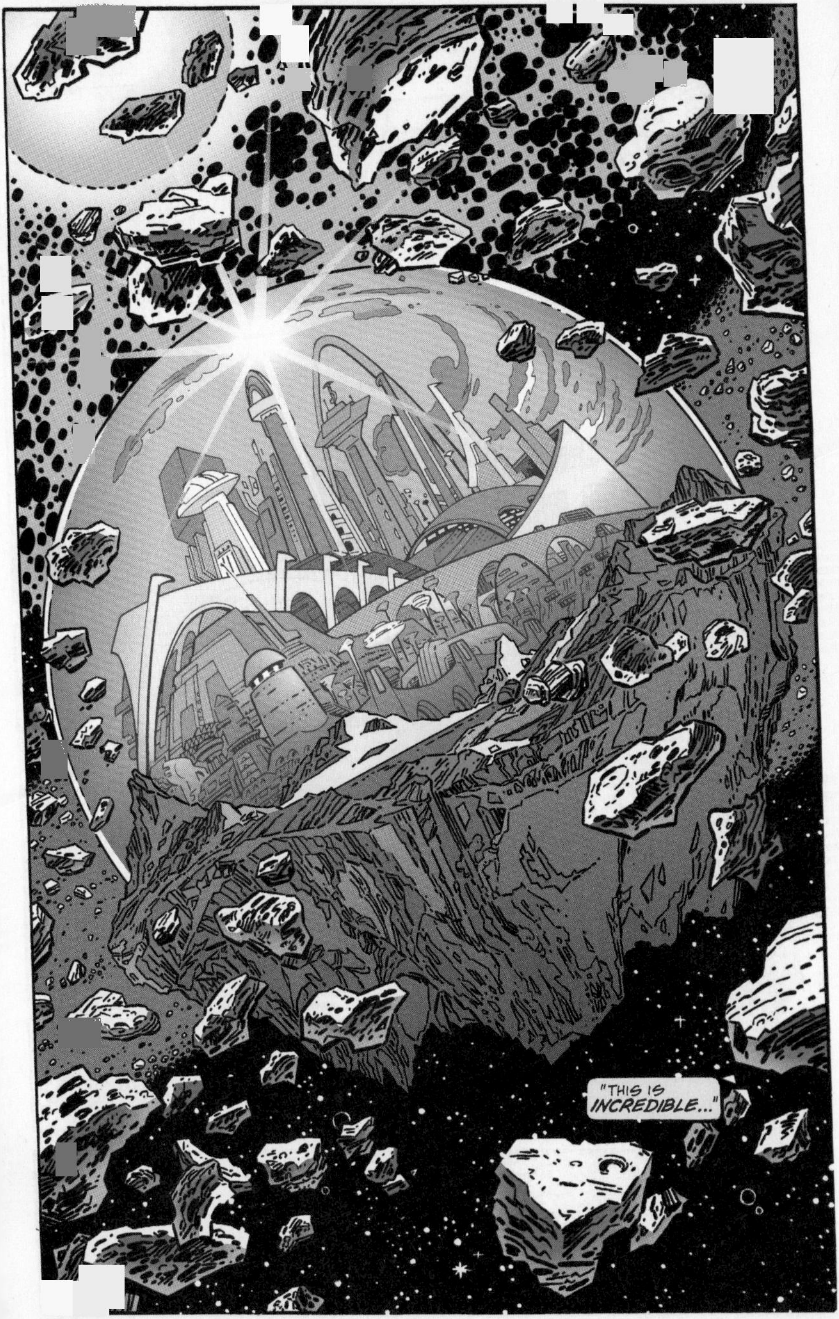
"THIS IS INCREDIBLE..."

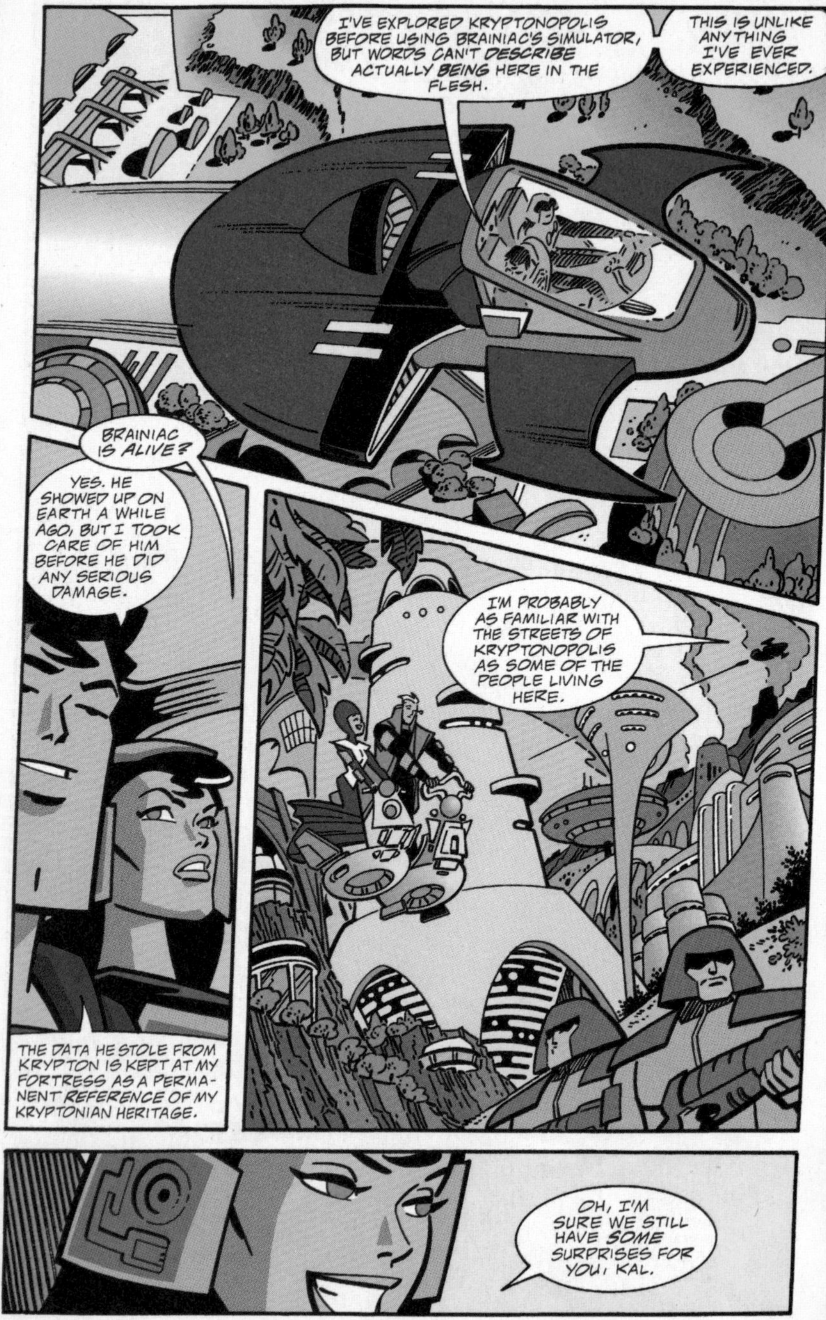

I'VE EXPLORED KRYPTONOPOLIS BEFORE USING BRAINIAC'S SIMULATOR, BUT WORDS CAN'T DESCRIBE ACTUALLY BEING HERE IN THE FLESH.
THIS IS UNLIKE ANYTHING I'VE EVER EXPERIENCED.
BRAINIAC IS ALIVE?
YES. HE SHOWED UP ON EARTH A WHILE AGO, BUT I TOOK CARE OF HIM BEFORE HE DID ANY SERIOUS DAMAGE.
THE DATA HE STOLE FROM KRYPTON IS KEPT AT MY FORTRESS AS A PERMANENT REFERENCE OF MY KRYPTONIAN HERITAGE.
I'M PROBABLY AS FAMILIAR WITH THE STREETS OF KRYPTONOPOLIS AS SOME OF THE PEOPLE LIVING HERE.
OH, I'M SURE WE STILL HAVE SOME SURPRISES FOR YOU, KAL.

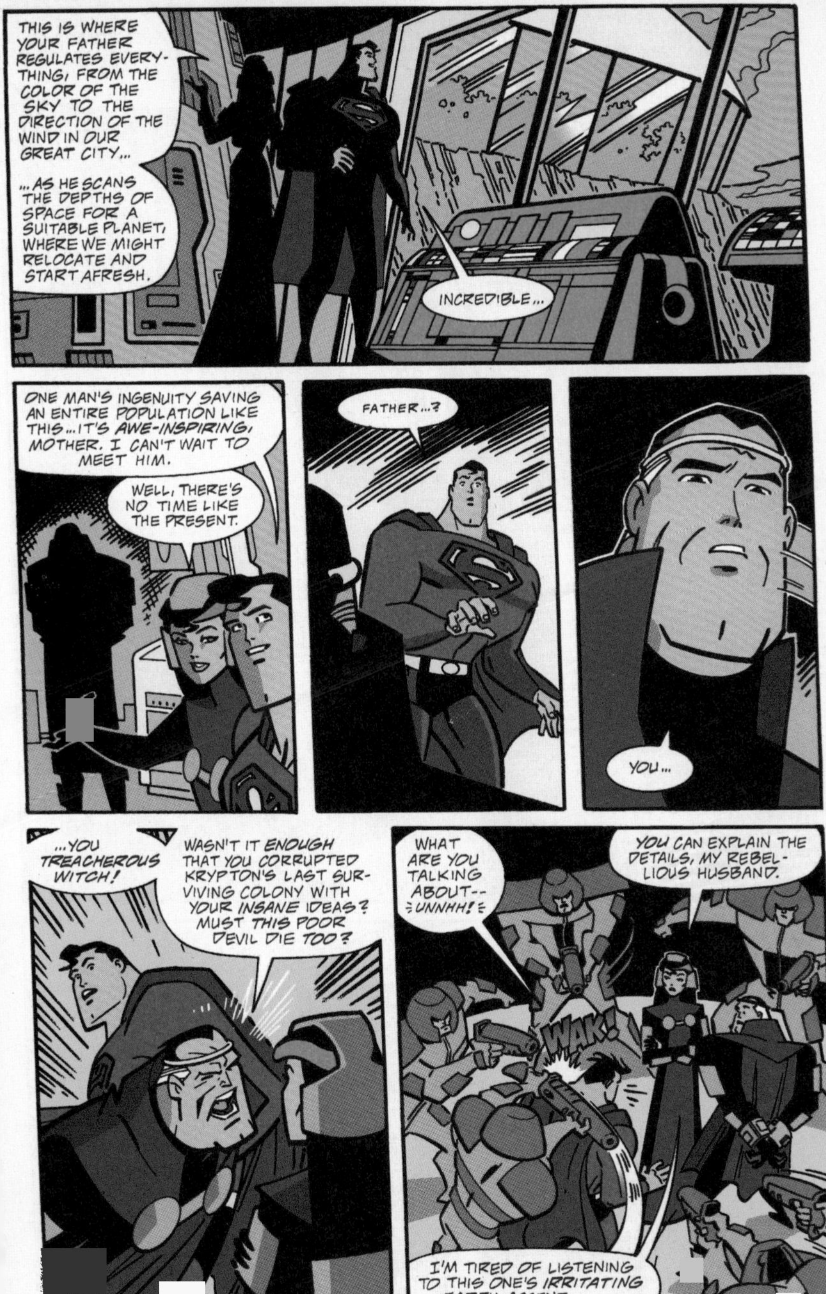
THIS IS WHERE YOUR FATHER REGULATES EVERY-THING, FROM THE COLOR OF THE SKY TO THE DIRECTION OF THE WIND IN OUR GREAT CITY...
...AS HE SCANS THE DEPTHS OF SPACE FOR A SUITABLE PLANET, WHERE WE MIGHT RELOCATE AND START AFRESH.
INCREDIBLE...
ONE MAN'S INGENUITY SAVING AN ENTIRE POPULATION LIKE THIS...IT'S AWE-INSPIRING, MOTHER. I CAN'T WAIT TO MEET HIM.
WELL, THERE'S NO TIME LIKE THE PRESENT.
FATHER...?
YOU...
...YOU TREACHEROUS WITCH!
WASN'T IT ENOUGH THAT YOU CORRUPTED KRYPTON'S LAST SUR-VIVING COLONY WITH YOUR INSANE IDEAS? MUST THIS POOR DEVIL DIE TOO?
WHAT ARE YOU TALKING ABOUT-- UNNHH!
YOU CAN EXPLAIN THE DETAILS, MY REBEL-LIOUS HUSBAND.
WAK!
I'M TIRED OF LISTENING TO THIS ONE'S IRRITATING EARTH ACCENT.

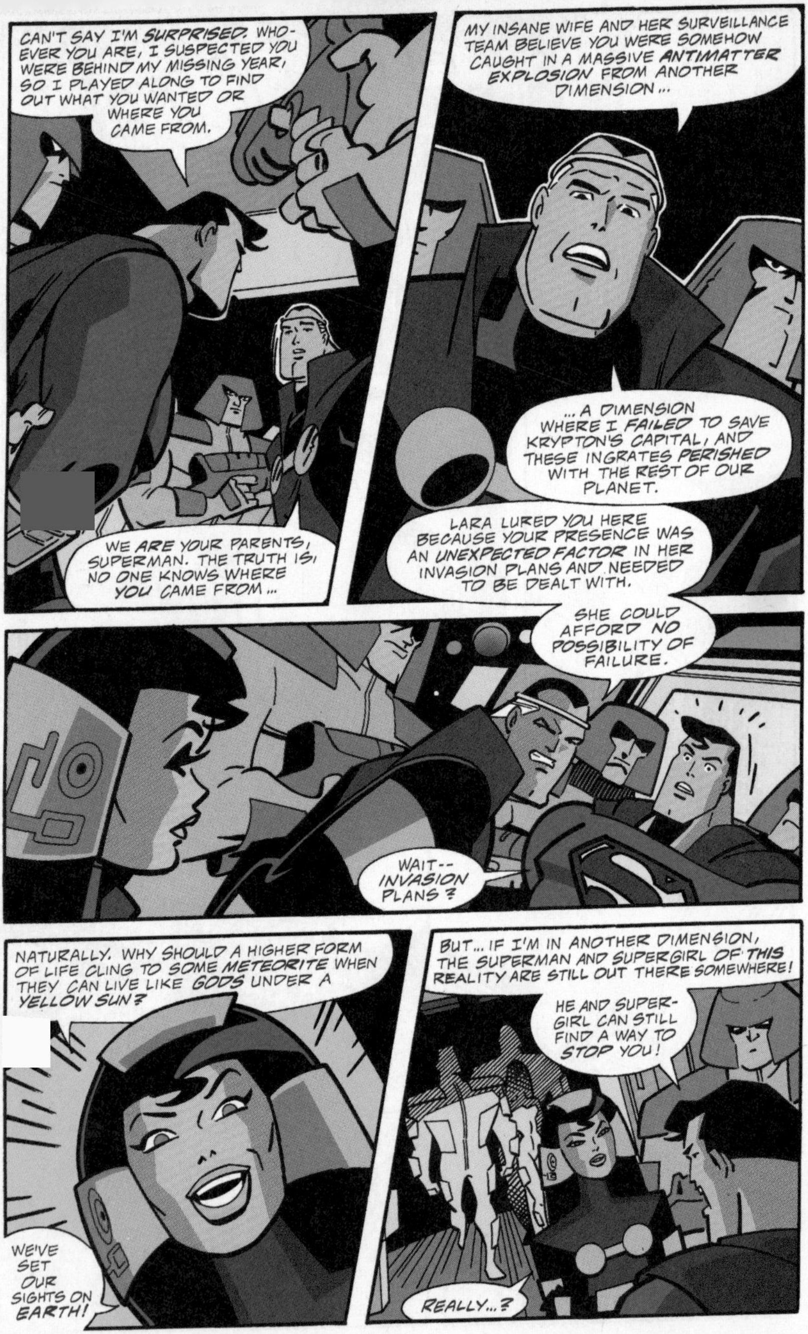
CAN'T SAY I'M SURPRISED. WHOEVER YOU ARE, I SUSPECTED YOU WERE BEHIND MY MISSING YEAR, SO I PLAYED ALONG TO FIND OUT WHAT YOU WANTED OR WHERE YOU CAME FROM.
WE ARE YOUR PARENTS, SUPERMAN. THE TRUTH IS, NO ONE KNOWS WHERE YOU CAME FROM...
MY INSANE WIFE AND HER SURVEILLANCE TEAM BELIEVE YOU WERE SOMEHOW CAUGHT IN A MASSIVE ANTIMATTER EXPLOSION FROM ANOTHER DIMENSION...
...A DIMENSION WHERE I FAILED TO SAVE KRYPTON'S CAPITAL, AND THESE INGRATES PERISHED WITH THE REST OF OUR PLANET.
LARA LURED YOU HERE BECAUSE YOUR PRESENCE WAS AN UNEXPECTED FACTOR IN HER INVASION PLANS AND NEEDED TO BE DEALT WITH.
SHE COULD AFFORD NO POSSIBILITY OF FAILURE.
WAIT-- INVASION PLANS?
NATURALLY. WHY SHOULD A HIGHER FORM OF LIFE CLING TO SOME METEORITE WHEN THEY CAN LIVE LIKE GODS UNDER A YELLOW SUN?
WE'VE SET OUR SIGHTS ON EARTH!
BUT... IF I'M IN ANOTHER DIMENSION, THE SUPERMAN AND SUPERGIRL OF THIS REALITY ARE STILL OUT THERE SOMEWHERE!
HE AND SUPERGIRL CAN STILL FIND A WAY TO STOP YOU!
REALLY...?

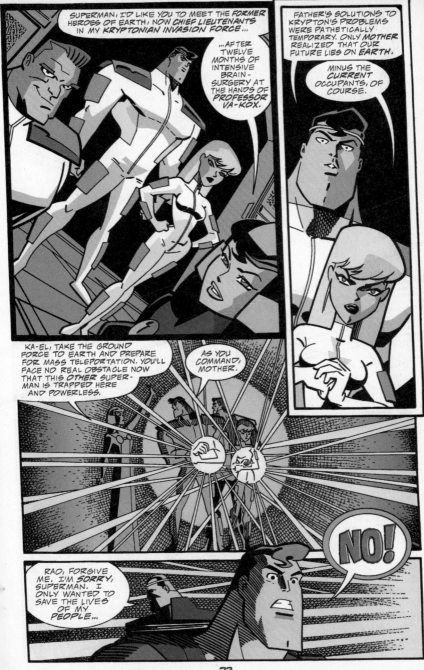

SUPERMAN, I'D LIKE YOU TO MEET THE *FORMER HEROES OF EARTH,* NOW *CHIEF LIEUTENANTS* IN MY *KRYPTONIAN INVASION FORCE...*

...AFTER TWELVE MONTHS OF INTENSIVE BRAIN-SURGERY AT THE HANDS OF *PROFESSOR VA-KOX.*

FATHER'S SOLUTIONS TO KRYPTON'S PROBLEMS WERE PATHETICALLY *TEMPORARY.* ONLY *MOTHER* REALIZED THAT OUR FUTURE LIES ON *EARTH.*

MINUS THE *CURRENT OCCUPANTS,* OF COURSE.

KA-EL, TAKE THE GROUND FORCE TO EARTH AND PREPARE FOR MASS TELEPORTATION. YOU'LL FACE NO REAL OBSTACLE NOW THAT THIS *OTHER* SUPER-MAN IS TRAPPED HERE AND POWERLESS.

AS YOU *COMMAND,* MOTHER.

NO!

RAO, FORGIVE ME. I'M *SORRY,* SUPERMAN. I ONLY WANTED TO SAVE THE LIVES OF MY *PEOPLE...*

23

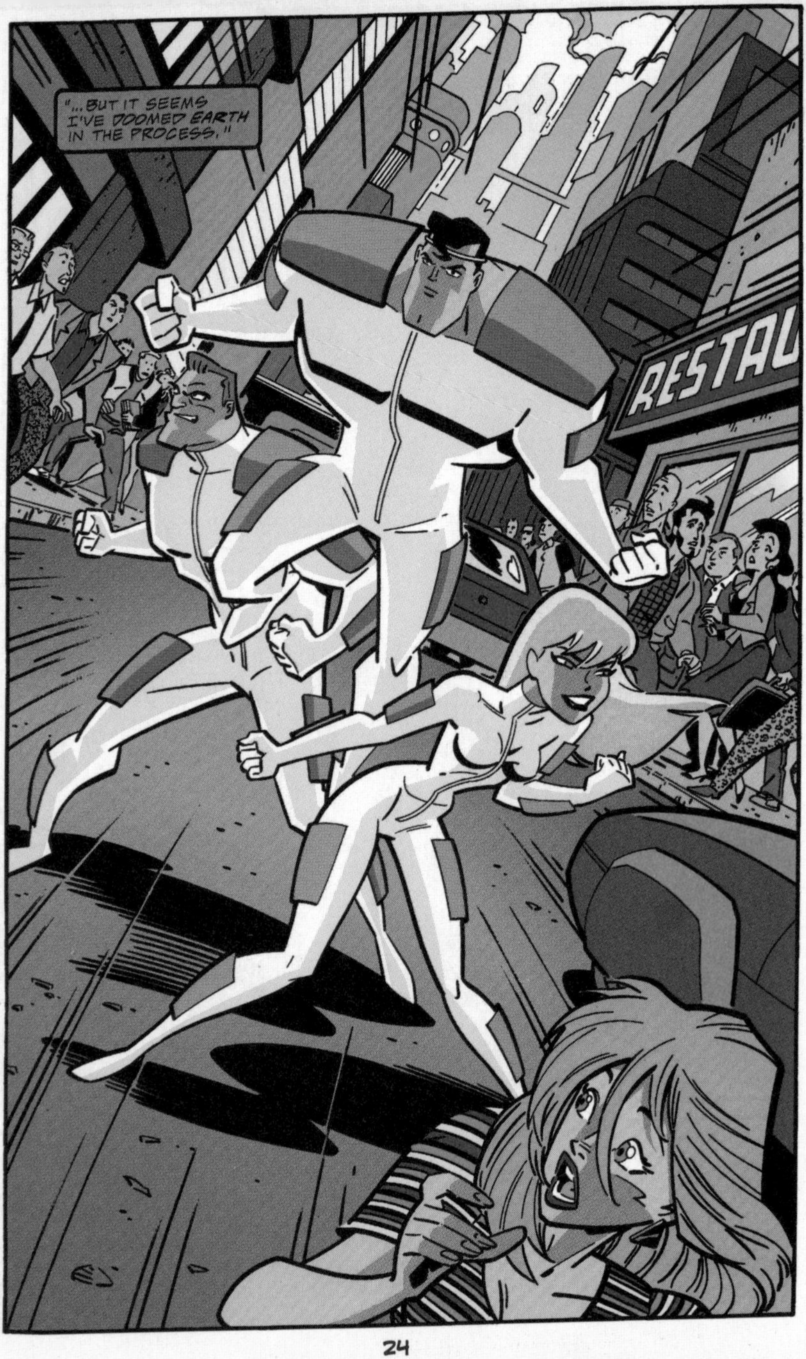
"...BUT IT SEEMS I'VE DOOMED EARTH IN THE PROCESS."
RESTAU

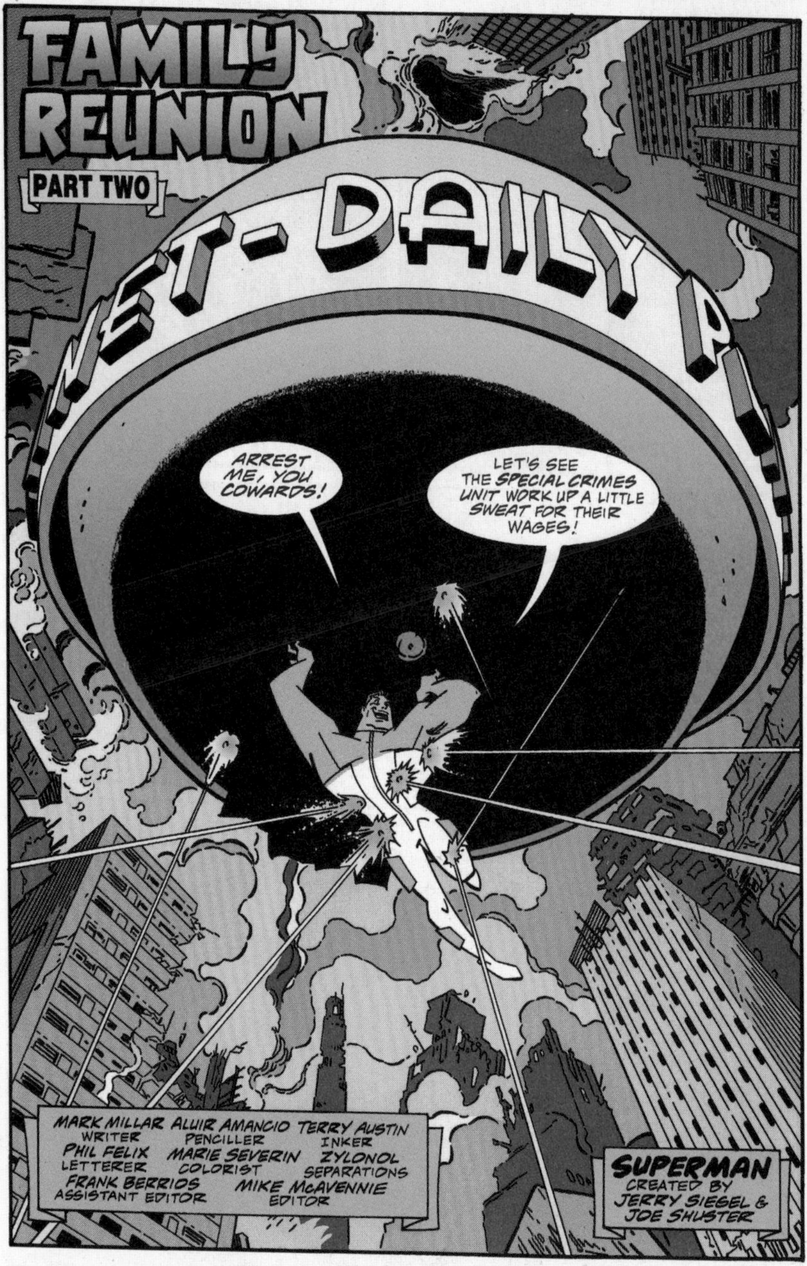
FAMILY REUNION
PART TWO
-NET- DAILY P
ARREST ME, YOU COWARDS!
LET'S SEE THE SPECIAL CRIMES UNIT WORK UP A LITTLE SWEAT FOR THEIR WAGES!
MARK MILLAR WRITER ALUIR AMANCIO PENCILLER TERRY AUSTIN INKER
PHIL FELIX LETTERER MARIE SEVERIN COLORIST ZYLONOL SEPARATIONS
FRANK BERRIOS ASSISTANT EDITOR MIKE McAVENNIE EDITOR
SUPERMAN CREATED BY JERRY SIEGEL & JOE SHUSTER

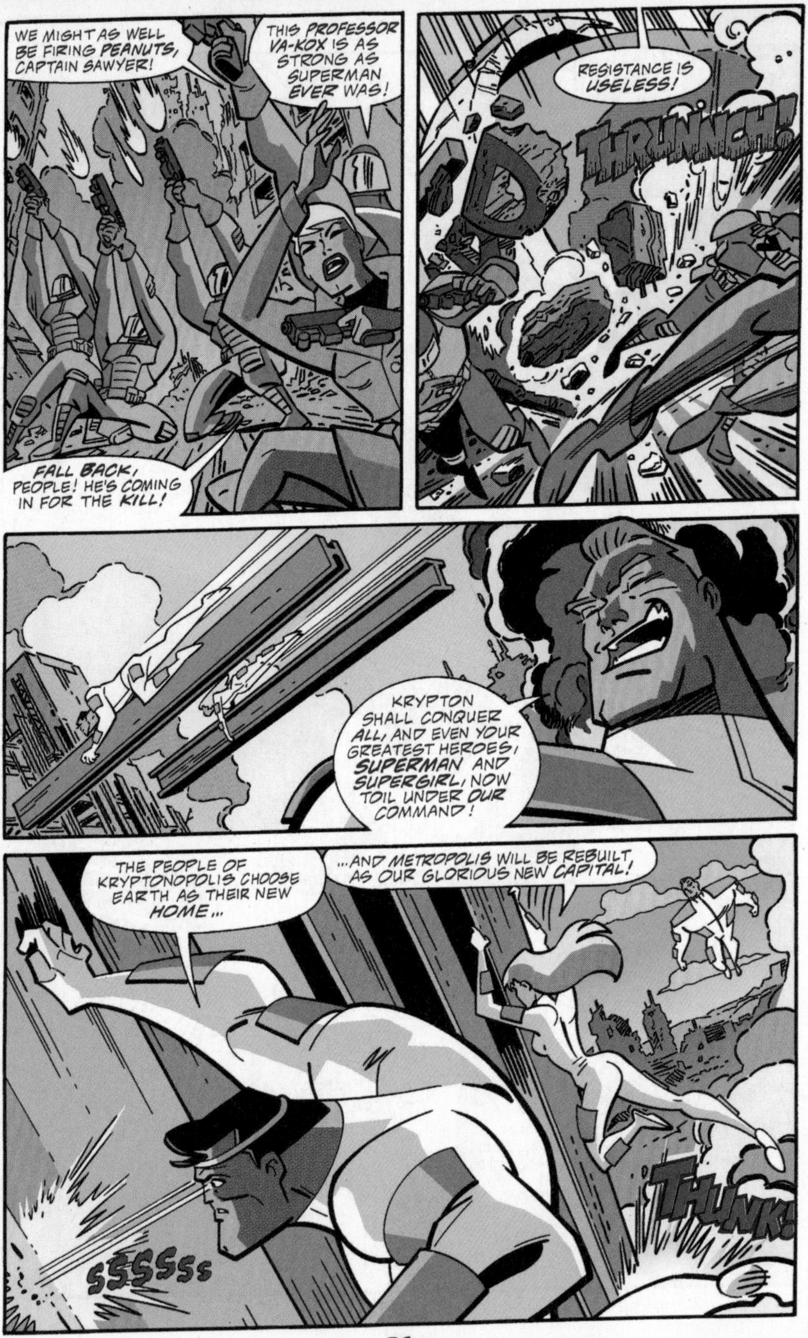

WE MIGHT AS WELL BE FIRING PEANUTS, CAPTAIN SAWYER!
THIS PROFESSOR VA-KOX IS AS STRONG AS SUPERMAN EVER WAS!
FALL BACK, PEOPLE! HE'S COMING IN FOR THE KILL!
RESISTANCE IS USELESS!
THRUNNCH!
KRYPTON SHALL CONQUER ALL, AND EVEN YOUR GREATEST HEROES, SUPERMAN AND SUPERGIRL, NOW TOIL UNDER OUR COMMAND!
THE PEOPLE OF KRYPTONOPOLIS CHOOSE EARTH AS THEIR NEW HOME...
...AND METROPOLIS WILL BE REBUILT AS OUR GLORIOUS NEW CAPITAL!
SSSSSSS
THUNK!

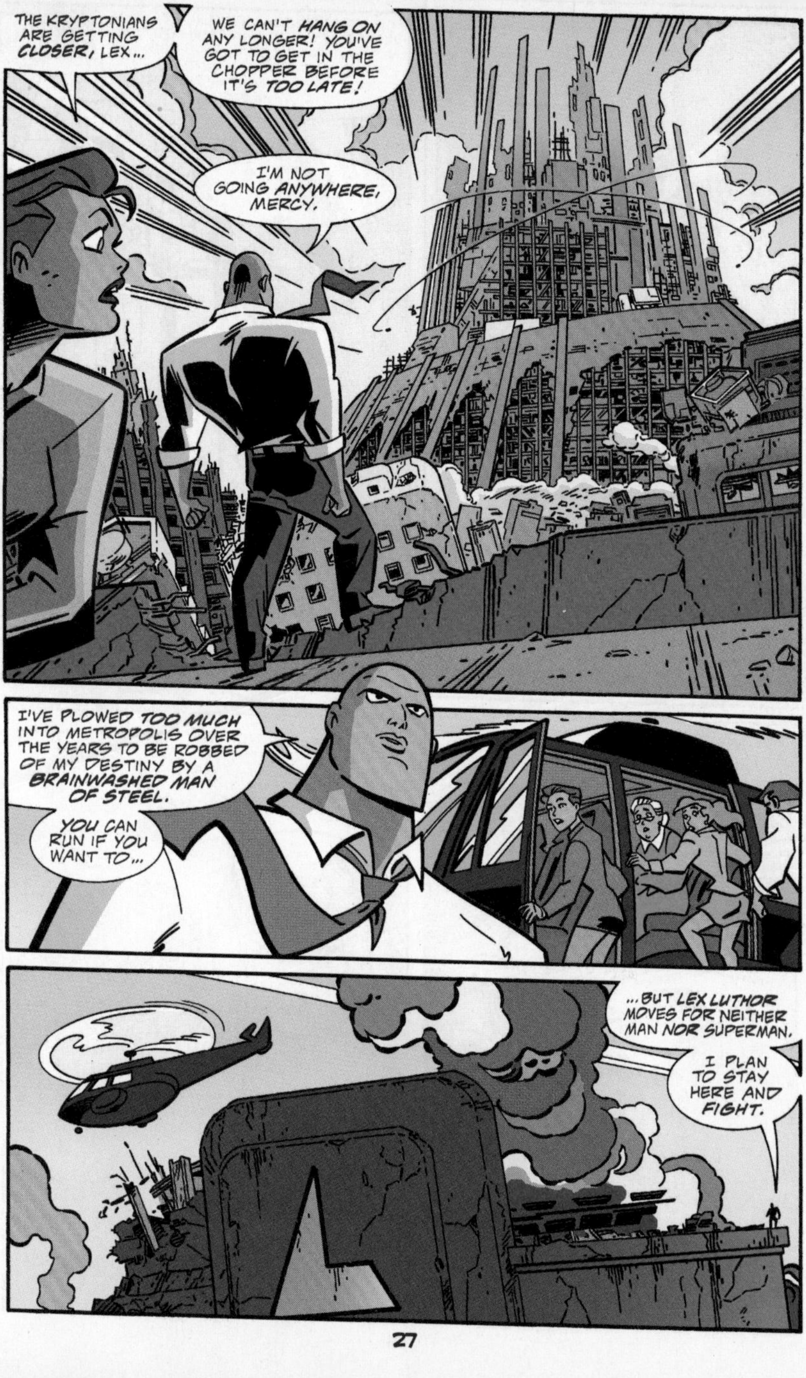
THE KRYPTONIANS ARE GETTING CLOSER, LEX...
WE CAN'T HANG ON ANY LONGER! YOU'VE GOT TO GET IN THE CHOPPER BEFORE IT'S TOO LATE!
I'M NOT GOING ANYWHERE, MERCY.
I'VE PLOWED TOO MUCH INTO METROPOLIS OVER THE YEARS TO BE ROBBED OF MY DESTINY BY A BRAINWASHED MAN OF STEEL.
YOU CAN RUN IF YOU WANT TO...
...BUT LEX LUTHOR MOVES FOR NEITHER MAN NOR SUPERMAN.
I PLAN TO STAY HERE AND FIGHT.

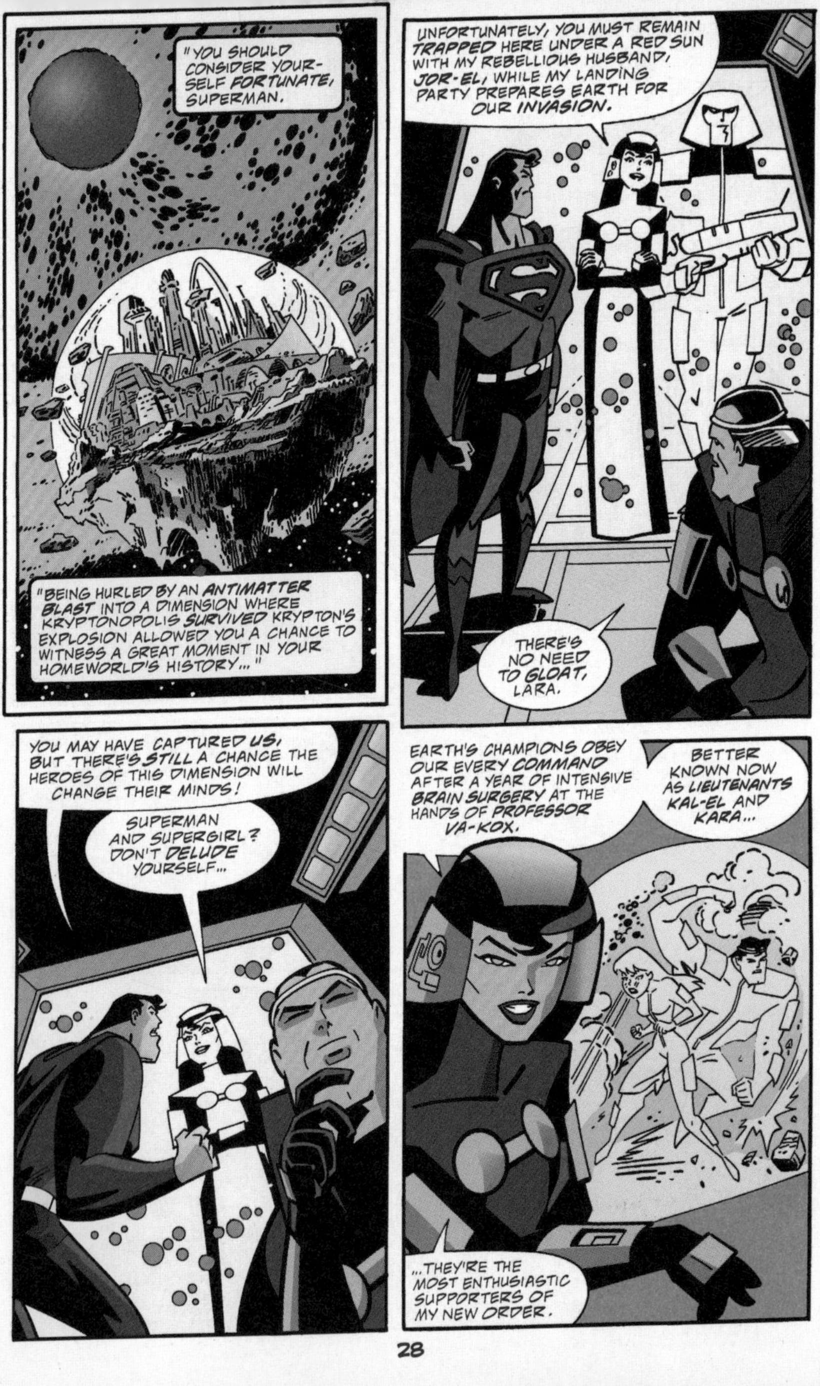
"YOU SHOULD CONSIDER YOURSELF FORTUNATE, SUPERMAN.
"BEING HURLED BY AN ANTIMATTER BLAST INTO A DIMENSION WHERE KRYPTONOPOLIS SURVIVED KRYPTON'S EXPLOSION ALLOWED YOU A CHANCE TO WITNESS A GREAT MOMENT IN YOUR HOMEWORLD'S HISTORY..."
UNFORTUNATELY, YOU MUST REMAIN TRAPPED HERE UNDER A RED SUN WITH MY REBELLIOUS HUSBAND, JOR-EL, WHILE MY LANDING PARTY PREPARES EARTH FOR OUR INVASION.
THERE'S NO NEED TO GLOAT, LARA.
YOU MAY HAVE CAPTURED US, BUT THERE'S STILL A CHANCE THE HEROES OF THIS DIMENSION WILL CHANGE THEIR MINDS!
SUPERMAN AND SUPERGIRL? DON'T DELUDE YOURSELF...
EARTH'S CHAMPIONS OBEY OUR EVERY COMMAND AFTER A YEAR OF INTENSIVE BRAIN SURGERY AT THE HANDS OF PROFESSOR VA-KOX.
BETTER KNOWN NOW AS LIEUTENANTS KAL-EL AND KARA...
...THEY'RE THE MOST ENTHUSIASTIC SUPPORTERS OF MY NEW ORDER.

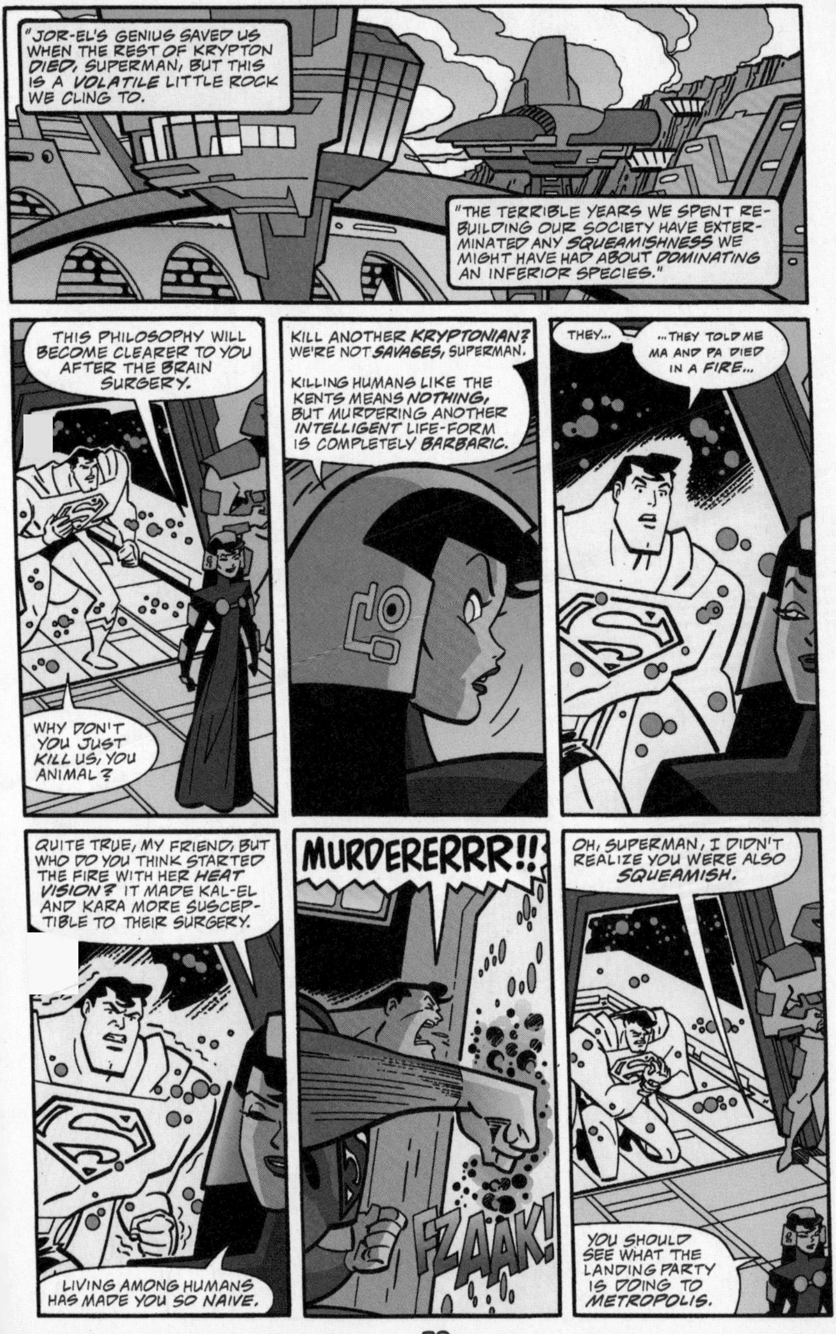
"JOR-EL'S GENIUS SAVED US WHEN THE REST OF KRYPTON DIED, SUPERMAN, BUT THIS IS A VOLATILE LITTLE ROCK WE CLING TO.
"THE TERRIBLE YEARS WE SPENT REBUILDING OUR SOCIETY HAVE EXTERMINATED ANY SQUEAMISHNESS WE MIGHT HAVE HAD ABOUT DOMINATING AN INFERIOR SPECIES."
THIS PHILOSOPHY WILL BECOME CLEARER TO YOU AFTER THE BRAIN SURGERY.
WHY DON'T YOU JUST KILL US, YOU ANIMAL?
KILL ANOTHER KRYPTONIAN? WE'RE NOT SAVAGES, SUPERMAN.
KILLING HUMANS LIKE THE KENTS MEANS NOTHING, BUT MURDERING ANOTHER INTELLIGENT LIFE-FORM IS COMPLETELY BARBARIC.
THEY...
...THEY TOLD ME MA AND PA DIED IN A FIRE...
QUITE TRUE, MY FRIEND, BUT WHO DO YOU THINK STARTED THE FIRE WITH HER HEAT VISION? IT MADE KAL-EL AND KARA MORE SUSCEPTIBLE TO THEIR SURGERY.
LIVING AMONG HUMANS HAS MADE YOU SO NAIVE.
MURDERERRR!!
FZAAK!
OH, SUPERMAN, I DIDN'T REALIZE YOU WERE ALSO SQUEAMISH.
YOU SHOULD SEE WHAT THE LANDING PARTY IS DOING TO METROPOLIS.

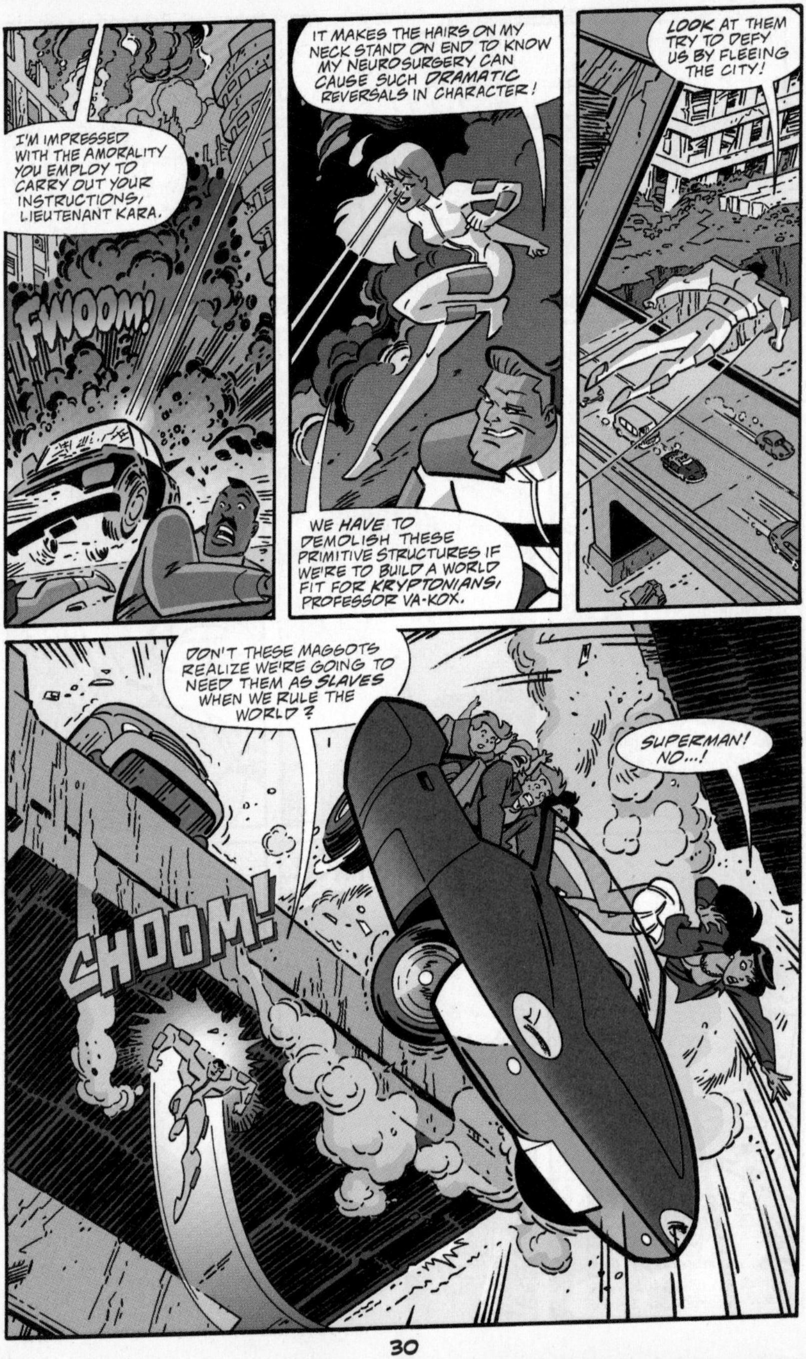
I'M IMPRESSED WITH THE AMORALITY YOU EMPLOY TO CARRY OUT YOUR INSTRUCTIONS, LIEUTENANT KARA.
FWOOM!
IT MAKES THE HAIRS ON MY NECK STAND ON END TO KNOW MY NEUROSURGERY CAN CAUSE SUCH DRAMATIC REVERSALS IN CHARACTER!
WE HAVE TO DEMOLISH THESE PRIMITIVE STRUCTURES IF WE'RE TO BUILD A WORLD FIT FOR KRYPTONIANS, PROFESSOR VA-KOX.
LOOK AT THEM TRY TO DEFY US BY FLEEING THE CITY!
DON'T THESE MAGGOTS REALIZE WE'RE GOING TO NEED THEM AS SLAVES WHEN WE RULE THE WORLD?
SUPERMAN! NO...!
CHOOM!

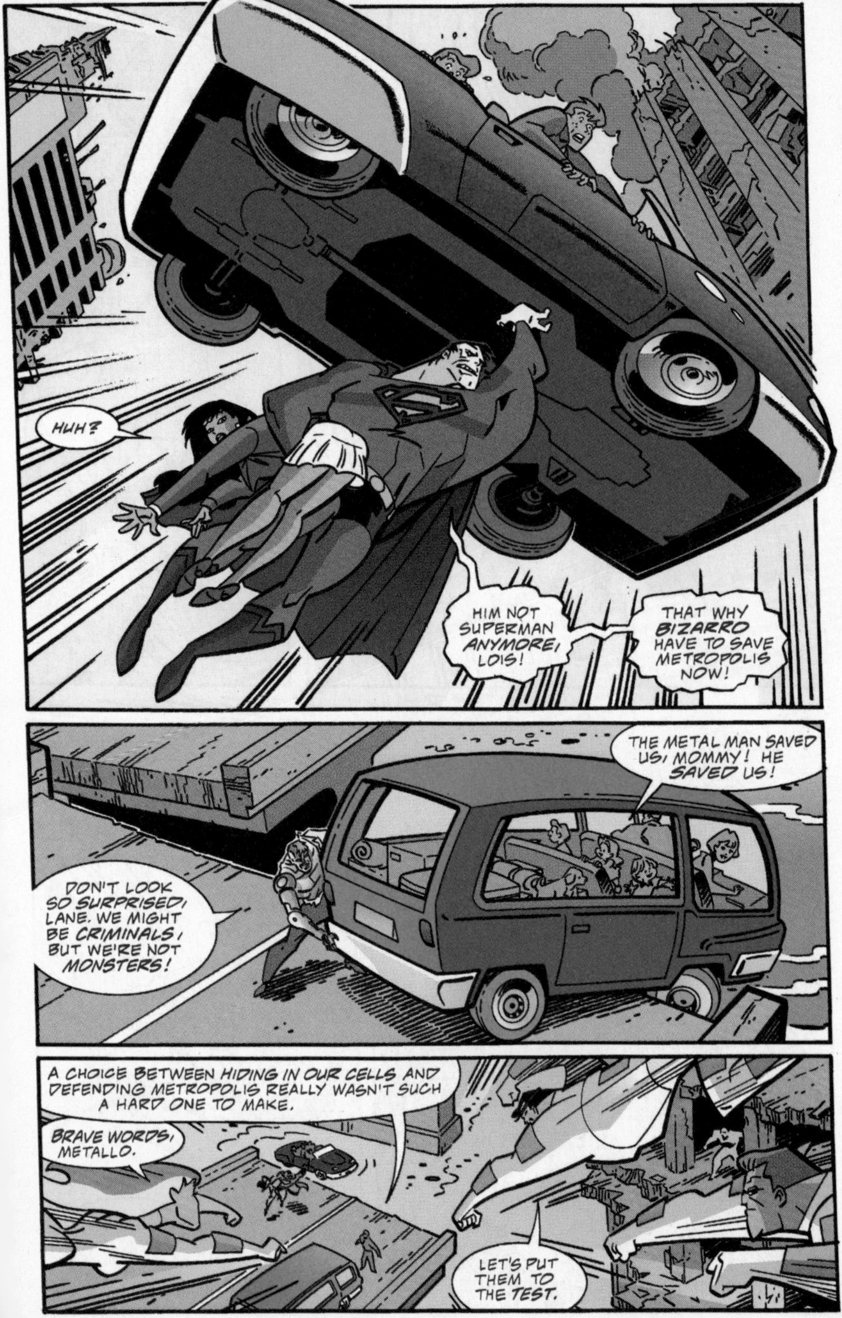
HUH?
HIM NOT SUPERMAN ANYMORE, LOIS!
THAT WHY BIZARRO HAVE TO SAVE METROPOLIS NOW!
THE METAL MAN SAVED US, MOMMY! HE SAVED US!
DON'T LOOK SO SURPRISED, LANE. WE MIGHT BE CRIMINALS, BUT WE'RE NOT MONSTERS!
A CHOICE BETWEEN HIDING IN OUR CELLS AND DEFENDING METROPOLIS REALLY WASN'T SUCH A HARD ONE TO MAKE.
BRAVE WORDS, METALLO.
LET'S PUT THEM TO THE TEST.

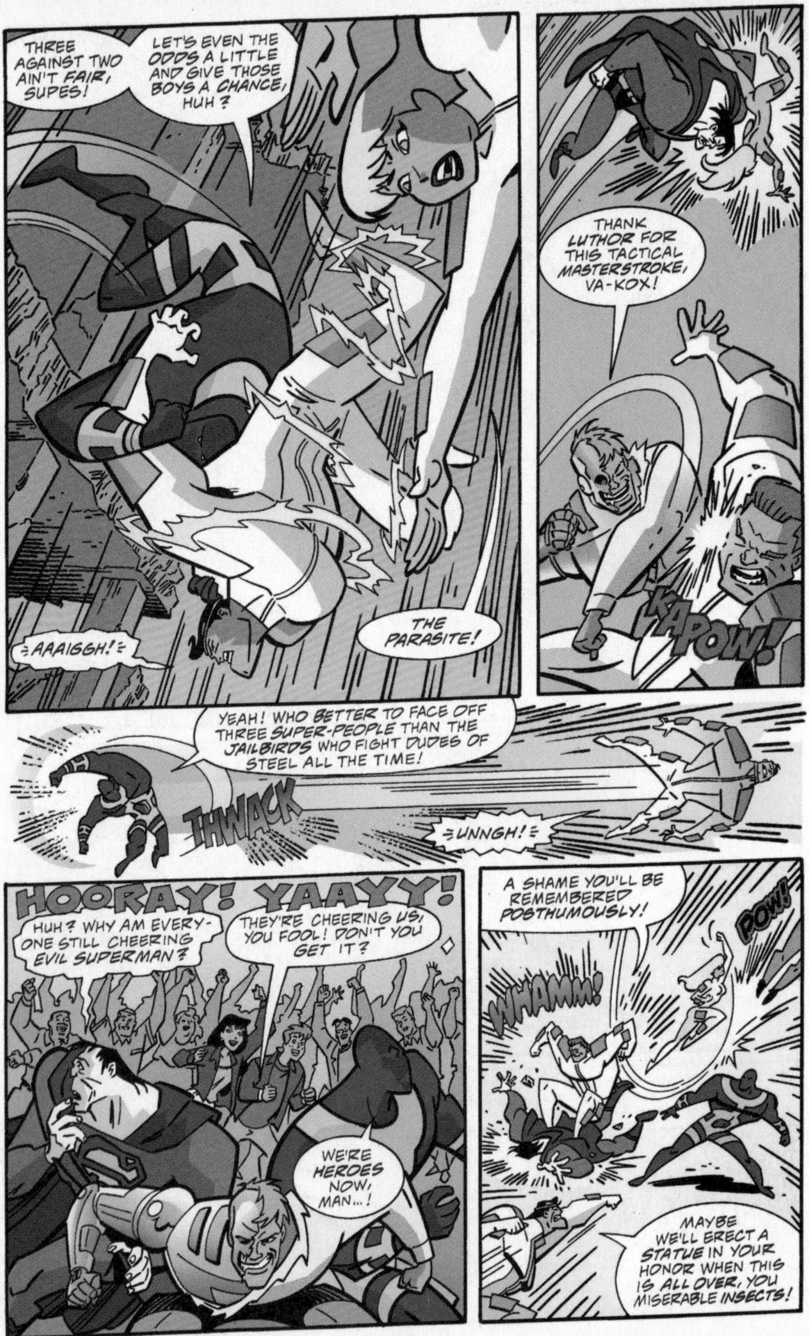
THREE AGAINST TWO AIN'T FAIR, SUPES!
LET'S EVEN THE ODDS A LITTLE AND GIVE THOSE BOYS A CHANCE, HUH?
AAAIGGH!
THE PARASITE!
THANK LUTHOR FOR THIS TACTICAL MASTERSTROKE, VA-KOX!
KAPOW!
YEAH! WHO BETTER TO FACE OFF THREE SUPER-PEOPLE THAN THE JAILBIRDS WHO FIGHT DUDES OF STEEL ALL THE TIME!
THWACK
UNNGH!
HOORAY! YAAYY!
HUH? WHY AM EVERY-ONE STILL CHEERING EVIL SUPERMAN?
THEY'RE CHEERING US, YOU FOOL! DON'T YOU GET IT?
WE'RE HEROES NOW, MAN...!
A SHAME YOU'LL BE REMEMBERED POSTHUMOUSLY!
POW!
WHAMM!
MAYBE WE'LL ERECT A STATUE IN YOUR HONOR WHEN THIS IS ALL OVER, YOU MISERABLE INSECTS!

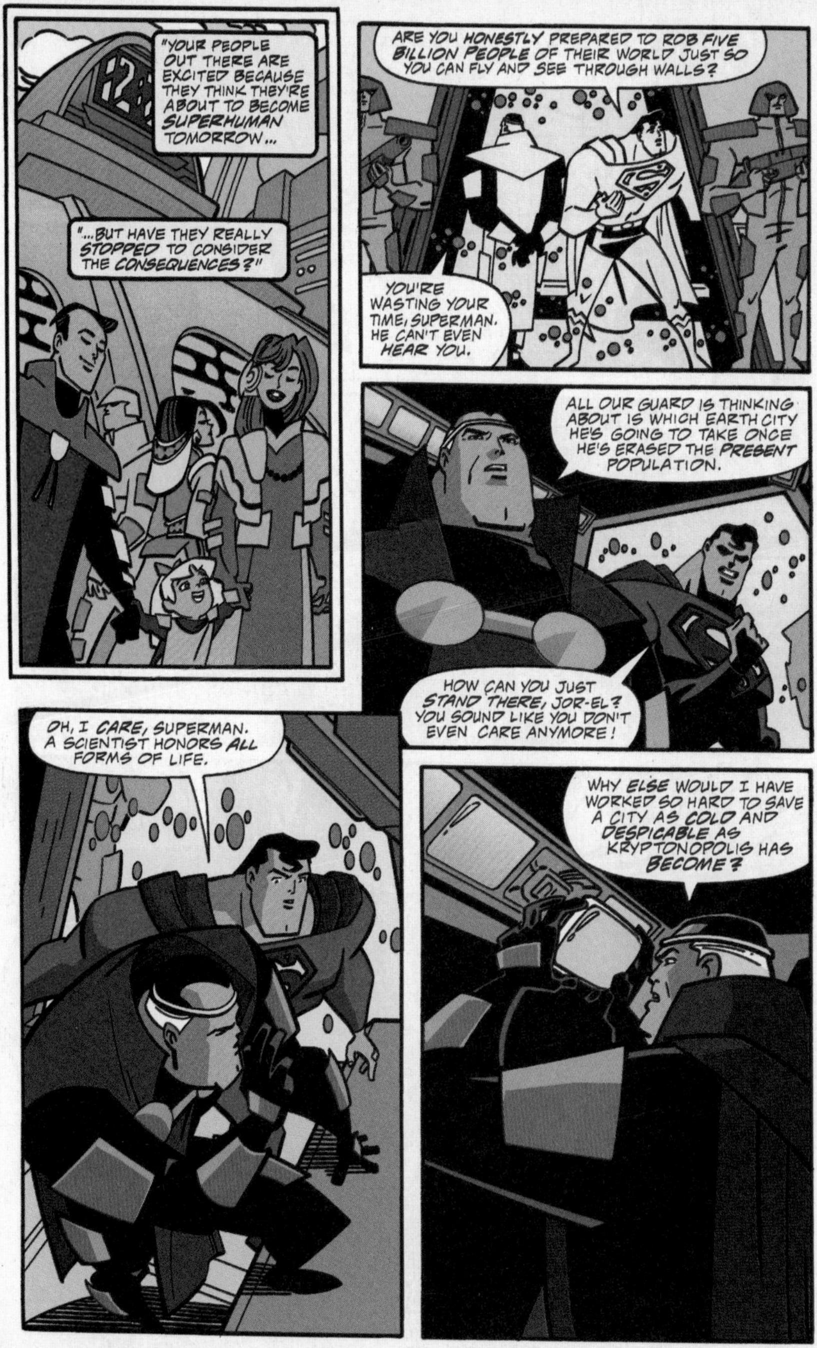
"YOUR PEOPLE OUT THERE ARE EXCITED BECAUSE THEY THINK THEY'RE ABOUT TO BECOME SUPERHUMAN TOMORROW...
"...BUT HAVE THEY REALLY STOPPED TO CONSIDER THE CONSEQUENCES?"
ARE YOU HONESTLY PREPARED TO ROB FIVE BILLION PEOPLE OF THEIR WORLD JUST SO YOU CAN FLY AND SEE THROUGH WALLS?
YOU'RE WASTING YOUR TIME, SUPERMAN. HE CAN'T EVEN HEAR YOU.
ALL OUR GUARD IS THINKING ABOUT IS WHICH EARTH CITY HE'S GOING TO TAKE ONCE HE'S ERASED THE PRESENT POPULATION.
HOW CAN YOU JUST STAND THERE, JOR-EL? YOU SOUND LIKE YOU DON'T EVEN CARE ANYMORE!
OH, I CARE, SUPERMAN. A SCIENTIST HONORS ALL FORMS OF LIFE.
WHY ELSE WOULD I HAVE WORKED SO HARD TO SAVE A CITY AS COLD AND DESPICABLE AS KRYPTONOPOLIS HAS BECOME?

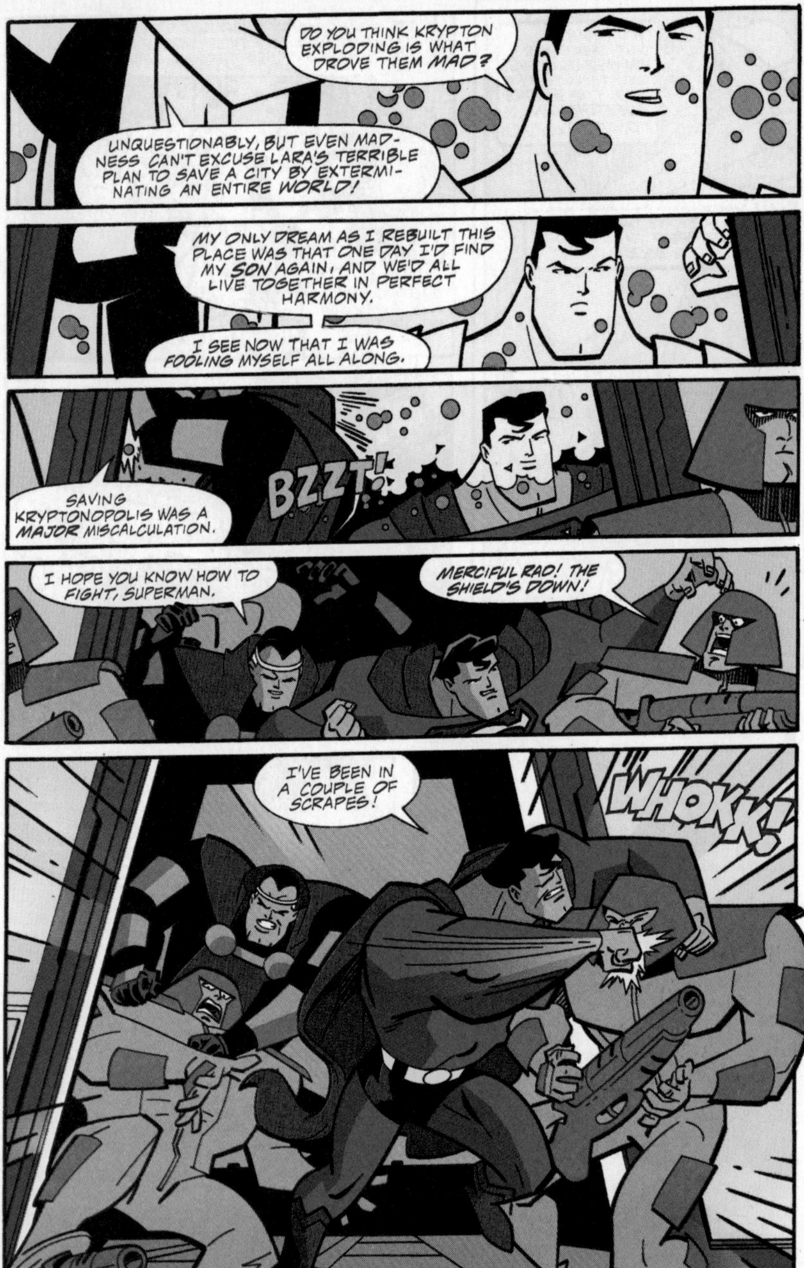
DO YOU THINK KRYPTON EXPLODING IS WHAT DROVE THEM MAD?
UNQUESTIONABLY, BUT EVEN MADNESS CAN'T EXCUSE LARA'S TERRIBLE PLAN TO SAVE A CITY BY EXTERMINATING AN ENTIRE WORLD!
MY ONLY DREAM AS I REBUILT THIS PLACE WAS THAT ONE DAY I'D FIND MY SON AGAIN, AND WE'D ALL LIVE TOGETHER IN PERFECT HARMONY.
I SEE NOW THAT I WAS FOOLING MYSELF ALL ALONG.
BZZT!
SAVING KRYPTONOPOLIS WAS A MAJOR MISCALCULATION.
I HOPE YOU KNOW HOW TO FIGHT, SUPERMAN.
MERCIFUL RAO! THE SHIELD'S DOWN!
I'VE BEEN IN A COUPLE OF SCRAPES!
WHOKK!

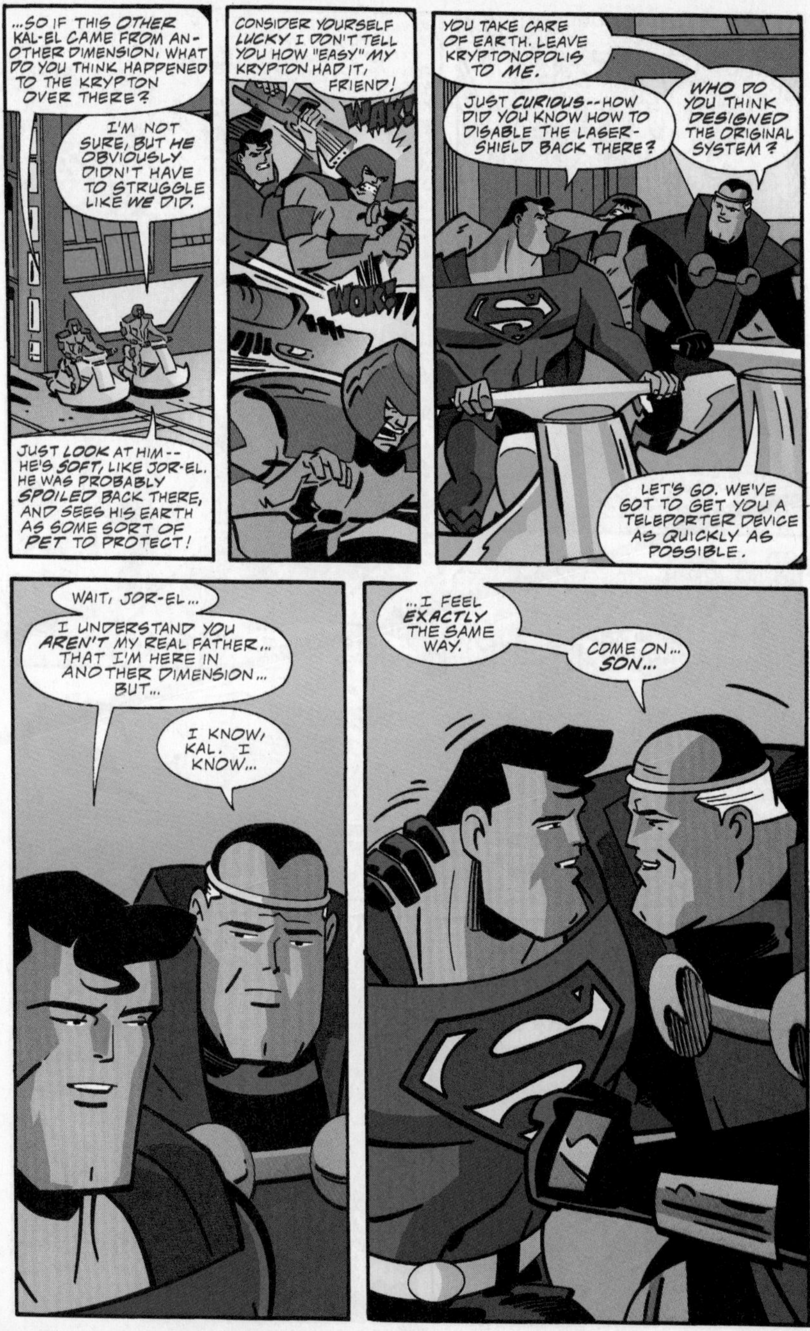
...SO IF THIS OTHER KAL-EL CAME FROM ANOTHER DIMENSION, WHAT DO YOU THINK HAPPENED TO THE KRYPTON OVER THERE?
I'M NOT SURE, BUT HE OBVIOUSLY DIDN'T HAVE TO STRUGGLE LIKE WE DID.
JUST LOOK AT HIM -- HE'S SOFT, LIKE JOR-EL. HE WAS PROBABLY SPOILED BACK THERE, AND SEES HIS EARTH AS SOME SORT OF PET TO PROTECT!
CONSIDER YOURSELF LUCKY I DON'T TELL YOU HOW "EASY" MY KRYPTON HAD IT, FRIEND!
WAK!
WOK!
YOU TAKE CARE OF EARTH. LEAVE KRYPTONOPOLIS TO ME.
JUST CURIOUS -- HOW DID YOU KNOW HOW TO DISABLE THE LASER-SHIELD BACK THERE?
WHO DO YOU THINK DESIGNED THE ORIGINAL SYSTEM?
LET'S GO. WE'VE GOT TO GET YOU A TELEPORTER DEVICE AS QUICKLY AS POSSIBLE.
WAIT, JOR-EL...
I UNDERSTAND YOU AREN'T MY REAL FATHER... THAT I'M HERE IN ANOTHER DIMENSION... BUT...
I KNOW, KAL. I KNOW...
...I FEEL EXACTLY THE SAME WAY.
COME ON... SON...

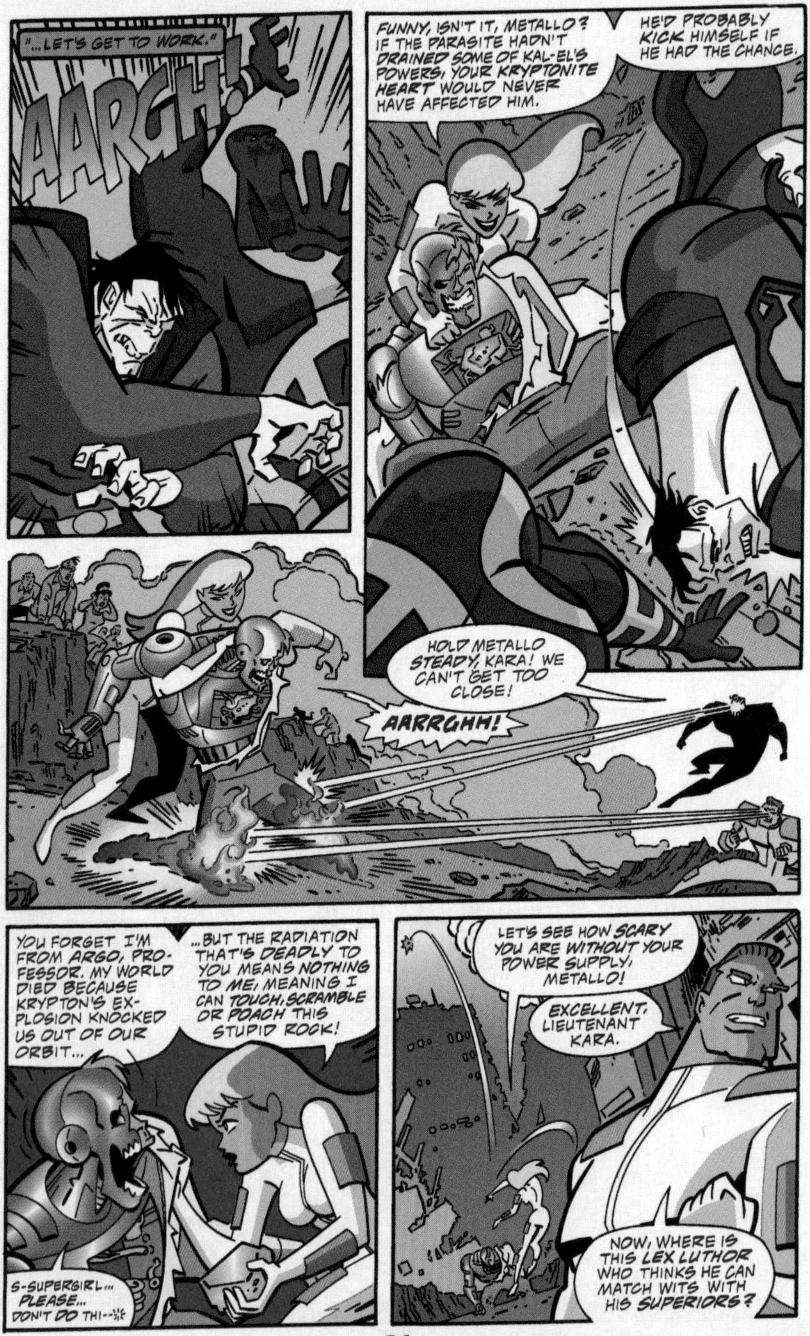
"...LET'S GET TO WORK."
AARGH!
FUNNY, ISN'T IT, METALLO? IF THE PARASITE HADN'T DRAINED SOME OF KAL-EL'S POWERS, YOUR KRYPTONITE HEART WOULD NEVER HAVE AFFECTED HIM.
HE'D PROBABLY KICK HIMSELF IF HE HAD THE CHANCE.
HOLD METALLO STEADY, KARA! WE CAN'T GET TOO CLOSE!
AARRGHH!
YOU FORGET I'M FROM ARGO, PROFESSOR. MY WORLD DIED BECAUSE KRYPTON'S EXPLOSION KNOCKED US OUT OF OUR ORBIT...
...BUT THE RADIATION THAT'S DEADLY TO YOU MEANS NOTHING TO ME, MEANING I CAN TOUCH, SCRAMBLE OR POACH THIS STUPID ROCK!
S-SUPERGIRL... PLEASE... DON'T DO THI--
LET'S SEE HOW SCARY YOU ARE WITHOUT YOUR POWER SUPPLY, METALLO!
EXCELLENT, LIEUTENANT KARA.
NOW, WHERE IS THIS LEX LUTHOR WHO THINKS HE CAN MATCH WITS WITH HIS SUPERIORS?

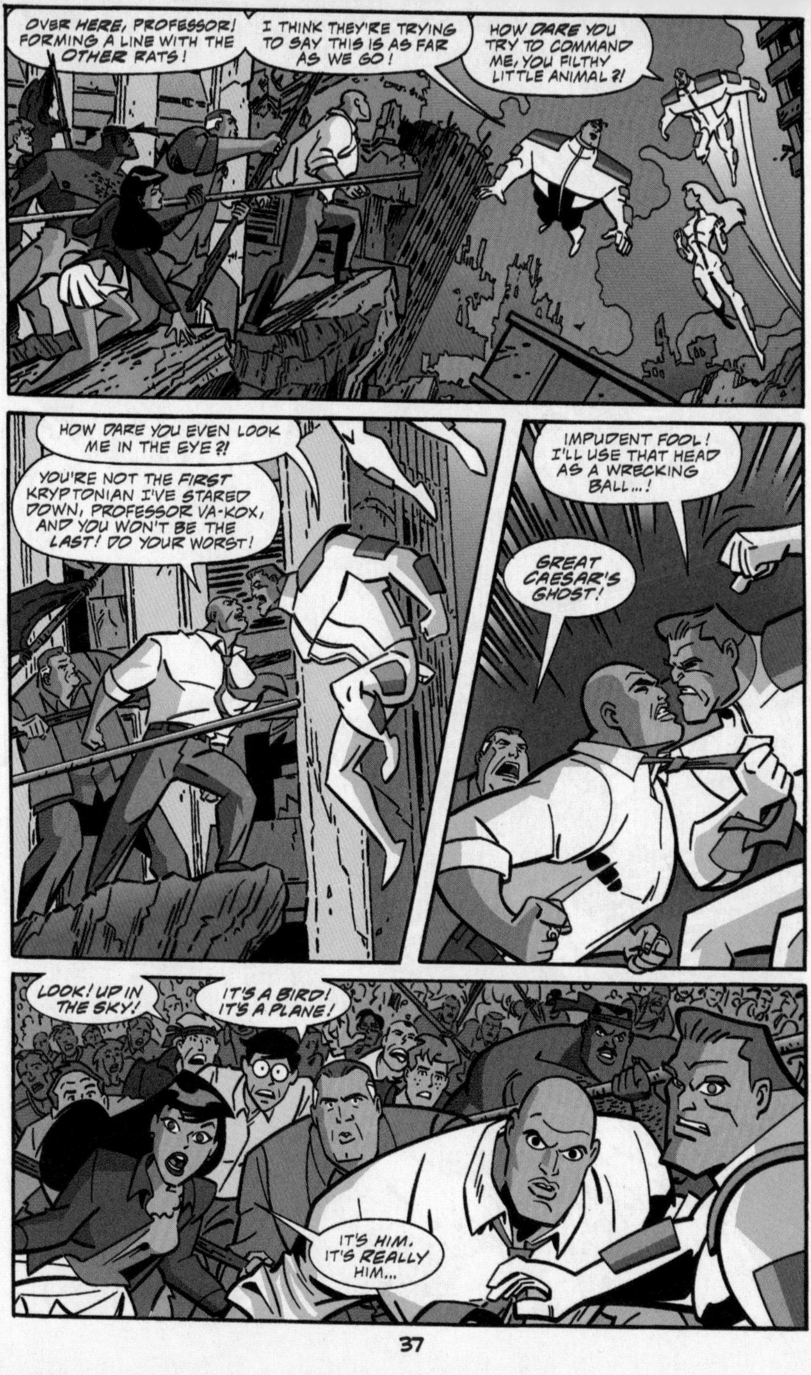
OVER HERE, PROFESSOR! FORMING A LINE WITH THE OTHER RATS!
I THINK THEY'RE TRYING TO SAY THIS IS AS FAR AS WE GO!
HOW DARE YOU TRY TO COMMAND ME, YOU FILTHY LITTLE ANIMAL?!
HOW DARE YOU EVEN LOOK ME IN THE EYE?!
YOU'RE NOT THE FIRST KRYPTONIAN I'VE STARED DOWN, PROFESSOR VA-KOX, AND YOU WON'T BE THE LAST! DO YOUR WORST!
IMPUDENT FOOL! I'LL USE THAT HEAD AS A WRECKING BALL...!
GREAT CAESAR'S GHOST!
LOOK! UP IN THE SKY!
IT'S A BIRD! IT'S A PLANE!
IT'S HIM. IT'S REALLY HIM...

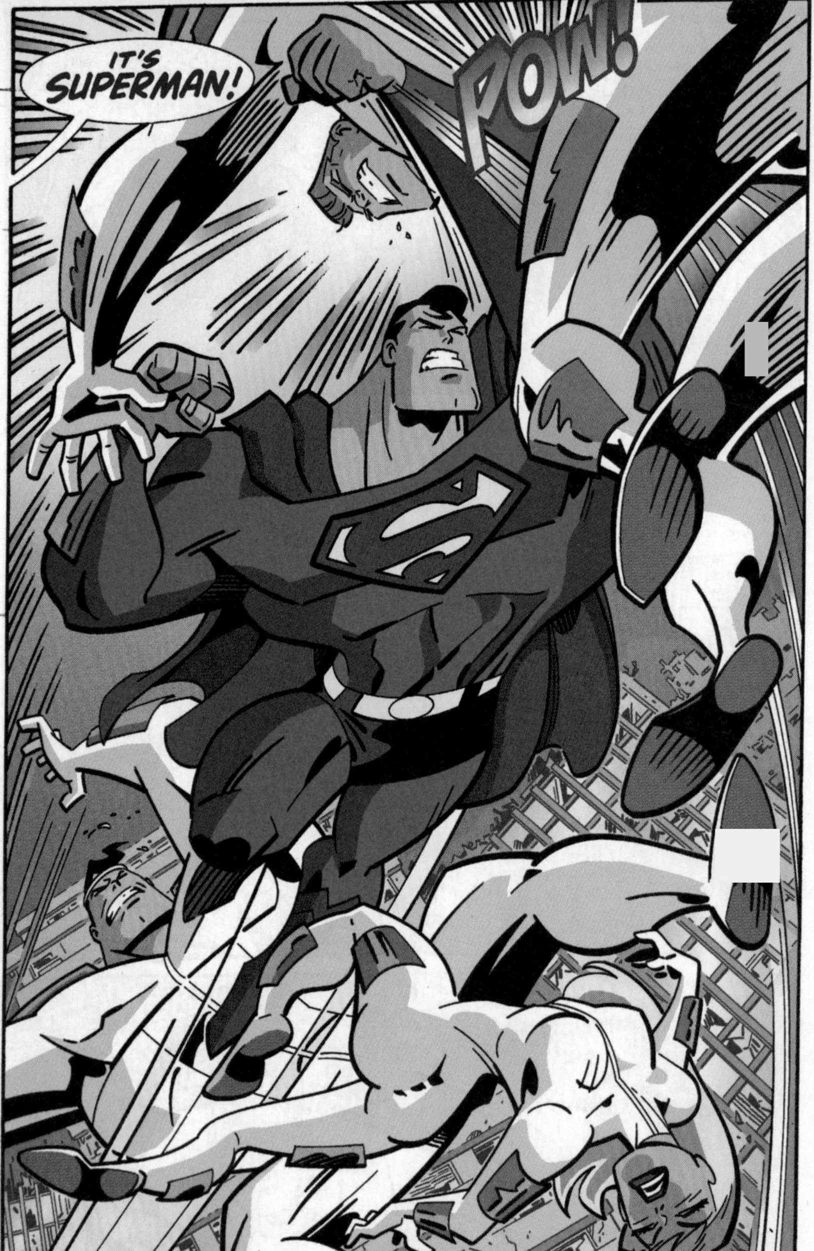
IT'S SUPERMAN!
POW!

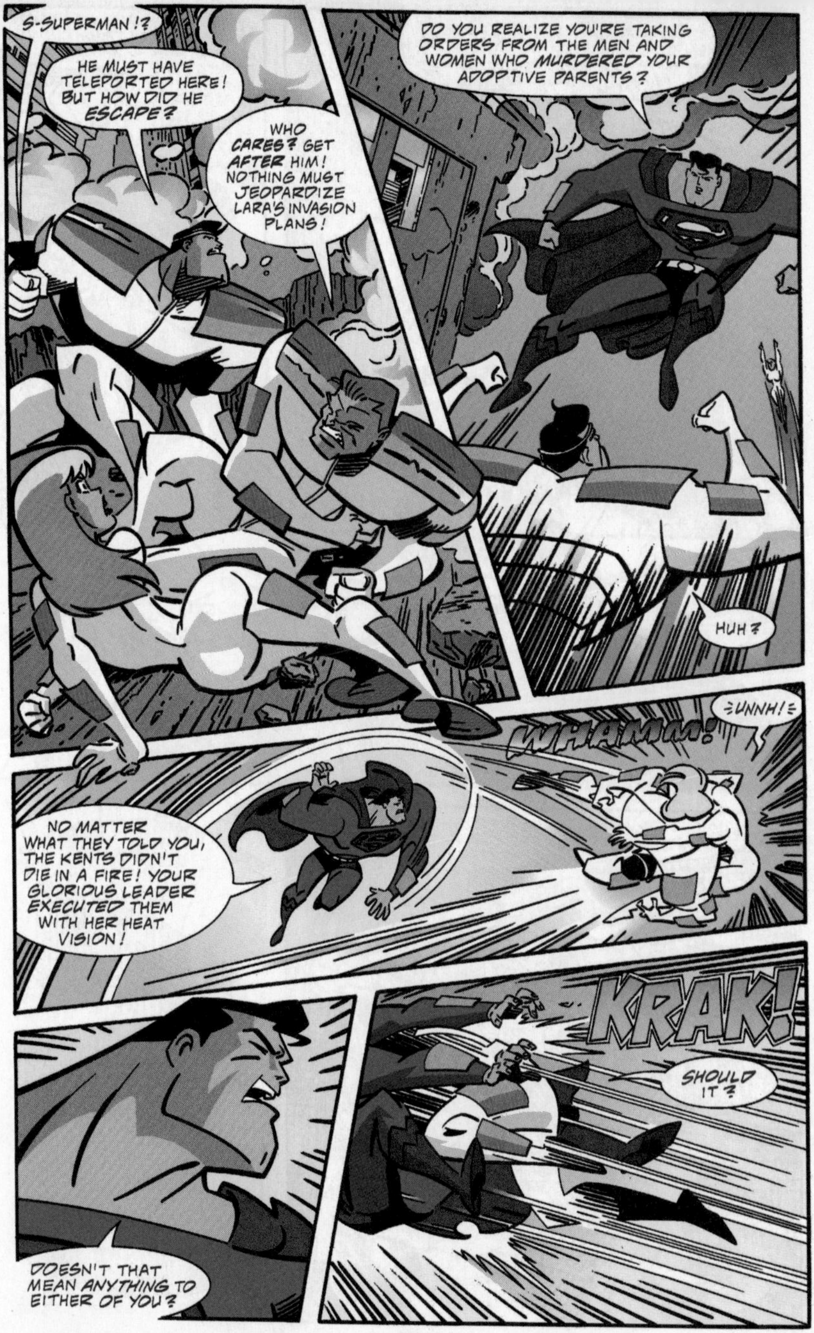

S-SUPERMAN!?
HE MUST HAVE TELEPORTED HERE! BUT HOW DID HE ESCAPE?
WHO CARES? GET AFTER HIM! NOTHING MUST JEOPARDIZE LARA'S INVASION PLANS!
DO YOU REALIZE YOU'RE TAKING ORDERS FROM THE MEN AND WOMEN WHO MURDERED YOUR ADOPTIVE PARENTS?
HUH?
WHAMM!
UNNH!
NO MATTER WHAT THEY TOLD YOU, THE KENTS DIDN'T DIE IN A FIRE! YOUR GLORIOUS LEADER EXECUTED THEM WITH HER HEAT VISION!
DOESN'T THAT MEAN ANYTHING TO EITHER OF YOU?
KRAK!
SHOULD IT?

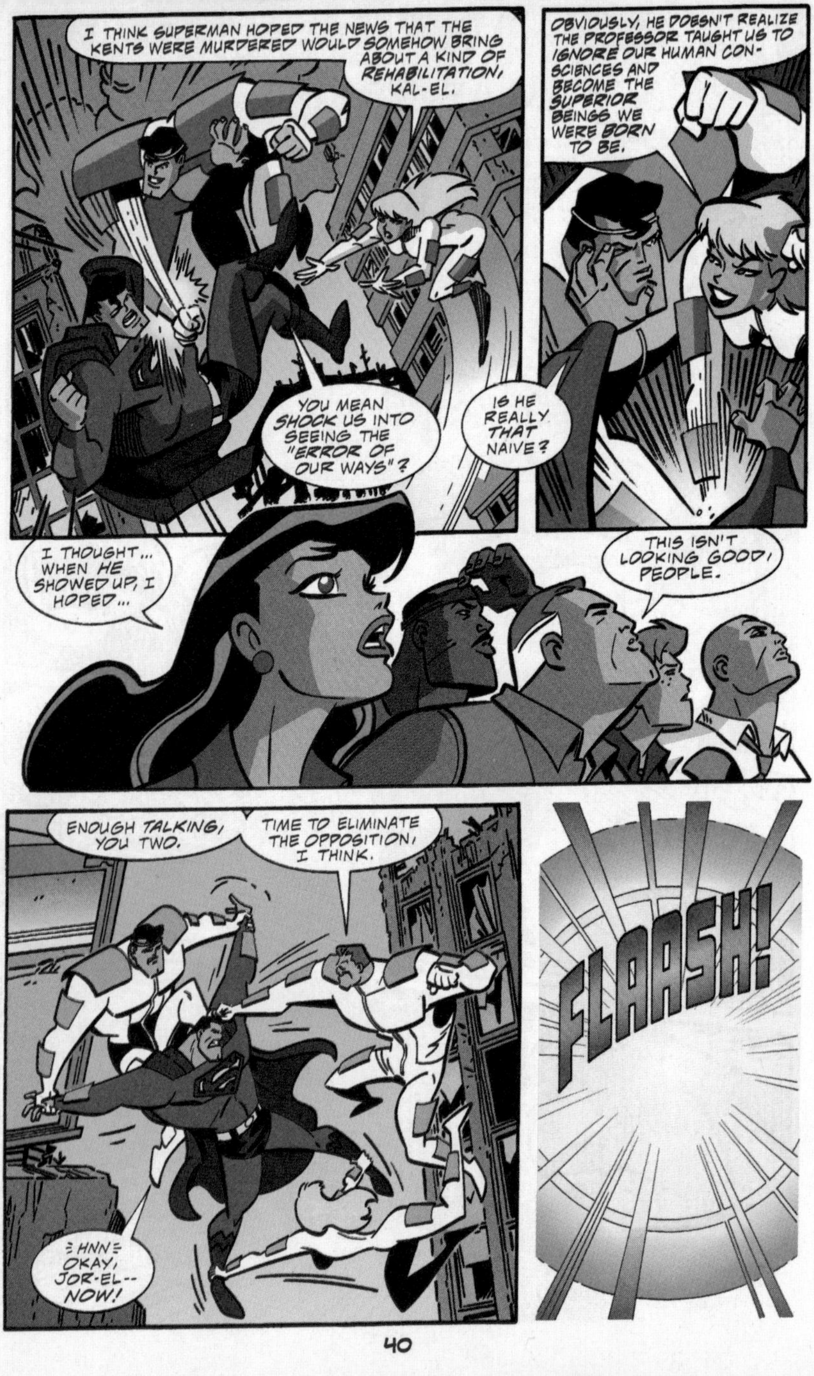
I THINK SUPERMAN HOPED THE NEWS THAT THE KENTS WERE MURDERED WOULD SOMEHOW BRING ABOUT A KIND OF REHABILITATION, KAL-EL.
YOU MEAN SHOCK US INTO SEEING THE "ERROR OF OUR WAYS"?
OBVIOUSLY, HE DOESN'T REALIZE THE PROFESSOR TAUGHT US TO IGNORE OUR HUMAN CON-SCIENCES AND BECOME THE SUPERIOR BEINGS WE WERE BORN TO BE.
IS HE REALLY THAT NAIVE?
I THOUGHT... WHEN HE SHOWED UP, I HOPED...
THIS ISN'T LOOKING GOOD, PEOPLE.
ENOUGH TALKING, YOU TWO.
TIME TO ELIMINATE THE OPPOSITION, I THINK.
HNN OKAY, JOR-EL-- NOW!
FLAASH!

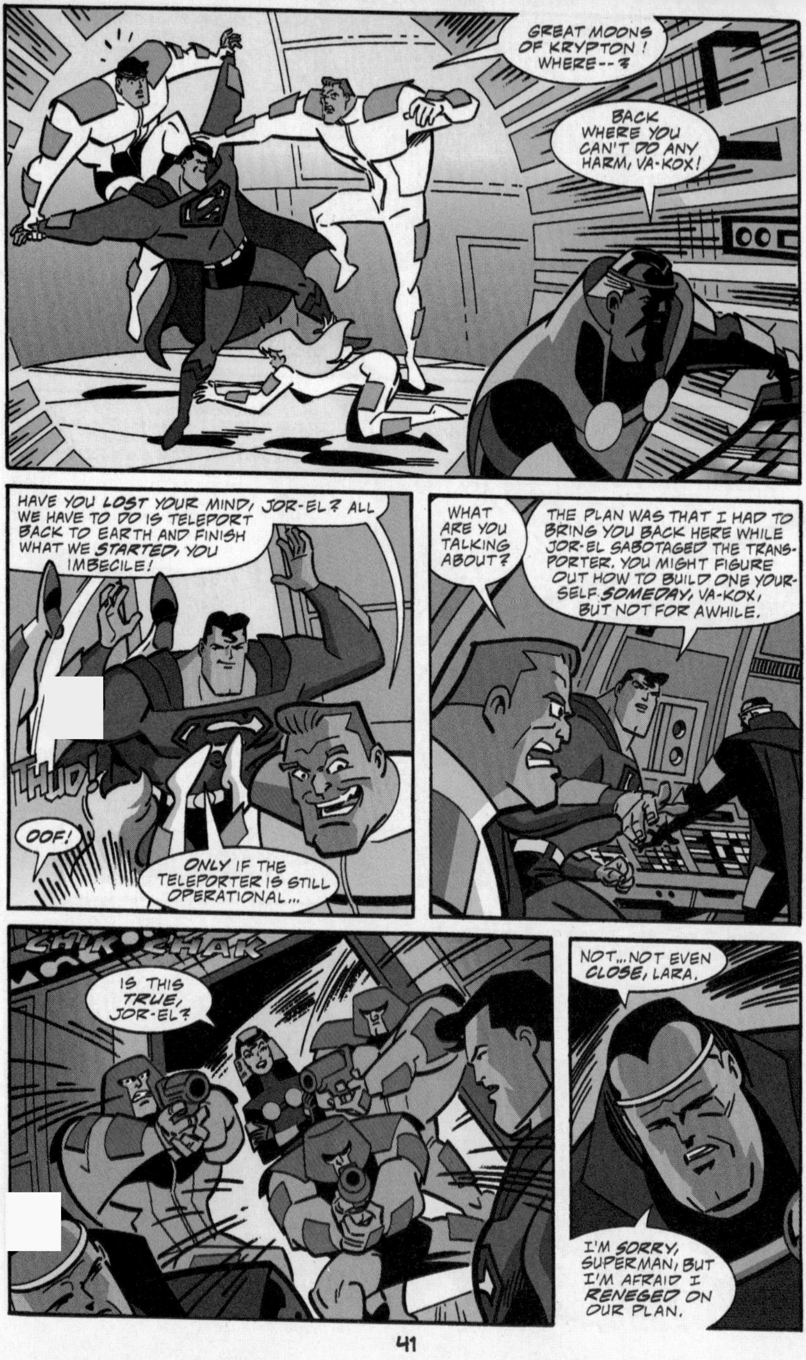
GREAT MOONS OF KRYPTON! WHERE--?
BACK WHERE YOU CAN'T DO ANY HARM, VA-KOX!
HAVE YOU LOST YOUR MIND, JOR-EL? ALL WE HAVE TO DO IS TELEPORT BACK TO EARTH AND FINISH WHAT WE STARTED, YOU IMBECILE!
THUD!
OOF!
ONLY IF THE TELEPORTER IS STILL OPERATIONAL...
WHAT ARE YOU TALKING ABOUT?
THE PLAN WAS THAT I HAD TO BRING YOU BACK HERE WHILE JOR-EL SABOTAGED THE TRANS-PORTER. YOU MIGHT FIGURE OUT HOW TO BUILD ONE YOUR-SELF SOMEDAY, VA-KOX, BUT NOT FOR AWHILE.
CHIK-CHAK
IS THIS TRUE, JOR-EL?
NOT...NOT EVEN CLOSE, LARA.
I'M SORRY, SUPERMAN, BUT I'M AFRAID I RENEGED ON OUR PLAN.

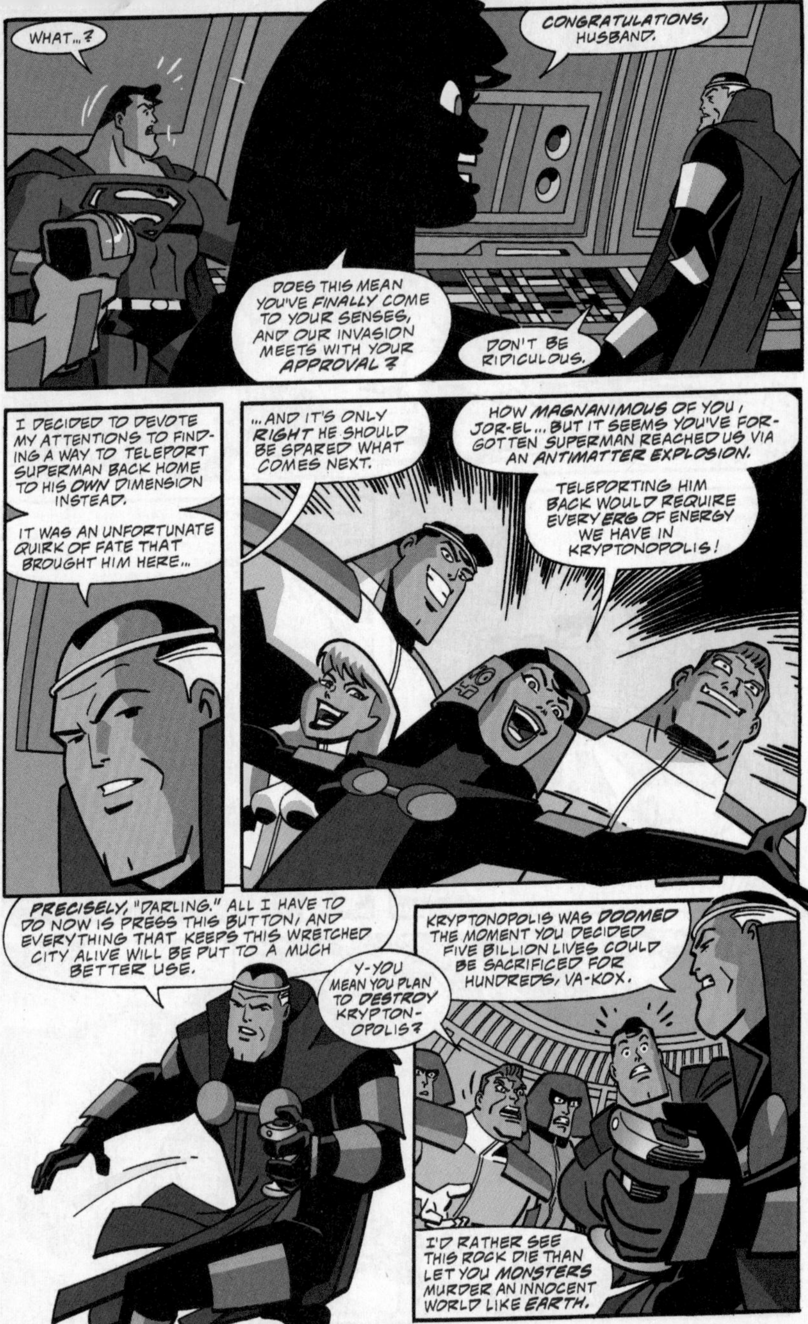

WHAT...?
CONGRATULATIONS, HUSBAND.
DOES THIS MEAN YOU'VE FINALLY COME TO YOUR SENSES, AND OUR INVASION MEETS WITH YOUR APPROVAL?
DON'T BE RIDICULOUS.
I DECIDED TO DEVOTE MY ATTENTIONS TO FINDING A WAY TO TELEPORT SUPERMAN BACK HOME TO HIS OWN DIMENSION INSTEAD.
IT WAS AN UNFORTUNATE QUIRK OF FATE THAT BROUGHT HIM HERE...
...AND IT'S ONLY RIGHT HE SHOULD BE SPARED WHAT COMES NEXT.
HOW MAGNANIMOUS OF YOU, JOR-EL... BUT IT SEEMS YOU'VE FORGOTTEN SUPERMAN REACHED US VIA AN ANTIMATTER EXPLOSION.
TELEPORTING HIM BACK WOULD REQUIRE EVERY ERG OF ENERGY WE HAVE IN KRYPTONOPOLIS!
PRECISELY, "DARLING." ALL I HAVE TO DO NOW IS PRESS THIS BUTTON, AND EVERYTHING THAT KEEPS THIS WRETCHED CITY ALIVE WILL BE PUT TO A MUCH BETTER USE.
Y-YOU MEAN YOU PLAN TO DESTROY KRYPTONOPOLIS?
KRYPTONOPOLIS WAS DOOMED THE MOMENT YOU DECIDED FIVE BILLION LIVES COULD BE SACRIFICED FOR HUNDREDS, VA-KOX.
I'D RATHER SEE THIS ROCK DIE THAN LET YOU MONSTERS MURDER AN INNOCENT WORLD LIKE EARTH.

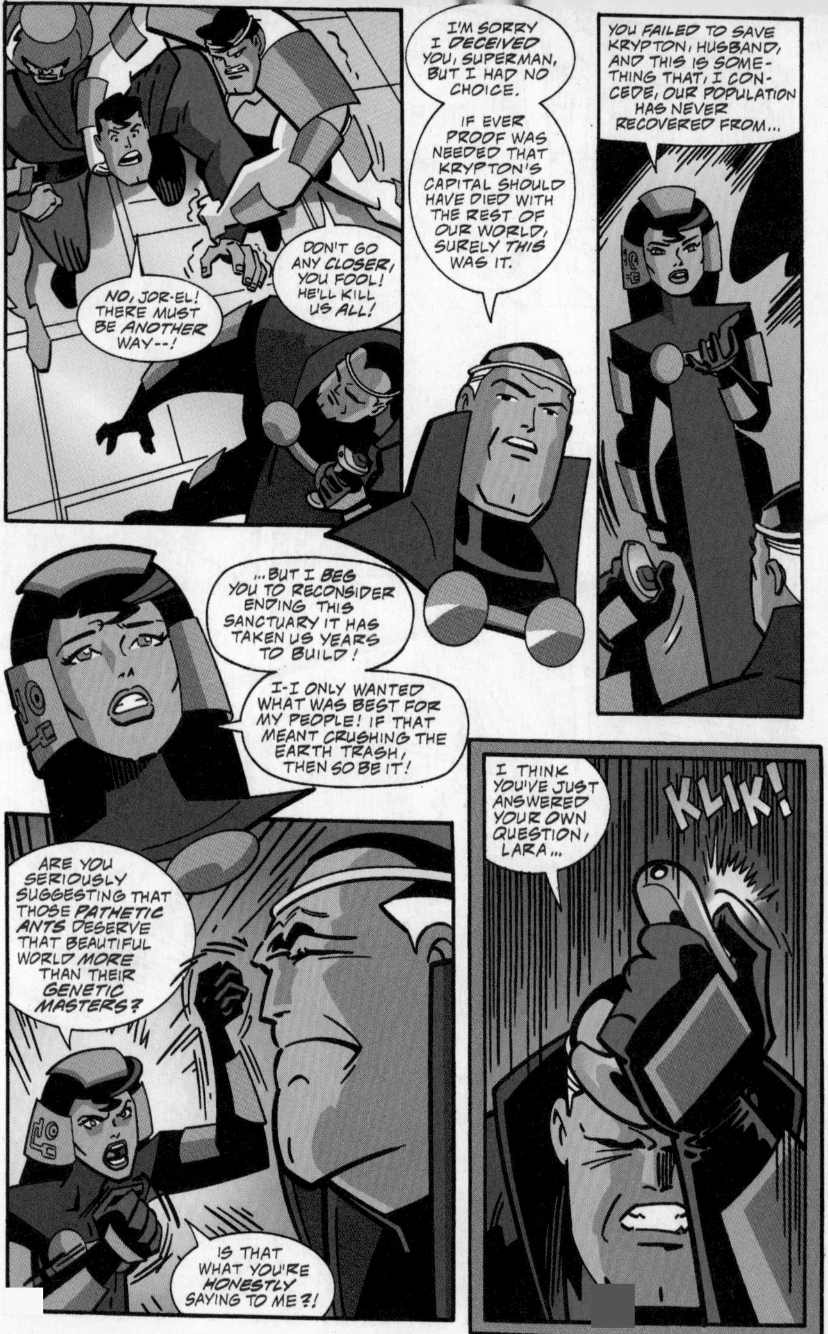
NO, JOR-EL! THERE MUST BE ANOTHER WAY--!
DON'T GO ANY CLOSER, YOU FOOL! HE'LL KILL US ALL!
I'M SORRY I DECEIVED YOU, SUPERMAN, BUT I HAD NO CHOICE.
IF EVER PROOF WAS NEEDED THAT KRYPTON'S CAPITAL SHOULD HAVE DIED WITH THE REST OF OUR WORLD, SURELY THIS WAS IT.
YOU FAILED TO SAVE KRYPTON, HUSBAND, AND THIS IS SOMETHING THAT, I CONCEDE, OUR POPULATION HAS NEVER RECOVERED FROM...
...BUT I BEG YOU TO RECONSIDER ENDING THIS SANCTUARY IT HAS TAKEN US YEARS TO BUILD!
I-I ONLY WANTED WHAT WAS BEST FOR MY PEOPLE! IF THAT MEANT CRUSHING THE EARTH TRASH, THEN SO BE IT!
ARE YOU SERIOUSLY SUGGESTING THAT THOSE PATHETIC ANTS DESERVE THAT BEAUTIFUL WORLD MORE THAN THEIR GENETIC MASTERS?
IS THAT WHAT YOU'RE HONESTLY SAYING TO ME?!
I THINK YOU'VE JUST ANSWERED YOUR OWN QUESTION, LARA...
KLIK!

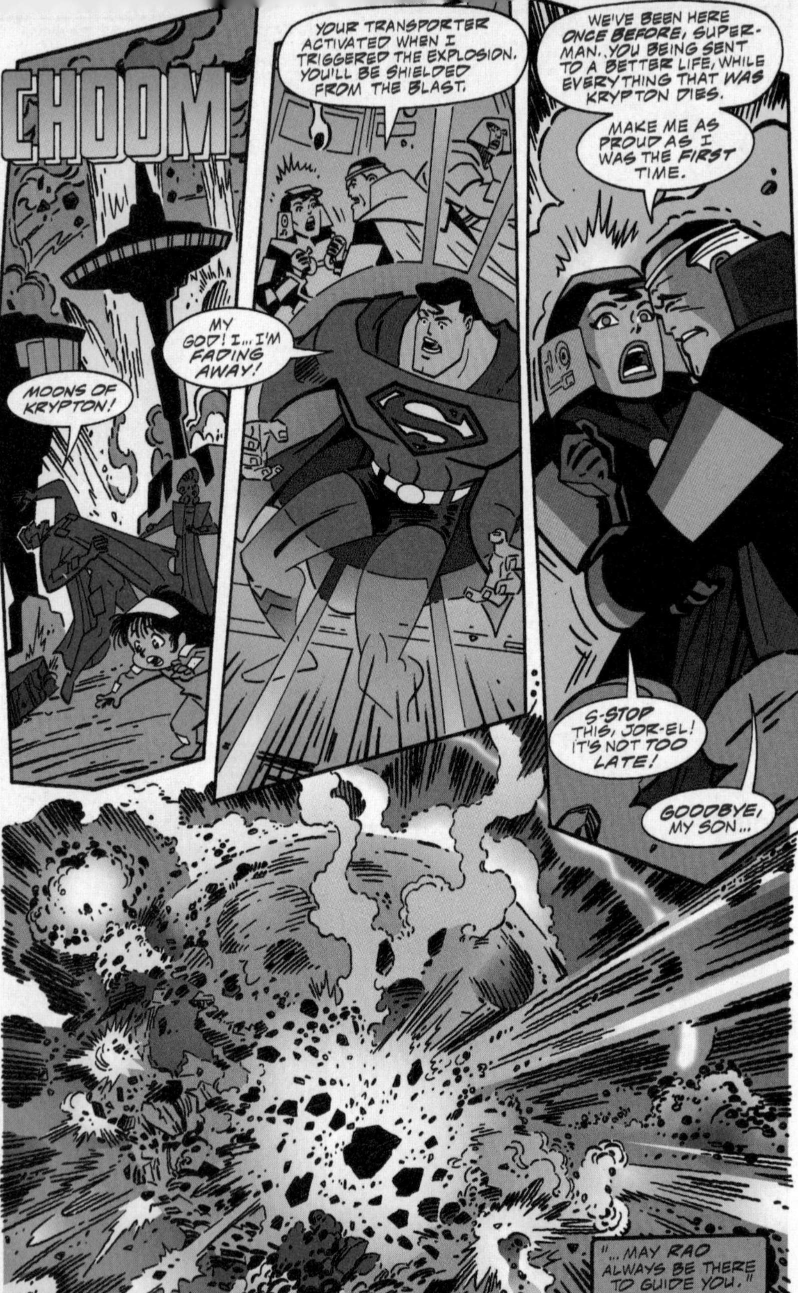
CHOOM
MOONS OF KRYPTON!
MY GOD! I... I'M FADING AWAY!
YOUR TRANSPORTER ACTIVATED WHEN I TRIGGERED THE EXPLOSION. YOU'LL BE SHIELDED FROM THE BLAST.
WE'VE BEEN HERE ONCE BEFORE, SUPERMAN. YOU BEING SENT TO A BETTER LIFE, WHILE EVERYTHING THAT WAS KRYPTON DIES.
MAKE ME AS PROUD AS I WAS THE FIRST TIME.
S-STOP THIS, JOR-EL! IT'S NOT TOO LATE!
GOODBYE, MY SON...
"...MAY RAO ALWAYS BE THERE TO GUIDE YOU."

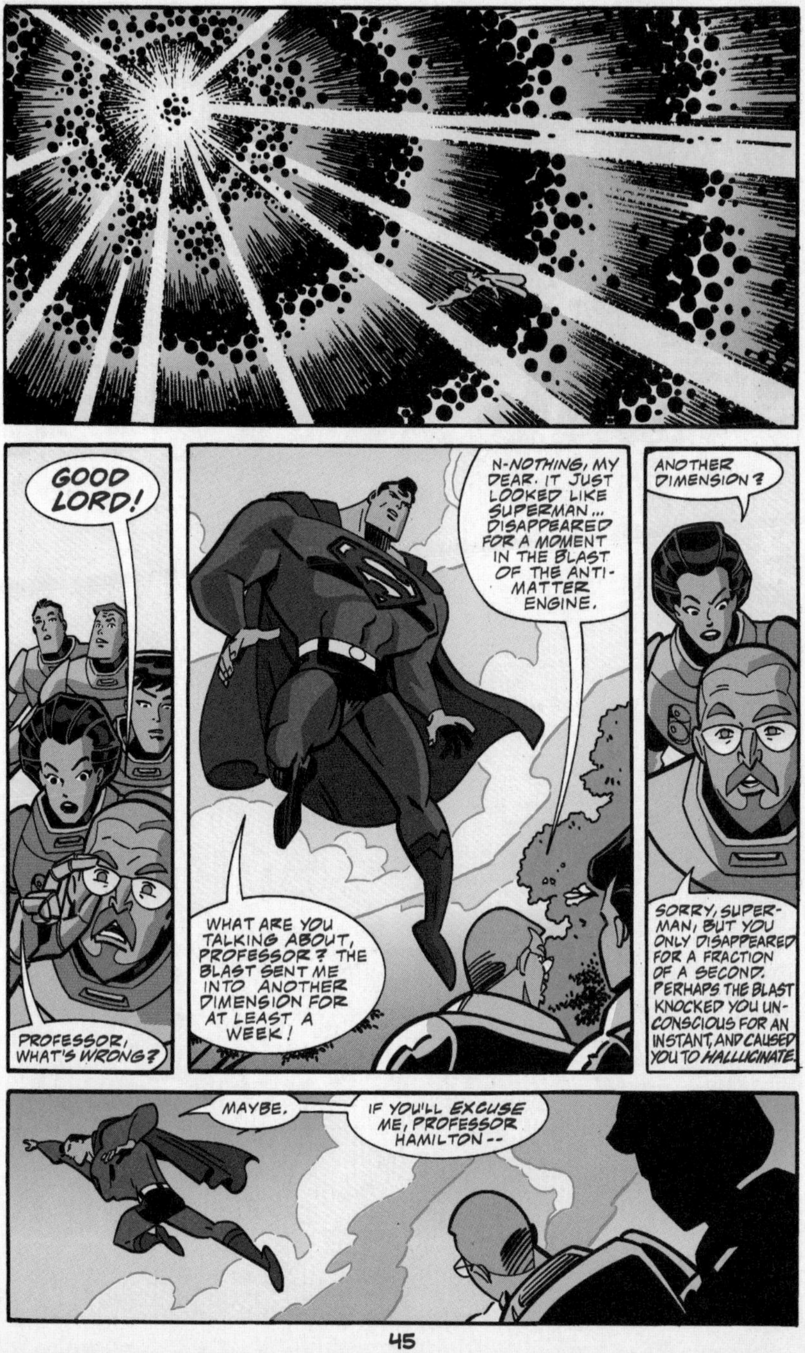
GOOD LORD!
PROFESSOR, WHAT'S WRONG?
N-NOTHING, MY DEAR. IT JUST LOOKED LIKE SUPERMAN... DISAPPEARED FOR A MOMENT IN THE BLAST OF THE ANTI-MATTER ENGINE.
WHAT ARE YOU TALKING ABOUT, PROFESSOR? THE BLAST SENT ME INTO ANOTHER DIMENSION FOR AT LEAST A WEEK!
ANOTHER DIMENSION?
SORRY, SUPERMAN, BUT YOU ONLY DISAPPEARED FOR A FRACTION OF A SECOND. PERHAPS THE BLAST KNOCKED YOU UNCONSCIOUS FOR AN INSTANT, AND CAUSED YOU TO HALLUCINATE.
MAYBE.
IF YOU'LL EXCUSE ME, PROFESSOR HAMILTON --

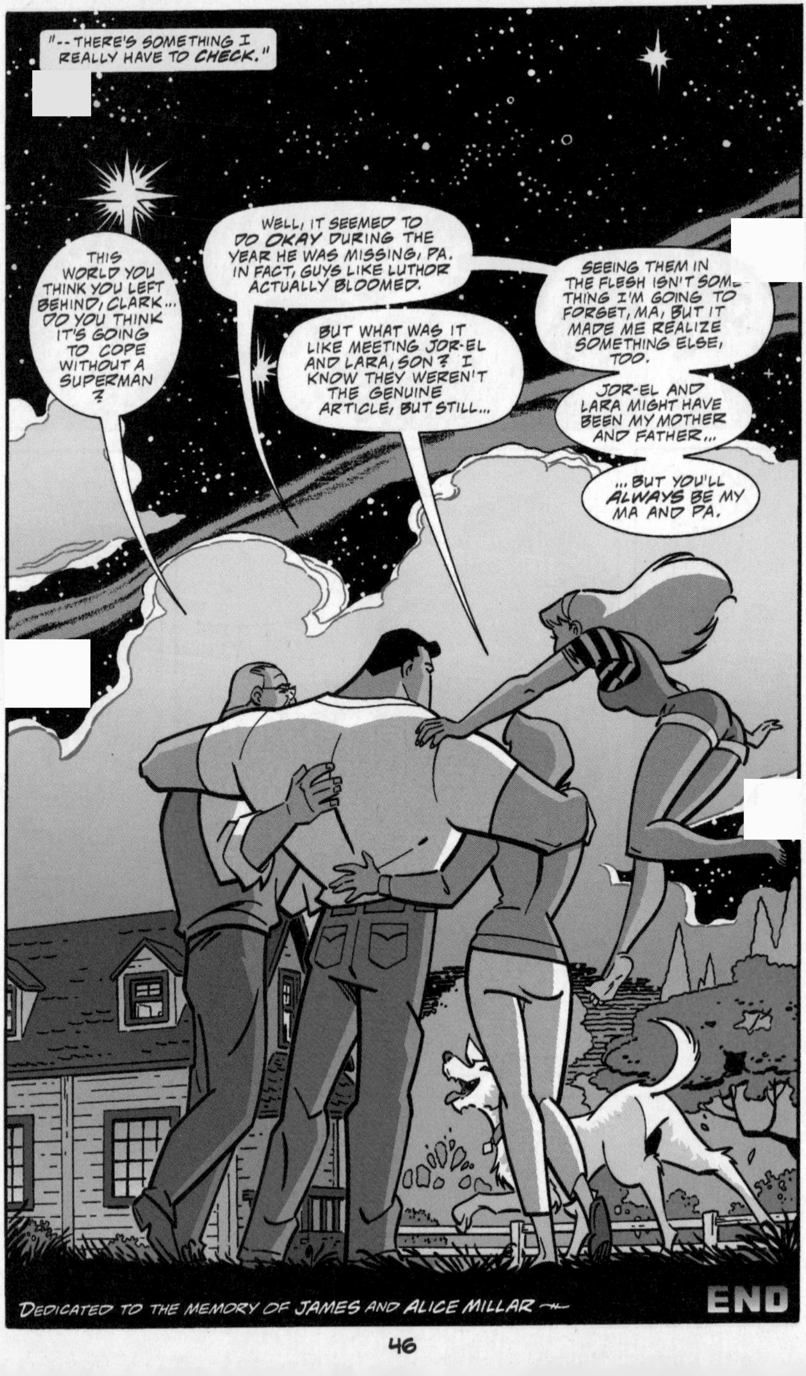
"--THERE'S SOMETHING I REALLY HAVE TO CHECK."
THIS WORLD YOU THINK YOU LEFT BEHIND, CLARK... DO YOU THINK IT'S GOING TO COPE WITHOUT A SUPERMAN?
WELL, IT SEEMED TO DO OKAY DURING THE YEAR HE WAS MISSING, PA. IN FACT, GUYS LIKE LUTHOR ACTUALLY BLOOMED.
BUT WHAT WAS IT LIKE MEETING JOR-EL AND LARA, SON? I KNOW THEY WEREN'T THE GENUINE ARTICLE, BUT STILL...
SEEING THEM IN THE FLESH ISN'T SOMETHING I'M GOING TO FORGET, MA, BUT IT MADE ME REALIZE SOMETHING ELSE, TOO.
JOR-EL AND LARA MIGHT HAVE BEEN MY MOTHER AND FATHER...
...BUT YOU'LL ALWAYS BE MY MA AND PA.
DEDICATED TO THE MEMORY OF JAMES AND ALICE MILLAR --M
END

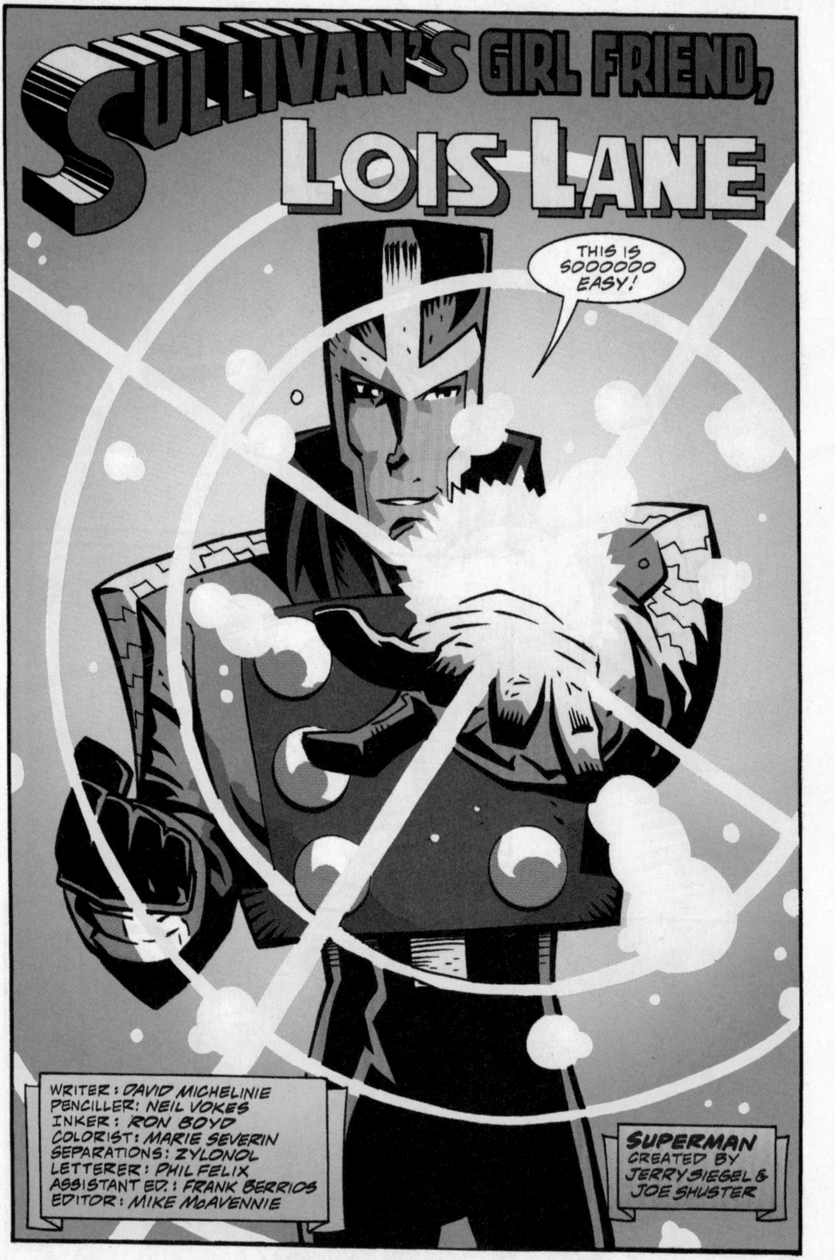
SULLIVAN'S GIRL FRIEND, LOIS LANE
THIS IS SOOOOOO EASY!
WRITER: DAVID MICHELINIE
PENCILLER: NEIL VOKES
INKER: RON BOYD
COLORIST: MARIE SEVERIN
SEPARATIONS: ZYLONOL
LETTERER: PHIL FELIX
ASSISTANT ED.: FRANK BERRIOS
EDITOR: MIKE McAVENNIE
SUPERMAN CREATED BY JERRY SIEGEL & JOE SHUSTER

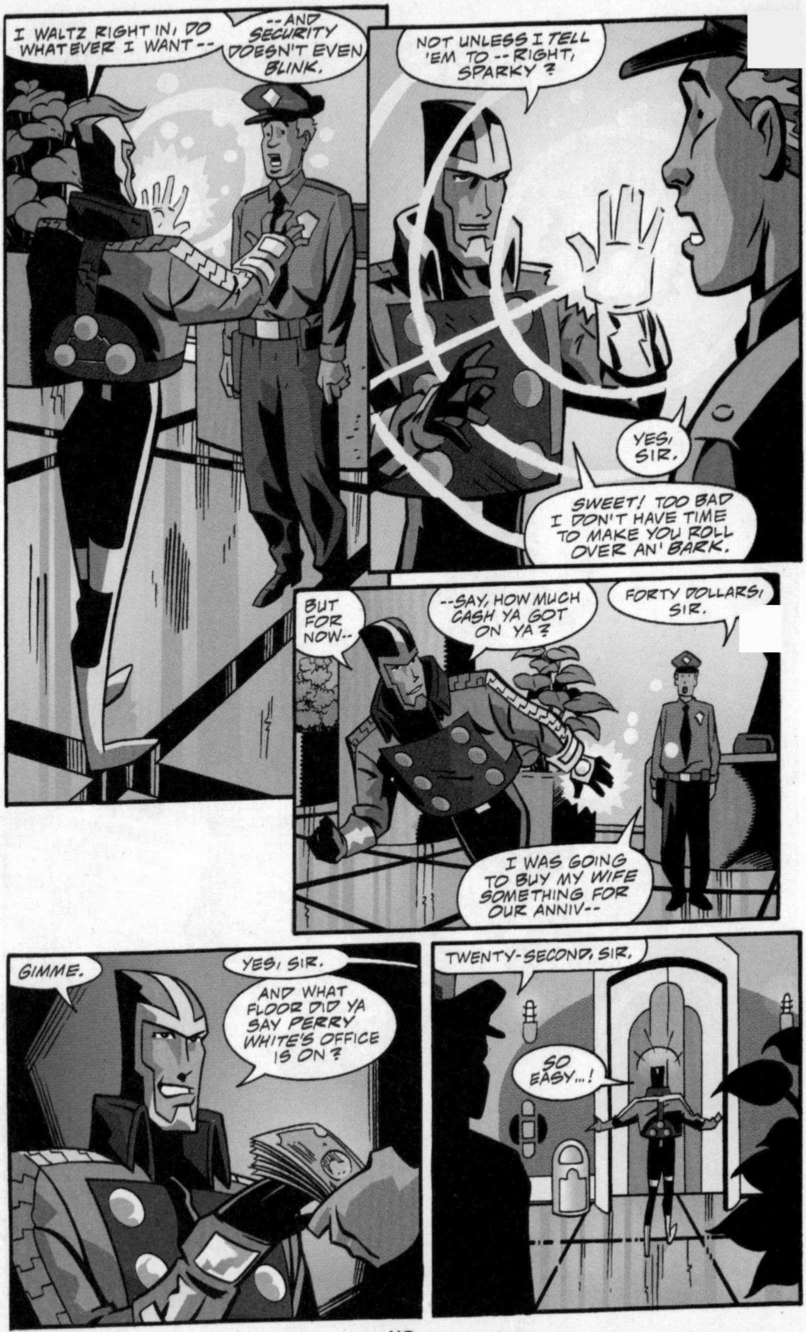
I WALTZ RIGHT IN, DO WHATEVER I WANT--
--AND SECURITY DOESN'T EVEN BLINK.
NOT UNLESS I TELL 'EM TO--RIGHT, SPARKY?
YES, SIR.
SWEET! TOO BAD I DON'T HAVE TIME TO MAKE YOU ROLL OVER AN' BARK.
BUT FOR NOW--
--SAY, HOW MUCH CASH YA GOT ON YA?
FORTY DOLLARS, SIR.
I WAS GOING TO BUY MY WIFE SOMETHING FOR OUR ANNIV--
GIMME.
YES, SIR.
AND WHAT FLOOR DID YA SAY PERRY WHITE'S OFFICE IS ON?
TWENTY-SECOND, SIR.
SO EASY...!

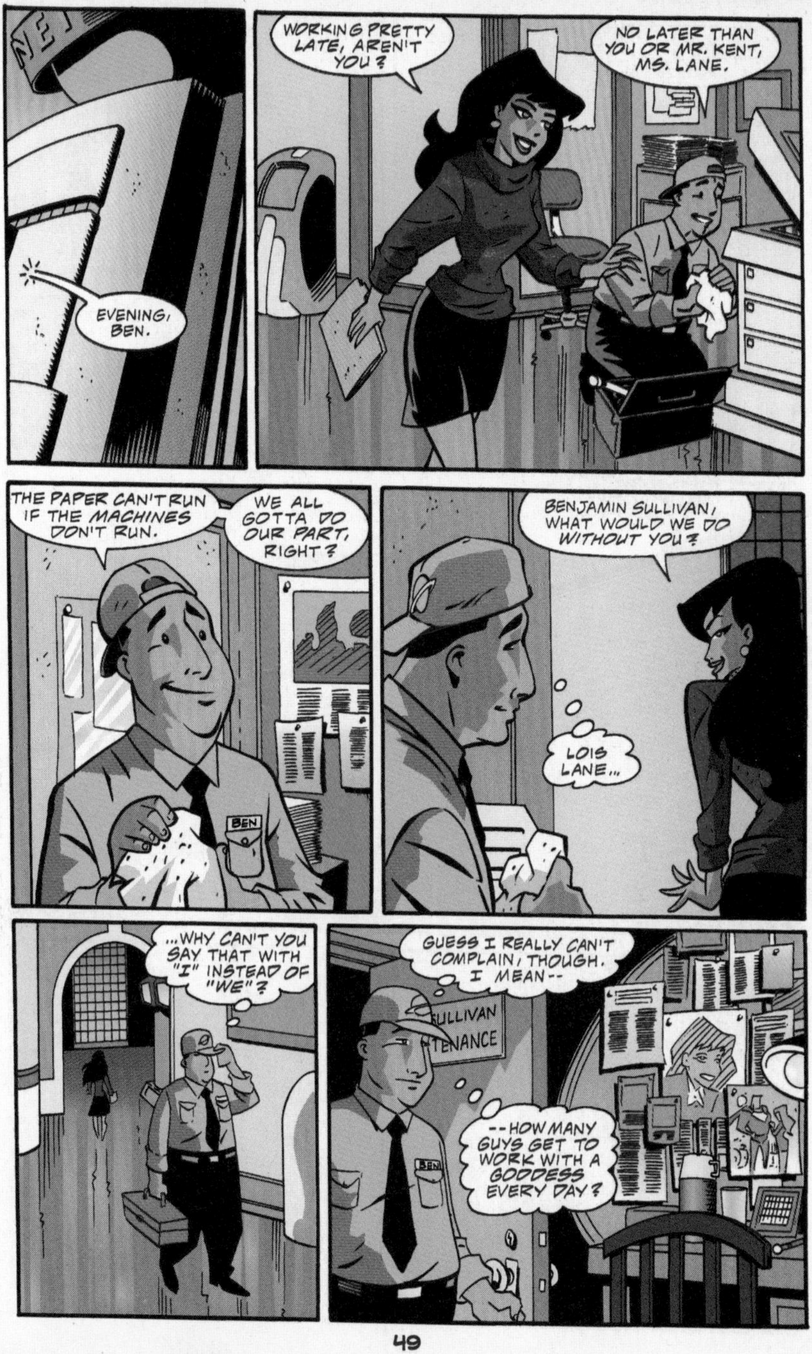

EVENING, BEN.
WORKING PRETTY LATE, AREN'T YOU?
NO LATER THAN YOU OR MR. KENT, MS. LANE.
THE PAPER CAN'T RUN IF THE MACHINES DON'T RUN.
WE ALL GOTTA DO OUR PART, RIGHT?
BENJAMIN SULLIVAN, WHAT WOULD WE DO WITHOUT YOU?
LOIS LANE...
BEN
...WHY CAN'T YOU SAY THAT WITH "I" INSTEAD OF "WE"?
GUESS I REALLY CAN'T COMPLAIN, THOUGH. I MEAN--
SULLIVAN
TENANCE
--HOW MANY GUYS GET TO WORK WITH A GODDESS EVERY DAY?
BEN

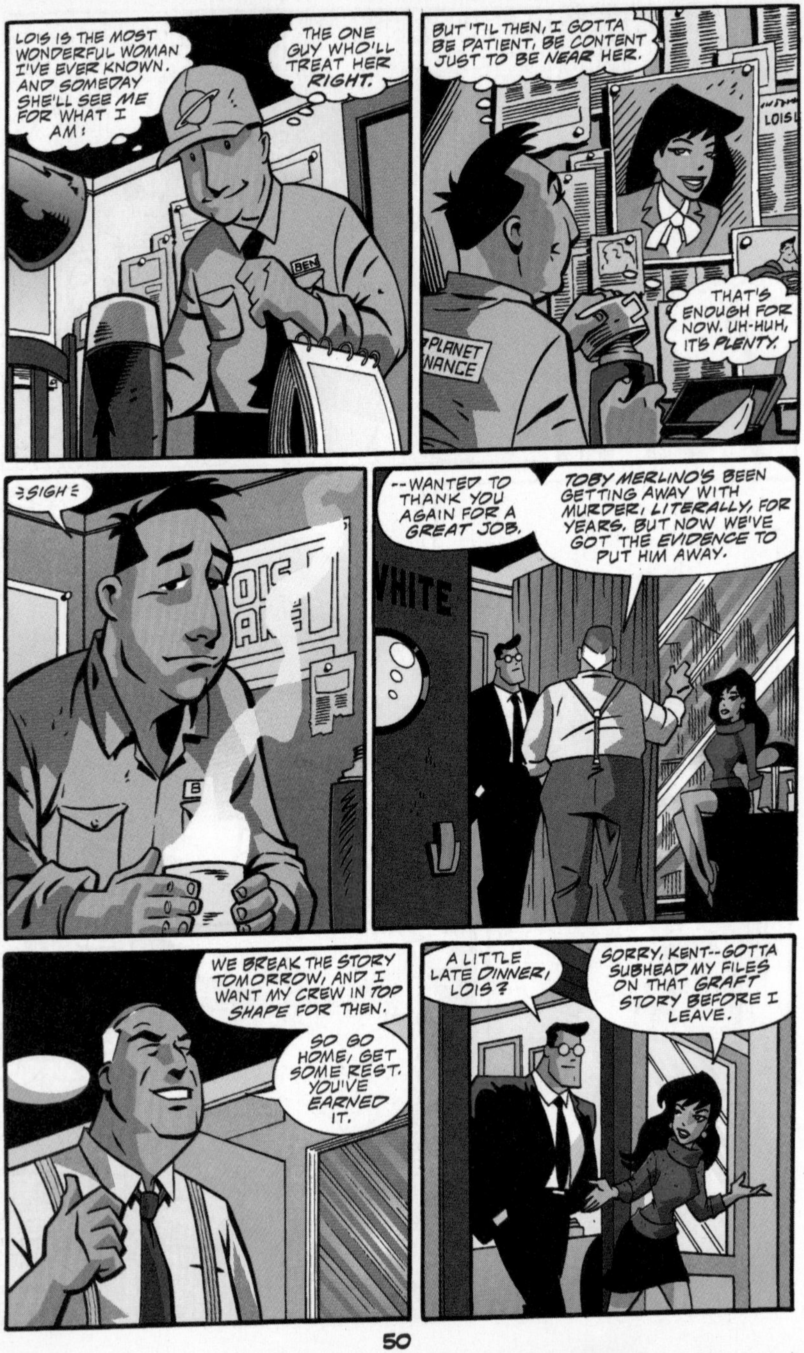
LOIS IS THE MOST WONDERFUL WOMAN I'VE EVER KNOWN. AND SOMEDAY SHE'LL SEE ME FOR WHAT I AM:
THE ONE GUY WHO'LL TREAT HER RIGHT.
BUT 'TIL THEN, I GOTTA BE PATIENT, BE CONTENT JUST TO BE NEAR HER.
THAT'S ENOUGH FOR NOW. UH-HUH, IT'S PLENTY.
SIGH
--WANTED TO THANK YOU AGAIN FOR A GREAT JOB.
TOBY MERLINO'S BEEN GETTING AWAY WITH MURDER, LITERALLY, FOR YEARS. BUT NOW WE'VE GOT THE EVIDENCE TO PUT HIM AWAY.
WHITE
WE BREAK THE STORY TOMORROW, AND I WANT MY CREW IN TOP SHAPE FOR THEN.
SO GO HOME, GET SOME REST. YOU'VE EARNED IT.
A LITTLE LATE DINNER, LOIS?
SORRY, KENT--GOTTA SUBHEAD MY FILES ON THAT GRAFT STORY BEFORE I LEAVE.

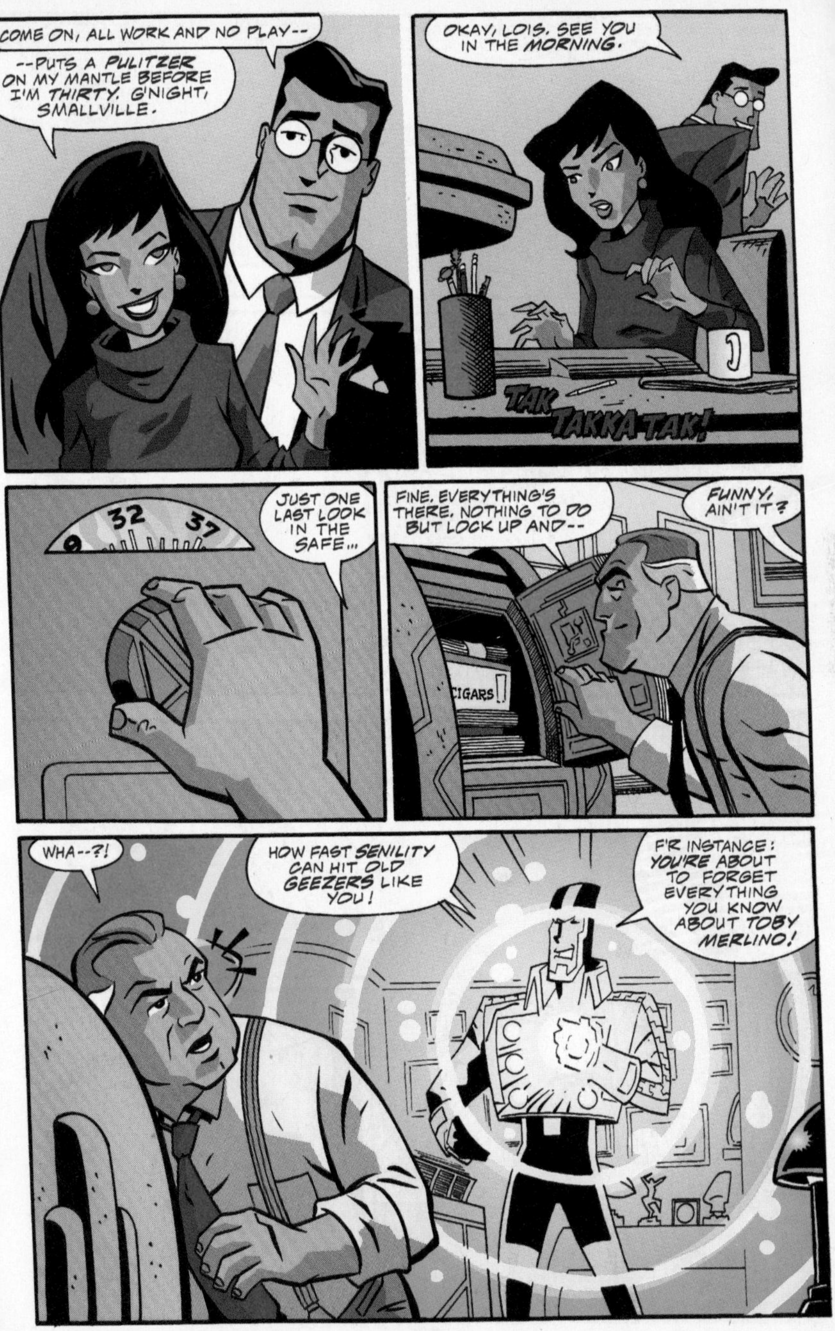
COME ON, ALL WORK AND NO PLAY--
--PUTS A PULITZER ON MY MANTLE BEFORE I'M THIRTY. G'NIGHT, SMALLVILLE.
OKAY, LOIS. SEE YOU IN THE MORNING.
TAK TAKKA TAK!
JUST ONE LAST LOOK IN THE SAFE...
FINE. EVERYTHING'S THERE. NOTHING TO DO BUT LOCK UP AND--
FUNNY, AIN'T IT?
CIGARS
WHA--?!
HOW FAST SENILITY CAN HIT OLD GEEZERS LIKE YOU!
F'R INSTANCE: YOU'RE ABOUT TO FORGET EVERYTHING YOU KNOW ABOUT TOBY MERLINO!

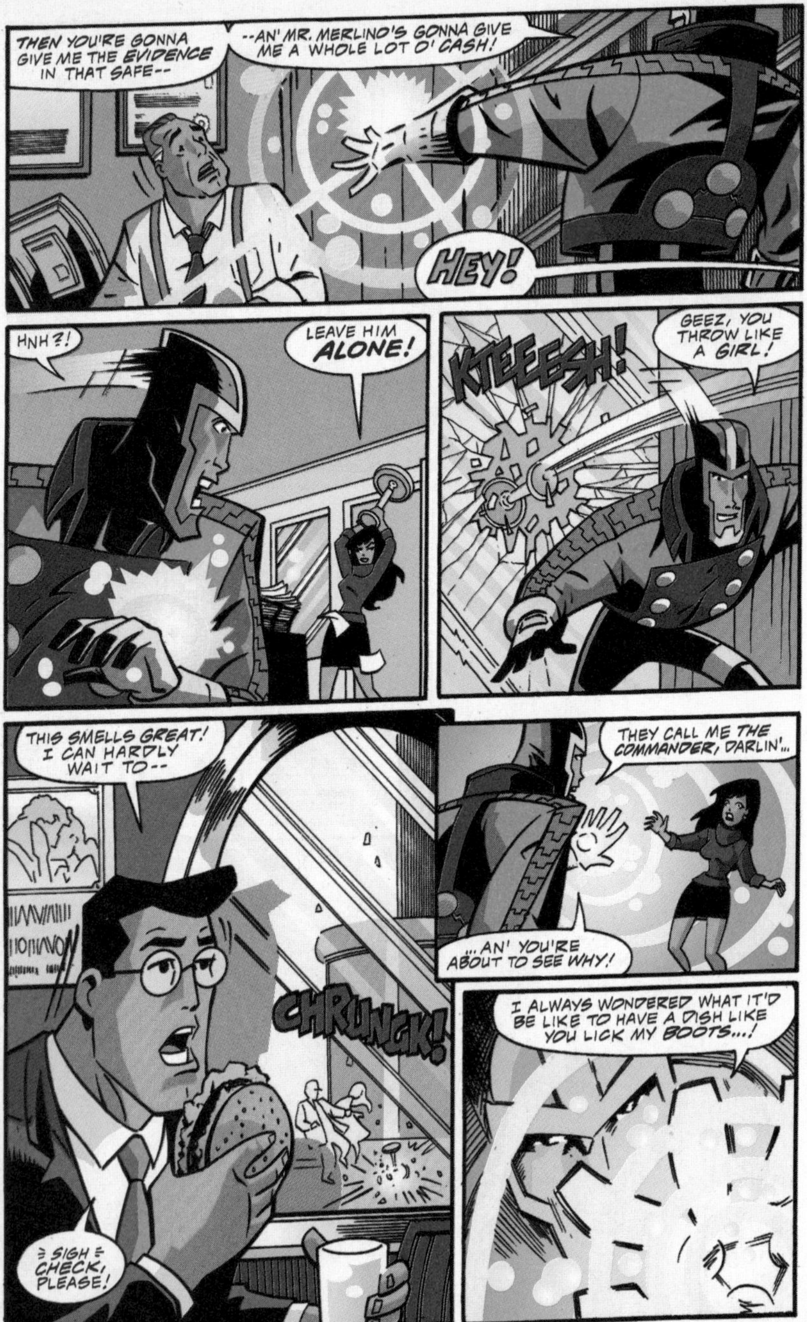
THEN YOU'RE GONNA GIVE ME THE EVIDENCE IN THAT SAFE--
--AN' MR. MERLINO'S GONNA GIVE ME A WHOLE LOT O' CASH!
HEY!
HNH?!
LEAVE HIM ALONE!
KTEEEESH!
GEEZ, YOU THROW LIKE A GIRL!
THIS SMELLS GREAT! I CAN HARDLY WAIT TO--
CHRUNGK!
SIGH
CHECK, PLEASE!
THEY CALL ME THE COMMANDER, DARLIN'...
...AN' YOU'RE ABOUT TO SEE WHY!
I ALWAYS WONDERED WHAT IT'D BE LIKE TO HAVE A DISH LIKE YOU LICK MY BOOTS...!

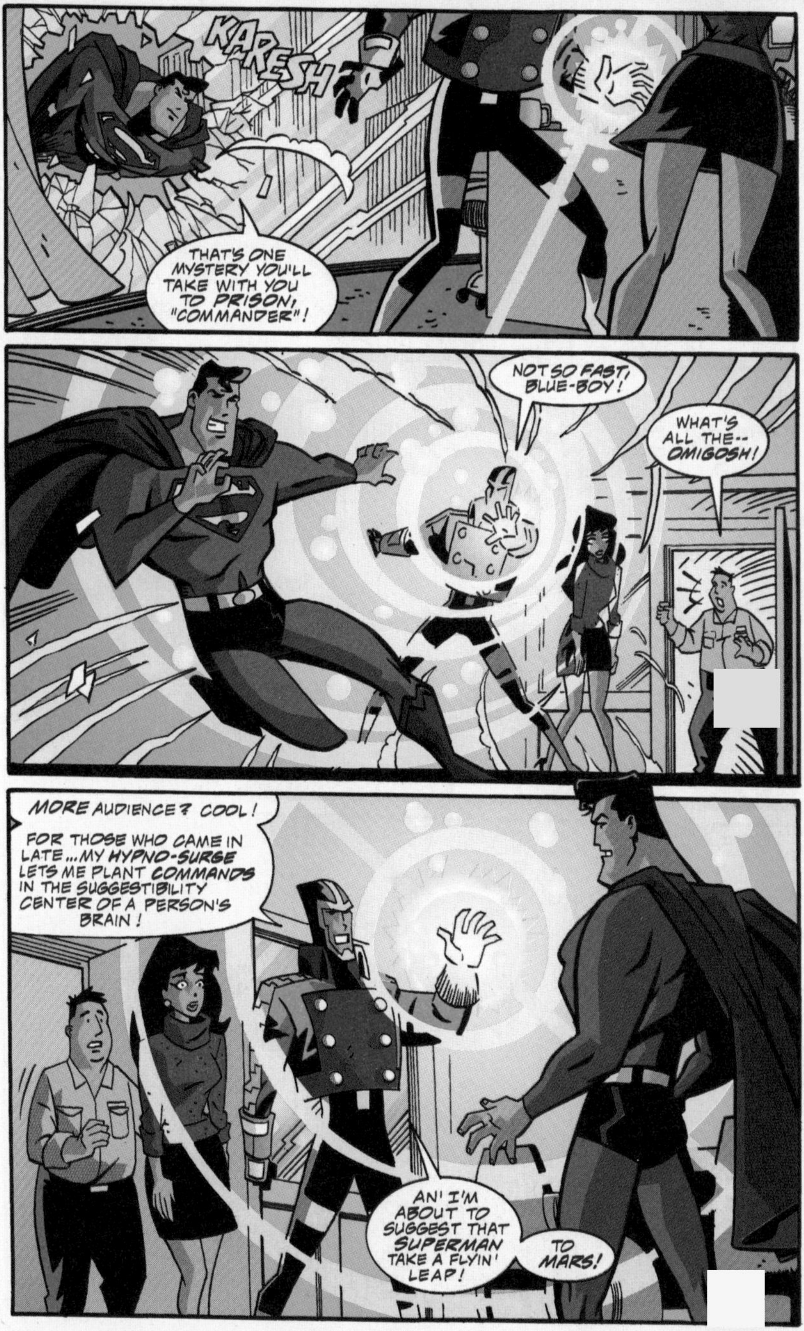
KARESH
THAT'S ONE MYSTERY YOU'LL TAKE WITH YOU TO PRISON, "COMMANDER"!
NOT SO FAST, BLUE-BOY!
WHAT'S ALL THE-- OMIGOSH!
MORE AUDIENCE? COOL!
FOR THOSE WHO CAME IN LATE... MY HYPNO-SURGE LETS ME PLANT COMMANDS IN THE SUGGESTIBILITY CENTER OF A PERSON'S BRAIN!
AN' I'M ABOUT TO SUGGEST THAT SUPERMAN TAKE A FLYIN' LEAP!
TO MARS!

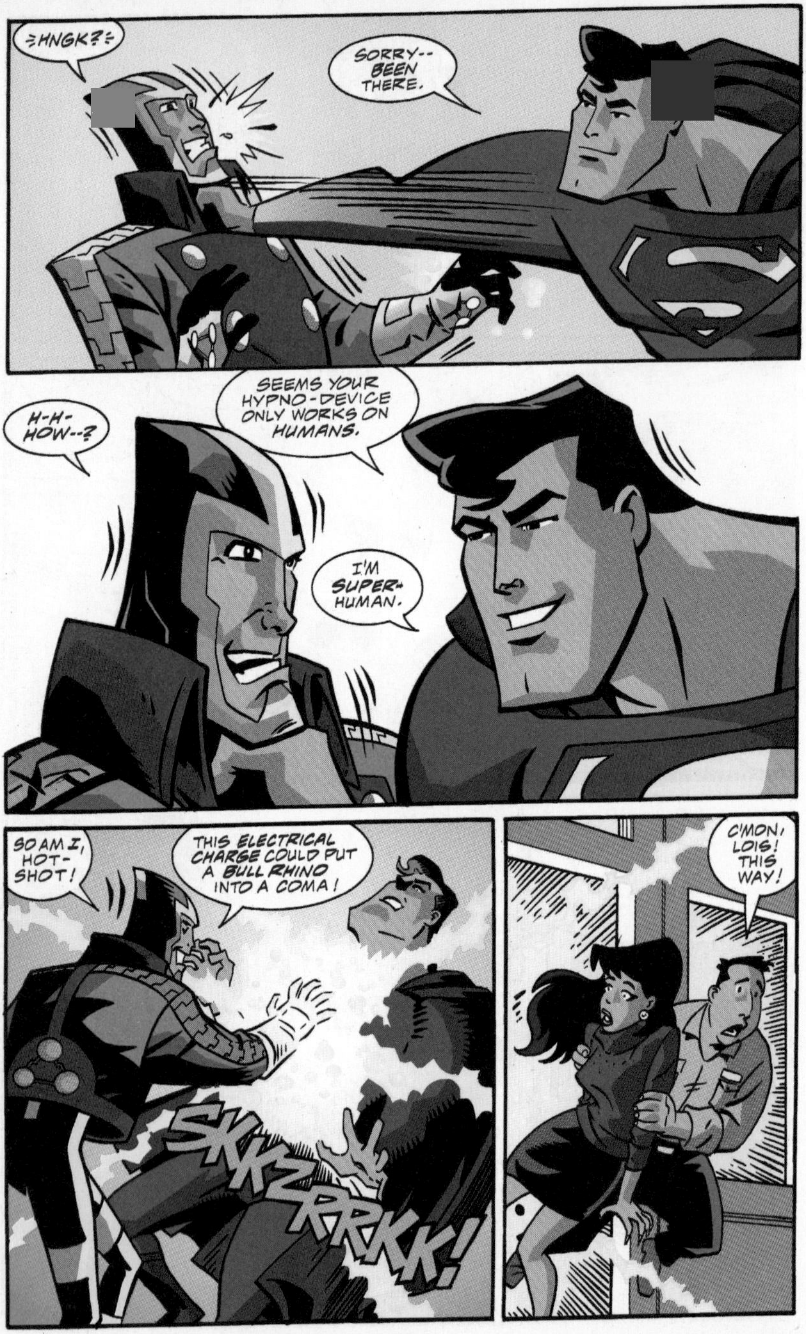
HNGK?
SORRY-- BEEN THERE.
SEEMS YOUR HYPNO-DEVICE ONLY WORKS ON HUMANS.
H-H-HOW--?
I'M SUPER-HUMAN.
SO AM I, HOT-SHOT!
THIS ELECTRICAL CHARGE COULD PUT A BULL RHINO INTO A COMA!
SKKZRRKK!
C'MON, LOIS! THIS WAY!

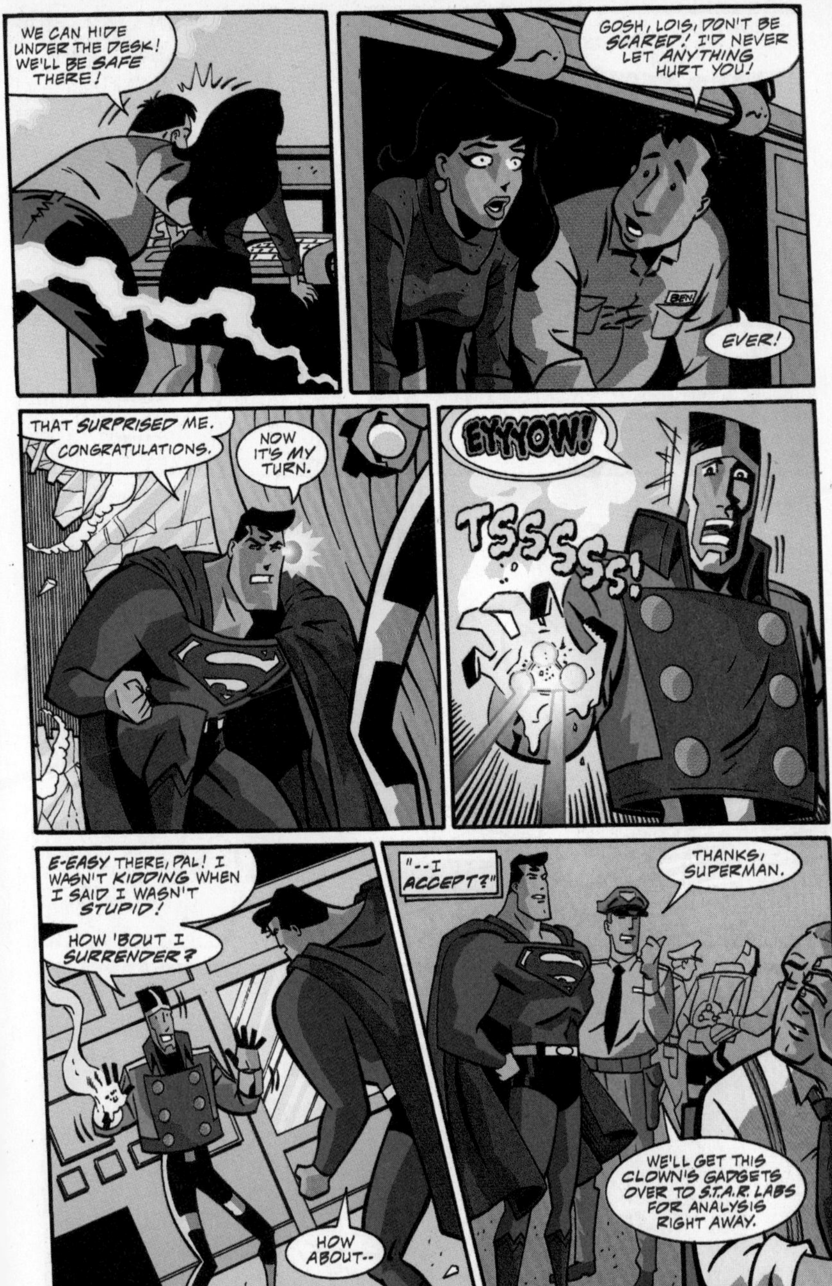
WE CAN HIDE UNDER THE DESK! WE'LL BE SAFE THERE!
GOSH, LOIS, DON'T BE SCARED! I'D NEVER LET ANYTHING HURT YOU!
EVER!
BEN
THAT SURPRISED ME.
CONGRATULATIONS.
NOW IT'S MY TURN.
EYYYOW!
TSSSSSS!
E-EASY THERE, PAL! I WASN'T KIDDING WHEN I SAID I WASN'T STUPID!
HOW 'BOUT I SURRENDER?
HOW ABOUT--
"--I ACCEPT?"
THANKS, SUPERMAN.
WE'LL GET THIS CLOWN'S GADGETS OVER TO S.T.A.R. LABS FOR ANALYSIS RIGHT AWAY.

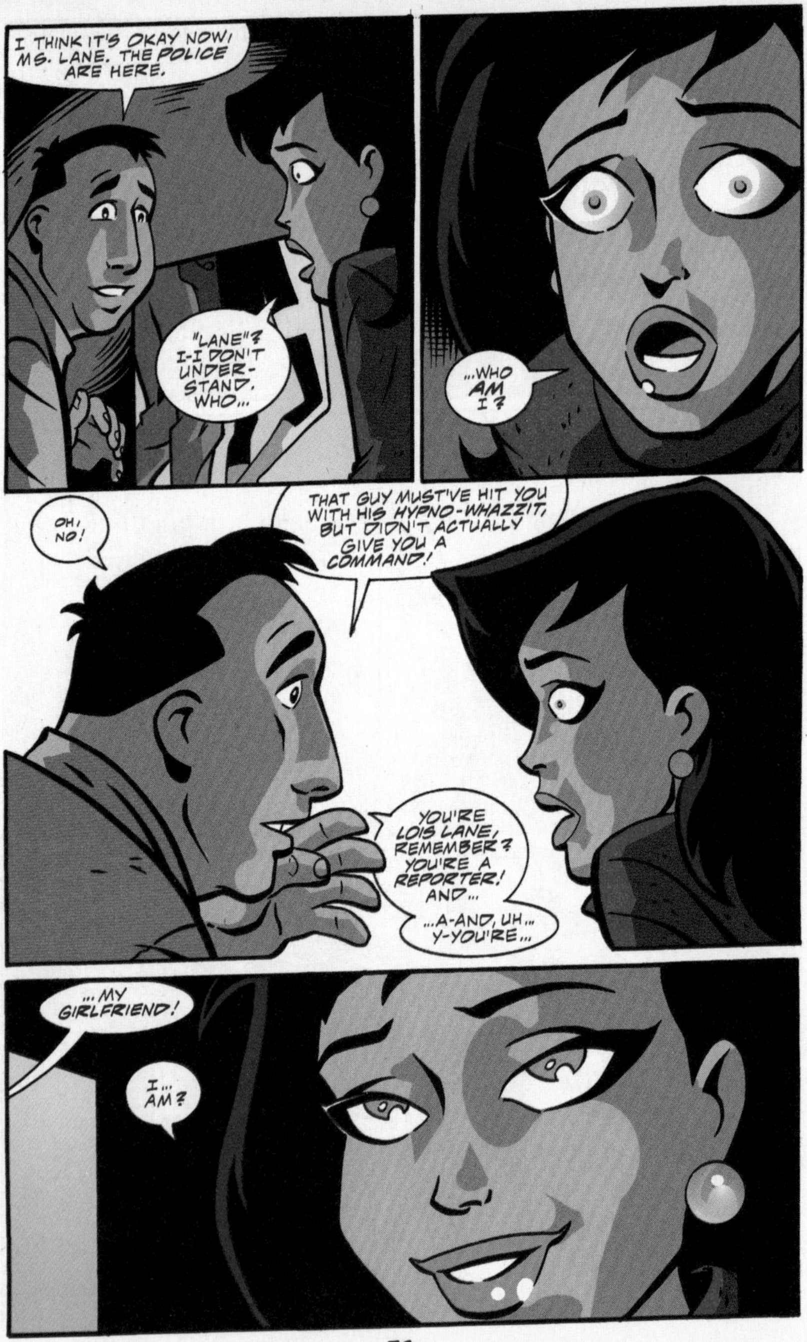
I THINK IT'S OKAY NOW, MS. LANE. THE POLICE ARE HERE.
"LANE"? I-I DON'T UNDER-STAND. WHO...
...WHO AM I?
OH, NO!
THAT GUY MUST'VE HIT YOU WITH HIS HYPNO-WHAZZIT, BUT DIDN'T ACTUALLY GIVE YOU A COMMAND!
YOU'RE LOIS LANE, REMEMBER? YOU'RE A REPORTER! AND...
...A-AND, UH... Y-YOU'RE...
...MY GIRLFRIEND!
I... AM?

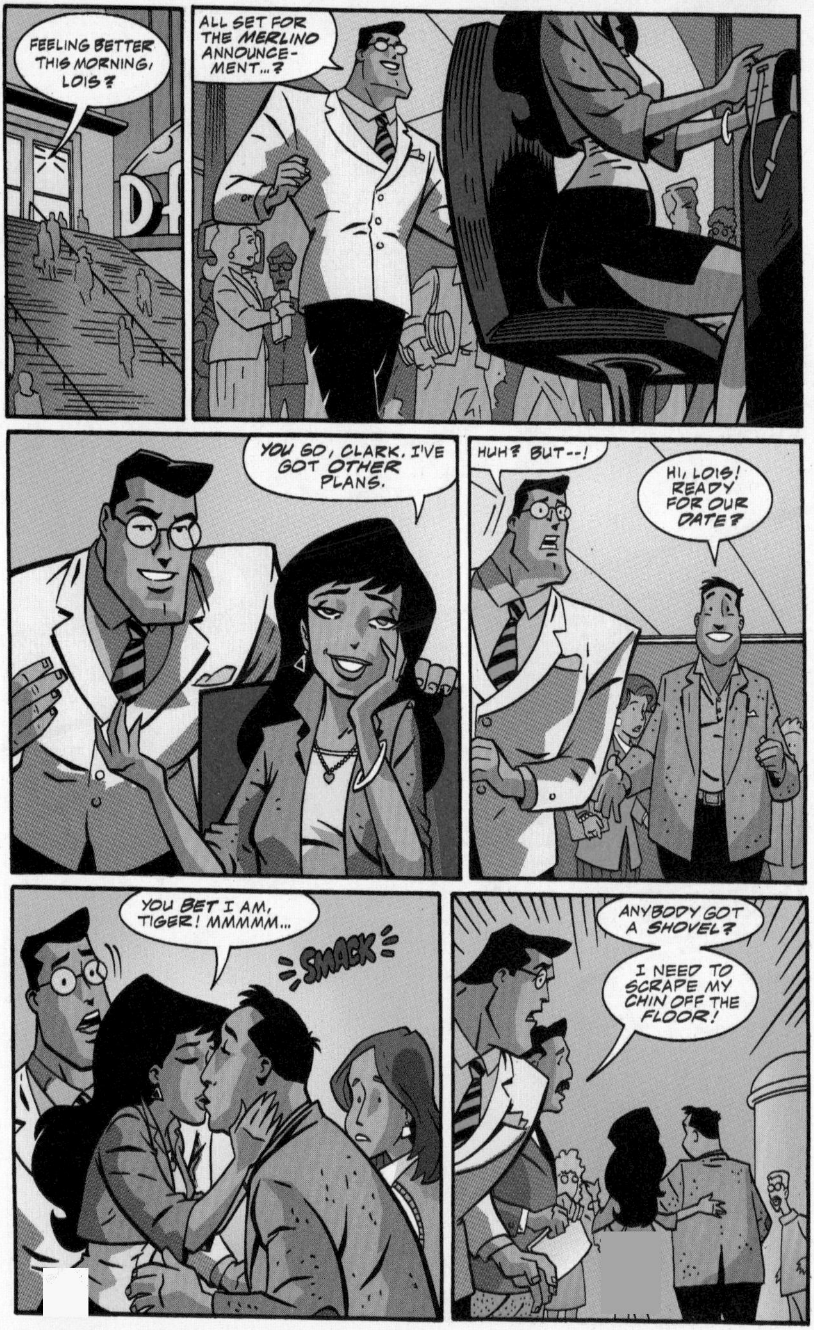
FEELING BETTER THIS MORNING, LOIS?
ALL SET FOR THE MERLINO ANNOUNCE-MENT...?
YOU GO, CLARK. I'VE GOT OTHER PLANS.
HUH? BUT--!
HI, LOIS! READY FOR OUR DATE?
YOU BET I AM, TIGER! MMMMM...
SMACK
ANYBODY GOT A SHOVEL?
I NEED TO SCRAPE MY CHIN OFF THE FLOOR!

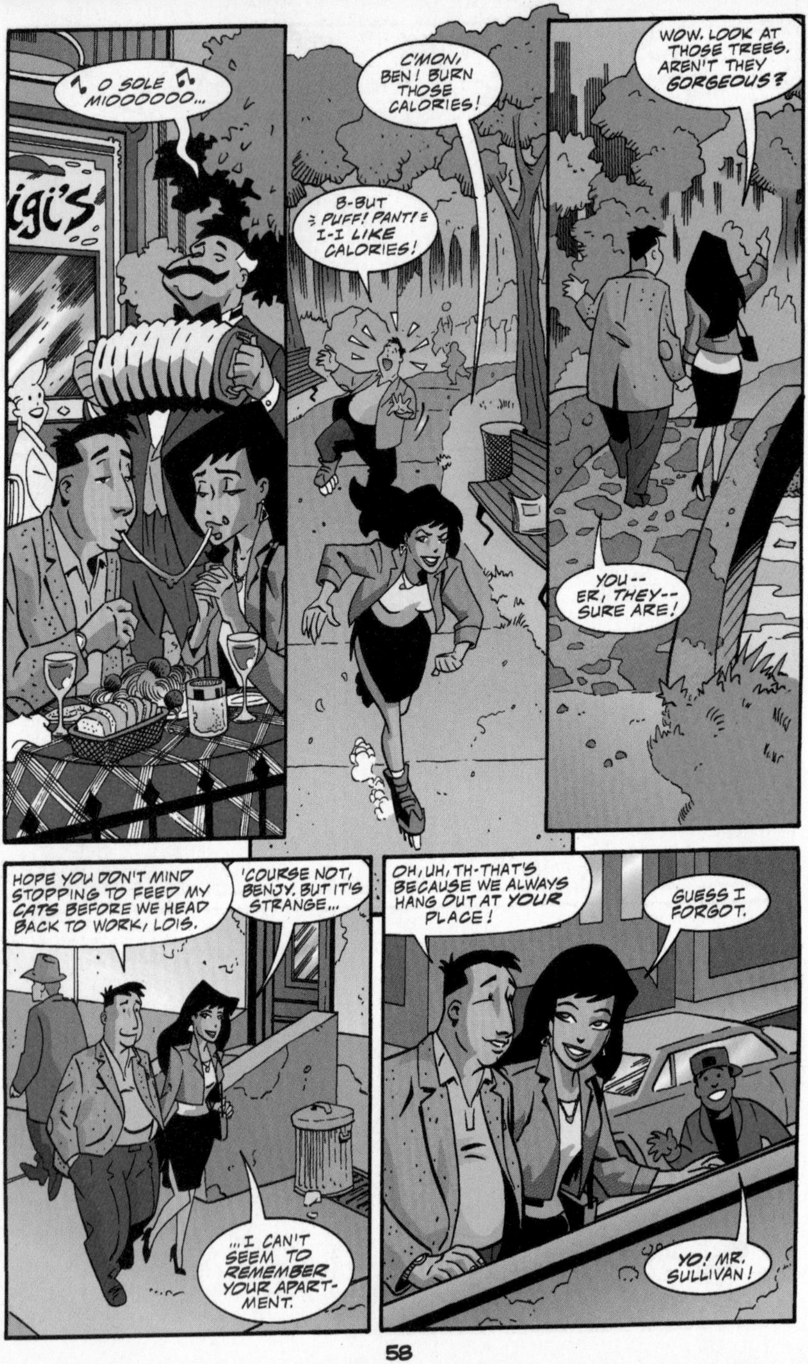
O SOLE MIOOOOOO...
igi's
C'MON, BEN! BURN THOSE CALORIES!
B-BUT PUFF! PANT! I-I LIKE CALORIES!
WOW. LOOK AT THOSE TREES. AREN'T THEY GORGEOUS?
YOU-- ER, THEY-- SURE ARE!
HOPE YOU DON'T MIND STOPPING TO FEED MY CATS BEFORE WE HEAD BACK TO WORK, LOIS.
'COURSE NOT, BENJY. BUT IT'S STRANGE...
...I CAN'T SEEM TO REMEMBER YOUR APARTMENT.
OH, UH, TH-THAT'S BECAUSE WE ALWAYS HANG OUT AT YOUR PLACE!
GUESS I FORGOT.
YO! MR. SULLIVAN!

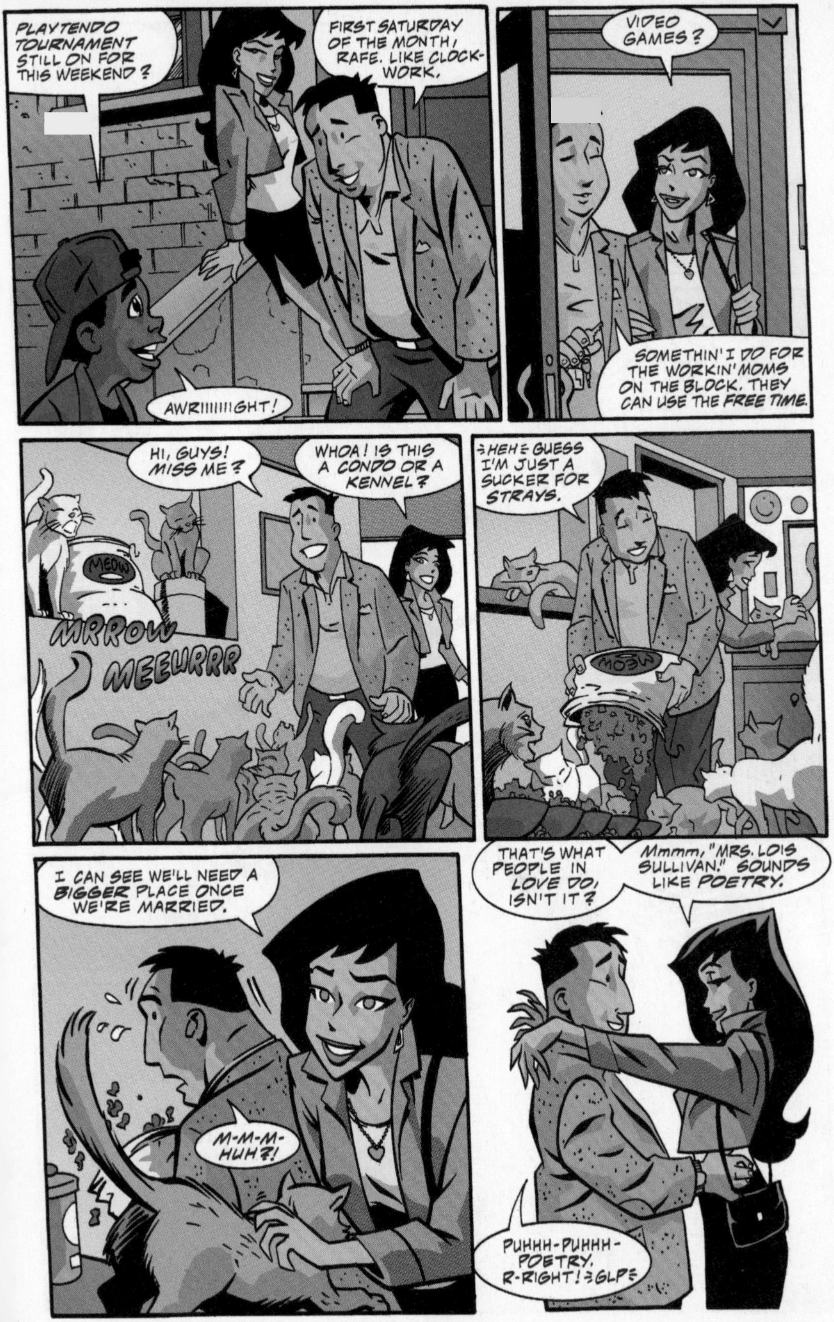
PLAYTENDO TOURNAMENT STILL ON FOR THIS WEEKEND?
FIRST SATURDAY OF THE MONTH, RAFE. LIKE CLOCK-WORK.
AWRIIIIIIIGHT!
VIDEO GAMES?
SOMETHIN' I DO FOR THE WORKIN' MOMS ON THE BLOCK. THEY CAN USE THE FREE TIME.
HI, GUYS! MISS ME?
WHOA! IS THIS A CONDO OR A KENNEL?
MEOW
MRROW
MEEURRR
HEH GUESS I'M JUST A SUCKER FOR STRAYS.
MEOW
I CAN SEE WE'LL NEED A BIGGER PLACE ONCE WE'RE MARRIED.
M-M-M-HUH?!
THAT'S WHAT PEOPLE IN LOVE DO, ISN'T IT?
Mmmm, "MRS. LOIS SULLIVAN." SOUNDS LIKE POETRY.
PUHHH-PUHHH-POETRY. R-RIGHT! GLP

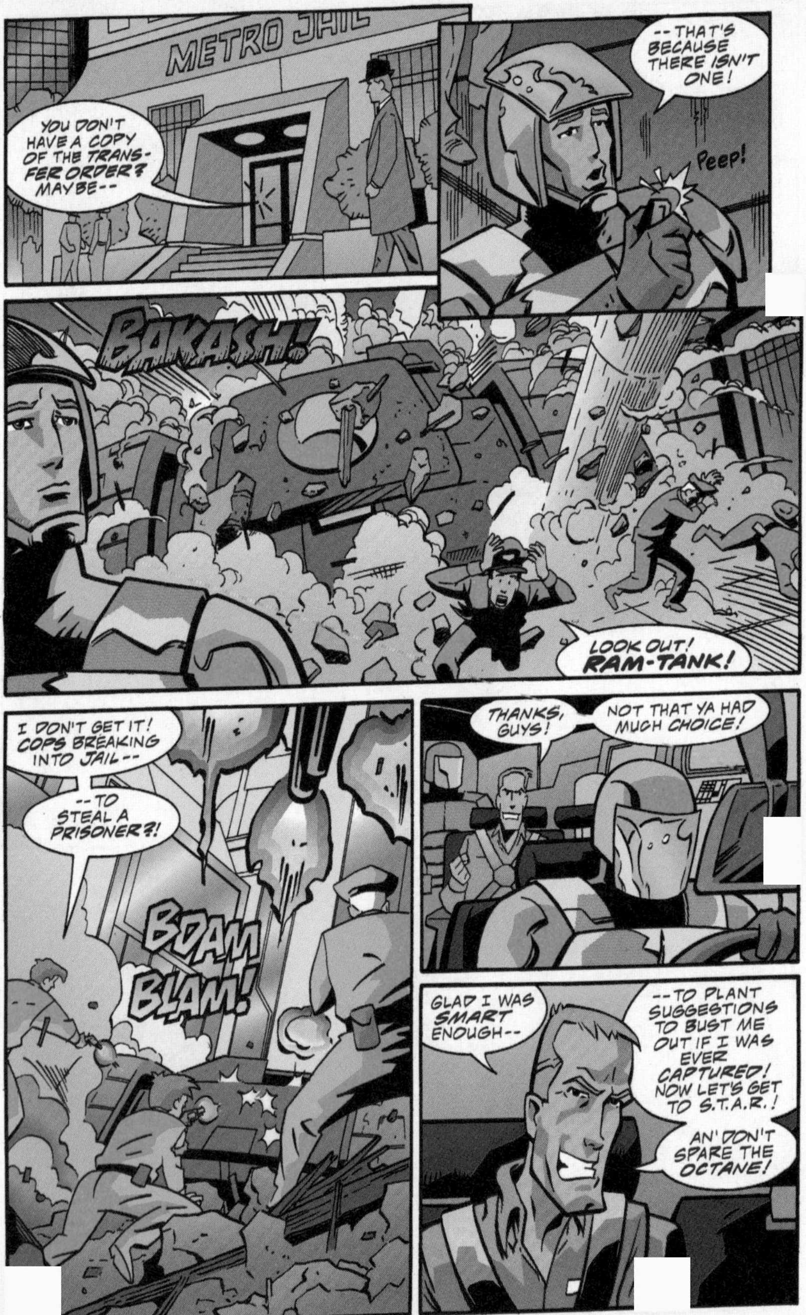
METRO JAIL
YOU DON'T HAVE A COPY OF THE TRANSFER ORDER? MAYBE--
--THAT'S BECAUSE THERE ISN'T ONE!
Peep!
BAKASH!
LOOK OUT! RAM-TANK!
I DON'T GET IT! COPS BREAKING INTO JAIL--
--TO STEAL A PRISONER?!
BDAM BLAM!
THANKS, GUYS!
NOT THAT YA HAD MUCH CHOICE!
GLAD I WAS SMART ENOUGH--
--TO PLANT SUGGESTIONS TO BUST ME OUT IF I WAS EVER CAPTURED! NOW LET'S GET TO S.T.A.R.!
AN' DON'T SPARE THE OCTANE!

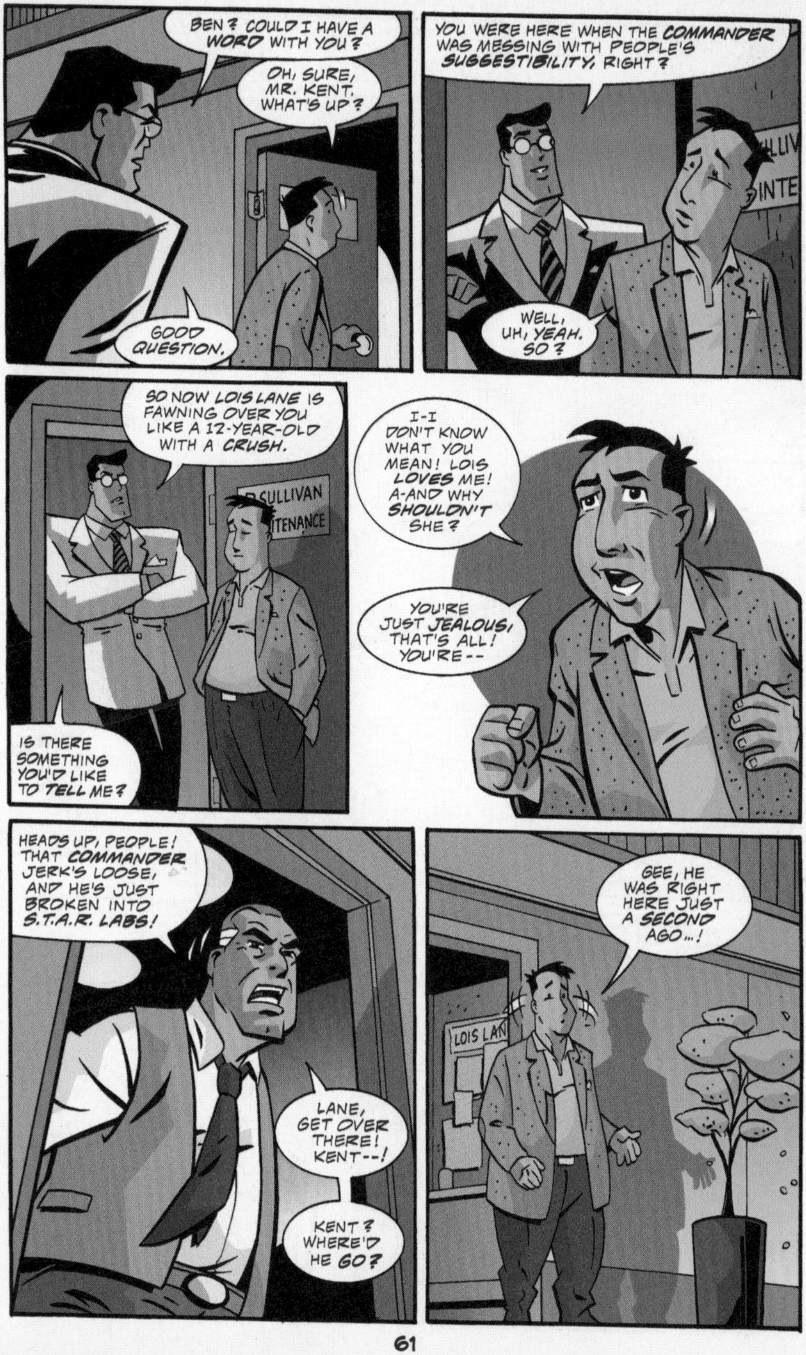

BEN? COULD I HAVE A WORD WITH YOU?
OH, SURE, MR. KENT. WHAT'S UP?
GOOD QUESTION.
YOU WERE HERE WHEN THE COMMANDER WAS MESSING WITH PEOPLE'S SUGGESTIBILITY, RIGHT?
WELL, UH, YEAH. SO?
SO NOW LOIS LANE IS FAWNING OVER YOU LIKE A 12-YEAR-OLD WITH A CRUSH.
SULLIVAN
IS THERE SOMETHING YOU'D LIKE TO TELL ME?
I-I DON'T KNOW WHAT YOU MEAN! LOIS LOVES ME! A-AND WHY SHOULDN'T SHE?
YOU'RE JUST JEALOUS, THAT'S ALL! YOU'RE--
HEADS UP, PEOPLE! THAT COMMANDER JERK'S LOOSE, AND HE'S JUST BROKEN INTO S.T.A.R. LABS!
LANE, GET OVER THERE! KENT--!
KENT? WHERE'D HE GO?
GEE, HE WAS RIGHT HERE JUST A SECOND AGO...!

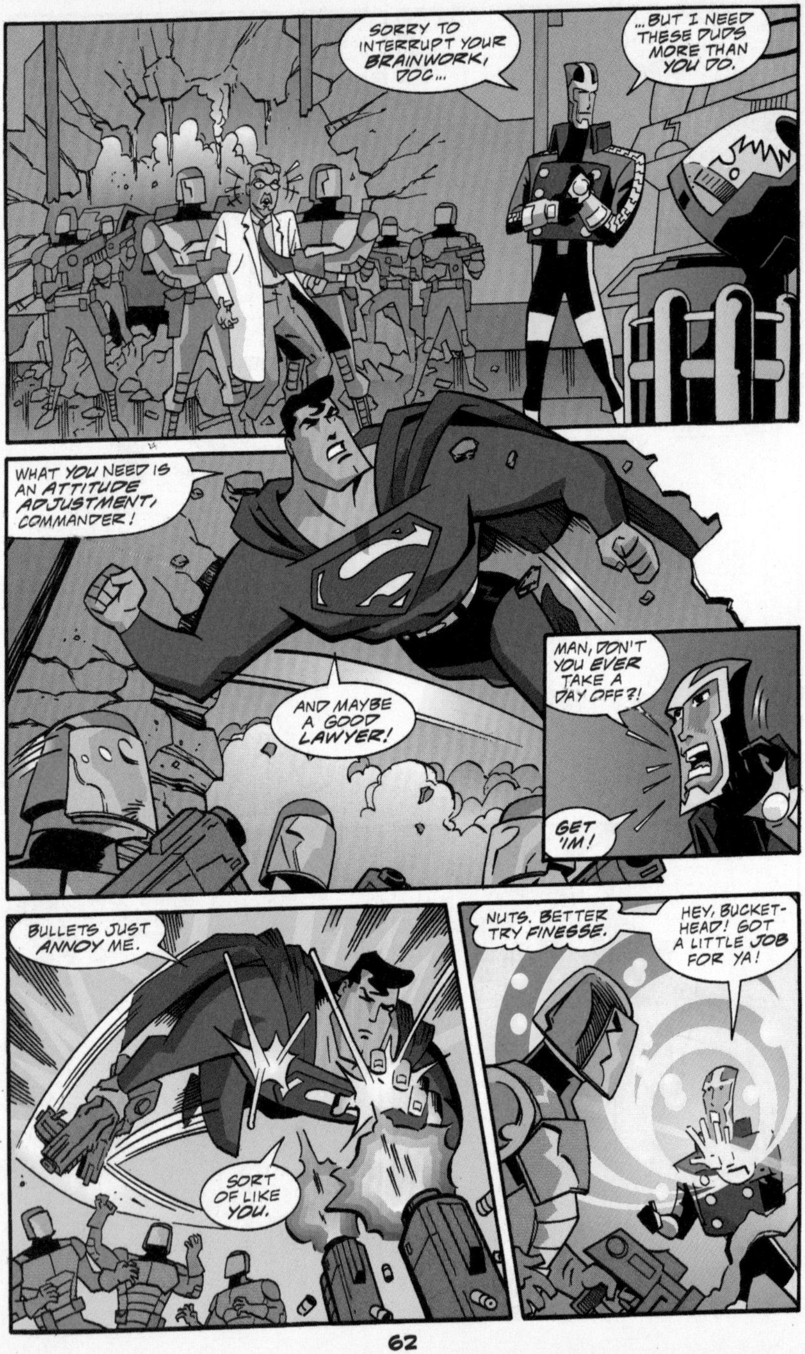
SORRY TO INTERRUPT YOUR BRAINWORK, DOC...
...BUT I NEED THESE DUDS MORE THAN YOU DO.
WHAT YOU NEED IS AN ATTITUDE ADJUSTMENT, COMMANDER!
AND MAYBE A GOOD LAWYER!
MAN, DON'T YOU EVER TAKE A DAY OFF?!
GET 'IM!
BULLETS JUST ANNOY ME.
SORT OF LIKE YOU.
NUTS. BETTER TRY FINESSE.
HEY, BUCKET-HEAD! GOT A LITTLE JOB FOR YA!

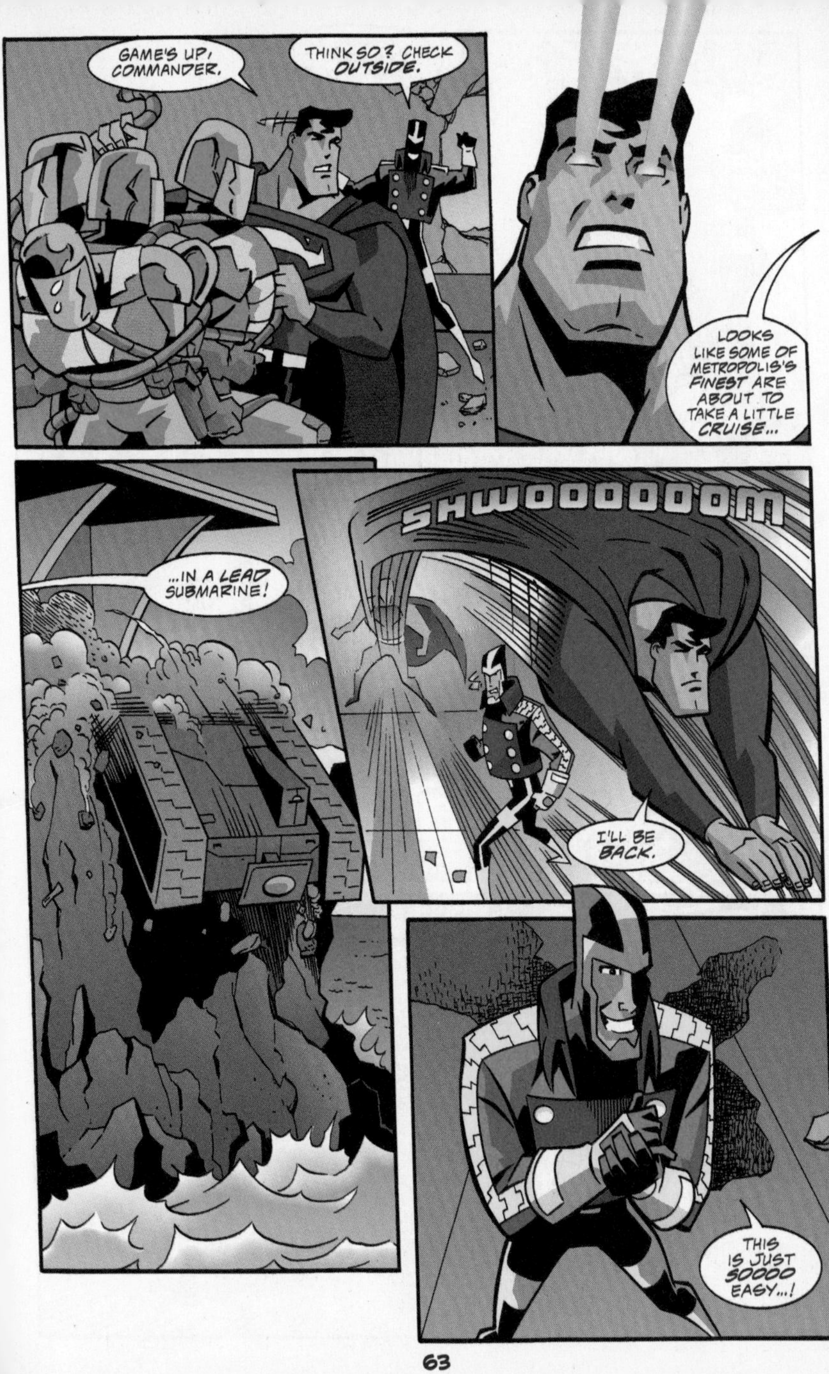
GAME'S UP, COMMANDER.
THINK SO? CHECK OUTSIDE.
LOOKS LIKE SOME OF METROPOLIS'S FINEST ARE ABOUT TO TAKE A LITTLE CRUISE...
...IN A LEAD SUBMARINE!
SHWOOOOOOOM
I'LL BE BACK.
THIS IS JUST SOOOO EASY...!

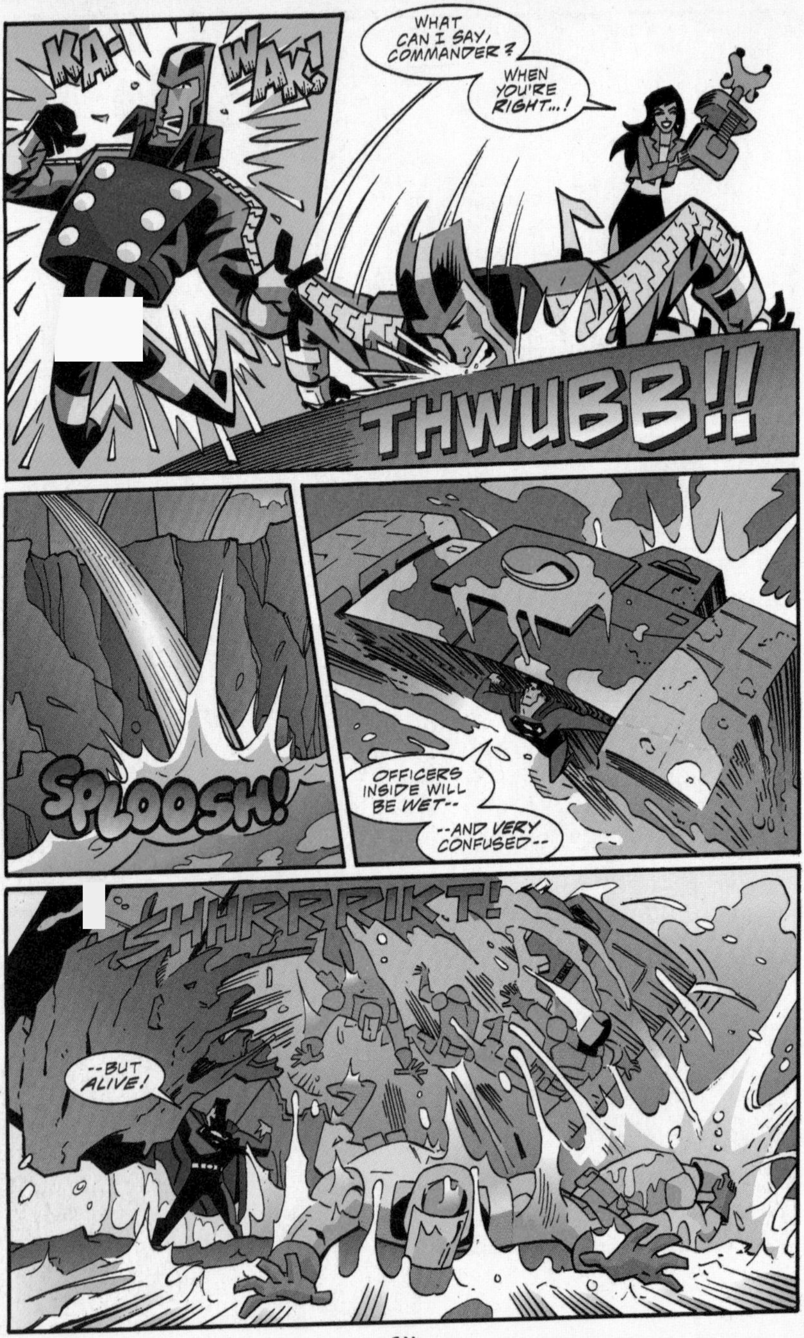
KA-WAK!
WHAT CAN I SAY, COMMANDER?
WHEN YOU'RE RIGHT...!
THWUBB!!
SPLOOSH!
OFFICERS INSIDE WILL BE WET--
--AND VERY CONFUSED--
SHHRRRIKT!
--BUT ALIVE!

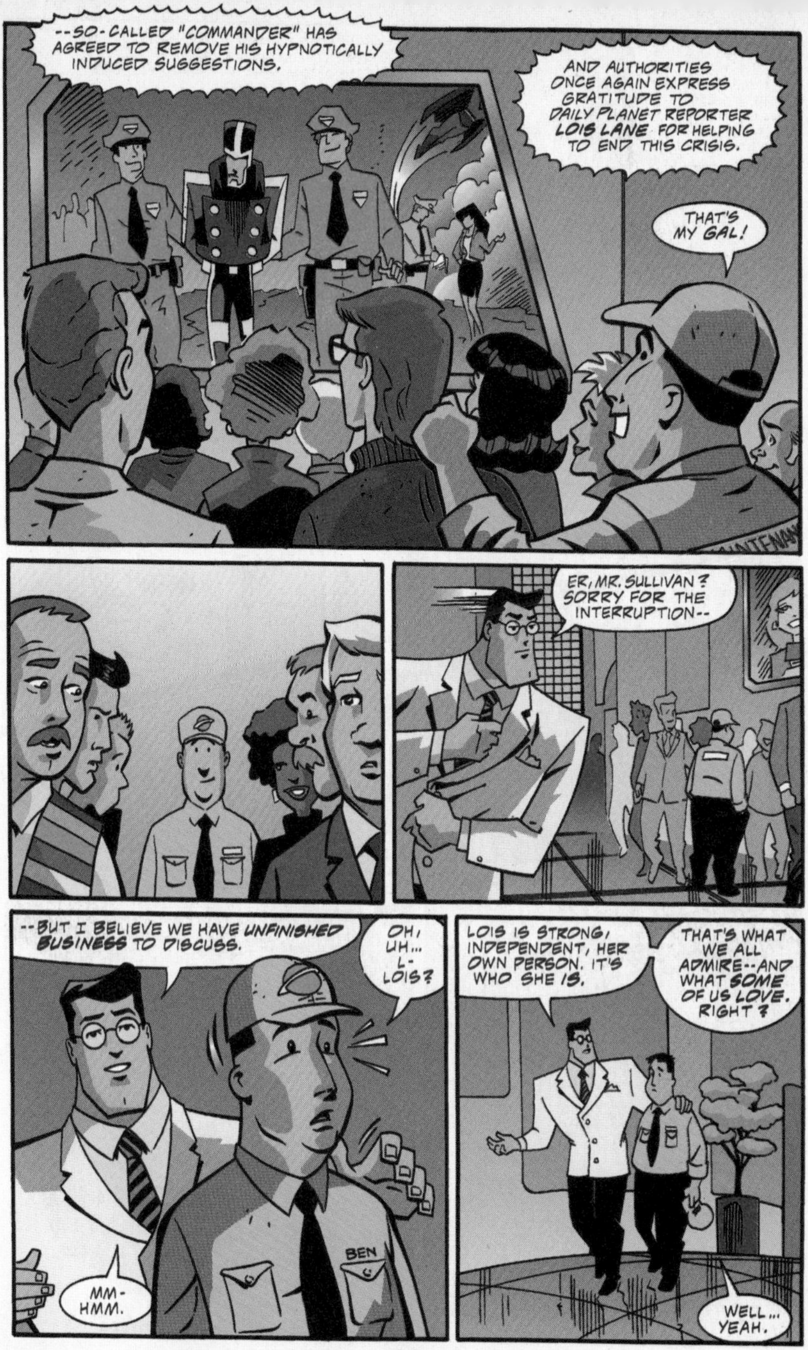
--SO-CALLED "COMMANDER" HAS AGREED TO REMOVE HIS HYPNOTICALLY INDUCED SUGGESTIONS.
AND AUTHORITIES ONCE AGAIN EXPRESS GRATITUDE TO DAILY PLANET REPORTER LOIS LANE FOR HELPING TO END THIS CRISIS.
THAT'S MY GAL!
ER, MR. SULLIVAN? SORRY FOR THE INTERRUPTION--
--BUT I BELIEVE WE HAVE UNFINISHED BUSINESS TO DISCUSS.
OH, UH... L-LOIS?
BEN
MM-HMM.
LOIS IS STRONG, INDEPENDENT, HER OWN PERSON. IT'S WHO SHE IS.
THAT'S WHAT WE ALL ADMIRE--AND WHAT SOME OF US LOVE. RIGHT?
WELL... YEAH.

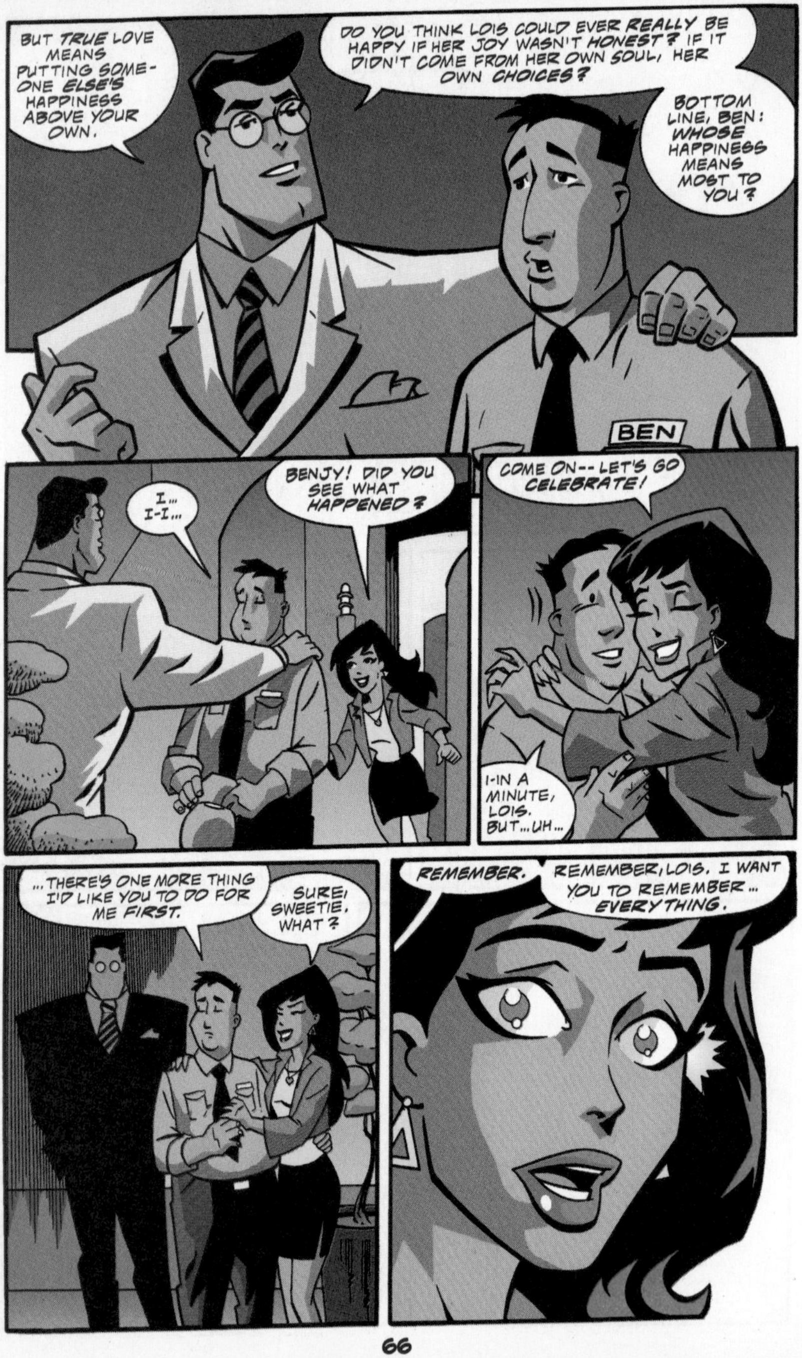
BUT TRUE LOVE MEANS PUTTING SOMEONE ELSE'S HAPPINESS ABOVE YOUR OWN.
DO YOU THINK LOIS COULD EVER REALLY BE HAPPY IF HER JOY WASN'T HONEST? IF IT DIDN'T COME FROM HER OWN SOUL, HER OWN CHOICES?
BOTTOM LINE, BEN: WHOSE HAPPINESS MEANS MOST TO YOU?
BEN
I... I-I...
BENJY! DID YOU SEE WHAT HAPPENED?
COME ON--LET'S GO CELEBRATE!
I-IN A MINUTE, LOIS. BUT...UH...
...THERE'S ONE MORE THING I'D LIKE YOU TO DO FOR ME FIRST.
SURE, SWEETIE. WHAT?
REMEMBER.
REMEMBER, LOIS. I WANT YOU TO REMEMBER... EVERYTHING.

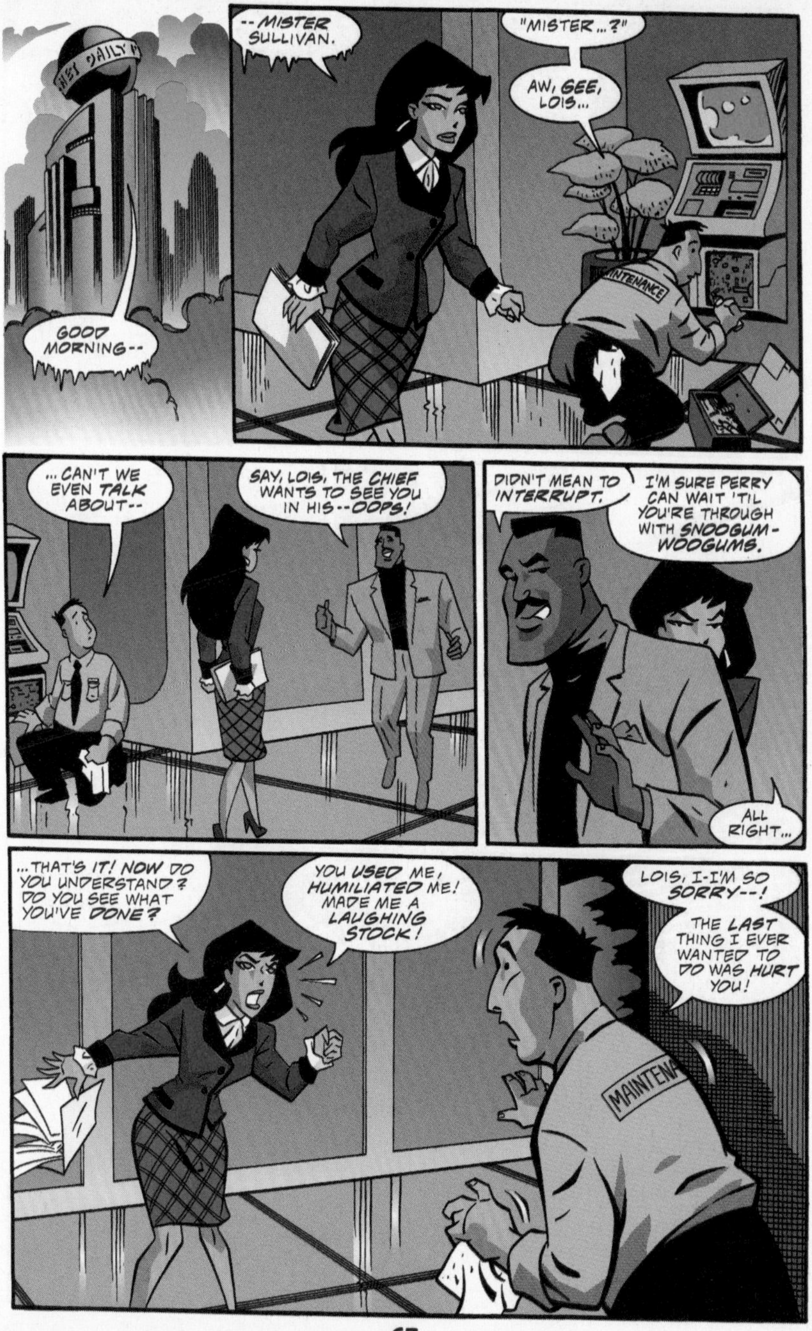
GOOD MORNING--
--MISTER SULLIVAN.
"MISTER...?"
AW, GEE, LOIS...
...CAN'T WE EVEN TALK ABOUT--
SAY, LOIS, THE CHIEF WANTS TO SEE YOU IN HIS--OOPS!
DIDN'T MEAN TO INTERRUPT.
I'M SURE PERRY CAN WAIT 'TIL YOU'RE THROUGH WITH SNOOGUM-WOOGUMS.
ALL RIGHT...
...THAT'S IT! NOW DO YOU UNDERSTAND? DO YOU SEE WHAT YOU'VE DONE?
YOU USED ME, HUMILIATED ME! MADE ME A LAUGHING STOCK!
LOIS, I-I'M SO SORRY--!
THE LAST THING I EVER WANTED TO DO WAS HURT YOU!
MAINTENANCE
MAINTENA

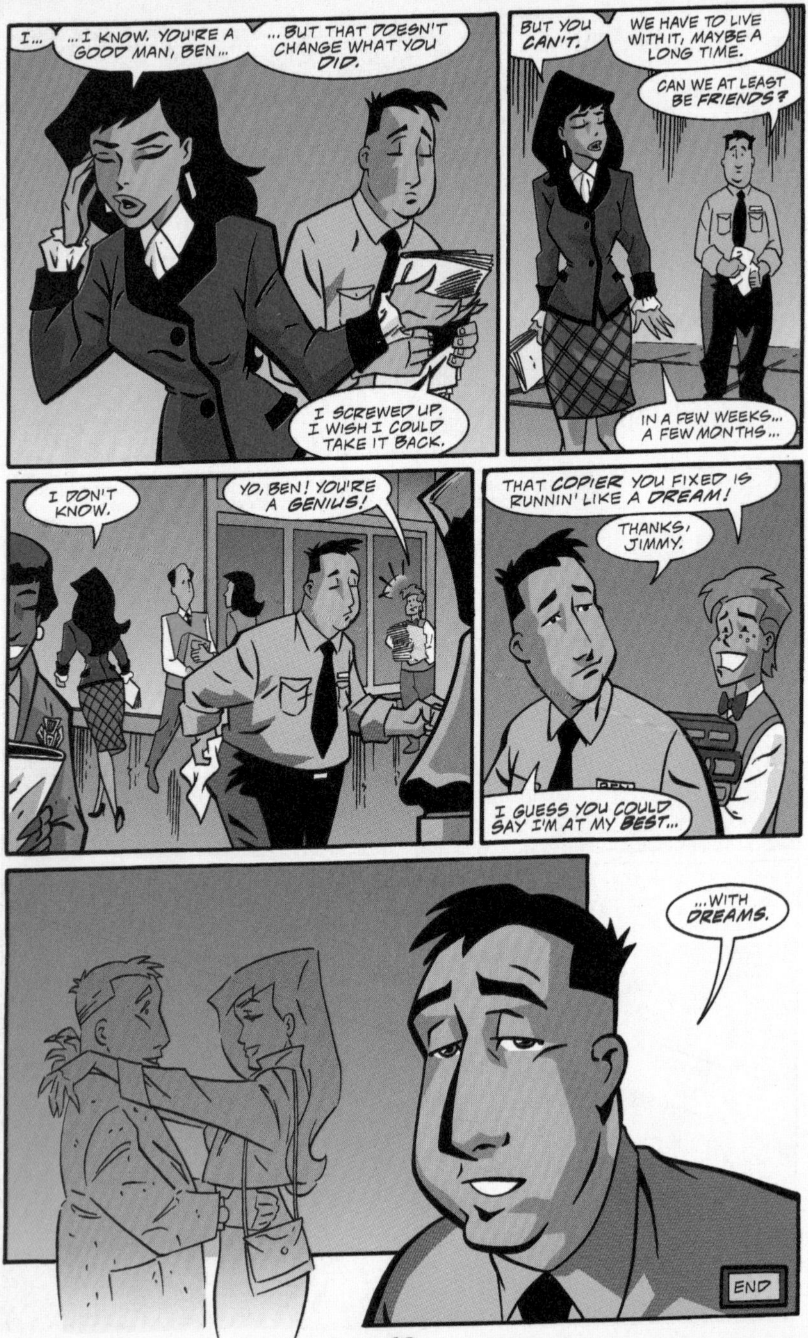
I...
...I KNOW. YOU'RE A GOOD MAN, BEN...
...BUT THAT DOESN'T CHANGE WHAT YOU DID.
I SCREWED UP. I WISH I COULD TAKE IT BACK.
BUT YOU CAN'T.
WE HAVE TO LIVE WITH IT, MAYBE A LONG TIME.
CAN WE AT LEAST BE FRIENDS?
IN A FEW WEEKS... A FEW MONTHS...
I DON'T KNOW.
YO, BEN! YOU'RE A GENIUS!
THAT COPIER YOU FIXED IS RUNNIN' LIKE A DREAM!
THANKS, JIMMY.
I GUESS YOU COULD SAY I'M AT MY BEST...
...WITH DREAMS.
END

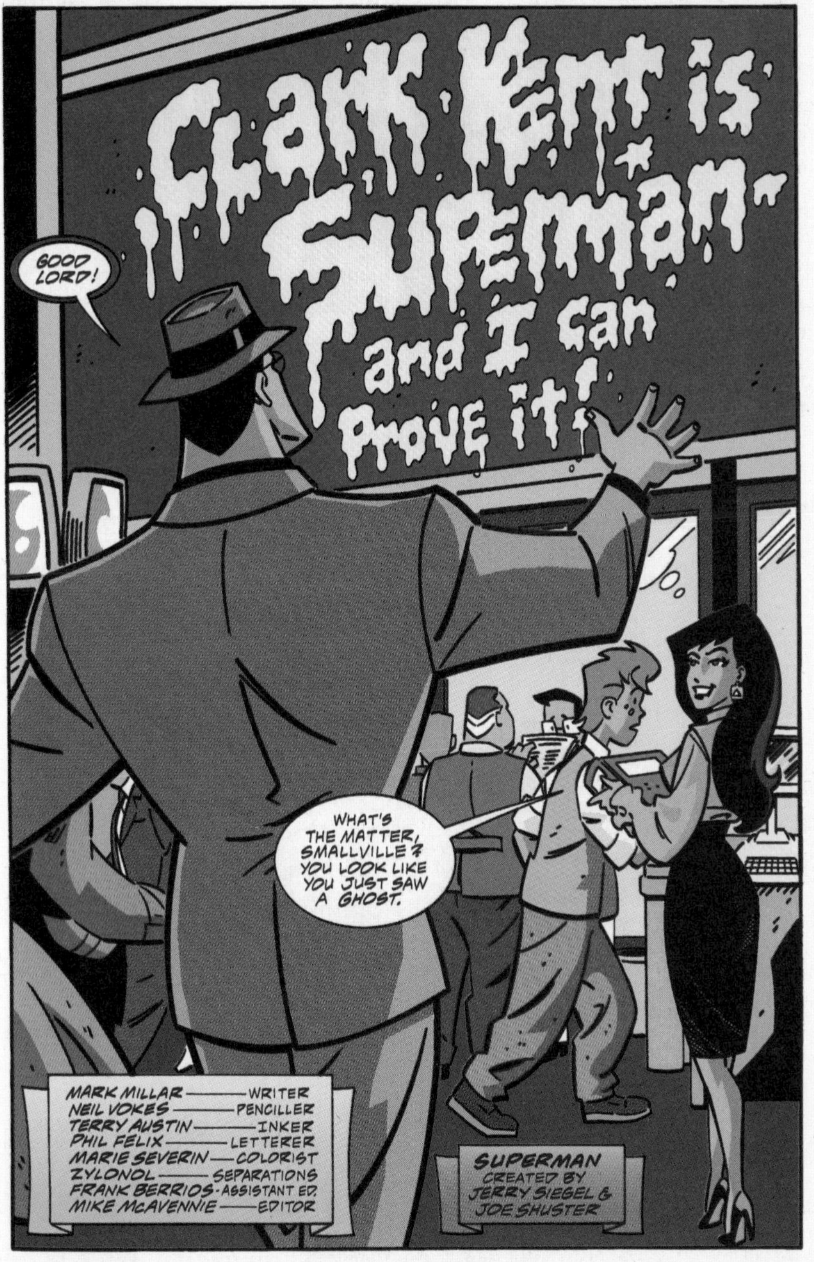
Clark Kent is Superman- and I can Prove it!
GOOD LORD!
WHAT'S THE MATTER, SMALLVILLE? YOU LOOK LIKE YOU JUST SAW A GHOST.
MARK MILLAR—WRITER
NEIL VOKES—PENCILLER
TERRY AUSTIN—INKER
PHIL FELIX—LETTERER
MARIE SEVERIN—COLORIST
ZYLONOL—SEPARATIONS
FRANK BERRIOS-ASSISTANT ED.
MIKE McAVENNIE—EDITOR
SUPERMAN CREATED BY JERRY SIEGEL & JOE SHUSTER

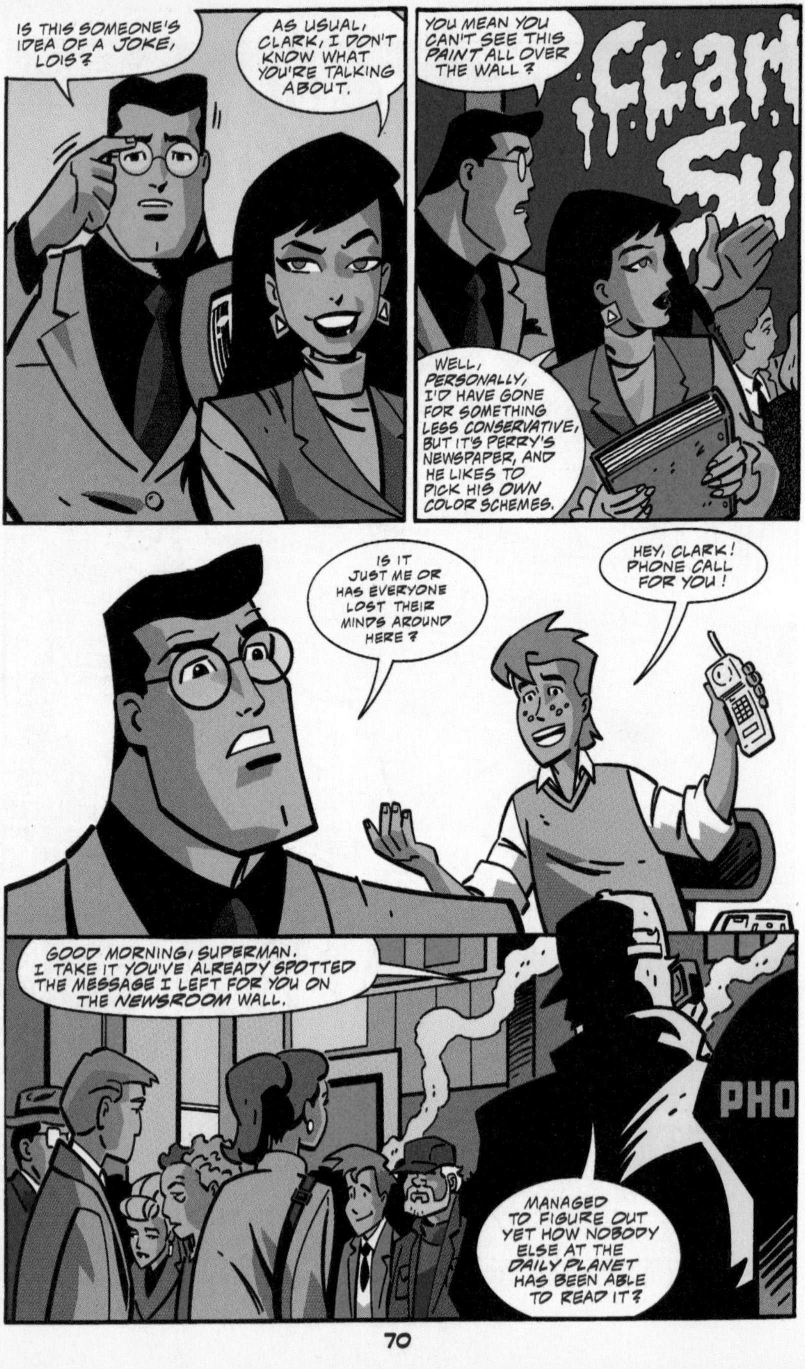
IS THIS SOMEONE'S IDEA OF A JOKE, LOIS?
AS USUAL, CLARK, I DON'T KNOW WHAT YOU'RE TALKING ABOUT.
YOU MEAN YOU CAN'T SEE THIS PAINT ALL OVER THE WALL?
WELL, PERSONALLY, I'D HAVE GONE FOR SOMETHING LESS CONSERVATIVE, BUT IT'S PERRY'S NEWSPAPER, AND HE LIKES TO PICK HIS OWN COLOR SCHEMES.
IS IT JUST ME OR HAS EVERYONE LOST THEIR MINDS AROUND HERE?
HEY, CLARK! PHONE CALL FOR YOU!
GOOD MORNING, SUPERMAN. I TAKE IT YOU'VE ALREADY SPOTTED THE MESSAGE I LEFT FOR YOU ON THE NEWSROOM WALL.
PHO
MANAGED TO FIGURE OUT YET HOW NOBODY ELSE AT THE DAILY PLANET HAS BEEN ABLE TO READ IT?

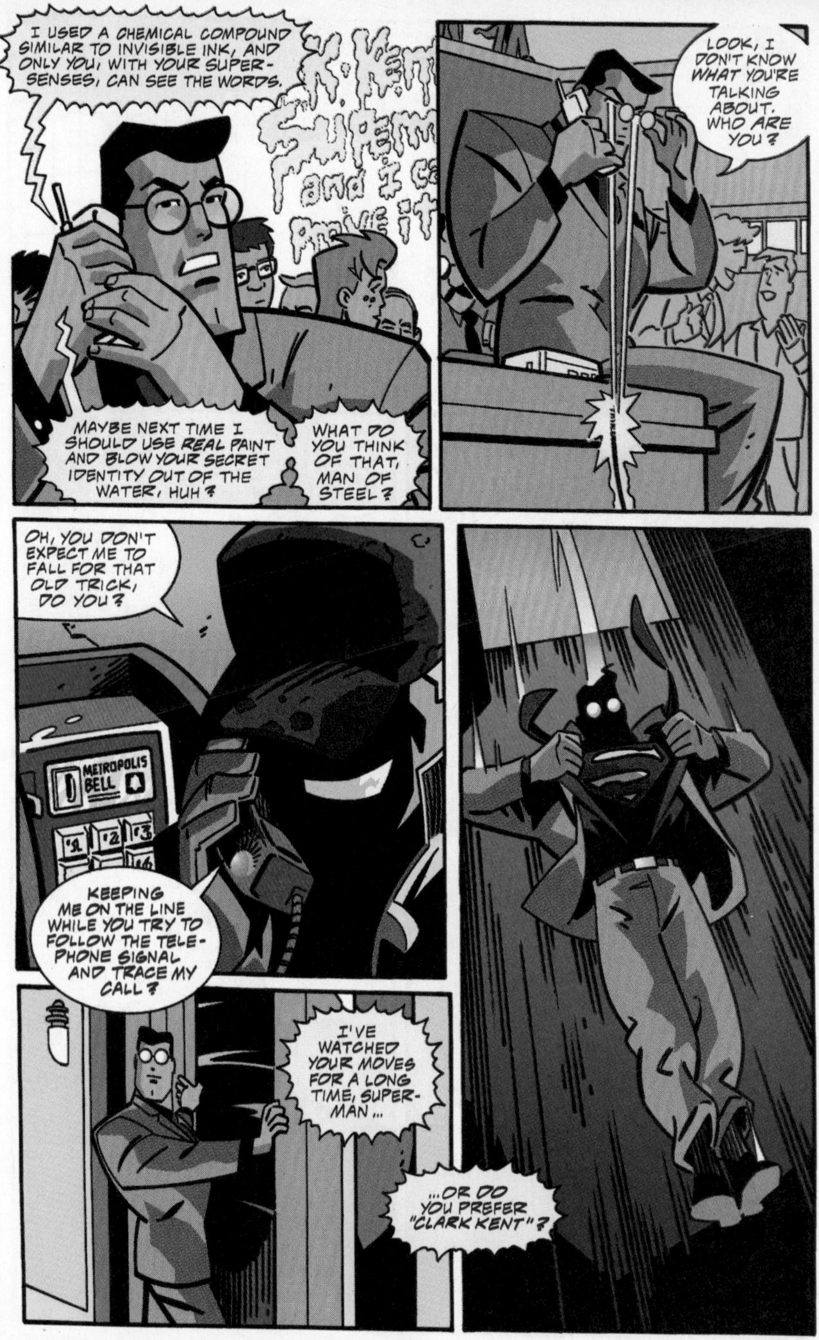
I USED A CHEMICAL COMPOUND SIMILAR TO INVISIBLE INK, AND ONLY YOU, WITH YOUR SUPER-SENSES, CAN SEE THE WORDS.
MAYBE NEXT TIME I SHOULD USE REAL PAINT AND BLOW YOUR SECRET IDENTITY OUT OF THE WATER, HUH?
WHAT DO YOU THINK OF THAT, MAN OF STEEL?
LOOK, I DON'T KNOW WHAT YOU'RE TALKING ABOUT. WHO ARE YOU?
OH, YOU DON'T EXPECT ME TO FALL FOR THAT OLD TRICK, DO YOU?
METROPOLIS BELL
KEEPING ME ON THE LINE WHILE YOU TRY TO FOLLOW THE TELE-PHONE SIGNAL AND TRACE MY CALL?
I'VE WATCHED YOUR MOVES FOR A LONG TIME, SUPER-MAN...
...OR DO YOU PREFER "CLARK KENT"?

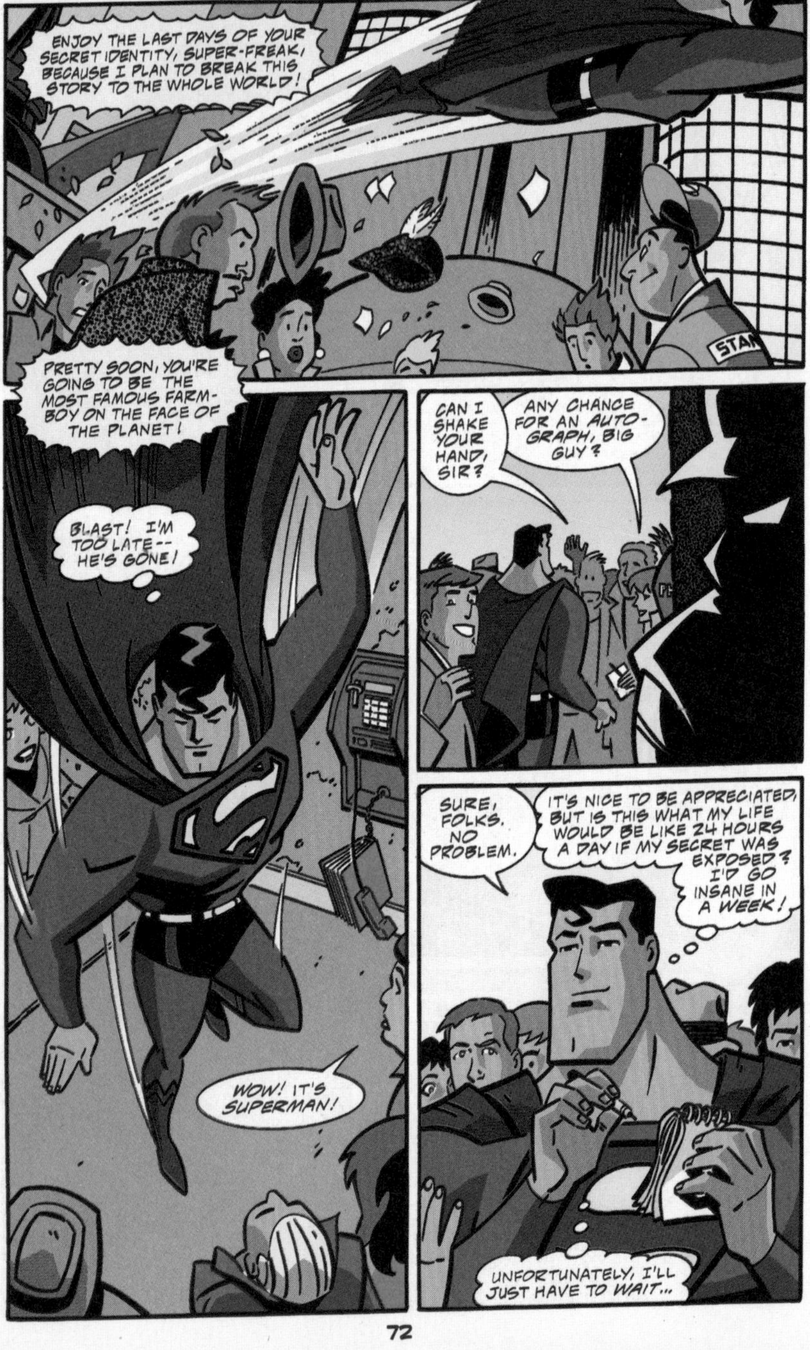
ENJOY THE LAST DAYS OF YOUR SECRET IDENTITY, SUPER-FREAK, BECAUSE I PLAN TO BREAK THIS STORY TO THE WHOLE WORLD!
PRETTY SOON, YOU'RE GOING TO BE THE MOST FAMOUS FARM-BOY ON THE FACE OF THE PLANET!
BLAST! I'M TOO LATE-- HE'S GONE!
WOW! IT'S SUPERMAN!
CAN I SHAKE YOUR HAND, SIR?
ANY CHANCE FOR AN AUTO-GRAPH, BIG GUY?
SURE, FOLKS. NO PROBLEM.
IT'S NICE TO BE APPRECIATED, BUT IS THIS WHAT MY LIFE WOULD BE LIKE 24 HOURS A DAY IF MY SECRET WAS EXPOSED? I'D GO INSANE IN A WEEK!
UNFORTUNATELY, I'LL JUST HAVE TO WAIT...

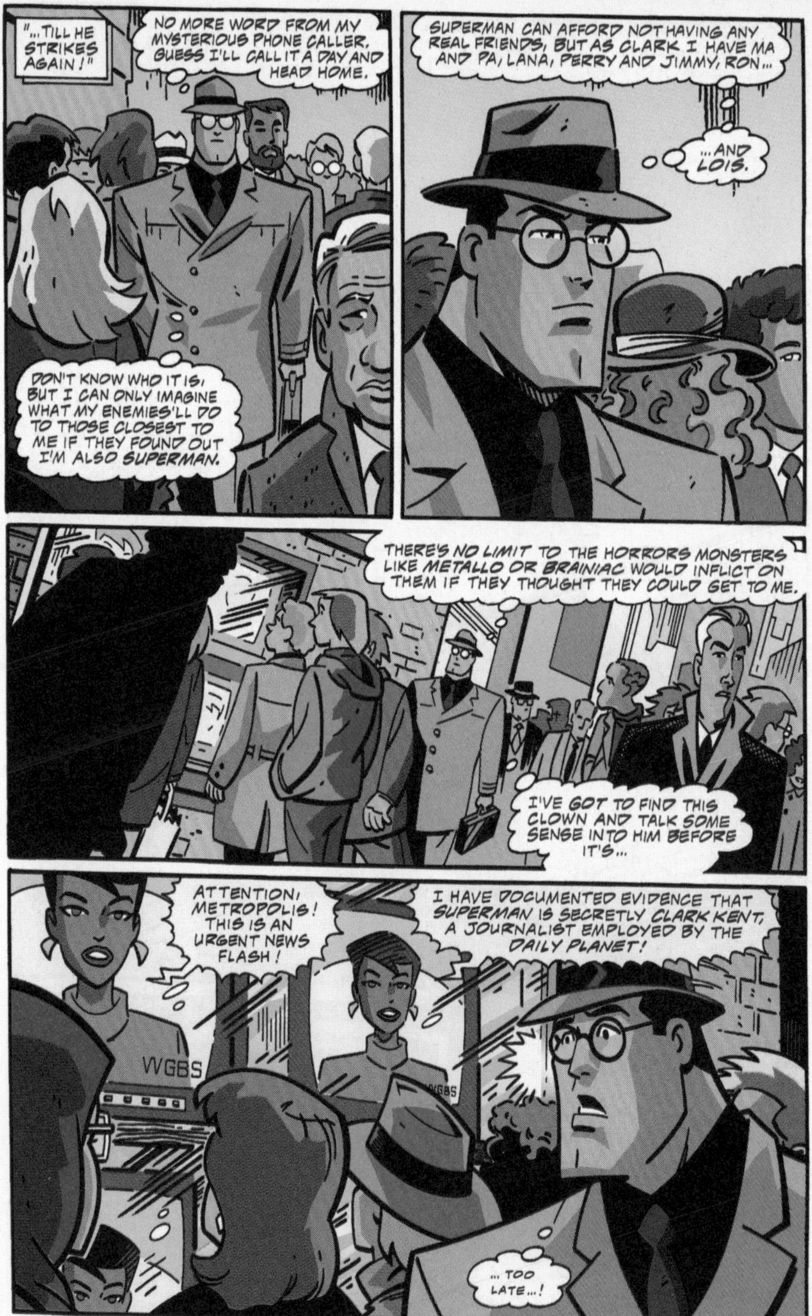
"...TILL HE STRIKES AGAIN!"
NO MORE WORD FROM MY MYSTERIOUS PHONE CALLER. GUESS I'LL CALL IT A DAY AND HEAD HOME.
DON'T KNOW WHO IT IS, BUT I CAN ONLY IMAGINE WHAT MY ENEMIES'LL DO TO THOSE CLOSEST TO ME IF THEY FOUND OUT I'M ALSO SUPERMAN.
SUPERMAN CAN AFFORD NOT HAVING ANY REAL FRIENDS, BUT AS CLARK I HAVE MA AND PA, LANA, PERRY AND JIMMY, RON...
...AND LOIS.
THERE'S NO LIMIT TO THE HORRORS MONSTERS LIKE METALLO OR BRAINIAC WOULD INFLICT ON THEM IF THEY THOUGHT THEY COULD GET TO ME.
I'VE GOT TO FIND THIS CLOWN AND TALK SOME SENSE INTO HIM BEFORE IT'S...
ATTENTION, METROPOLIS! THIS IS AN URGENT NEWS FLASH!
I HAVE DOCUMENTED EVIDENCE THAT SUPERMAN IS SECRETLY CLARK KENT, A JOURNALIST EMPLOYED BY THE DAILY PLANET!
WGBS
WGBS
...TOO LATE...!

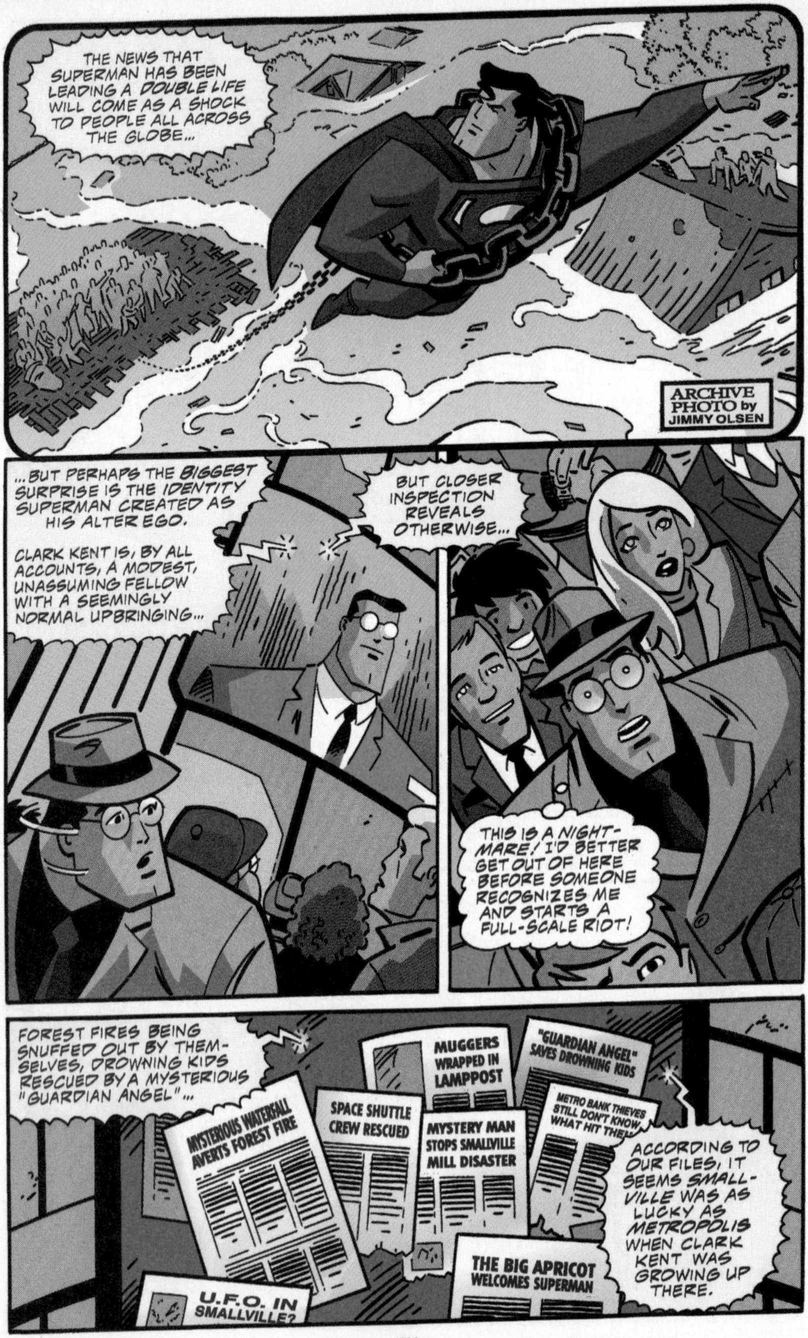
THE NEWS THAT SUPERMAN HAS BEEN LEADING A DOUBLE LIFE WILL COME AS A SHOCK TO PEOPLE ALL ACROSS THE GLOBE...
ARCHIVE PHOTO by JIMMY OLSEN
...BUT PERHAPS THE BIGGEST SURPRISE IS THE IDENTITY SUPERMAN CREATED AS HIS ALTER EGO.
CLARK KENT IS, BY ALL ACCOUNTS, A MODEST, UNASSUMING FELLOW WITH A SEEMINGLY NORMAL UPBRINGING...
BUT CLOSER INSPECTION REVEALS OTHERWISE...
THIS IS A NIGHT-MARE! I'D BETTER GET OUT OF HERE BEFORE SOMEONE RECOGNIZES ME AND STARTS A FULL-SCALE RIOT!
FOREST FIRES BEING SNUFFED OUT BY THEM-SELVES, DROWNING KIDS RESCUED BY A MYSTERIOUS "GUARDIAN ANGEL"...
MUGGERS WRAPPED IN LAMPPOST
"GUARDIAN ANGEL" SAVES DROWNING KIDS
MYSTERIOUS WATERFALL AVERTS FOREST FIRE
SPACE SHUTTLE CREW RESCUED
MYSTERY MAN STOPS SMALLVILLE MILL DISASTER
METRO BANK THIEVES STILL DON'T KNOW WHAT HIT THEM
THE BIG APRICOT WELCOMES SUPERMAN
U.F.O. IN SMALLVILLE?
ACCORDING TO OUR FILES, IT SEEMS SMALL-VILLE WAS AS LUCKY AS METROPOLIS WHEN CLARK KENT WAS GROWING UP THERE.

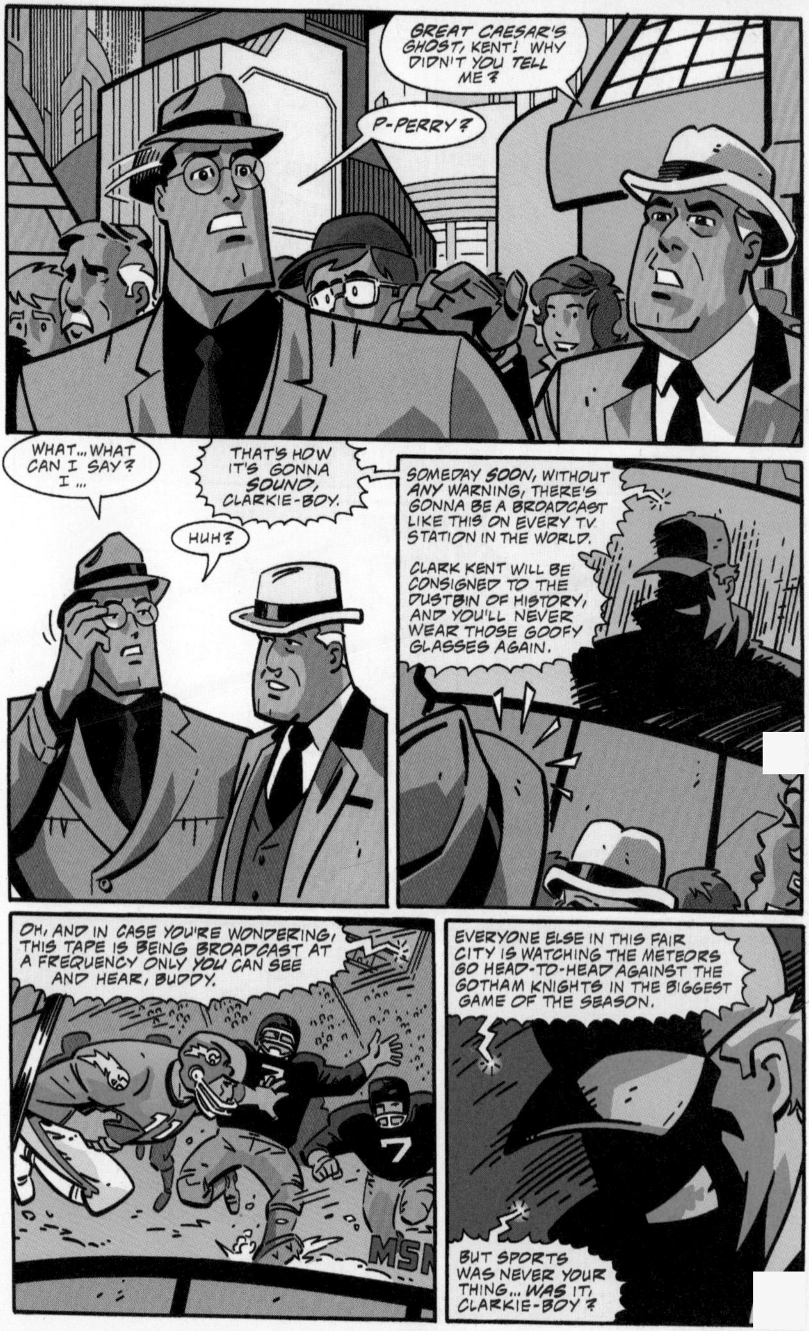
GREAT CAESAR'S GHOST, KENT! WHY DIDN'T YOU TELL ME?
P-PERRY?
WHAT... WHAT CAN I SAY? I ...
THAT'S HOW IT'S GONNA SOUND, CLARKIE-BOY.
HUH?
SOMEDAY SOON, WITHOUT ANY WARNING, THERE'S GONNA BE A BROADCAST LIKE THIS ON EVERY TV STATION IN THE WORLD.
CLARK KENT WILL BE CONSIGNED TO THE DUSTBIN OF HISTORY, AND YOU'LL NEVER WEAR THOSE GOOFY GLASSES AGAIN.
OH, AND IN CASE YOU'RE WONDERING, THIS TAPE IS BEING BROADCAST AT A FREQUENCY ONLY YOU CAN SEE AND HEAR, BUDDY.
MSN
EVERYONE ELSE IN THIS FAIR CITY IS WATCHING THE METEORS GO HEAD-TO-HEAD AGAINST THE GOTHAM KNIGHTS IN THE BIGGEST GAME OF THE SEASON.
BUT SPORTS WAS NEVER YOUR THING... WAS IT, CLARKIE-BOY?

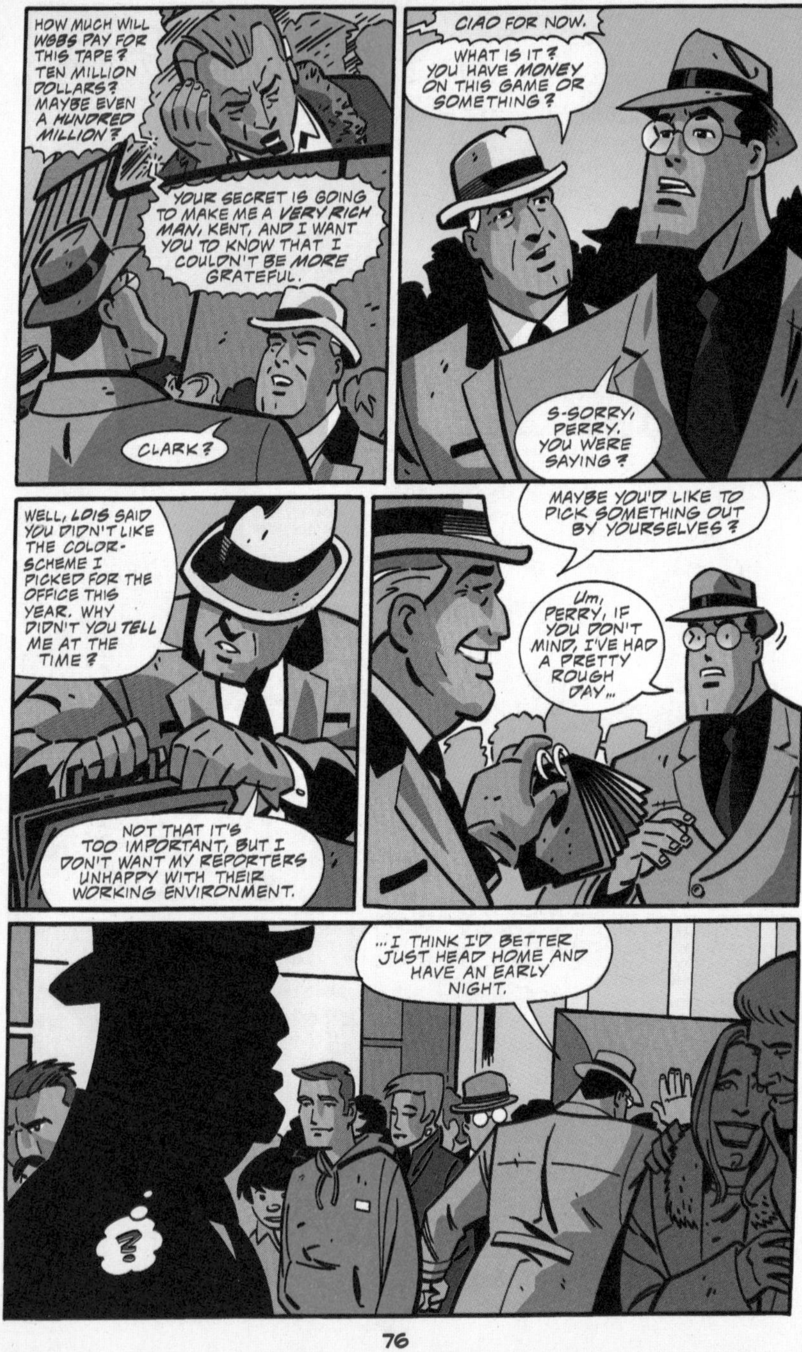
HOW MUCH WILL WEBS PAY FOR THIS TAPE? TEN MILLION DOLLARS? MAYBE EVEN A HUNDRED MILLION?
YOUR SECRET IS GOING TO MAKE ME A VERY RICH MAN, KENT, AND I WANT YOU TO KNOW THAT I COULDN'T BE MORE GRATEFUL.
CLARK?
CIAO FOR NOW.
WHAT IS IT? YOU HAVE MONEY ON THIS GAME OR SOMETHING?
S-SORRY, PERRY. YOU WERE SAYING?
WELL, LOIS SAID YOU DIDN'T LIKE THE COLOR-SCHEME I PICKED FOR THE OFFICE THIS YEAR. WHY DIDN'T YOU TELL ME AT THE TIME?
NOT THAT IT'S TOO IMPORTANT, BUT I DON'T WANT MY REPORTERS UNHAPPY WITH THEIR WORKING ENVIRONMENT.
MAYBE YOU'D LIKE TO PICK SOMETHING OUT BY YOURSELVES?
Um, PERRY, IF YOU DON'T MIND, I'VE HAD A PRETTY ROUGH DAY...
...I THINK I'D BETTER JUST HEAD HOME AND HAVE AN EARLY NIGHT.
?

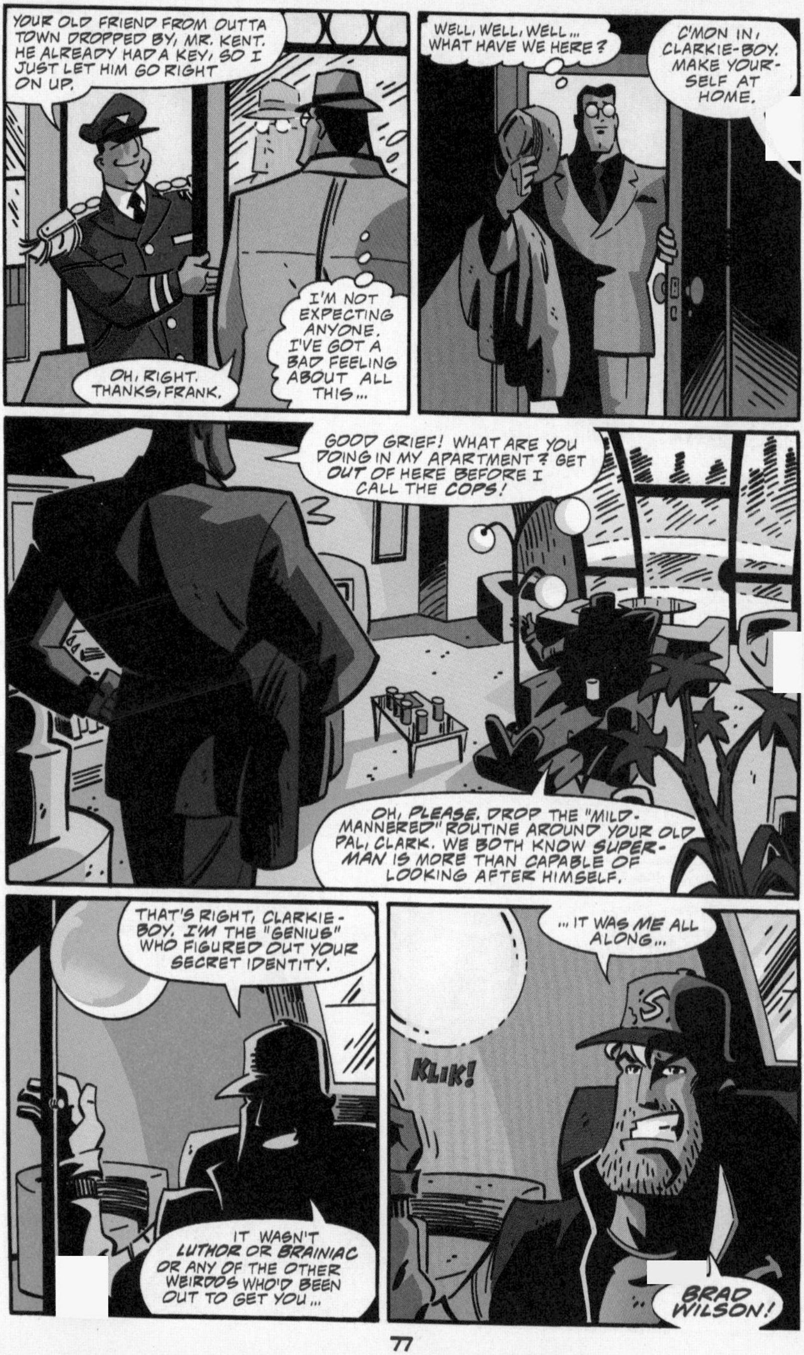

YOUR OLD FRIEND FROM OUTTA TOWN DROPPED BY, MR. KENT. HE ALREADY HAD A KEY, SO I JUST LET HIM GO RIGHT ON UP.
OH, RIGHT. THANKS, FRANK.
I'M NOT EXPECTING ANYONE. I'VE GOT A BAD FEELING ABOUT ALL THIS...
WELL, WELL, WELL... WHAT HAVE WE HERE?
C'MON IN, CLARKIE-BOY. MAKE YOURSELF AT HOME.
GOOD GRIEF! WHAT ARE YOU DOING IN MY APARTMENT? GET OUT OF HERE BEFORE I CALL THE COPS!
OH, PLEASE. DROP THE "MILD-MANNERED" ROUTINE AROUND YOUR OLD PAL, CLARK. WE BOTH KNOW SUPERMAN IS MORE THAN CAPABLE OF LOOKING AFTER HIMSELF.
THAT'S RIGHT, CLARKIE-BOY. I'M THE "GENIUS" WHO FIGURED OUT YOUR SECRET IDENTITY.
IT WASN'T LUTHOR OR BRAINIAC OR ANY OF THE OTHER WEIRDOS WHO'D BEEN OUT TO GET YOU...
...IT WAS ME ALL ALONG...
KLIK!
BRAD WILSON!

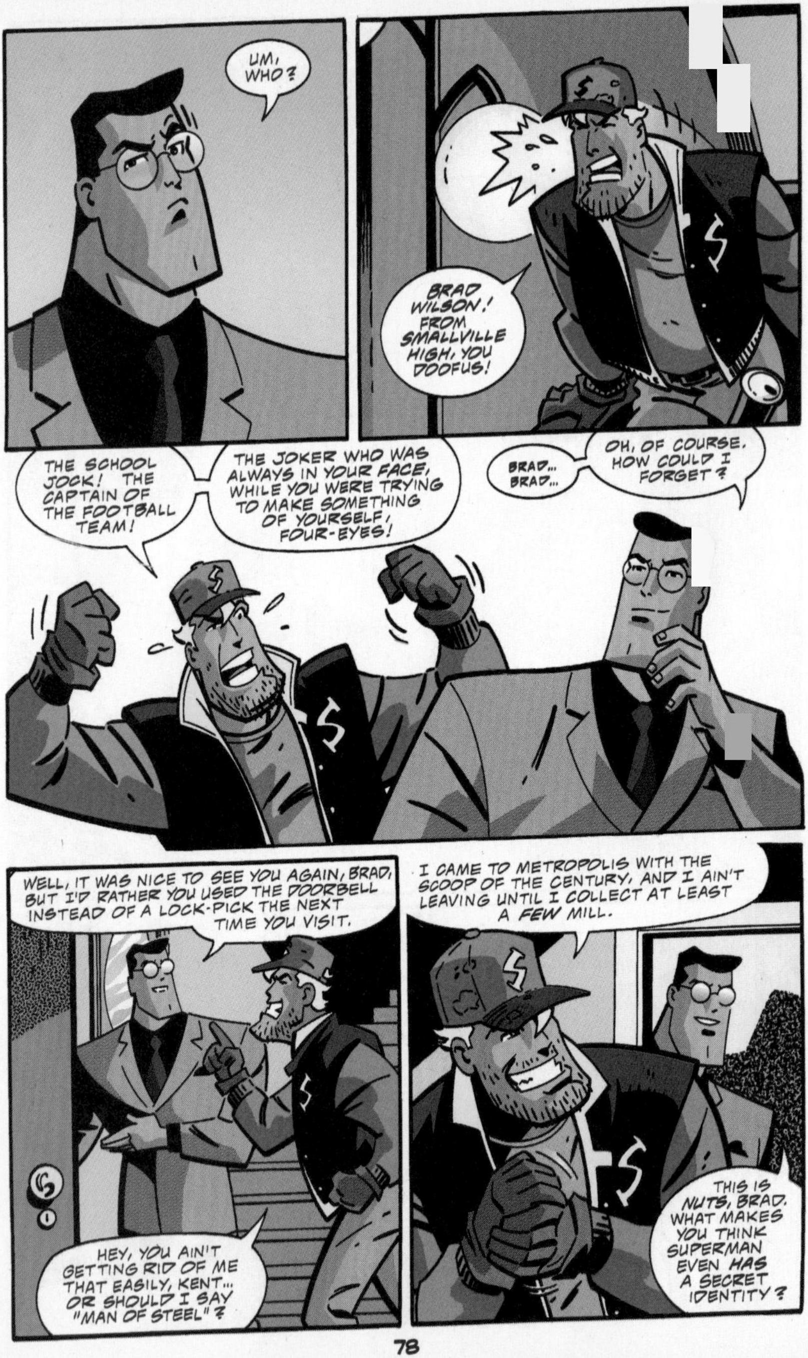
UM, WHO?
BRAD WILSON! FROM SMALLVILLE HIGH, YOU DOOFUS!
THE SCHOOL JOCK! THE CAPTAIN OF THE FOOTBALL TEAM!
THE JOKER WHO WAS ALWAYS IN YOUR FACE, WHILE YOU WERE TRYING TO MAKE SOMETHING OF YOURSELF, FOUR-EYES!
BRAD... BRAD...
OH, OF COURSE. HOW COULD I FORGET?
WELL, IT WAS NICE TO SEE YOU AGAIN, BRAD, BUT I'D RATHER YOU USED THE DOORBELL INSTEAD OF A LOCK-PICK THE NEXT TIME YOU VISIT.
HEY, YOU AIN'T GETTING RID OF ME THAT EASILY, KENT... OR SHOULD I SAY "MAN OF STEEL"?
I CAME TO METROPOLIS WITH THE SCOOP OF THE CENTURY, AND I AIN'T LEAVING UNTIL I COLLECT AT LEAST A FEW MILL.
THIS IS NUTS, BRAD. WHAT MAKES YOU THINK SUPERMAN EVEN HAS A SECRET IDENTITY?

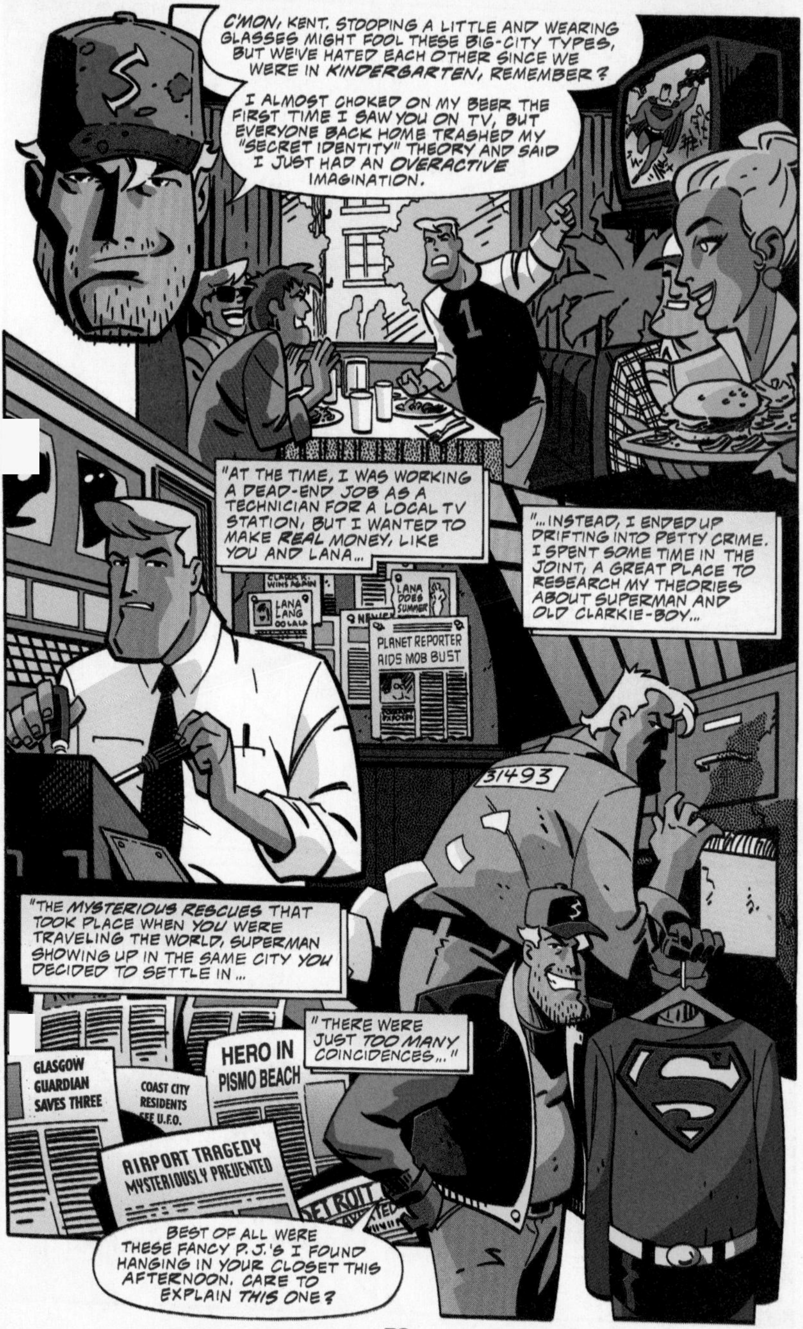
C'MON, KENT. STOOPING A LITTLE AND WEARING GLASSES MIGHT FOOL THESE BIG-CITY TYPES, BUT WE'VE HATED EACH OTHER SINCE WE WERE IN KINDERGARTEN, REMEMBER?
I ALMOST CHOKED ON MY BEER THE FIRST TIME I SAW YOU ON TV, BUT EVERYONE BACK HOME TRASHED MY "SECRET IDENTITY" THEORY AND SAID I JUST HAD AN OVERACTIVE IMAGINATION.
"AT THE TIME, I WAS WORKING A DEAD-END JOB AS A TECHNICIAN FOR A LOCAL TV STATION, BUT I WANTED TO MAKE REAL MONEY, LIKE YOU AND LANA...
"...INSTEAD, I ENDED UP DRIFTING INTO PETTY CRIME. I SPENT SOME TIME IN THE JOINT, A GREAT PLACE TO RESEARCH MY THEORIES ABOUT SUPERMAN AND OLD CLARKIE-BOY...
PLANET REPORTER AIDS MOB BUST
LANA LANG
31493
"THE MYSTERIOUS RESCUES THAT TOOK PLACE WHEN YOU WERE TRAVELING THE WORLD, SUPERMAN SHOWING UP IN THE SAME CITY YOU DECIDED TO SETTLE IN...
"THERE WERE JUST TOO MANY COINCIDENCES..."
GLASGOW GUARDIAN SAVES THREE
COAST CITY RESIDENTS SEE U.F.O.
HERO IN PISMO BEACH
AIRPORT TRAGEDY MYSTERIOUSLY PREVENTED
DETROIT
BEST OF ALL WERE THESE FANCY P.J.'S I FOUND HANGING IN YOUR CLOSET THIS AFTERNOON. CARE TO EXPLAIN THIS ONE?

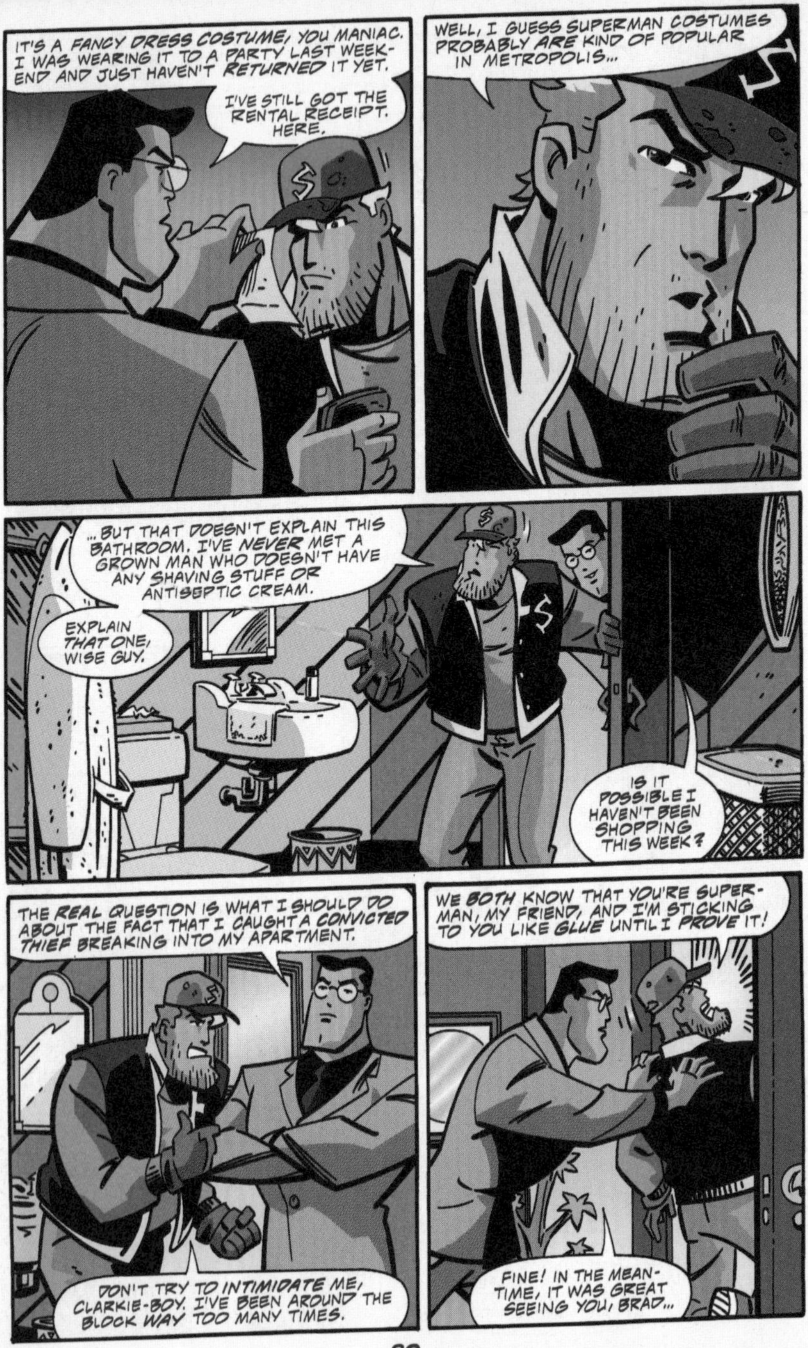
IT'S A FANCY DRESS COSTUME, YOU MANIAC. I WAS WEARING IT TO A PARTY LAST WEEK-END AND JUST HAVEN'T RETURNED IT YET.
I'VE STILL GOT THE RENTAL RECEIPT. HERE.
WELL, I GUESS SUPERMAN COSTUMES PROBABLY ARE KIND OF POPULAR IN METROPOLIS...
...BUT THAT DOESN'T EXPLAIN THIS BATHROOM. I'VE NEVER MET A GROWN MAN WHO DOESN'T HAVE ANY SHAVING STUFF OR ANTISEPTIC CREAM.
EXPLAIN THAT ONE, WISE GUY.
IS IT POSSIBLE I HAVEN'T BEEN SHOPPING THIS WEEK?
THE REAL QUESTION IS WHAT I SHOULD DO ABOUT THE FACT THAT I CAUGHT A CONVICTED THIEF BREAKING INTO MY APARTMENT.
DON'T TRY TO INTIMIDATE ME, CLARKIE-BOY. I'VE BEEN AROUND THE BLOCK WAY TOO MANY TIMES.
WE BOTH KNOW THAT YOU'RE SUPER-MAN, MY FRIEND, AND I'M STICKING TO YOU LIKE GLUE UNTIL I PROVE IT!
FINE! IN THE MEAN-TIME, IT WAS GREAT SEEING YOU, BRAD...

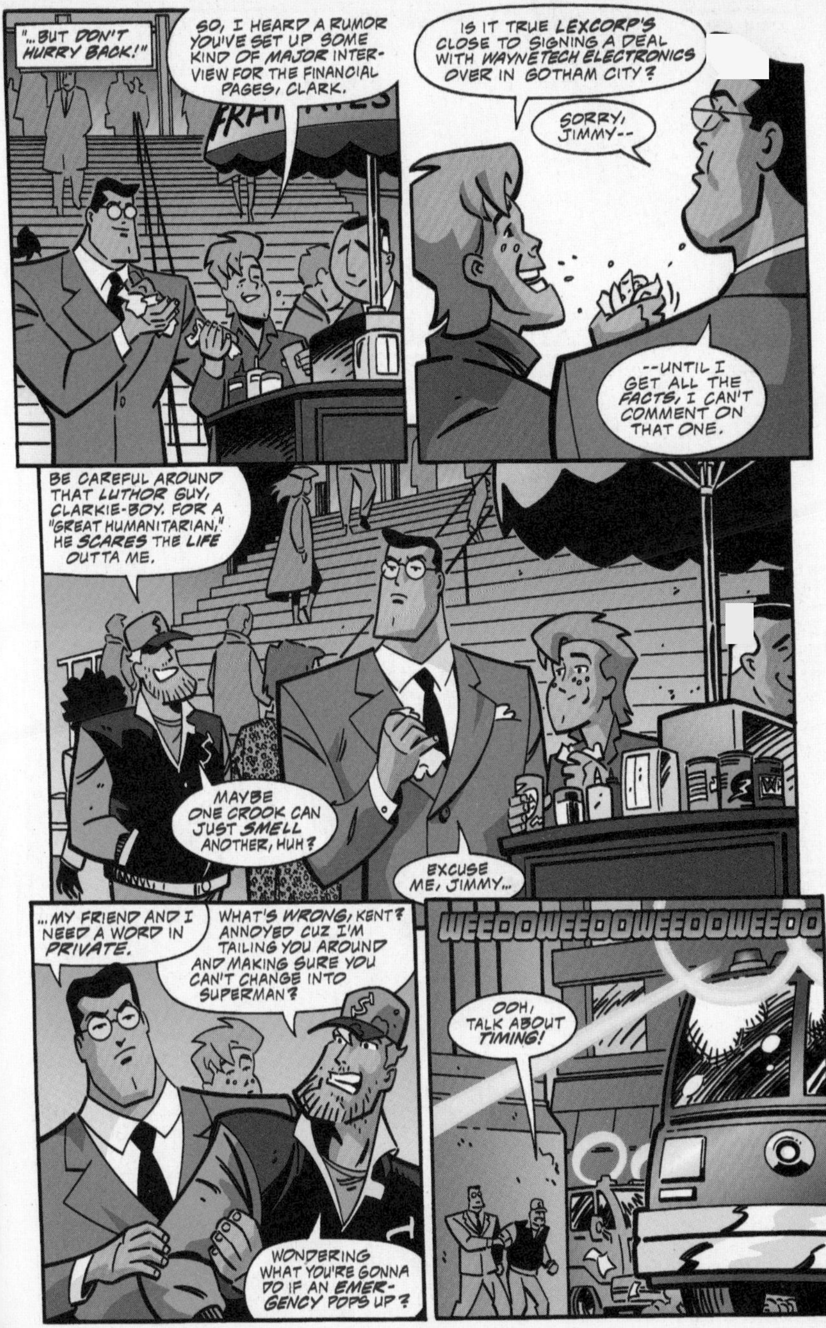
"...BUT DON'T HURRY BACK!"
SO, I HEARD A RUMOR YOU'VE SET UP SOME KIND OF MAJOR INTERVIEW FOR THE FINANCIAL PAGES, CLARK.
IS IT TRUE LEXCORP'S CLOSE TO SIGNING A DEAL WITH WAYNETECH ELECTRONICS OVER IN GOTHAM CITY?
SORRY, JIMMY--
--UNTIL I GET ALL THE FACTS, I CAN'T COMMENT ON THAT ONE.
BE CAREFUL AROUND THAT LUTHOR GUY, CLARKIE-BOY. FOR A "GREAT HUMANITARIAN," HE SCARES THE LIFE OUTTA ME.
MAYBE ONE CROOK CAN JUST SMELL ANOTHER, HUH?
EXCUSE ME, JIMMY...
...MY FRIEND AND I NEED A WORD IN PRIVATE.
WHAT'S WRONG, KENT? ANNOYED CUZ I'M TAILING YOU AROUND AND MAKING SURE YOU CAN'T CHANGE INTO SUPERMAN?
WONDERING WHAT YOU'RE GONNA DO IF AN EMERGENCY POPS UP?
WEEDOWEEDOWEEDOWEEDOO
OOH, TALK ABOUT TIMING!

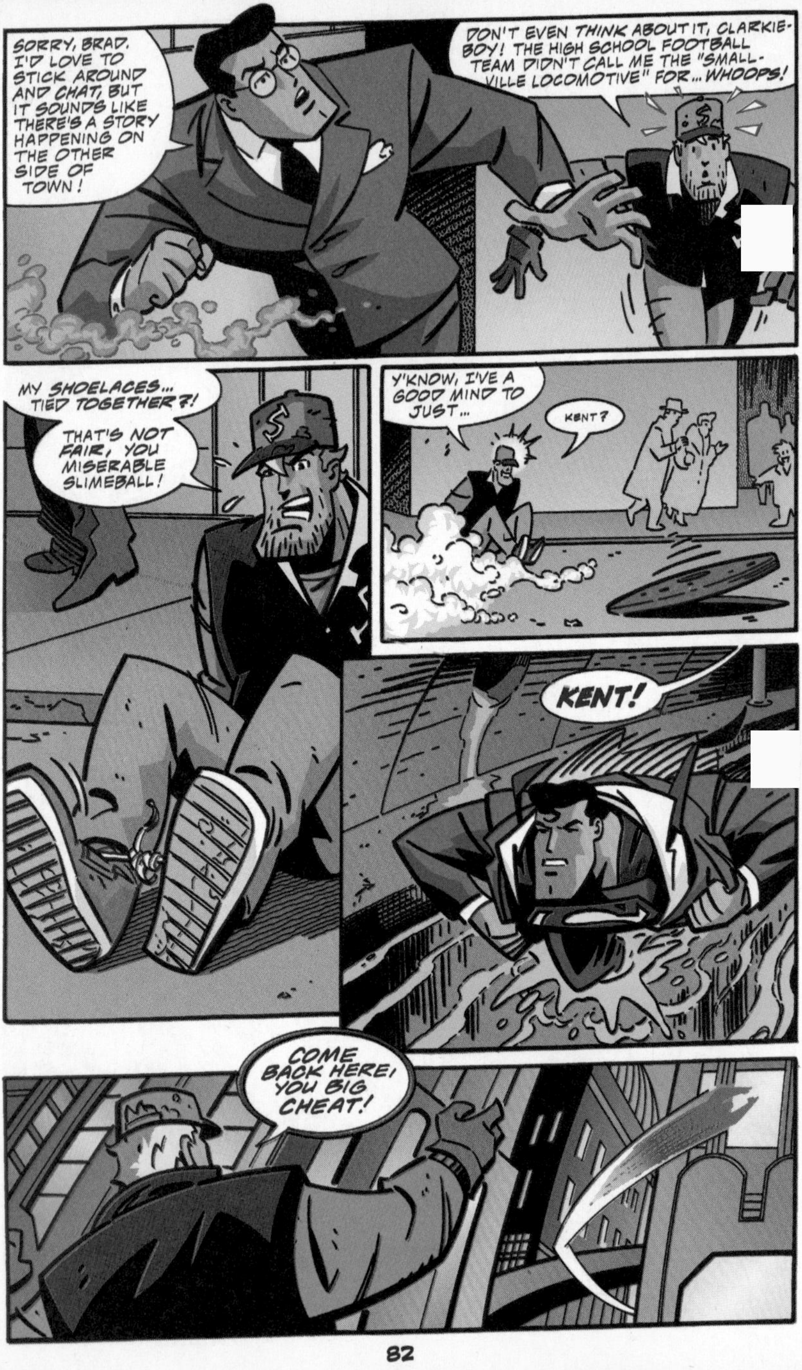
SORRY, BRAD. I'D LOVE TO STICK AROUND AND CHAT, BUT IT SOUNDS LIKE THERE'S A STORY HAPPENING ON THE OTHER SIDE OF TOWN!
DON'T EVEN THINK ABOUT IT, CLARKIE-BOY! THE HIGH SCHOOL FOOTBALL TEAM DIDN'T CALL ME THE "SMALL-VILLE LOCOMOTIVE" FOR... WHOOPS!
MY SHOELACES... TIED TOGETHER?!
THAT'S NOT FAIR, YOU MISERABLE SLIMEBALL!
Y'KNOW, I'VE A GOOD MIND TO JUST...
KENT?
KENT!
COME BACK HERE, YOU BIG CHEAT!

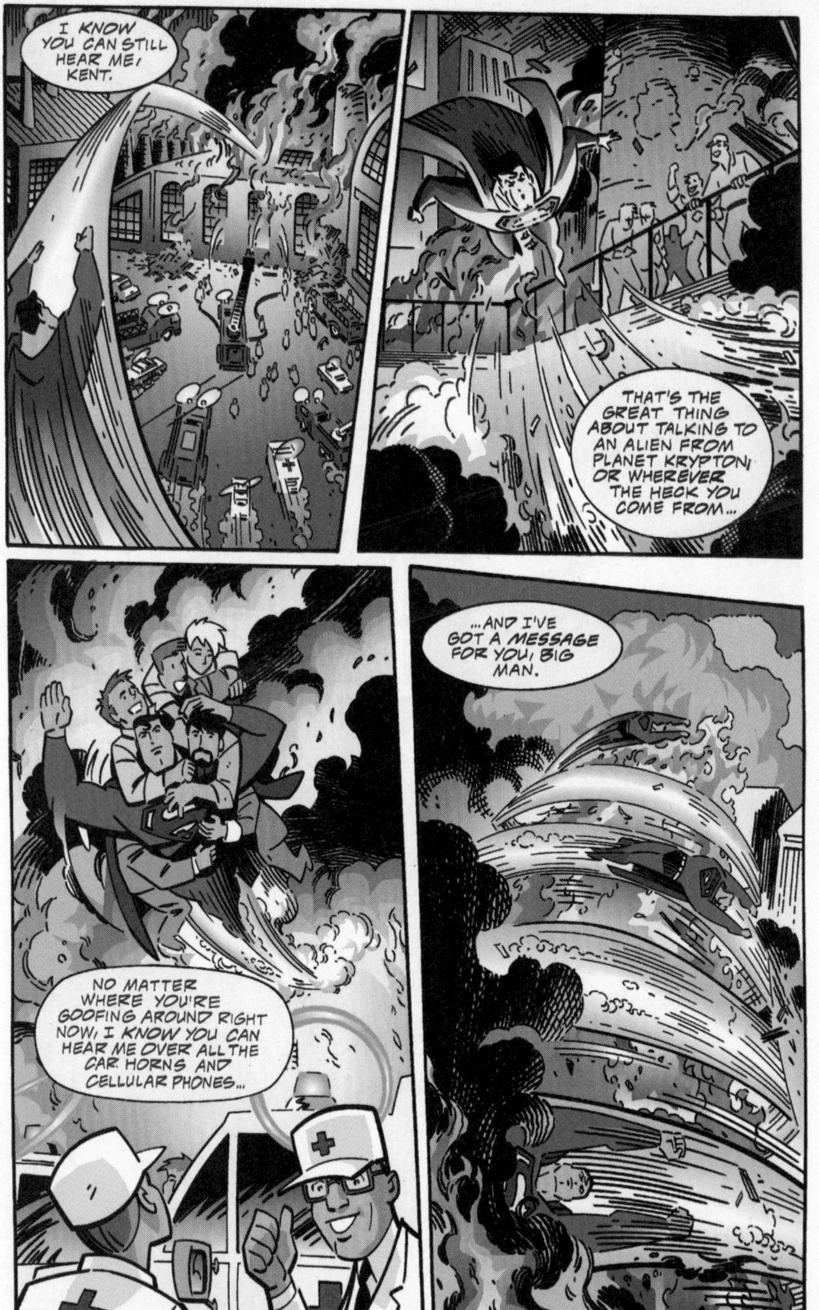
I KNOW YOU CAN STILL HEAR ME, KENT.
THAT'S THE GREAT THING ABOUT TALKING TO AN ALIEN FROM PLANET KRYPTON, OR WHEREVER THE HECK YOU COME FROM...
NO MATTER WHERE YOU'RE GOOFING AROUND RIGHT NOW, I KNOW YOU CAN HEAR ME OVER ALL THE CAR HORNS AND CELLULAR PHONES...
...AND I'VE GOT A MESSAGE FOR YOU, BIG MAN.

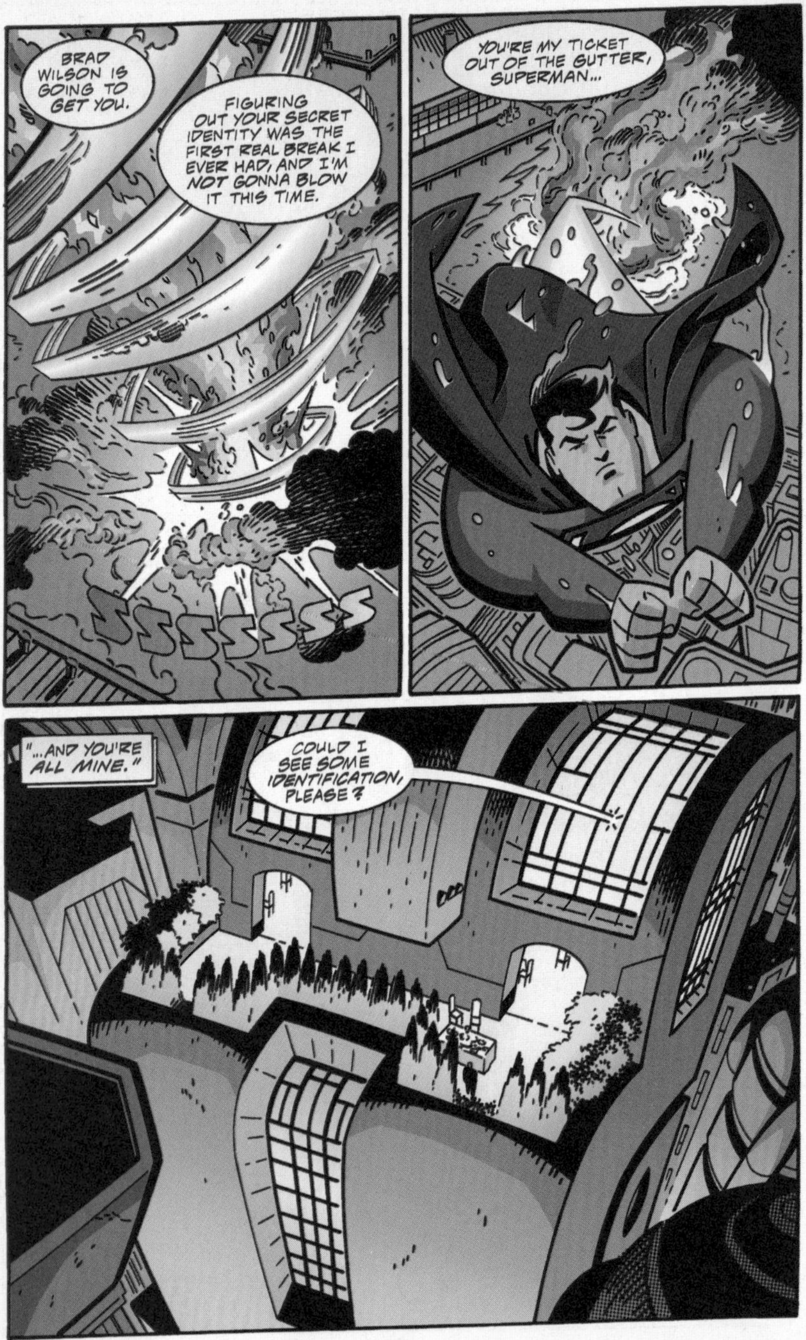
BRAD WILSON IS GOING TO GET YOU.
FIGURING OUT YOUR SECRET IDENTITY WAS THE FIRST REAL BREAK I EVER HAD, AND I'M NOT GONNA BLOW IT THIS TIME.
SSSSSS
YOU'RE MY TICKET OUT OF THE GUTTER, SUPERMAN...
"...AND YOU'RE ALL MINE."
COULD I SEE SOME IDENTIFICATION, PLEASE?

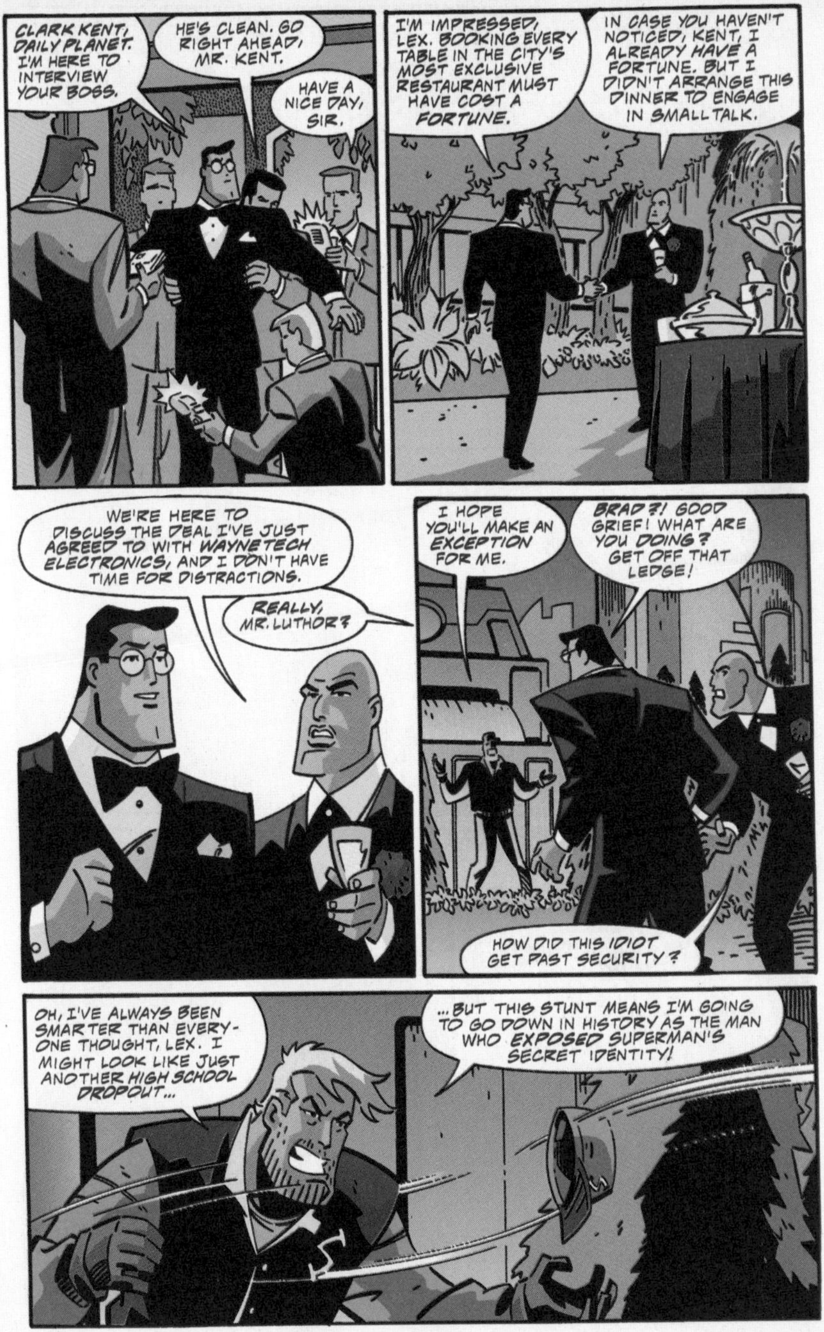
CLARK KENT, DAILY PLANET. I'M HERE TO INTERVIEW YOUR BOSS.
HE'S CLEAN. GO RIGHT AHEAD, MR. KENT.
HAVE A NICE DAY, SIR.
I'M IMPRESSED, LEX. BOOKING EVERY TABLE IN THE CITY'S MOST EXCLUSIVE RESTAURANT MUST HAVE COST A FORTUNE.
IN CASE YOU HAVEN'T NOTICED, KENT, I ALREADY HAVE A FORTUNE. BUT I DIDN'T ARRANGE THIS DINNER TO ENGAGE IN SMALL TALK.
WE'RE HERE TO DISCUSS THE DEAL I'VE JUST AGREED TO WITH WAYNETECH ELECTRONICS, AND I DON'T HAVE TIME FOR DISTRACTIONS.
REALLY, MR. LUTHOR?
I HOPE YOU'LL MAKE AN EXCEPTION FOR ME.
BRAD?! GOOD GRIEF! WHAT ARE YOU DOING? GET OFF THAT LEDGE!
HOW DID THIS IDIOT GET PAST SECURITY?
OH, I'VE ALWAYS BEEN SMARTER THAN EVERY-ONE THOUGHT, LEX. I MIGHT LOOK LIKE JUST ANOTHER HIGH SCHOOL DROPOUT...
...BUT THIS STUNT MEANS I'M GOING TO GO DOWN IN HISTORY AS THE MAN WHO EXPOSED SUPERMAN'S SECRET IDENTITY!

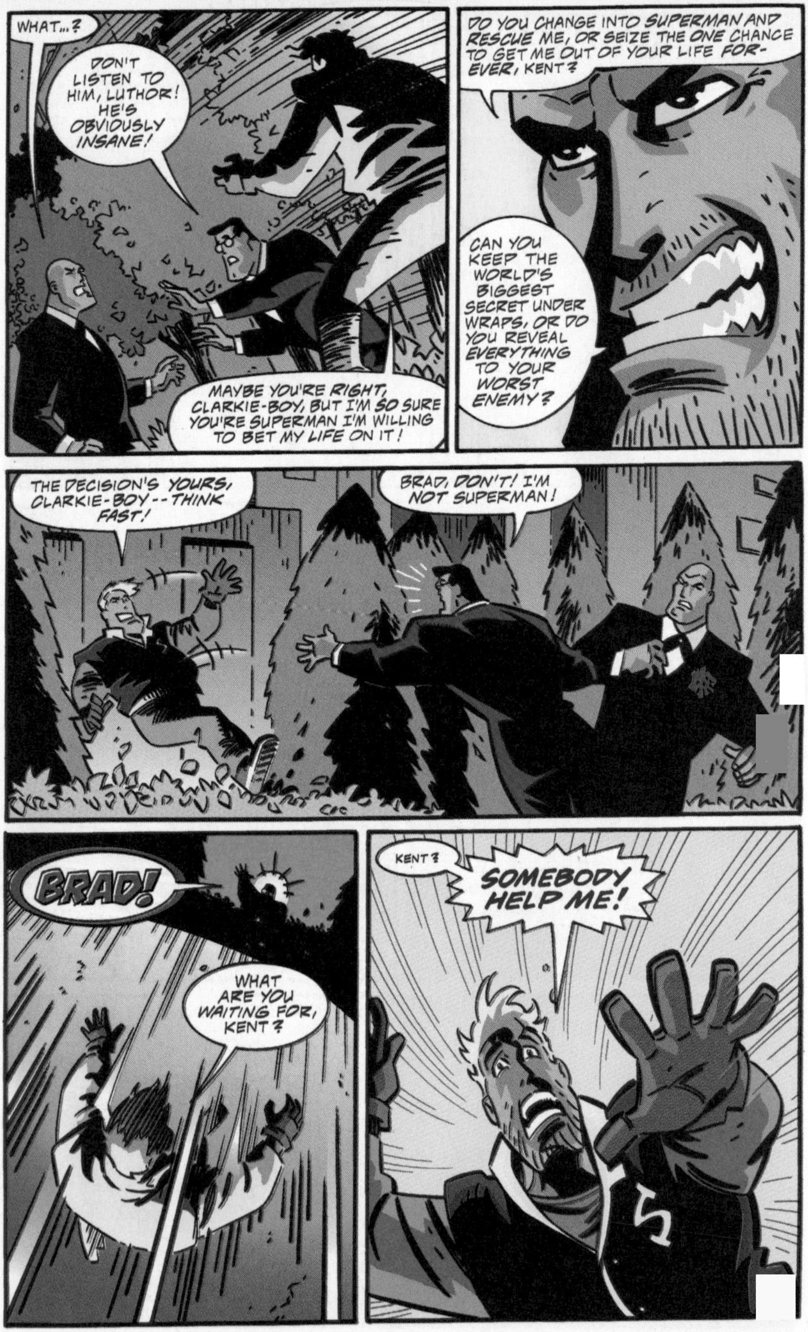
WHAT...?
DON'T LISTEN TO HIM, LUTHOR! HE'S OBVIOUSLY INSANE!
MAYBE YOU'RE RIGHT, CLARKIE-BOY, BUT I'M SO SURE YOU'RE SUPERMAN I'M WILLING TO BET MY LIFE ON IT!
DO YOU CHANGE INTO SUPERMAN AND RESCUE ME, OR SEIZE THE ONE CHANCE TO GET ME OUT OF YOUR LIFE FOREVER, KENT?
CAN YOU KEEP THE WORLD'S BIGGEST SECRET UNDER WRAPS, OR DO YOU REVEAL EVERYTHING TO YOUR WORST ENEMY?
THE DECISION'S YOURS, CLARKIE-BOY--THINK FAST!
BRAD, DON'T! I'M NOT SUPERMAN!
BRAD!
WHAT ARE YOU WAITING FOR, KENT?
KENT?
SOMEBODY HELP ME!

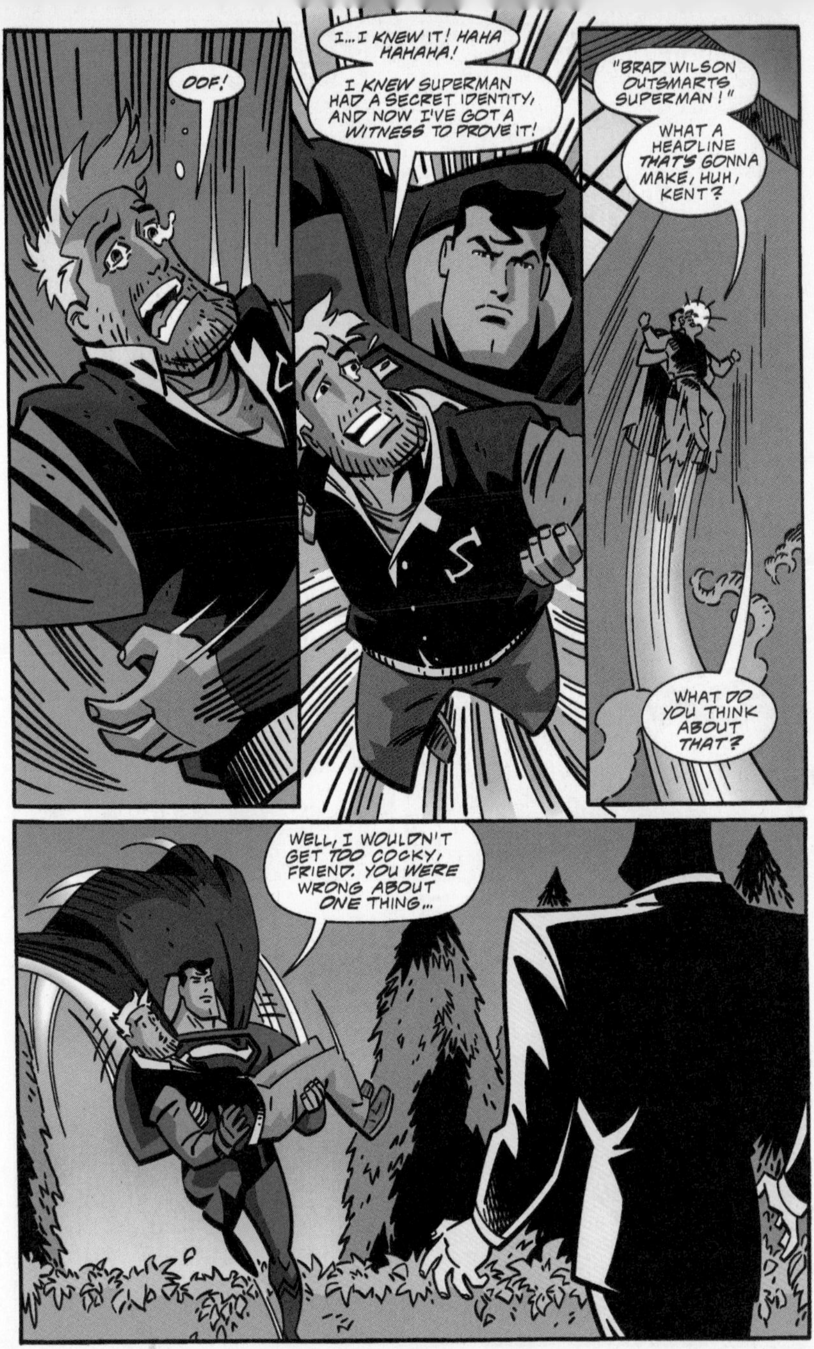
OOF!
I... I KNEW IT! HAHA HAHAHA!
I KNEW SUPERMAN HAD A SECRET IDENTITY, AND NOW I'VE GOT A WITNESS TO PROVE IT!
"BRAD WILSON OUTSMARTS SUPERMAN!"
WHAT A HEADLINE THAT'S GONNA MAKE, HUH, KENT?
WHAT DO YOU THINK ABOUT THAT?
WELL, I WOULDN'T GET TOO COCKY, FRIEND. YOU WERE WRONG ABOUT ONE THING...

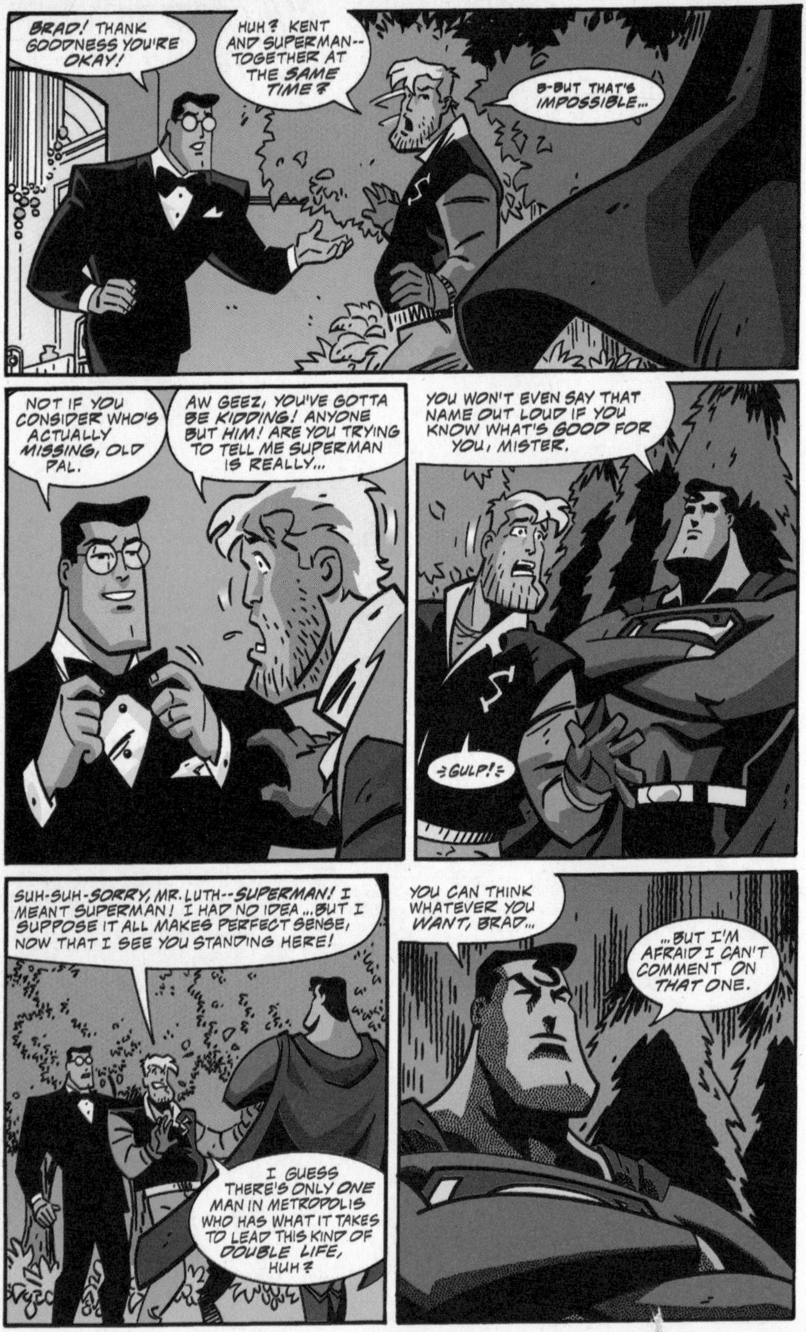
BRAD! THANK GOODNESS YOU'RE OKAY!
HUH? KENT AND SUPERMAN--TOGETHER AT THE SAME TIME?
B-BUT THAT'S IMPOSSIBLE...
NOT IF YOU CONSIDER WHO'S ACTUALLY MISSING, OLD PAL.
AW GEEZ, YOU'VE GOTTA BE KIDDING! ANYONE BUT HIM! ARE YOU TRYING TO TELL ME SUPERMAN IS REALLY...
YOU WON'T EVEN SAY THAT NAME OUT LOUD IF YOU KNOW WHAT'S GOOD FOR YOU, MISTER.
GULP!
SUH-SUH-SORRY, MR. LUTH--SUPERMAN! I MEANT SUPERMAN! I HAD NO IDEA ...BUT I SUPPOSE IT ALL MAKES PERFECT SENSE, NOW THAT I SEE YOU STANDING HERE!
I GUESS THERE'S ONLY ONE MAN IN METROPOLIS WHO HAS WHAT IT TAKES TO LEAD THIS KIND OF DOUBLE LIFE, HUH?
YOU CAN THINK WHATEVER YOU WANT, BRAD...
...BUT I'M AFRAID I CAN'T COMMENT ON THAT ONE.

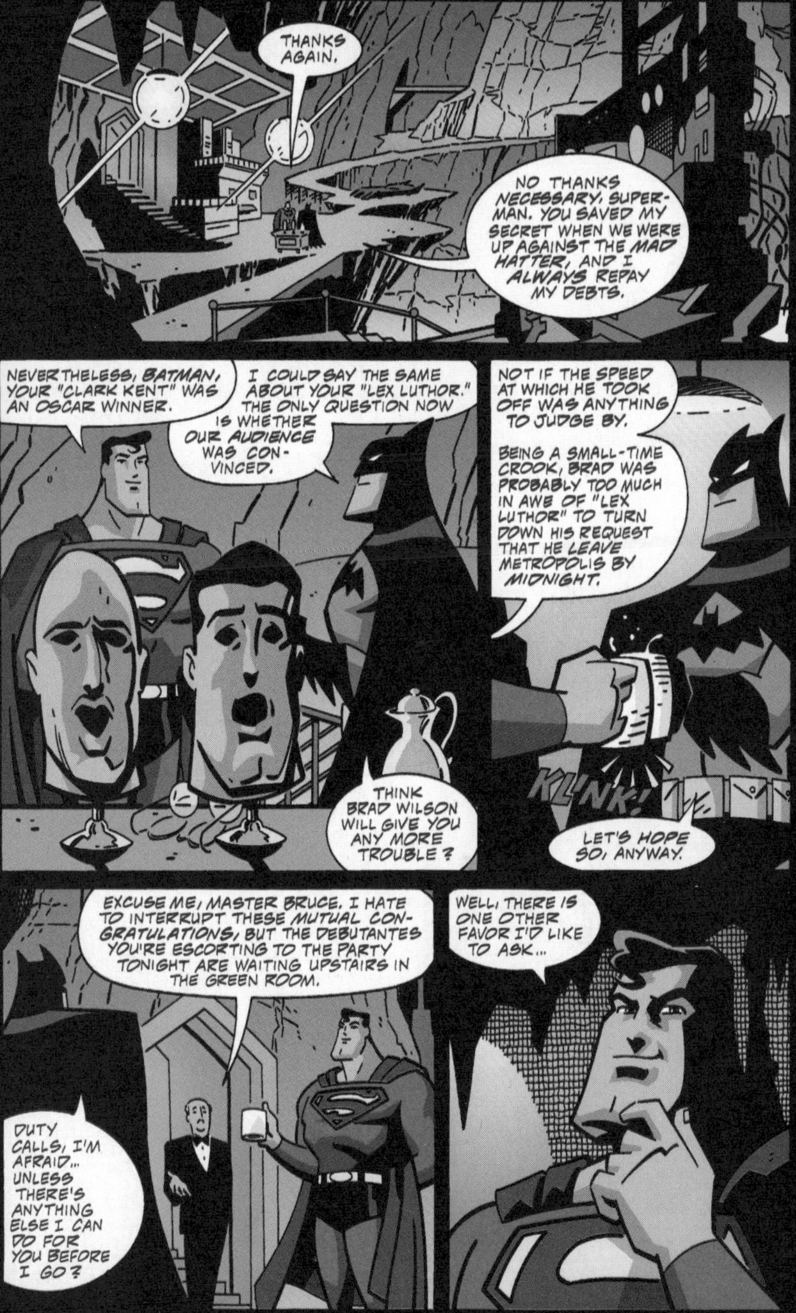
THANKS AGAIN.
NO THANKS NECESSARY, SUPERMAN. YOU SAVED MY SECRET WHEN WE WERE UP AGAINST THE MAD HATTER, AND I ALWAYS REPAY MY DEBTS.
NEVERTHELESS, BATMAN, YOUR "CLARK KENT" WAS AN OSCAR WINNER.
I COULD SAY THE SAME ABOUT YOUR "LEX LUTHOR." THE ONLY QUESTION NOW IS WHETHER OUR AUDIENCE WAS CONVINCED.
THINK BRAD WILSON WILL GIVE YOU ANY MORE TROUBLE ?
NOT IF THE SPEED AT WHICH HE TOOK OFF WAS ANYTHING TO JUDGE BY.
BEING A SMALL-TIME CROOK, BRAD WAS PROBABLY TOO MUCH IN AWE OF "LEX LUTHOR" TO TURN DOWN HIS REQUEST THAT HE LEAVE METROPOLIS BY MIDNIGHT.
KLINK!
LET'S HOPE SO, ANYWAY.
EXCUSE ME, MASTER BRUCE. I HATE TO INTERRUPT THESE MUTUAL CONGRATULATIONS, BUT THE DEBUTANTES YOU'RE ESCORTING TO THE PARTY TONIGHT ARE WAITING UPSTAIRS IN THE GREEN ROOM.
DUTY CALLS, I'M AFRAID... UNLESS THERE'S ANYTHING ELSE I CAN DO FOR YOU BEFORE I GO ?
WELL, THERE IS ONE OTHER FAVOR I'D LIKE TO ASK...

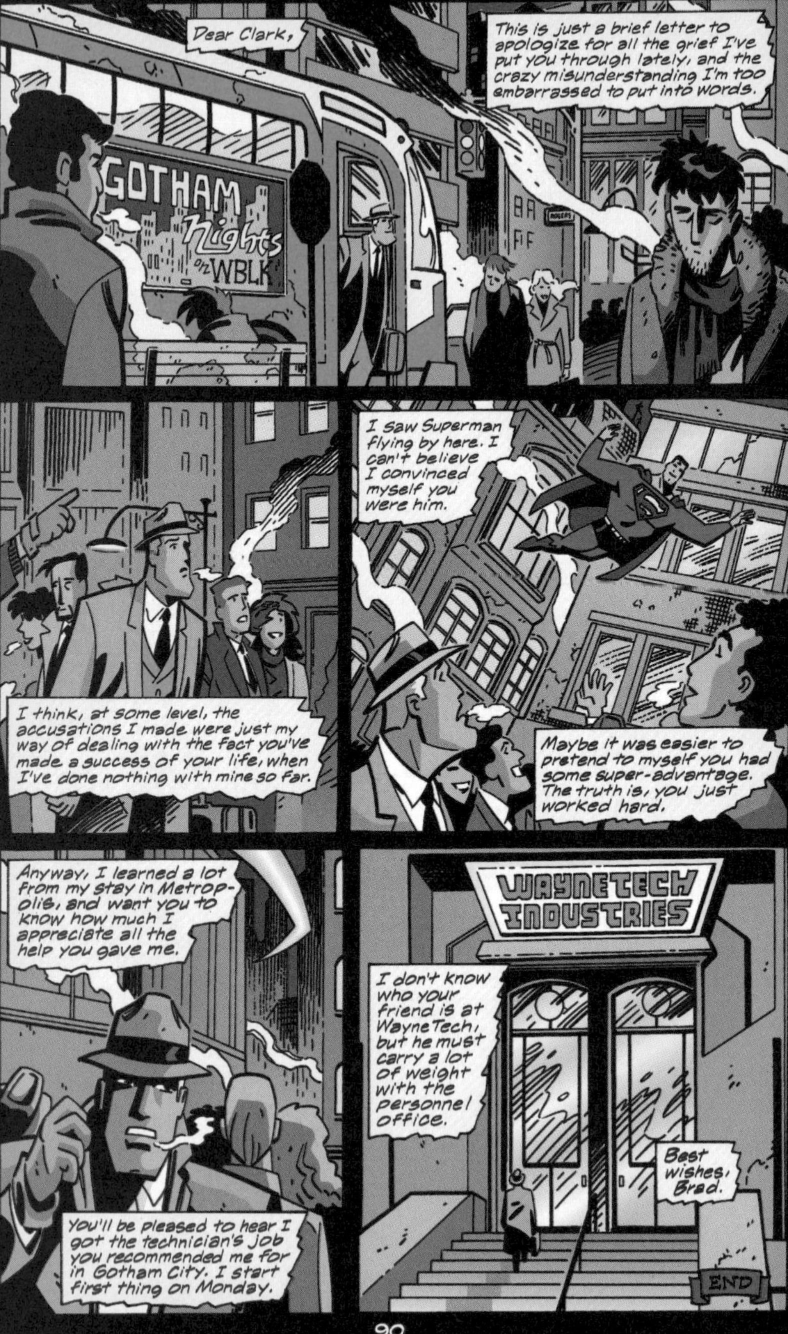
Dear Clark,
This is just a brief letter to apologize for all the grief I've put you through lately, and the crazy misunderstanding I'm too embarrassed to put into words.
GOTHAM Nights on WBLK
I think, at some level, the accusations I made were just my way of dealing with the fact you've made a success of your life, when I've done nothing with mine so far.
I saw Superman flying by here. I can't believe I convinced myself you were him.
Maybe it was easier to pretend to myself you had some super-advantage. The truth is, you just worked hard.
Anyway, I learned a lot from my stay in Metropolis, and want you to know how much I appreciate all the help you gave me.
You'll be pleased to hear I got the technician's job you recommended me for in Gotham City. I start first thing on Monday.
WAYNETECH INDUSTRIES
I don't know who your friend is at WayneTech, but he must carry a lot of weight with the personnel office.
Best wishes, Brad.
END

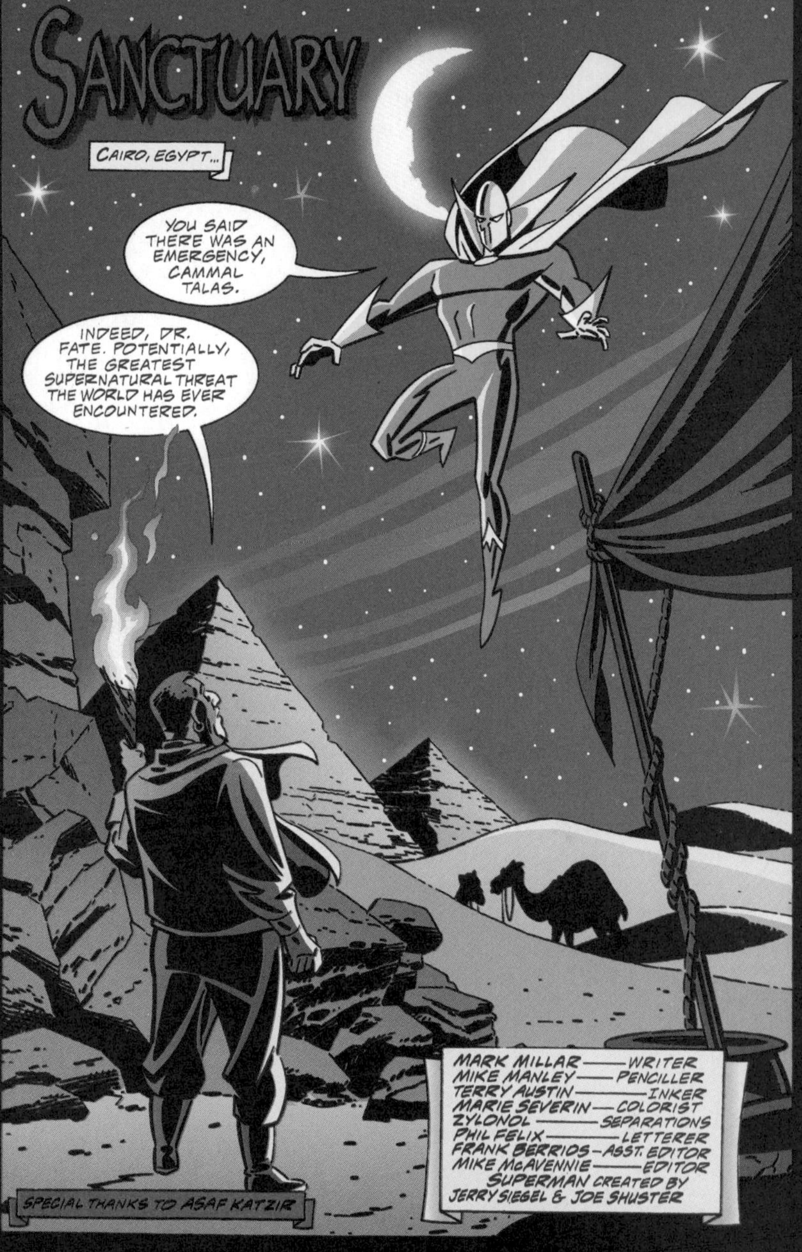
SANCTUARY
CAIRO, EGYPT...
YOU SAID THERE WAS AN EMERGENCY, CAMMAL TALAS.
INDEED, DR. FATE. POTENTIALLY, THE GREATEST SUPERNATURAL THREAT THE WORLD HAS EVER ENCOUNTERED.
MARK MILLAR—WRITER
MIKE MANLEY—PENCILLER
TERRY AUSTIN—INKER
MARIE SEVERIN—COLORIST
ZYLONOL—SEPARATIONS
PHIL FELIX—LETTERER
FRANK BERRIOS—ASST. EDITOR
MIKE McAVENNIE—EDITOR
SUPERMAN CREATED BY JERRY SIEGEL & JOE SHUSTER
SPECIAL THANKS TO ASAF KATZIR

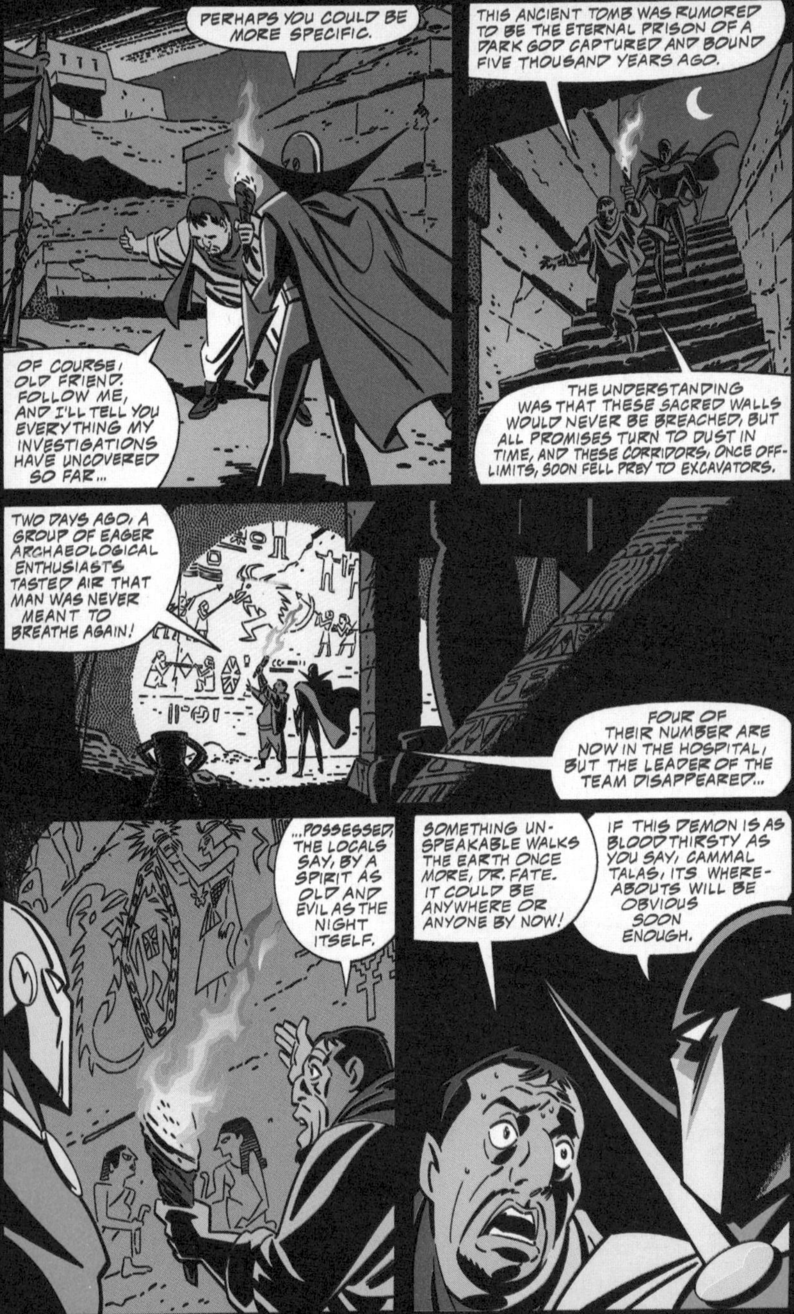
PERHAPS YOU COULD BE MORE SPECIFIC.
OF COURSE, OLD FRIEND. FOLLOW ME, AND I'LL TELL YOU EVERYTHING MY INVESTIGATIONS HAVE UNCOVERED SO FAR...
THIS ANCIENT TOMB WAS RUMORED TO BE THE ETERNAL PRISON OF A DARK GOD CAPTURED AND BOUND FIVE THOUSAND YEARS AGO.
THE UNDERSTANDING WAS THAT THESE SACRED WALLS WOULD NEVER BE BREACHED, BUT ALL PROMISES TURN TO DUST IN TIME, AND THESE CORRIDORS, ONCE OFF-LIMITS, SOON FELL PREY TO EXCAVATORS.
TWO DAYS AGO, A GROUP OF EAGER ARCHAEOLOGICAL ENTHUSIASTS TASTED AIR THAT MAN WAS NEVER MEANT TO BREATHE AGAIN!
FOUR OF THEIR NUMBER ARE NOW IN THE HOSPITAL, BUT THE LEADER OF THE TEAM DISAPPEARED...
...POSSESSED, THE LOCALS SAY, BY A SPIRIT AS OLD AND EVIL AS THE NIGHT ITSELF.
SOMETHING UN-SPEAKABLE WALKS THE EARTH ONCE MORE, DR. FATE. IT COULD BE ANYWHERE OR ANYONE BY NOW!
IF THIS DEMON IS AS BLOODTHIRSTY AS YOU SAY, CAMMAL TALAS, ITS WHERE-ABOUTS WILL BE OBVIOUS SOON ENOUGH.

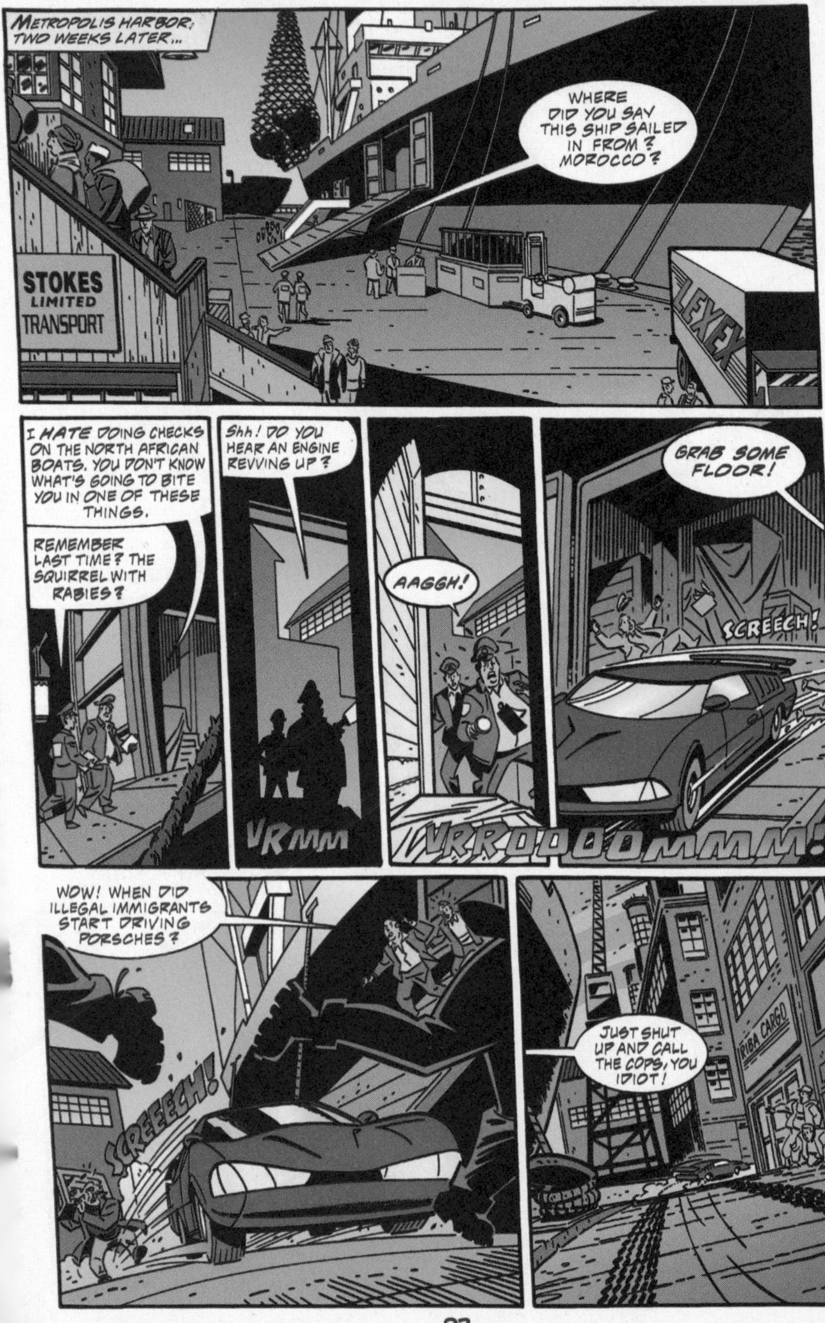
METROPOLIS HARBOR; TWO WEEKS LATER...
STOKES LIMITED TRANSPORT
WHERE DID YOU SAY THIS SHIP SAILED IN FROM? MOROCCO?
LEXEX
I HATE DOING CHECKS ON THE NORTH AFRICAN BOATS. YOU DON'T KNOW WHAT'S GOING TO BITE YOU IN ONE OF THESE THINGS.
REMEMBER LAST TIME? THE SQUIRREL WITH RABIES?
Shh! DO YOU HEAR AN ENGINE REVVING UP?
VRMM
AAGGH!
GRAB SOME FLOOR!
SCREECH!
VRROOOOOMMMM!
WOW! WHEN DID ILLEGAL IMMIGRANTS START DRIVING PORSCHES?
SCREEECH!
JUST SHUT UP AND CALL THE COPS, YOU IDIOT!
RIBA CARGO

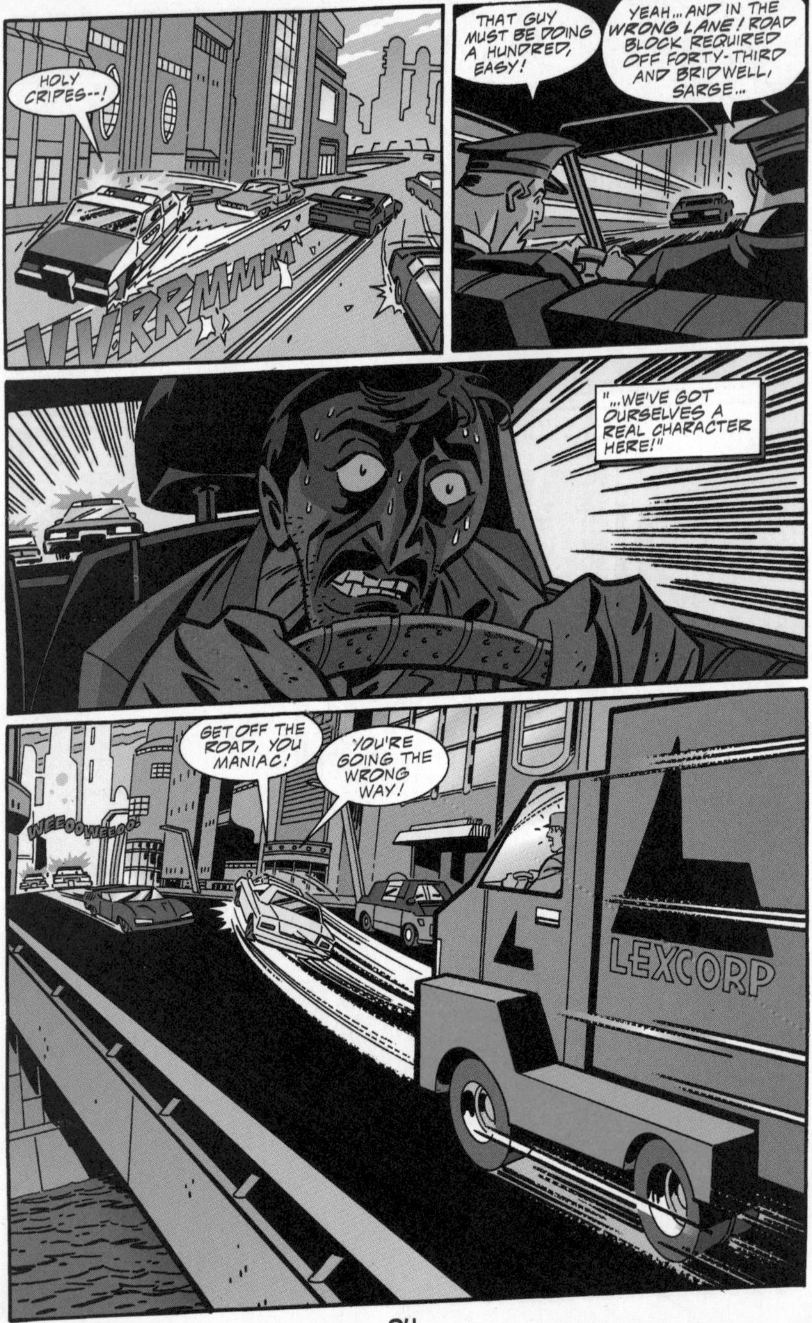
HOLY CRIPES--!
VVRRMMMM
THAT GUY MUST BE DOING A HUNDRED, EASY!
YEAH... AND IN THE WRONG LANE! ROAD BLOCK REQUIRED OFF FORTY-THIRD AND BRIDWELL, SARGE...
"...WE'VE GOT OURSELVES A REAL CHARACTER HERE!"
WEEOOWEEOO
GET OFF THE ROAD, YOU MANIAC!
YOU'RE GOING THE WRONG WAY!
LEXCORP

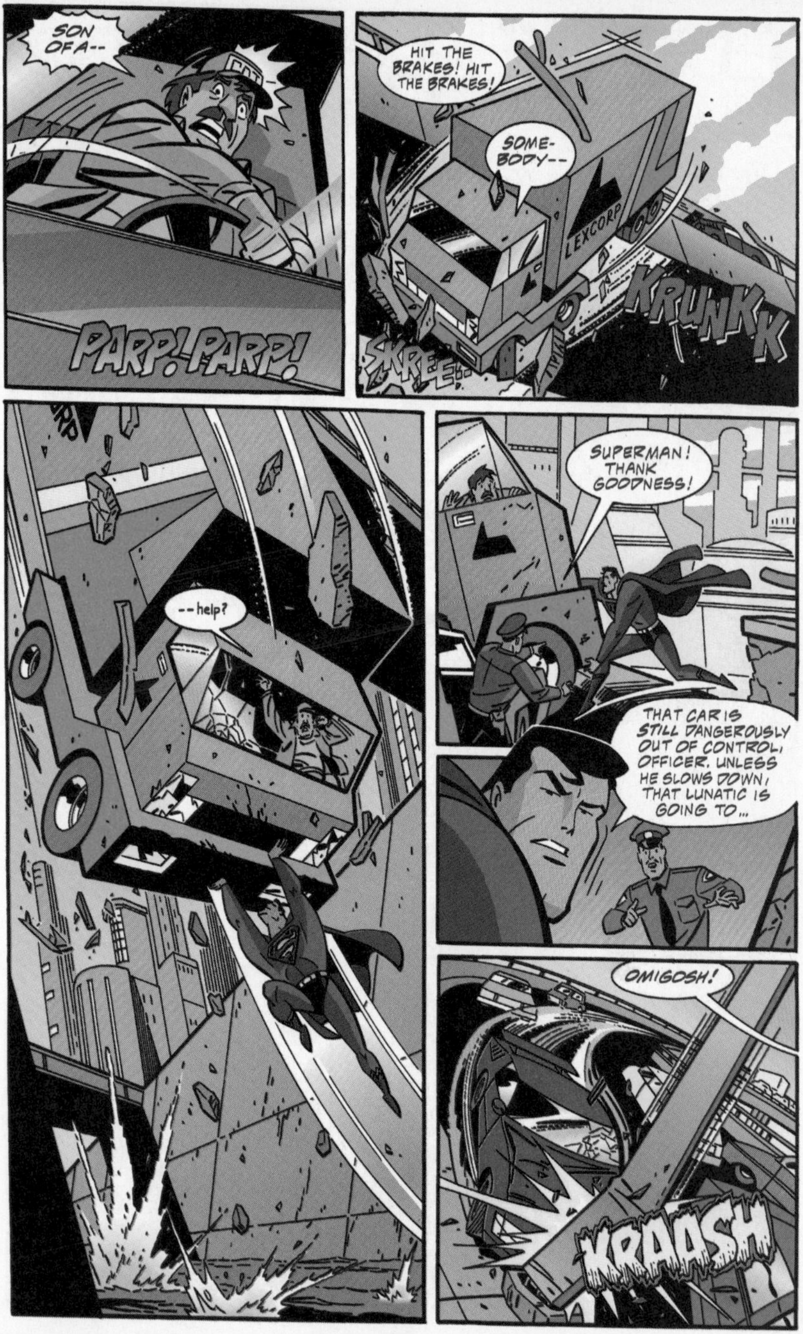
SON OF A--
PARP! PARP!
HIT THE BRAKES! HIT THE BRAKES!
SOME-BODY--
LEXCORP
SKREE!
KRUNKK
--help?
SUPERMAN! THANK GOODNESS!
THAT CAR IS STILL DANGEROUSLY OUT OF CONTROL, OFFICER. UNLESS HE SLOWS DOWN, THAT LUNATIC IS GOING TO...
OMIGOSH!
KRAASH

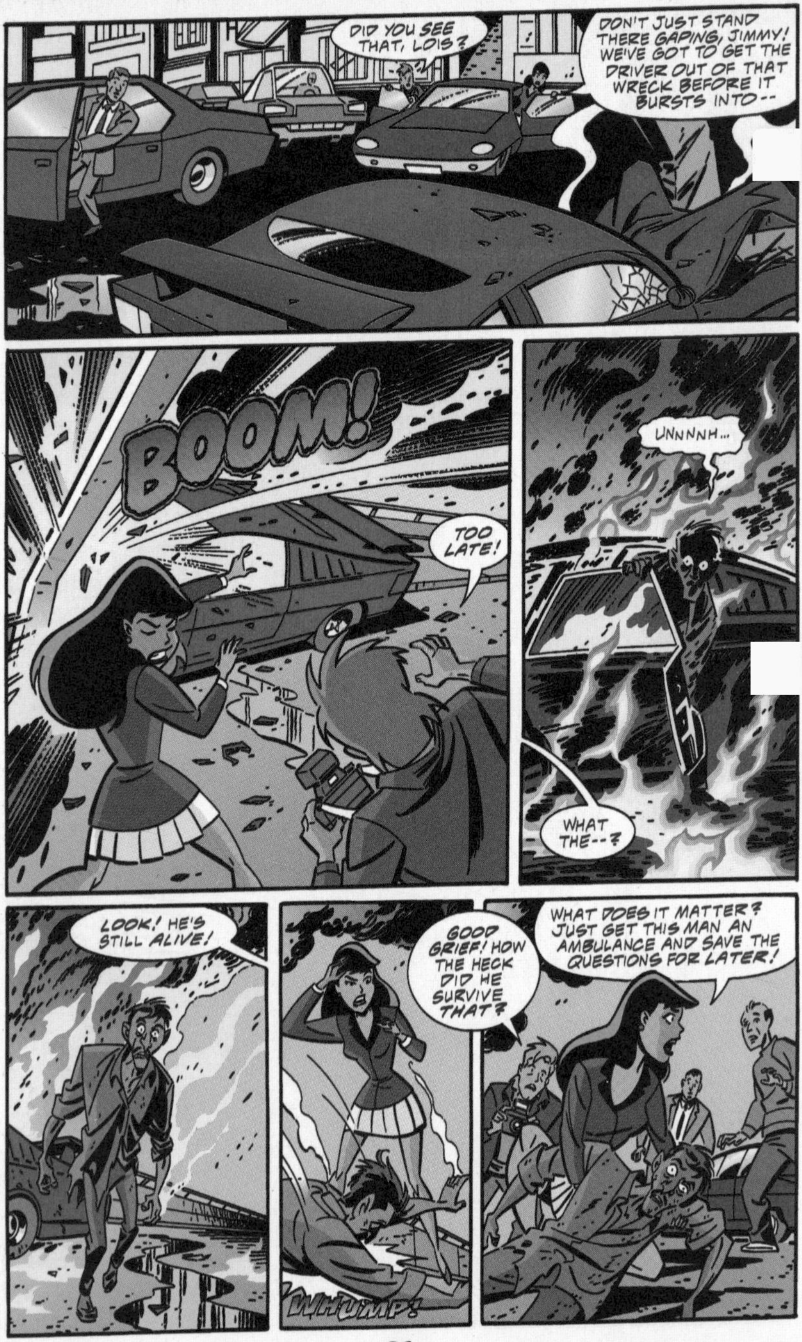
DID YOU SEE THAT, LOIS?
DON'T JUST STAND THERE GAPING, JIMMY! WE'VE GOT TO GET THE DRIVER OUT OF THAT WRECK BEFORE IT BURSTS INTO--
BOOM!
TOO LATE!
UNNNNH...
WHAT THE--?
LOOK! HE'S STILL ALIVE!
GOOD GRIEF! HOW THE HECK DID HE SURVIVE THAT?
WHUMP!
WHAT DOES IT MATTER? JUST GET THIS MAN AN AMBULANCE AND SAVE THE QUESTIONS FOR LATER!

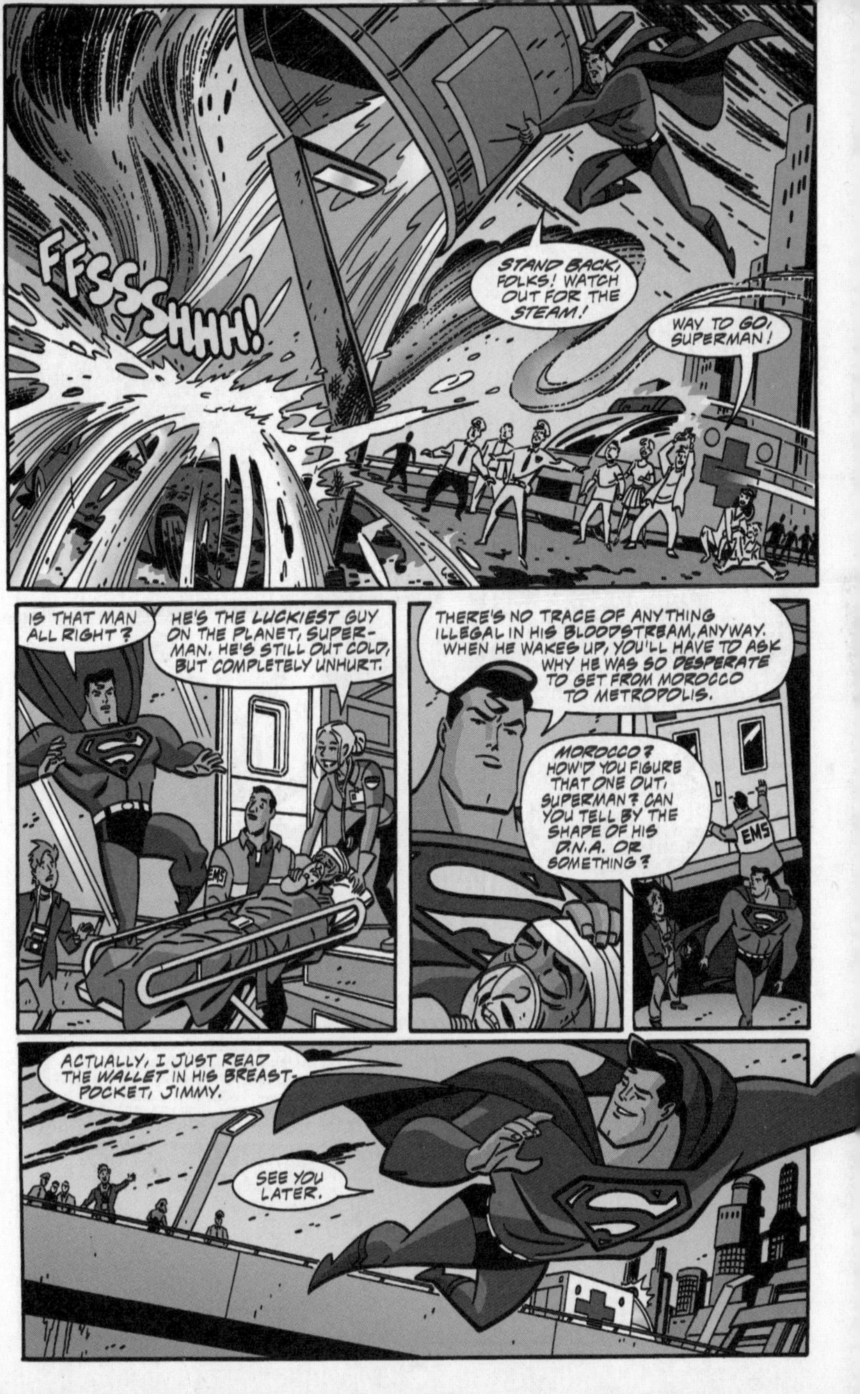
FFSSSHHH!
STAND BACK, FOLKS! WATCH OUT FOR THE STEAM!
WAY TO GO, SUPERMAN!
IS THAT MAN ALL RIGHT?
HE'S THE LUCKIEST GUY ON THE PLANET, SUPERMAN. HE'S STILL OUT COLD, BUT COMPLETELY UNHURT.
EMS
THERE'S NO TRACE OF ANYTHING ILLEGAL IN HIS BLOODSTREAM, ANYWAY. WHEN HE WAKES UP, YOU'LL HAVE TO ASK WHY HE WAS SO DESPERATE TO GET FROM MOROCCO TO METROPOLIS.
MOROCCO? HOW'D YOU FIGURE THAT ONE OUT, SUPERMAN? CAN YOU TELL BY THE SHAPE OF HIS D.N.A. OR SOMETHING?
EMS
ACTUALLY, I JUST READ THE WALLET IN HIS BREAST-POCKET, JIMMY.
SEE YOU LATER.

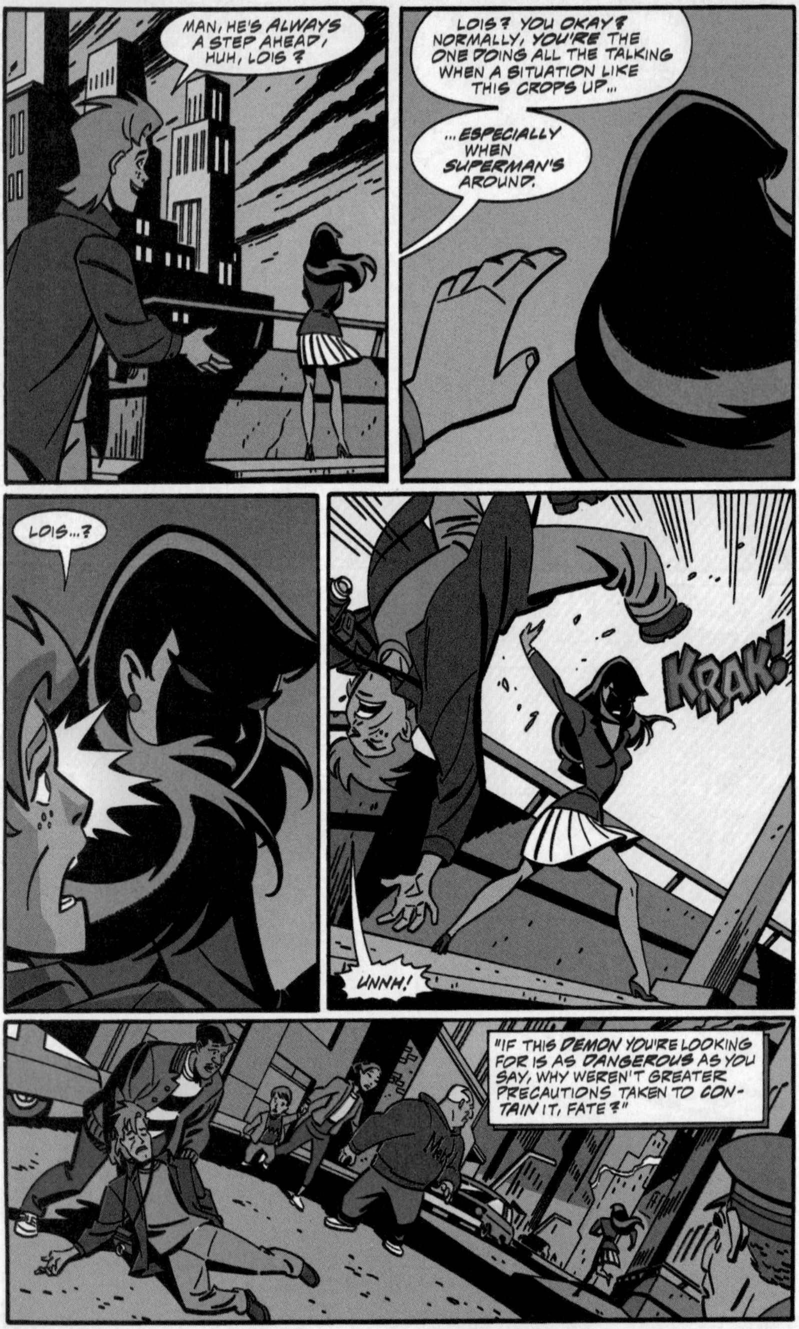
MAN, HE'S ALWAYS A STEP AHEAD, HUH, LOIS?
LOIS? YOU OKAY? NORMALLY, YOU'RE THE ONE DOING ALL THE TALKING WHEN A SITUATION LIKE THIS CROPS UP...
...ESPECIALLY WHEN SUPERMAN'S AROUND.
LOIS...?
KRAK!
UNNH!
"IF THIS DEMON YOU'RE LOOKING FOR IS AS DANGEROUS AS YOU SAY, WHY WEREN'T GREATER PRECAUTIONS TAKEN TO CONTAIN IT, FATE?"

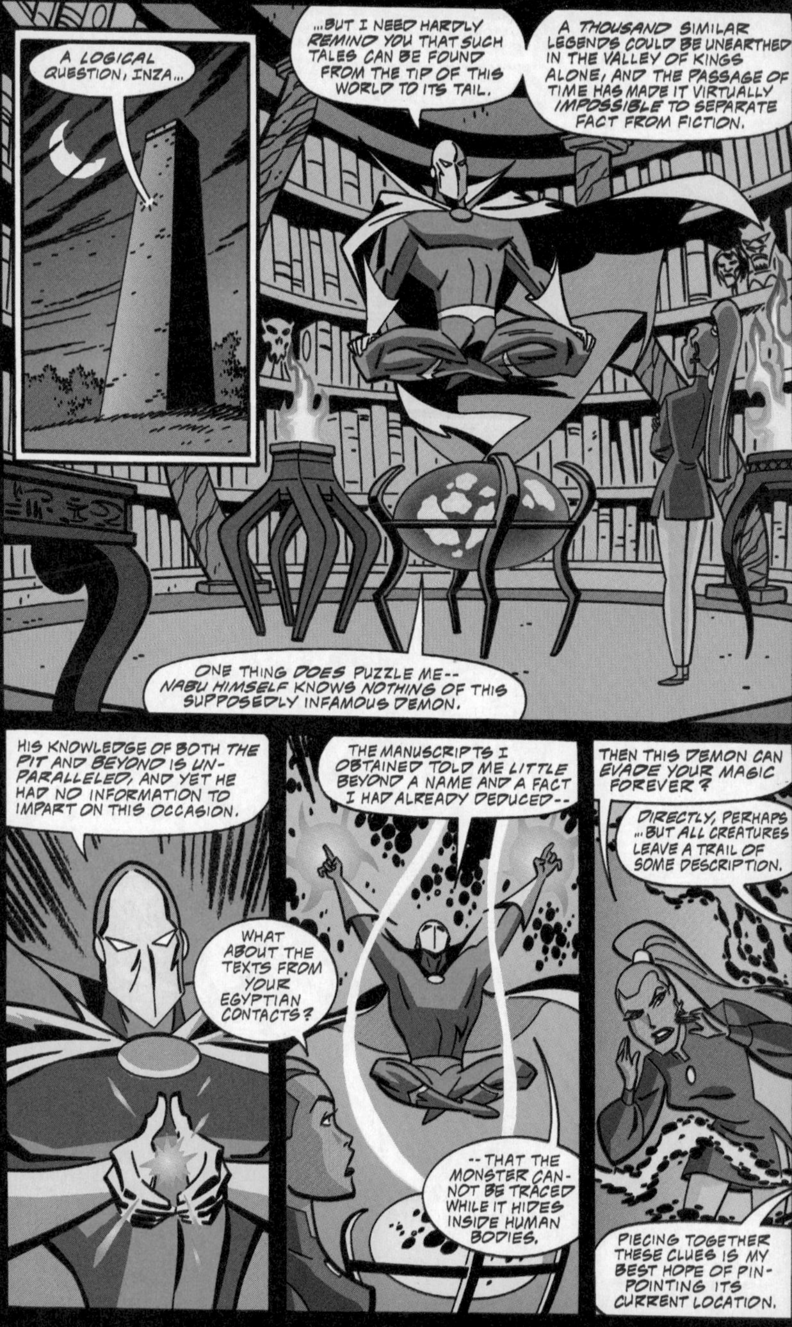
A LOGICAL QUESTION, INZA...
...BUT I NEED HARDLY REMIND YOU THAT SUCH TALES CAN BE FOUND FROM THE TIP OF THIS WORLD TO ITS TAIL.
A THOUSAND SIMILAR LEGENDS COULD BE UNEARTHED IN THE VALLEY OF KINGS ALONE, AND THE PASSAGE OF TIME HAS MADE IT VIRTUALLY IMPOSSIBLE TO SEPARATE FACT FROM FICTION.
ONE THING DOES PUZZLE ME-- NABU HIMSELF KNOWS NOTHING OF THIS SUPPOSEDLY INFAMOUS DEMON.
HIS KNOWLEDGE OF BOTH THE PIT AND BEYOND IS UN-PARALLELED, AND YET HE HAD NO INFORMATION TO IMPART ON THIS OCCASION.
WHAT ABOUT THE TEXTS FROM YOUR EGYPTIAN CONTACTS?
THE MANUSCRIPTS I OBTAINED TOLD ME LITTLE BEYOND A NAME AND A FACT I HAD ALREADY DEDUCED--
--THAT THE MONSTER CAN-NOT BE TRACED WHILE IT HIDES INSIDE HUMAN BODIES.
THEN THIS DEMON CAN EVADE YOUR MAGIC FOREVER?
DIRECTLY, PERHAPS ...BUT ALL CREATURES LEAVE A TRAIL OF SOME DESCRIPTION.
PIECING TOGETHER THESE CLUES IS MY BEST HOPE OF PIN-POINTING ITS CURRENT LOCATION.

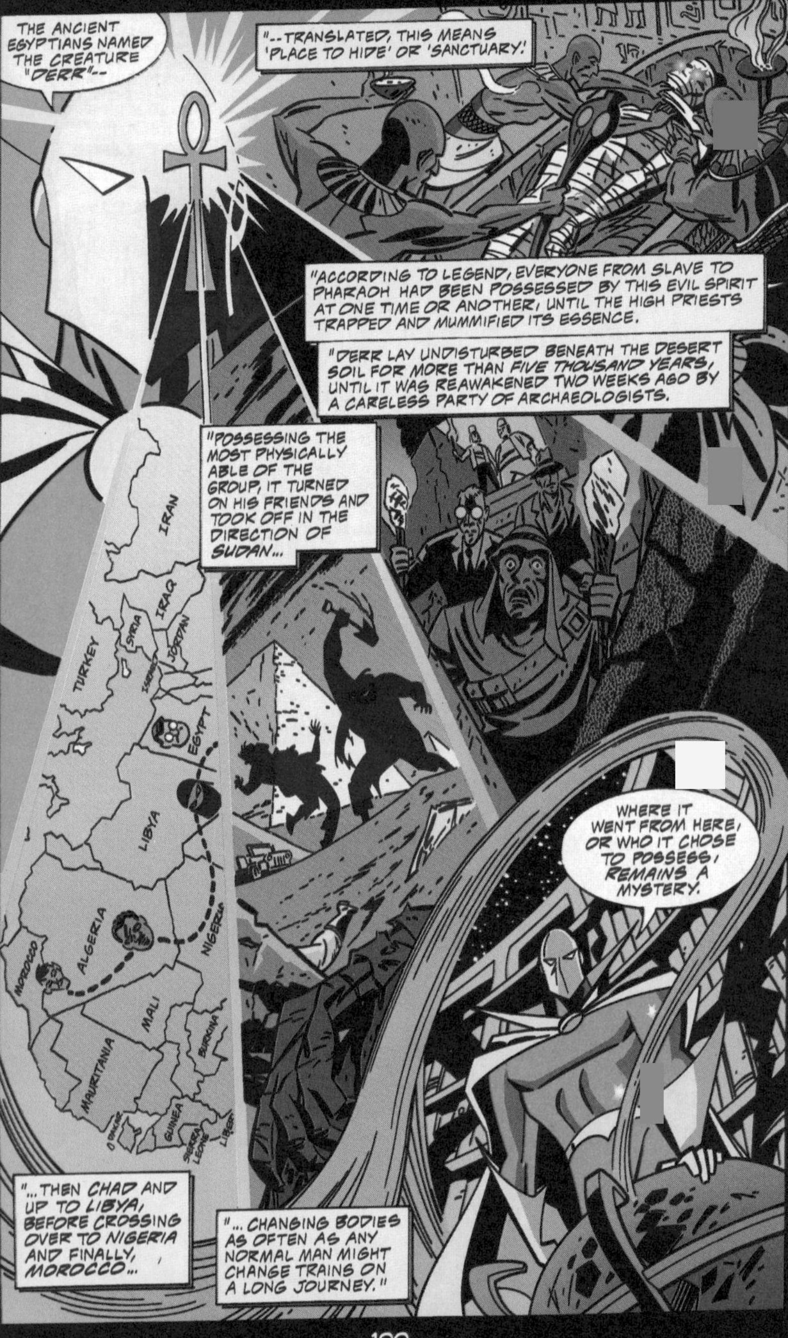

THE ANCIENT EGYPTIANS NAMED THE CREATURE "DERR"--
"--TRANSLATED, THIS MEANS 'PLACE TO HIDE' OR 'SANCTUARY.'
"ACCORDING TO LEGEND, EVERYONE FROM SLAVE TO PHARAOH HAD BEEN POSSESSED BY THIS EVIL SPIRIT AT ONE TIME OR ANOTHER, UNTIL THE HIGH PRIESTS TRAPPED AND MUMMIFIED ITS ESSENCE.
"DERR LAY UNDISTURBED BENEATH THE DESERT SOIL FOR MORE THAN FIVE THOUSAND YEARS, UNTIL IT WAS REAWAKENED TWO WEEKS AGO BY A CARELESS PARTY OF ARCHAEOLOGISTS.
"POSSESSING THE MOST PHYSICALLY ABLE OF THE GROUP, IT TURNED ON HIS FRIENDS AND TOOK OFF IN THE DIRECTION OF SUDAN...
IRAN
IRAQ
SYRIA
JORDAN
TURKEY
EGYPT
LIBYA
ALGERIA
MOROCCO
MALI
BURKINA
MAURITANIA
DAKAR
GUINEA
SIERRA LEONE
"...THEN CHAD AND UP TO LIBYA, BEFORE CROSSING OVER TO NIGERIA AND FINALLY, MOROCCO...
"...CHANGING BODIES AS OFTEN AS ANY NORMAL MAN MIGHT CHANGE TRAINS ON A LONG JOURNEY."
WHERE IT WENT FROM HERE, OR WHO IT CHOSE TO POSSESS, REMAINS A MYSTERY.

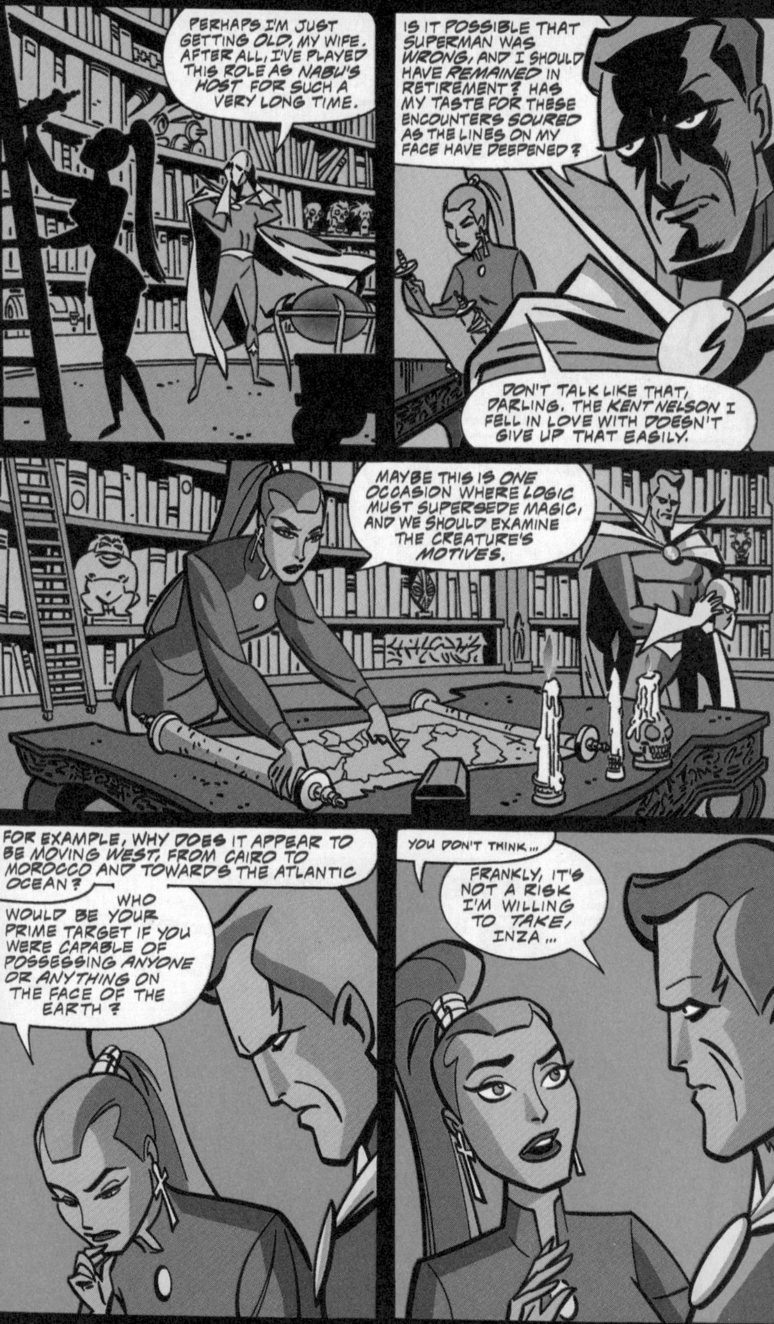
PERHAPS I'M JUST GETTING OLD, MY WIFE. AFTER ALL, I'VE PLAYED THIS ROLE AS NABU'S HOST FOR SUCH A VERY LONG TIME.
IS IT POSSIBLE THAT SUPERMAN WAS WRONG, AND I SHOULD HAVE REMAINED IN RETIREMENT? HAS MY TASTE FOR THESE ENCOUNTERS SOURED AS THE LINES ON MY FACE HAVE DEEPENED?
DON'T TALK LIKE THAT, DARLING. THE KENT NELSON I FELL IN LOVE WITH DOESN'T GIVE UP THAT EASILY.
MAYBE THIS IS ONE OCCASION WHERE LOGIC MUST SUPERSEDE MAGIC, AND WE SHOULD EXAMINE THE CREATURE'S MOTIVES.
FOR EXAMPLE, WHY DOES IT APPEAR TO BE MOVING WEST, FROM CAIRO TO MOROCCO AND TOWARDS THE ATLANTIC OCEAN?
WHO WOULD BE YOUR PRIME TARGET IF YOU WERE CAPABLE OF POSSESSING ANYONE OR ANYTHING ON THE FACE OF THE EARTH?
YOU DON'T THINK...
FRANKLY, IT'S NOT A RISK I'M WILLING TO TAKE, INZA...

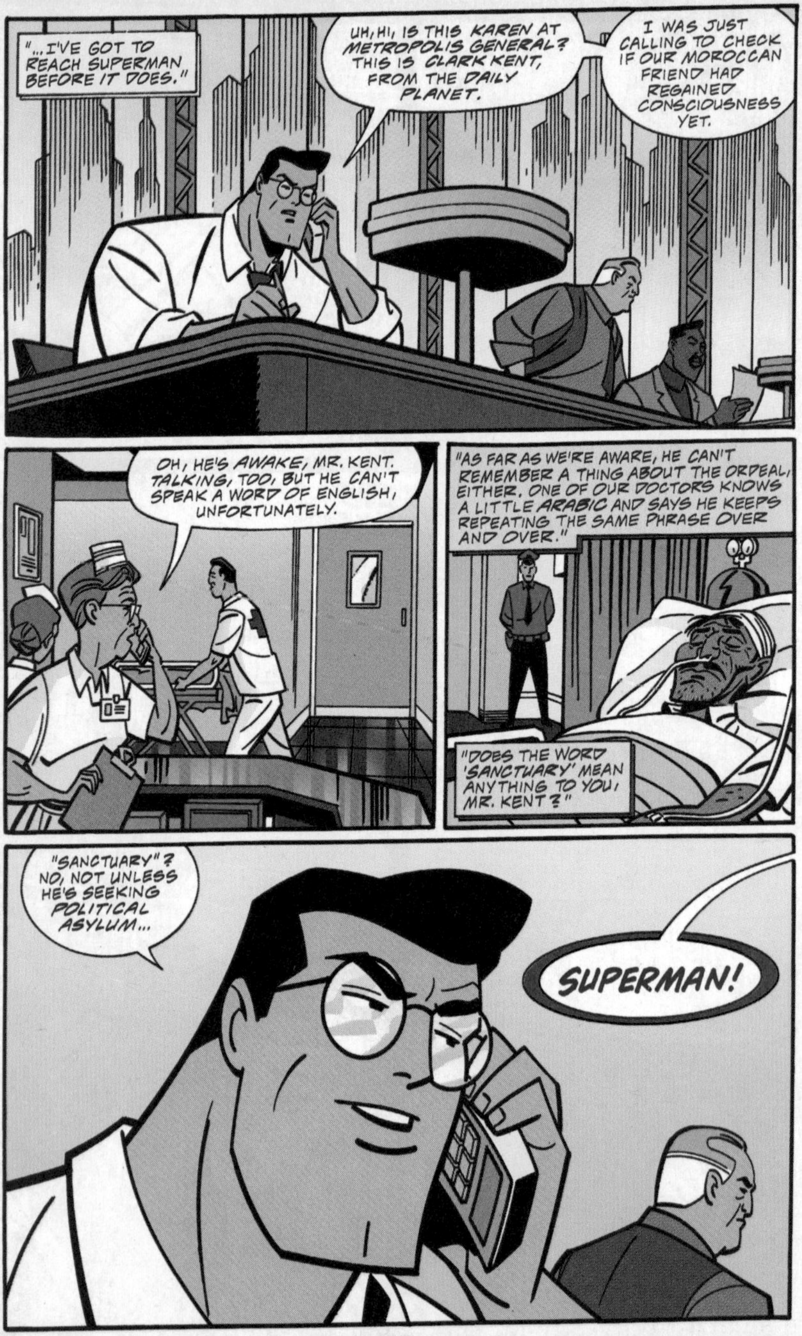
"...I'VE GOT TO REACH SUPERMAN BEFORE IT DOES."
UH, HI, IS THIS KAREN AT METROPOLIS GENERAL? THIS IS CLARK KENT, FROM THE DAILY PLANET.
I WAS JUST CALLING TO CHECK IF OUR MOROCCAN FRIEND HAD REGAINED CONSCIOUSNESS YET.
OH, HE'S AWAKE, MR. KENT. TALKING, TOO, BUT HE CAN'T SPEAK A WORD OF ENGLISH, UNFORTUNATELY.
"AS FAR AS WE'RE AWARE, HE CAN'T REMEMBER A THING ABOUT THE ORDEAL, EITHER. ONE OF OUR DOCTORS KNOWS A LITTLE ARABIC AND SAYS HE KEEPS REPEATING THE SAME PHRASE OVER AND OVER."
"DOES THE WORD 'SANCTUARY' MEAN ANYTHING TO YOU, MR. KENT?"
"SANCTUARY"? NO, NOT UNLESS HE'S SEEKING POLITICAL ASYLUM...
SUPERMAN!

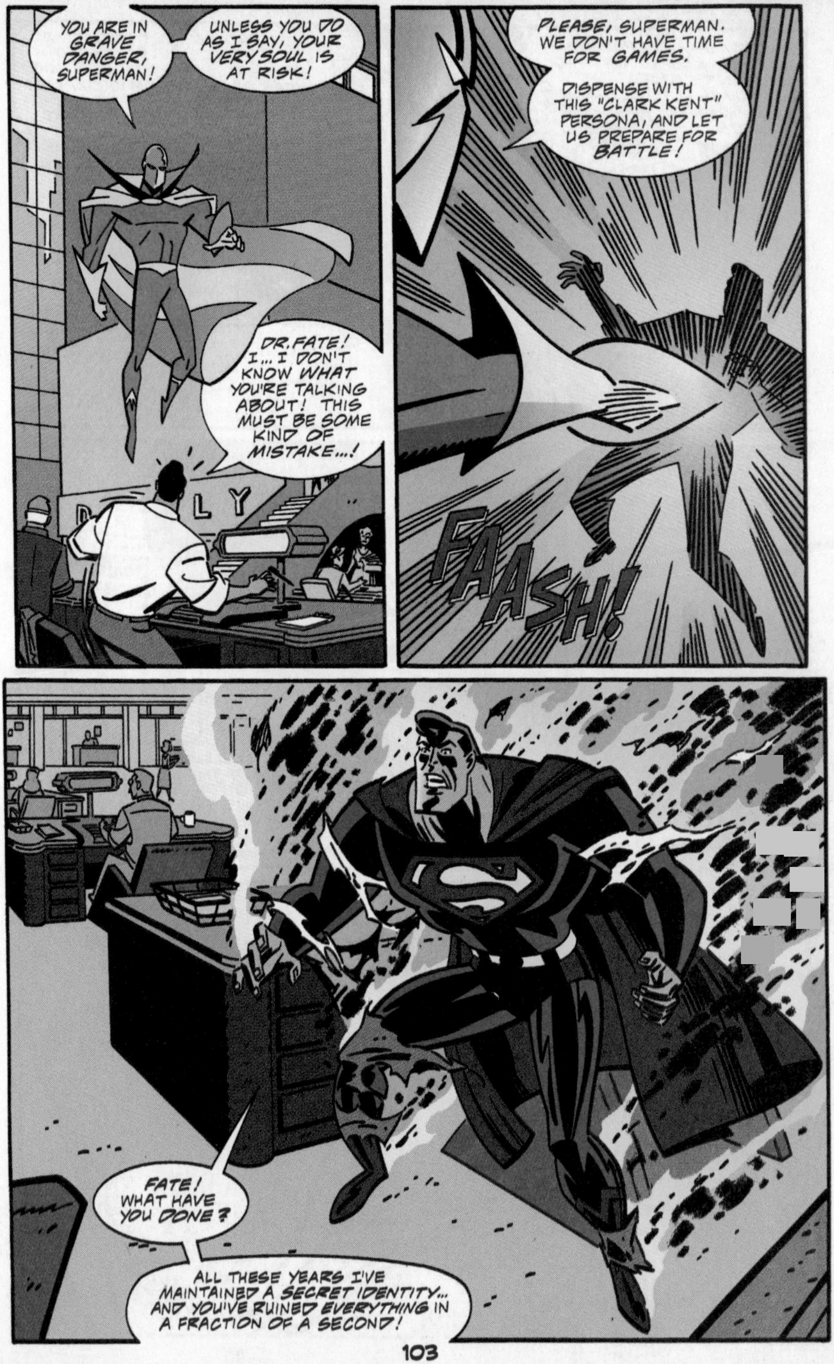
YOU ARE IN GRAVE DANGER, SUPERMAN!
UNLESS YOU DO AS I SAY, YOUR VERY SOUL IS AT RISK!
DR. FATE! I... I DON'T KNOW WHAT YOU'RE TALKING ABOUT! THIS MUST BE SOME KIND OF MISTAKE...!
PLEASE, SUPERMAN. WE DON'T HAVE TIME FOR GAMES.
DISPENSE WITH THIS "CLARK KENT" PERSONA, AND LET US PREPARE FOR BATTLE!
FAASH!
FATE! WHAT HAVE YOU DONE?
ALL THESE YEARS I'VE MAINTAINED A SECRET IDENTITY... AND YOU'VE RUINED EVERYTHING IN A FRACTION OF A SECOND!

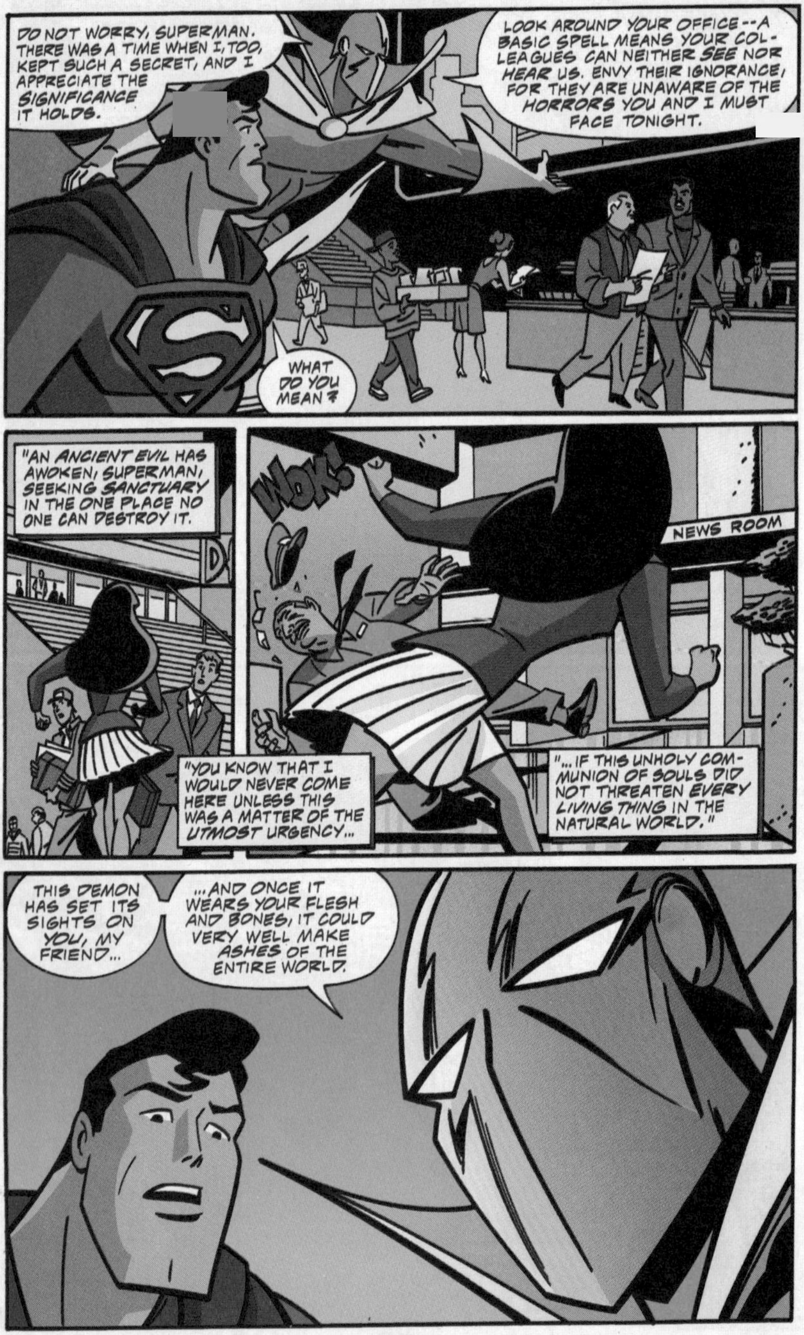
DO NOT WORRY, SUPERMAN. THERE WAS A TIME WHEN I, TOO, KEPT SUCH A SECRET, AND I APPRECIATE THE SIGNIFICANCE IT HOLDS.
LOOK AROUND YOUR OFFICE--A BASIC SPELL MEANS YOUR COL-LEAGUES CAN NEITHER SEE NOR HEAR US. ENVY THEIR IGNORANCE, FOR THEY ARE UNAWARE OF THE HORRORS YOU AND I MUST FACE TONIGHT.
WHAT DO YOU MEAN?
"AN ANCIENT EVIL HAS AWOKEN, SUPERMAN, SEEKING SANCTUARY IN THE ONE PLACE NO ONE CAN DESTROY IT.
WOK!
NEWS ROOM
"YOU KNOW THAT I WOULD NEVER COME HERE UNLESS THIS WAS A MATTER OF THE UTMOST URGENCY...
"...IF THIS UNHOLY COM-MUNION OF SOULS DID NOT THREATEN EVERY LIVING THING IN THE NATURAL WORLD."
THIS DEMON HAS SET ITS SIGHTS ON YOU, MY FRIEND...
...AND ONCE IT WEARS YOUR FLESH AND BONES, IT COULD VERY WELL MAKE ASHES OF THE ENTIRE WORLD.

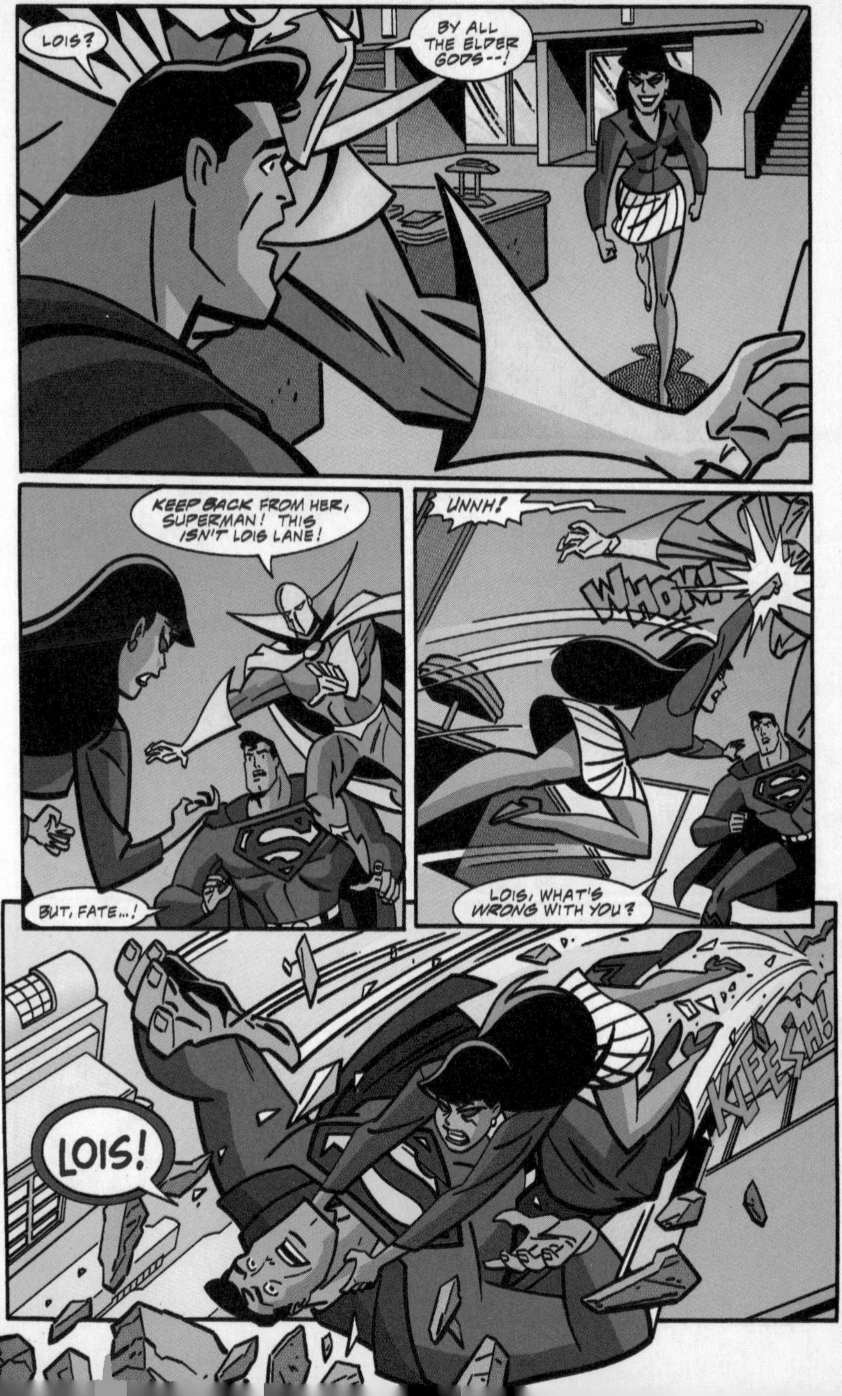
LOIS?
BY ALL THE ELDER GODS--!
KEEP BACK FROM HER, SUPERMAN! THIS ISN'T LOIS LANE!
BUT, FATE...!
UNNH!
WHOK!
LOIS, WHAT'S WRONG WITH YOU?
KLEESH!
LOIS!

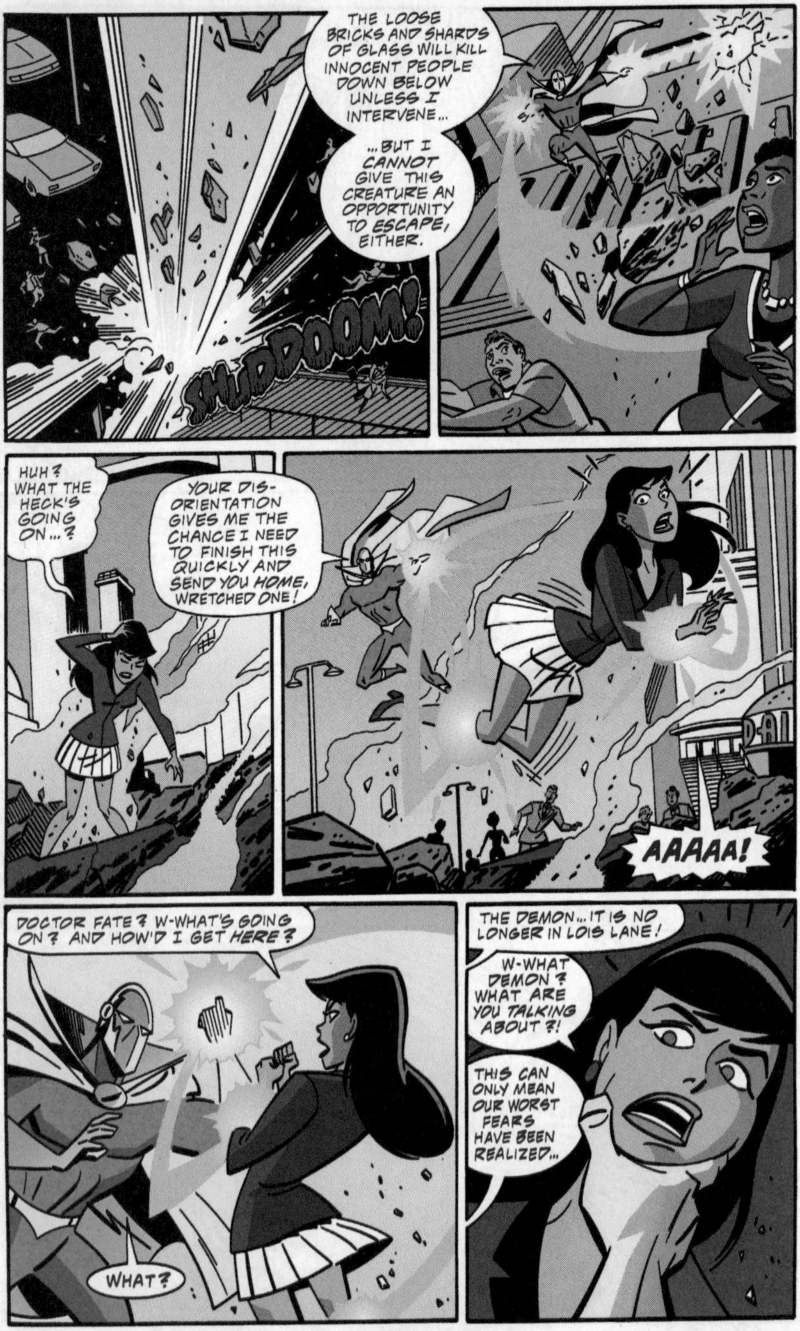
THE LOOSE BRICKS AND SHARDS OF GLASS WILL KILL INNOCENT PEOPLE DOWN BELOW UNLESS I INTERVENE...
...BUT I CANNOT GIVE THIS CREATURE AN OPPORTUNITY TO ESCAPE, EITHER.
SHUDDOOM!
HUH? WHAT THE HECK'S GOING ON...?
YOUR DIS-ORIENTATION GIVES ME THE CHANCE I NEED TO FINISH THIS QUICKLY AND SEND YOU HOME, WRETCHED ONE!
AAAAA!
DOCTOR FATE? W-WHAT'S GOING ON? AND HOW'D I GET HERE?
WHAT?
THE DEMON... IT IS NO LONGER IN LOIS LANE!
W-WHAT DEMON? WHAT ARE YOU TALKING ABOUT?!
THIS CAN ONLY MEAN OUR WORST FEARS HAVE BEEN REALIZED...

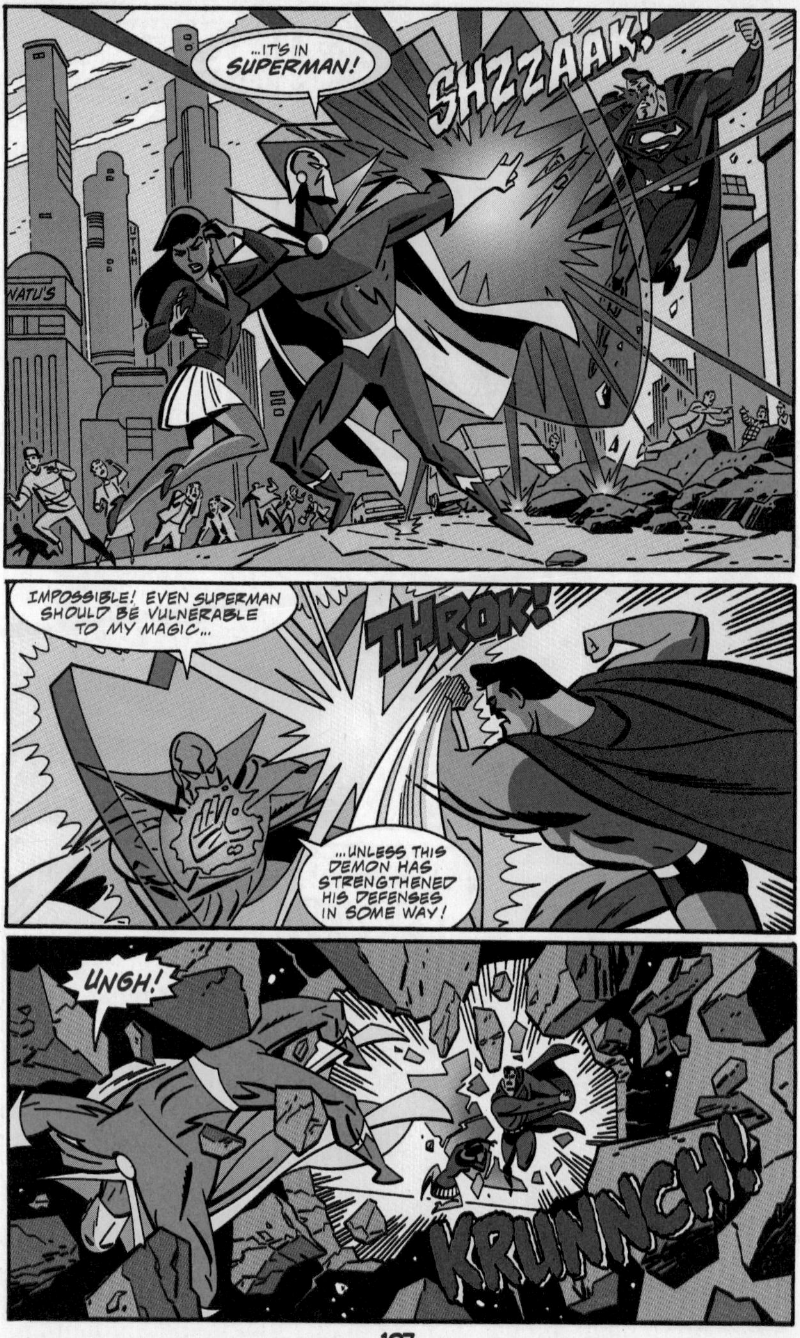
...IT'S IN SUPERMAN!
SHZZAAK!
NATU'S
UTAH
IMPOSSIBLE! EVEN SUPERMAN SHOULD BE VULNERABLE TO MY MAGIC...
THROK!
...UNLESS THIS DEMON HAS STRENGTHENED HIS DEFENSES IN SOME WAY!
UNGH!
KRUNNCH!

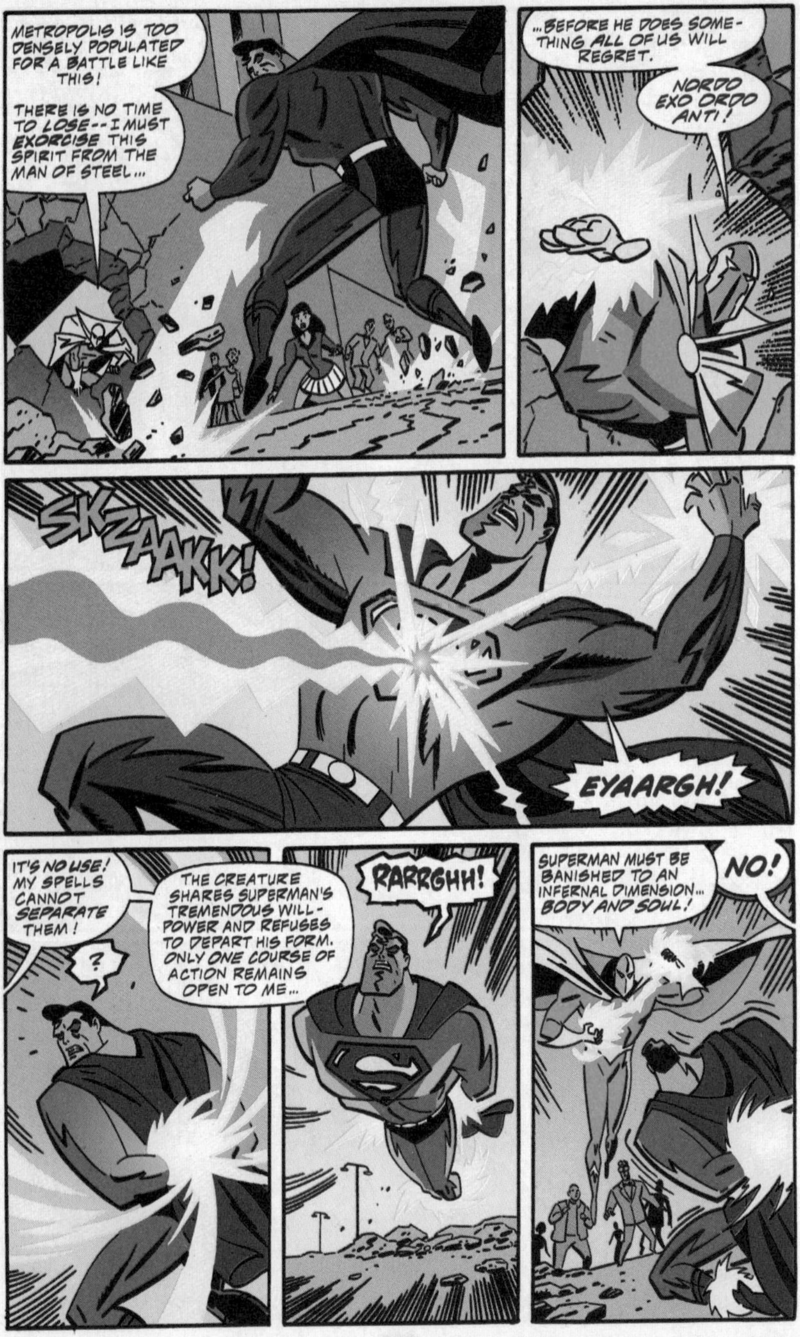
METROPOLIS IS TOO DENSELY POPULATED FOR A BATTLE LIKE THIS!
THERE IS NO TIME TO LOSE--I MUST EXORCISE THIS SPIRIT FROM THE MAN OF STEEL...
...BEFORE HE DOES SOMETHING ALL OF US WILL REGRET.
NORDO EXO ORDO ANTI!
SKZAAKK!
EYAARGH!
IT'S NO USE! MY SPELLS CANNOT SEPARATE THEM!
?
THE CREATURE SHARES SUPERMAN'S TREMENDOUS WILL-POWER AND REFUSES TO DEPART HIS FORM. ONLY ONE COURSE OF ACTION REMAINS OPEN TO ME...
RARRGHH!
SUPERMAN MUST BE BANISHED TO AN INFERNAL DIMENSION... BODY AND SOUL!
NO!

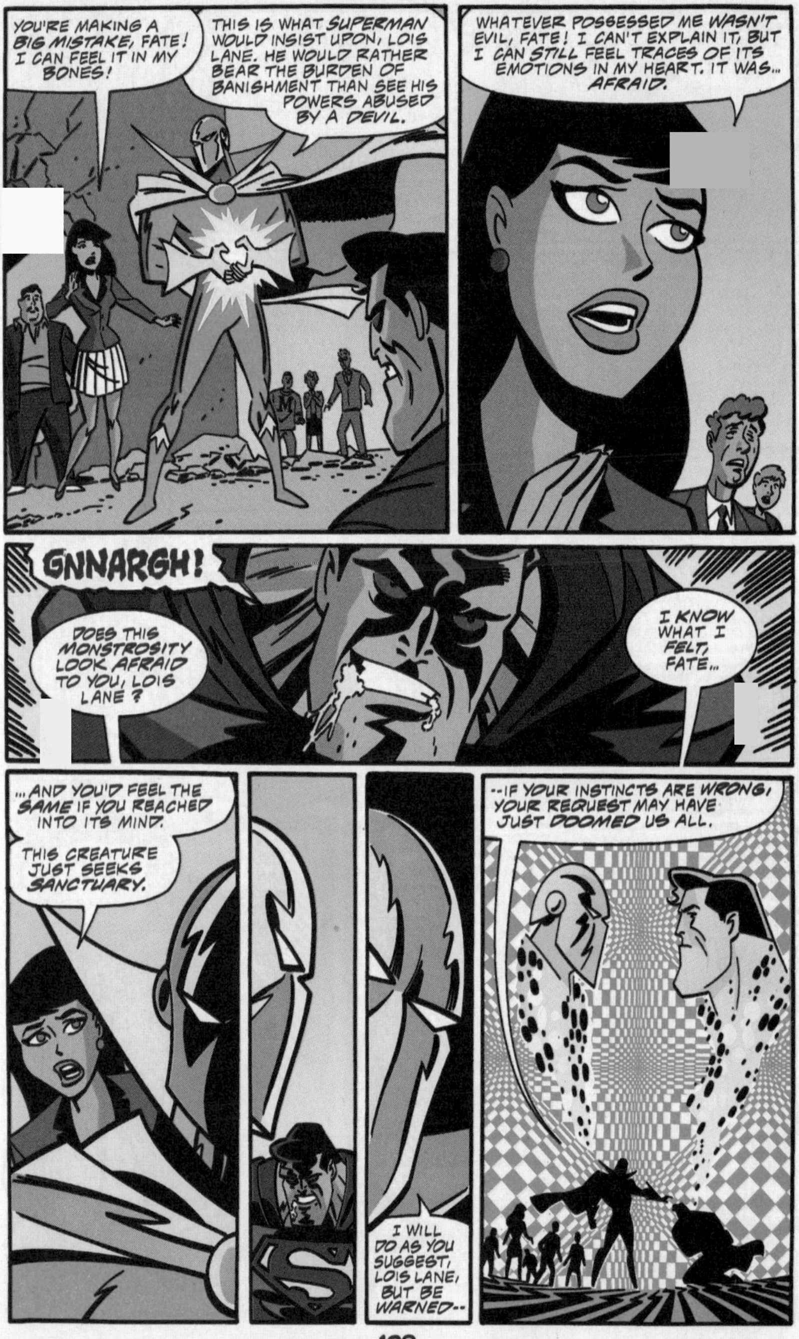
YOU'RE MAKING A BIG MISTAKE, FATE! I CAN FEEL IT IN MY BONES!
THIS IS WHAT SUPERMAN WOULD INSIST UPON, LOIS LANE. HE WOULD RATHER BEAR THE BURDEN OF BANISHMENT THAN SEE HIS POWERS ABUSED BY A DEVIL.
WHATEVER POSSESSED ME WASN'T EVIL, FATE! I CAN'T EXPLAIN IT, BUT I CAN STILL FEEL TRACES OF ITS EMOTIONS IN MY HEART. IT WAS... AFRAID.
GNNARGH!
DOES THIS MONSTROSITY LOOK AFRAID TO YOU, LOIS LANE?
I KNOW WHAT I FELT, FATE...
...AND YOU'D FEEL THE SAME IF YOU REACHED INTO ITS MIND.
THIS CREATURE JUST SEEKS SANCTUARY.
I WILL DO AS YOU SUGGEST, LOIS LANE, BUT BE WARNED--
--IF YOUR INSTINCTS ARE WRONG, YOUR REQUEST MAY HAVE JUST DOOMED US ALL.

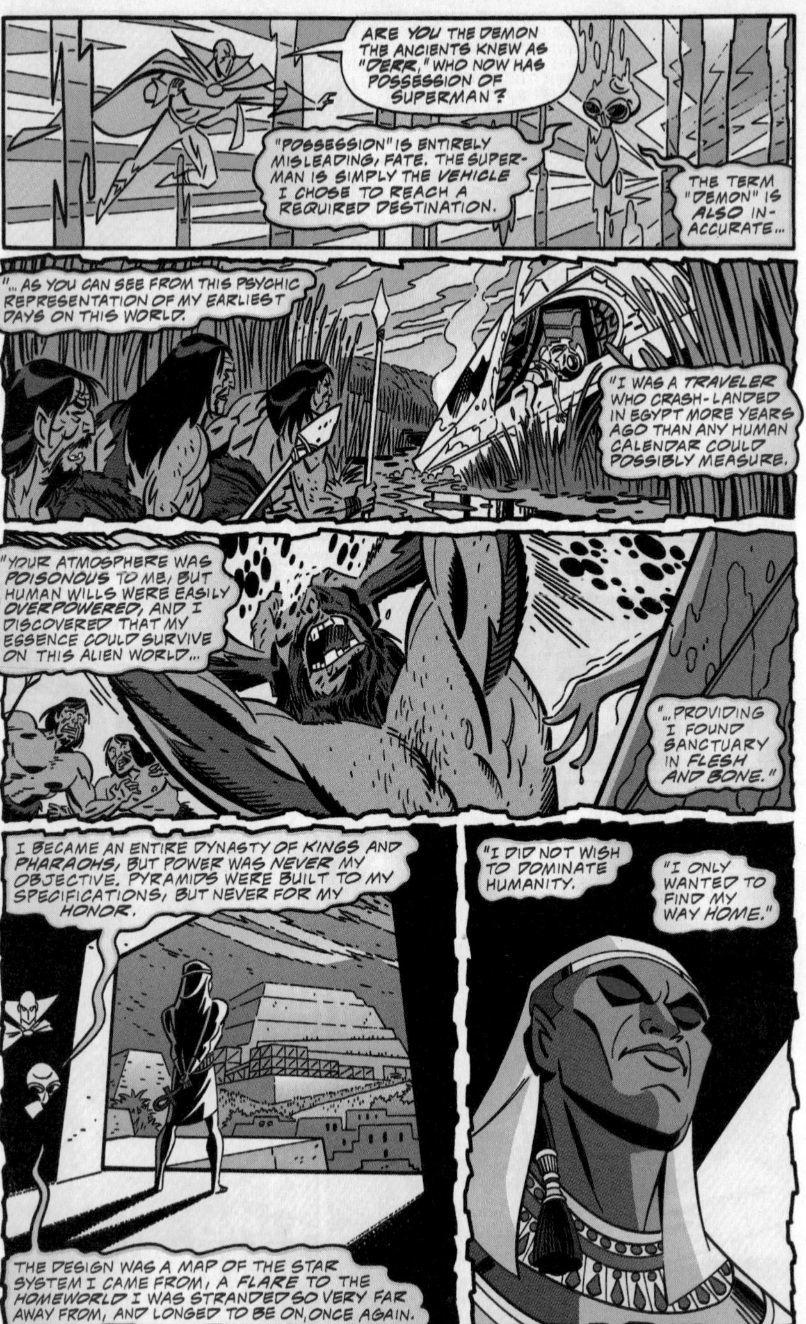
ARE YOU THE DEMON THE ANCIENTS KNEW AS "DERR," WHO NOW HAS POSSESSION OF SUPERMAN?
"POSSESSION" IS ENTIRELY MISLEADING, FATE. THE SUPERMAN IS SIMPLY THE VEHICLE I CHOSE TO REACH A REQUIRED DESTINATION.
THE TERM "DEMON" IS ALSO INACCURATE...
"...AS YOU CAN SEE FROM THIS PSYCHIC REPRESENTATION OF MY EARLIEST DAYS ON THIS WORLD.
"I WAS A TRAVELER WHO CRASH-LANDED IN EGYPT MORE YEARS AGO THAN ANY HUMAN CALENDAR COULD POSSIBLY MEASURE.
"YOUR ATMOSPHERE WAS POISONOUS TO ME, BUT HUMAN WILLS WERE EASILY OVERPOWERED, AND I DISCOVERED THAT MY ESSENCE COULD SURVIVE ON THIS ALIEN WORLD...
"...PROVIDING I FOUND SANCTUARY IN FLESH AND BONE."
I BECAME AN ENTIRE DYNASTY OF KINGS AND PHARAOHS, BUT POWER WAS NEVER MY OBJECTIVE. PYRAMIDS WERE BUILT TO MY SPECIFICATIONS, BUT NEVER FOR MY HONOR.
THE DESIGN WAS A MAP OF THE STAR SYSTEM I CAME FROM, A FLARE TO THE HOMEWORLD I WAS STRANDED SO VERY FAR AWAY FROM, AND LONGED TO BE ON, ONCE AGAIN.
"I DID NOT WISH TO DOMINATE HUMANITY.
"I ONLY WANTED TO FIND MY WAY HOME."

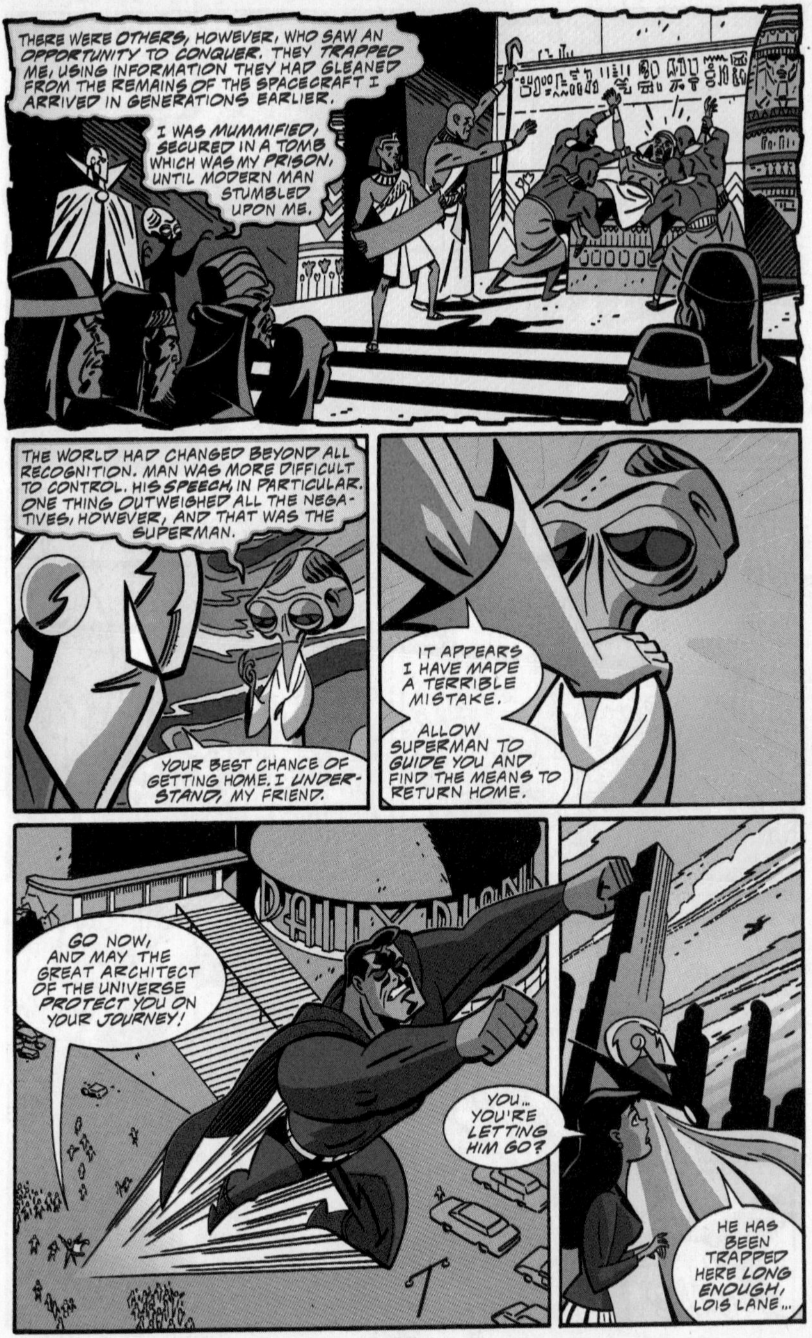
THERE WERE OTHERS, HOWEVER, WHO SAW AN OPPORTUNITY TO CONQUER. THEY TRAPPED ME, USING INFORMATION THEY HAD GLEANED FROM THE REMAINS OF THE SPACECRAFT I ARRIVED IN GENERATIONS EARLIER.
I WAS MUMMIFIED, SECURED IN A TOMB WHICH WAS MY PRISON, UNTIL MODERN MAN STUMBLED UPON ME.
THE WORLD HAD CHANGED BEYOND ALL RECOGNITION. MAN WAS MORE DIFFICULT TO CONTROL. HIS SPEECH, IN PARTICULAR. ONE THING OUTWEIGHED ALL THE NEGATIVES, HOWEVER, AND THAT WAS THE SUPERMAN.
YOUR BEST CHANCE OF GETTING HOME. I UNDERSTAND, MY FRIEND.
IT APPEARS I HAVE MADE A TERRIBLE MISTAKE.
ALLOW SUPERMAN TO GUIDE YOU AND FIND THE MEANS TO RETURN HOME.
GO NOW, AND MAY THE GREAT ARCHITECT OF THE UNIVERSE PROTECT YOU ON YOUR JOURNEY!
YOU... YOU'RE LETTING HIM GO?
HE HAS BEEN TRAPPED HERE LONG ENOUGH, LOIS LANE...

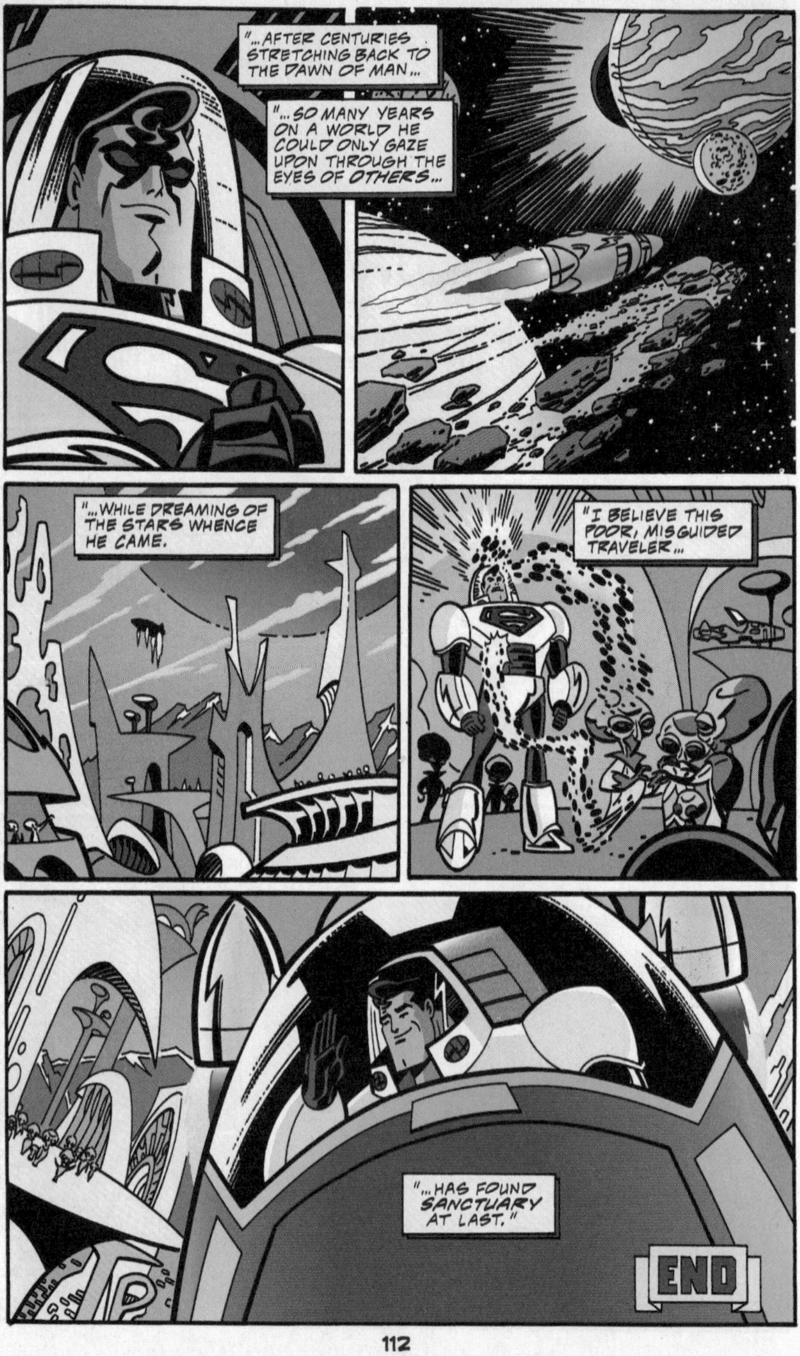
"...AFTER CENTURIES STRETCHING BACK TO THE DAWN OF MAN...
"...SO MANY YEARS ON A WORLD HE COULD ONLY GAZE UPON THROUGH THE EYES OF OTHERS...
"...WHILE DREAMING OF THE STARS WHENCE HE CAME.
"I BELIEVE THIS POOR, MISGUIDED TRAVELER...
"...HAS FOUND SANCTUARY AT LAST."
END